James received a diagnosis for bipolar affective disorder in his late teens, when it was still known as manic depression. In addition to the little experiences gained, like sitting cross-legged on a psych-ward floor, too medicated to move and dribbling into his lap, there were psychoses. For some with bipolar, psychosis creates a spiritual dis-ease.

Psychosis in bipolar is a mania induced state of mind where reality becomes non-reality. However, for the sufferer, the non-reality appears real. This is a strange world of things seen, heard and tasted beyond that which others can sense. However, it is one which fuels imagination. Drawing on these many experiences through the years, he has channelled them creatively and compassionately into his work.

His many internal journeys and brushes with the mental health system stirred a responsibility and a passion to support vulnerable others with complex needs. With many of them affected by mental health and homelessness, he has sought to empower them, so they can find their own voices.

Mixing commercial, academic and support type work with the experiences of the unreal, a vision crystallised to write about the existence of many lifetimes towards understanding the relationship and dis-ease between the Earth and after world. And why, the Earth and the after world systems were fashioned in the way they are, making them critically dependent upon each other.

Although living in the flatness of Norfolk, in reality, like eagles, he prefers mountains.

James Gabrian

THE CRUCIAL STEP

AUSTIN MACAULEY PUBLISHERS™
LONDON * CAMBRIDGE * NEW YORK * SHARJAH

Copyright © James Gabrian 2023

The right of James Gabrian to be identified as author of this work has been asserted by the author in accordance with sections 77 and 78 of the Copyright, Designs and Patents Act 1988.

All rights reserved. No part of this publication may be reproduced, stored in a retrieval system or transmitted in any form or by any means, electronic, mechanical, photocopying, recording or otherwise, without the prior permission of the publishers.

Any person who commits any unauthorised act in relation to this publication may be liable to criminal prosecution and civil claims for damages.

A CIP catalogue record for this title is available from the British Library.

ISBN 9781398412149 (Paperback)
ISBN 9781398412156 (ePub e-book)

www.austinmacauley.com

First Published 2023
Austin Macauley Publishers Ltd®
1 Canada Square
Canary Wharf
London
E14 5AA

Divine Factoring

The small matter of finding a way to 'rebalance the Earth with the after world', in the face of a climate catastrophe, was starting to gain momentum. In addition to friends, families and communities in the spirit world, high planers, those with a greater developed sense of 'knowing', held the greatest concern.

Knowing is a spiritual term for a state of connected consciousness. Although the ability to 'know' is available to Earth dwellers, it is only the most interested who gain it beyond knowledge and wisdom. Knowing is achieved via spiritually guided intuition, enabling the connection into the collective consciousness. This is a bank of both world's experiences and knowledge, where thoughts, emotions and intuitions from all life forms are kept in accessible storage.

Their ability to link into collective consciousness provided a deeper insight into the future of Earth and the worlds beyond, should climate change escalate to affect world populations.

Realm Five high planers had already sought counsel with Realm Six concerning the consequences for all worlds, should the Earth be damaged further. Those in Realm Seven remained connected to all events. These beings were the closest to evolving to become part of the Collective, the collective knowing and consciousness orchestrating all life in all worlds.

We, Alana, our Harpy friends and I were residents of Realm Four, the archetypal heaven as such, who were guided by those in the higher realms. In truth, ideas and insights flowed both ways and higher planers accepted and were empathic towards lower realm inhabitant's development and growing awareness. In Realm Five, it was Tarquin and Nevaeh who were our direct mentors. Nevaeh being Alana and my only daughter, conceived in our first lifetime on Earth, nearly five hundred years ago. Her existence had been concealed from us until the revelations of that first lifetime were finally revealed to us by Tarquin, two weeks ago.

The last two Earth weeks since freeing Simon and arriving back from our 'border patrol', in Between Worlds, had been spent coming to know more of Neveah. Our sharing's, of lifetimes and memories, both happy and sad demonstrated how each of us had had very different experiences of Earth. Although this reunion was a happy time, on a carefully shrouded level and one only known to me, Alana held a sadness. This was not a loss; it was a feeling of unfulfilled longing.

Alana and I had been first born Harpies. This meant that we had been created a Harpy spirit's essence evolving back into the Collective when they had grown in knowing past the level of the realm seven existence. In contrast, Neveah was a reincarnated Harpy, one who had been born to us along a journey of many lifetimes. Although she was still ours in an Earth sense and we loved one another, the feeling of 'belonging to' and its seemingly possessive and unconditional connection, was not the same as the Earth experience of parenthood. This illusion enjoyed and despaired over by many as they parented generations on Earth, was so because reincarnation was not an accepted life fact to the majority on Earth.

Our experience of having Nevaeh, was like the experience of many surrogate loving and compassionate parents on Earth and was like that of adoption. This haunted me, as it was something else that the Collective kept hidden from the Earthbound. The system however, as always, covered its tracks so Earth dwellers were unable to uncover the truth beyond theirs. Alana yearned for an essence child, like she and I had been. This was the closest thing to a child born to us if we had been Harpies living on Earth before we became extinct. Her sadness was that we had passed both opportunities in our spirit world development and would no longer be reincarnated back on Earth.

Tarquin and Nevaeh had called for a gathering to sound ideas and thoughts as to how we, as after world dwellers, might work together to halt or slow down the damage currently being sustained by the Earth. Tarquin had previously approached Alana and I, seeking our involvement, because of our tenacity to challenge existing systems and after world guidelines.

The gathering included a cross section of spirit folk with different functions and whom might contribute and influence others opinion. It was Tarquin who opened the address.

"We are gathered here together, because the Earth needs help. Whilst there are a whole host of reasons for the increase in carbon dioxide in the Earth's atmosphere causing global warming, population growth and warming are directly linked. It is the increase in each extra human consumer's carbon footprint which far out paces the progress of carbon reduction achieved by increasing renewable energy sources. Let's not be under any illusion, overpopulation causes climate change."

"I thought it was to do with the continual use and burning of fossil fuels to create energy and to power industry that had caused the issue," added Melanie, one of the Earth guides.

Tarquin clarified that the production of greenhouse gases, carbon dioxide and methane through the burning of fossil fuels, oil, gas and coal, had created the problem. However, each additional human born consumes, as does every other Earth born human and therefore the demand for energy increases. As the Earth did not have renewable energy infrastructures sophisticated or widespread enough to meet the demand for energy, the use of fossil fuels would continue.

"In addition, those countries with fossil fuel reserves, treat those reserves as bank accounts to maintain economies and nations and support other nations, albeit for a profit, to meet the energy needs of their consumers," said Tarquin answering her question.

"Why not build more windmills and install solar panels on buildings or in deserts, or harness tidal energy? Then people could drive around in electric cars," Melanie replied.

"Who would agree to fund the infrastructure and technology to make that happen on a global basis? Governments, energy producers or suppliers; the oil, gas and coal industries? Or perhaps the consumers themselves through taxation? Whoever funds, the public uptake of such changes, it would happen too slowly to avoid the effects of climate change and everything that comes with it. We need to work with them," defended Tarquin.

"I think everybody should become vegetarians and drink soya milk!" proposed Stuart, one of the catchers, a catcher being an after-world spirit who met Earth dwellers when they had just died and accompanied them to the after world.

"And how would that help?"

"There are nearly 95 million cattle in the US alone. Cows fart 100kg of methane per year or 9.5 billion kg a year collectively in the US. Methane is about thirty times more destructive to the climate than carbon dioxide and 9.5 billion kg of methane is equivalent to 220 billion kg of carbon dioxide. The Earth has about 1.5 billion head of cattle. Being vegetarian would take some of the wind out of the problem," he said.

I heard Scout, my close friend from the Harpy horse lines, snart nervously, followed by his voice in my head, saying, 'and after the cattle are all gone, which species would be next, horses'? Snarting was his method of disguising untimely flatulence by snorting at the same time. I told him not to worry, as horses don't fart as much as cattle, although it might be debatable in his case. But I did seriously support his point. The voices in the room started to increase in number, as I heard their suggestions:

"Protect the rainforests and plant more trees; plant more kelp meadows; improve public transport and subsidise it; introduce a planet tax; make governments and countries work together closer and effectively sharing technology; ban cars; better recycling systems and waste disposal; cut global defence spending and internationally redirect funds into renewable energy production and supply infrastructure!"

Neveah rose and took up the points.

"I find it interesting how we can come up with many ideas and solutions; however, these are Earth instigated countermeasures to the problem, not things we can directly influence."

The fact was, we were dead to them or floating around on clouds, playing harps. Even with the additional resources we held in terms of personal abilities, the system and the Collective's methods, we were forbidden from making our voices heard on Earth. Admittedly, we could 'seed' by placing thought and ideas into their unconscious, but not in a way to immediately convince the recipient of a positive change in direction which would be acted upon collectively as a race on the Earth.

Although the Earth born and spirit shared the same connected essence, unlike them, we were not consumers in the way they were. Changes in behaviour were adopted not only via the experience propelling it, but more importantly through security.

We knew from our populations over here, security provided the impetus to engage will and like Earth humans, by embracing it, change evolves. The problem was that ironically and in the main, denial of the Earth's issues was now veiled by leisure, as was procrastination but the Earth bound no longer had this leisure time to decide their best course of action.

"There are an increasing number of the Earth bound who fear the worst and they do for good reason," said Nevaeh, "as realistically the perception of what they fear as the worst, is on its way."

There were murmurs and momentary disquiet from all of us who were present and the audible message emerging from most, was 'what effect will this have on us, our world as well as the Earth world'. Alana slipped her hand into mine and squeezed it gently. I caught her thought and replied:

"I don't know if we will cease to exist. This is bad," I then spoke into the group.

"What can we do if anything. We only have guides under the current system who can seed and hopefully, help to provide insight to change or clarify potential direction. That is, when and if the seeds become conscious? How can we realistically help the planet?" I asked.

"I am glad you said help James and not save." replied Nevaeh. "As Tarquin said, let us not be under any illusions. We cannot save the Earth as it is and neither can they with the resources and timeframes available. Rather than saving, what can be done will serve to limit and slow down the damage occurring, to enable time to create systems and infrastructure to manage changes as they occur," injected Nevaeh.

"But you speak as though the different nations are going to cooperate and work together for the global good," I said. "There is too much power at stake and non-equality of resources for them to reach any kind of constructive plan which will benefit all of human kind, or those who will survive. Is it not an illusion to think that nations will come together, at a time when war, separation, independence and exclusion seem to be of greater importance than engagement in a common cause?" I said.

I cited the examples of the reduction of international aid, or non-military aid, or a country's population voting for separation from others in the name of greater independence and assumed power, as had happened in Europe. It was likely nations would continue to look after their own, or those who could afford to. If charity was needed, it always began at home, that was unless there was an opportunity for a trade-off.

"James, what you are quoting is the evolutionary, albeit reoccurring history of humanity. Global cooperation does and has happened, admittedly at a cost, but in the last century, it happened to counteract the Nazi dictatorship. However, in this warming situation, nations will battle with the effects of the planet responding to the careless wounds caused by some of those nations. Like individuals, nations must take responsibility for the actions of their predecessors whose misguided or ignorant acts have caused this situation."

"Ideally yes," I replied with a degree of reserve. "After all, they are the ones with the greatest levels of accumulated wealth. What are your suggestions for making this happen?"

Nevaeh addressed the group.

"I said we would try to reduce the rate that damage is occurring. However, this is where we run into our own after world issues of how to."

Nevaeh explained there were hypothetical ideas, whose input may be possible, however, we found ourselves in a similar scenario to the Earth bound. Whilst they faced the planet and its unknown reactions, we faced the Collective, its system and the question of its ability and willingness to rectify and change the Earth's imbalance.

Both populations, here and on Earth, were unable to predict the response, impact and over what time scale any induced changes may occur.

"As Tarquin said, climate change goes hand in hand with population change. Therefore, as our main impetus, we need to somehow slow down population growth on Earth," Nevaeh concluded.

"This is heresy!" said Matteo, one of the religious group leaders of Realm Four. "Who are you to question what is ordained by God, or the Collective, as you label him. Ask yourself whether it is in fact your personal designs to become more God like, in your attempt to embrace the powers he alone commands. Is what I am detecting, a coup from those residing in Realm Five?"

In addition to high planers, guides and catchers, after world representatives from the Earth's main religions, were also present. Alana, Audaz, Scout, Simon, Sarah and I were present, representing the Harpy lines. Some of the religious groups, retained their beliefs even in the after world and even with more of its truth revealed to them. As with the Earth bound, the ability and will to choose, remained open to all in the after-world realms. Nevaeh then chose to defend the high planer viewpoint.

"Matteo, this is not heresy nor blasphemy. The power we seek is the power invested by God or the Collective in us, to help maintain balance upon the Earth and in our world, so as to serve to preserve the Collective. We do not have the foresight to speculate on the potential damage which may be incurred by the Collective or in fact our world, should events on Earth escalate to a point where world populations are decimated. Our aim is to find a pathway to the Collective, not unlike Moses did to God in your religion. We must engage in some sort of exchange with it, so we can work together and with strategy to reduce this immanent threat which will affect all of us," replied Nevaeh.

"God is above us," jeered Matteo. "He is not dependent upon us. What gives you the right to challenge what he sees fit as his plan for all of us. In addition, what makes you think that he will grant any kind of an audience with you, let alone entertain any suggestions you may have to interfere with his divine plan?". Tarquin then chose to strengthen his and Nevaeh's position.

"Why do we, gathered here today, believe that the after world exists? I would say, it is because we exist in it. It is our experience. On Earth, those who believe in our world's existence do not 'know' it exists. Histories aside, religions evolved to provide and educate Earth dwellers with a moral code along the lines of 'do unto others, as you would have done to yourself'. The religious elders maintained these edicts through the centuries and the believer network maintained the status quo through their acceptable behaviours. I do not pull rank as a high planer; however, you may liken my development to that of the religious leaders on Earth. That being said, my development and others like me from the progressive realms beyond Realm Four, know more than those who can only believe at their level of development. This is also part of God's plan."

Matteo maintained his eye contact with Tarquin throughout his response, his face considerate, yet unemotionally expressive.

Tarquin continued by telling him he believed that God or the Collective was not dependent upon us. Yet he was aware of the additional positive thought energy accumulated via spiritual development on Earth, which was donated to the Collective upon our entrance to this realm, Realm Four. This energy surrender which the Collective uses, was not only used to create new life, but also to power the system which maintained the realms including life on Earth. This energy, produced by the majority, did not harm any environment, unlike the energy required on Earth to fuel their growing needs.

"I suggest, in fact know, our spiritual existence is not self-sustaining, we fulfil a symbiotic relationship. The Collective, the after world and Earth, all need each other," Tarquin asserted.

"I respect your status as a high planer and your levels of achieved knowing. However, I do not know what degree of your knowing, is based on your belief that you know. Your knowing could arguably be placed there by high planers beyond your realm who propagate your knowing to orchestrate your belief?" Matteo replied.

"Am I correct in saying that on Earth it is the cardinals and to a degree, the archbishops, who orchestrate strategy within your religion to effect change, both advising and informing their leader of the need to change?" said Tarquin.

"You are pulling rank, Tarquin! I think or believe, the whole after world thought energy system is a myth. God is a self-sustaining, all knowing and benevolent God, who holds man's best interests at heart and will choose to save Earth, if it so pleases him. Reading into my Muslim friend and colleague's mind, I think you will find that he also shares my views on this matter," stated Matteo.

From the periphery of my vision, I could see the guide group becoming more unsettled and Arthur, my lighthouse guide friend, preparing himself to be heard. Before he could speak, Alana cut in.

"How can we encourage the nations on Earth to work together, if we cannot agree on how our own world works to best find a way forward. Matteo, you speak in terms of God acting in man's best interests. What about all of the other creatures who share the Earth with man, who will not have a voice in this? They have no power to protect themselves, their families or their habitats. It is not only man who is being affected; it is all of the Earth born."

"Only a number of animals have growing consciousness and God has provided man with animals to serve him. Most live their shortened lives through instinct," he replied.

Alana transformed to her osprey form right in front of him. I could see his eyes widen and nostrils flare. She then questioned him directly on whether he had any idea about the internal relationship between instinct and consciousness? Did he know what level of knowing, instinct could provide to animals and extinction rates amongst animals were currently beyond a thousand times greater than recorded natural extinction rates? If climate alteration due man's behaviour did not change, it was estimated that thirty to fifty percent of Earth's animal species would be extinct by 2050. She continued.

"You, as part of your race has never faced extinction, other than your Jewish colleague David here, whose people were hunted and systematically exterminated for their beliefs. A process my kind are sadly aware of. If world powers had not cooperated and fought to maintain the right to choose and live peacefully, millions more like David would have lost their lives. However, we are talking now about billions losing their lives and multi-billions when you include animals and organisms containing life essence. My Harpy friends and I know what it is like to be extinct. The after world allows revolution back to Earth to further gain knowing, but we cannot return in our natural form. We are forced to revolve as other species. Being extinct imprisons us and takes away our right of choice to enjoy the Earth plain as we were meant to, as God designed us to. We must strive to work together to help all life."

"I am not familiar with your kind. I sense that you are part human and part bird and something from myths and legends rather than evolution. Perhaps a deviance from what is natural?" Matteo arrogantly retorted.

I could not mind link fast enough to intervene with the simultaneous transformation of Scout, Simon and Audaz. I caught Nevaeh's eye as she shimmered but maintained her human form, as did Sarah and I. I spoke via mind link directly to Audaz, whose impetuousness part of his nature, had initiated him powering up.

"Power down, Audaz. I mean it, now! Matteo must not sense a threat from us, regardless of his limited awareness," Audaz then responded through our mind link.

"I am a Harpy and proud. It is his attitude that others held in the past, which led to our extinction. He is an idiot, Joao."

"We learn from his prejudice, Audaz. It deepens the knowing."

"Tether your birds' high planers. I question what real truth they can bring? As for Pegasus here, you are not telling me he is real too?"

Scout, being of the Harpy horse line, had the ability to transform into a winged horse, as the others transformed to birds of prey.

"Would you have me tethered as well, Matteo?" questioned Nevaeh.

Nevaeh, transformed to her Sea Eagle, edged in white light and an emotional expression finally emerged upon Matteo's face, which could only be translated as shock, followed by an acknowledgement of respect.

"Perhaps you did not expect a 'deviance' as you unfortunately term it, to have reached a level of knowing required to become a high planer? And by the way, although you may wrestle with the difference, the Collective was obviously happy with it, otherwise it would not have let me enter my current realm. Come on!" "Everyone, let us not be caught by Earthly differences and conflict. The Collective needs our help and so does Earth."

"I stand corrected and humbled by your declaration and apologise to you and the others of your race for the use of my label. I am aware through the thoughts of my religious colleagues that in their numbers, my views are in the minority. But on Earth our followers are not," said Matteo, reasserting part of his authority. "I understand that as high planers, you may choose to exclude me from your plans and progress; however, I would respectfully welcome your choice to maintain my involvement. I believe I speak for my colleagues also."

"Your input and guidance are welcome and necessary," responded Tarquin.

"Although I do not wish to elevate my status in these proceedings, are my colleagues and I the prime representatives of our worldly religions?"

"At present, none of us are. This is a pilot meeting. Other meetings will take place across the realm shortly to introduce the notion to offer aid. Final representatives will be selected in due course. You are at liberty to consult with your colleagues, perhaps after their meetings, to pool ideas and voice concerns. I think we should take a break and meet back here in five Earth hours. By the way, Arthur, I can hear you loud and clear, you are like a light house sending out a beacon and we will hear your thoughts on our return."

"Thank you, Tarquin," he replied.

"Thank you, ladies and gentlemen, see you shortly," Tarquin concluded.

Sarah's mind linked a message to our group to meet back at her ranch for a glass of cool dandelion tune juice and spring water.

Deviance

Our Harpy group dematerialised and landed simultaneously at the ranch, with instantaneous chatter from all present other than Simon.

"A deviance from what is natural?" quoted Alana.

"We are not real!" snorted Scout.

"I know. I think we should all calm down and put what he said into perspective. On a slightly lighter note, err not, I cannot believe that you were considering blasting the guy Audaz?" I said with a degree of humour laced into my message of shock.

"Well, as I said, he was an idiot and I stand by my judgement!"

It was Sarah who sought to bring insight to Audaz' potentially devastating faux pas, asking him if he would accept what she thought had just happened?

"My intention is not to wound. We have come to know each other more over the past few weeks, as we have flown together and spoken some of our truths."

Audaz hesitated, ruffled his feathers and elevated the tip of his beak slightly skyward.

"If you translate the gesture you have just made, as a way to seek personal truth, I think it may help you to see what I see and now gently deliver to you," she said.

"You are my friend, Sarah. Friends deliver judgement with love. I trust your insights. Shoot!" he replied.

"Thank you and I am glad you did not. Matteo delivered a judgement based on his awareness and the historical doctrines of his church. He has chosen to belong to their group through beliefs based on their interpretation of the truth aligning with his own. Regardless of religions, difference breeds a fear of the unknown and as we all know, security, a fundamental need for all living creatures, is created by knowing more. I heard your response of pride, when James asked you to power down and you responded to Matteo's label for us, by labelling him an idiot. In your view, what constitutes him being an idiot?"

Audaz felt it was arrogant to consider yourself, or the group or race you are part of, to be better than others because they were different. On reading Matteo's thoughts, he considered his race to be natural and ours deviant. What was more, Audaz knew that the teachings within the religions with the greatest number of followers, state that you will not reside in heaven or paradise if you are the slightest bit arrogant.

"And yet he is here! That must show him that assumed truth is not always what is real!"

"You make a good argument," said Sarah.

"Thank you, I am a Harpy eagle."

Everyone burst out laughing. Audaz was a South American Harpy eagle in his natural Earth form and lovably, a little self-important.

"What?" exclaimed Audaz.

"But what made you rise to anger and potential attack?" Sarah then asked.

Audaz dropped his beak ground ward this time and raised his shoulders.

"I think I see. I am proud to be a Harpy and just because we are small in number does not mean we should be dismissed by those of larger numbers who think they are right. My pride is not something that I am wholly proud of. In fact, there are aspects of it that I do not like," Audaz admitted and Sarah responded.

"Growing awareness of ourselves allows us to show ourselves compassion, as we learn from whatever age we start. It also allows us to be compassionate with others, at the stage of their learning. Without awareness, we attack the parts of others which we least like but sense without recognising them in ourselves. Your pride connected to his arrogance and you moved to anger out of fear. If we are defensive out of fear, we are not truly seen by others, nor do we truly see others and fear then collectively evolves further," guided Sarah.

"As I said before, you are my friend, Sarah, and I hope that you can truly see that which I now see and accept as a greater truth about myself. I am humbled my friends and I am sorry that a part of me overwhelmed my compassion for Matteo and myself. I realise this may have caused untold damage if James had not interrupted me. In addition, I would like to say that the reason I was able to see this part of myself, albeit with Sarah's help, is because I am a Harpy eagle and…"

We all were poised with baited breath…

"I now accept that I am also a work in progress!" he concluded.

Cheers and well-done's rang out in support of Audaz' apology and insight. It was Simon's voice that now entered the airwaves. I had noticed he had remained quiet since we had arrived and was carefully considering the events of this morning's gathering.

"Tune juice and spring water anyone?" he asked.

Tune Juice was not alcoholic, in the sense of being chemically mind altering. The light energies from the different flower nectars it was made from, stimulated tones, scales and music inside the head when consumed. The effect may vary between the melodic and the invigorating.

One of the pleasures of being in spirit was being able to search for varieties of flowers you had not heard before and absorb yourself in blending the light nectar essences from different ones to compose your own musical experience. There were not only the millions of species of Earth flower available in the realm, but also those ones which had gone extinct since flora life had existed.

Like alcohol, it was a soother, much how a choice of music might sooth, but not addictive. It was also fun, not just in experimentation, but when with mind links you could introduce the tune you were experiencing into others heads, many hours of guessing origins was a popular game. The other benefit was, it tasted heavenly, that's if heaven could be.

Simon handed out glasses to eager recipients, before placing a glass and a flower in front of Sarah who was sitting at the side of the table.

"Thanks, darling." She reached up and playfully twisted his feather on his temple, a symbol of Harpy heritage present in Harpies of the human line. "Do you wish to say what you are thinking about the situation?"

"I think it is important to voice it, yes," he replied.

Simon fully empathised with Audaz' behaviour, although the 'deviance' comment had only raised his anger to a point of transformation. He had spent four hundred years in Between Worlds, a prejudgement and contemplation existence on Earth, where dwellers, having passed on from their earthly lives, remained undetectable to the Earth populations.

In the last century of his time there, he had battled groups of Leaves who in their force chose to impact upon his choice to live fairly and to help others. To the Leaves, those who chose not to pass to the after world, he was a Leaf like them, not a Harpy as he was now aware, but all the same, he was in the minority for aiding others.

When he had lived on Earth, he had turned his back on the church because judgements were made upon him being told he would face punishment for his deed, as written in the scriptures. What's more, these punishments would be lessened if he chose to hide a truth about Nevaeh being Alana's child. He felt this had contributed to Alana's judgement as a witch and death.

His deed was the accidental death of his brother whom I was in my first lifetime. When he chose to remain in Between Worlds and not pass to the after world, he did so out of the fear he held provided by the church, that he would go to hell if he ever decided to pass over.

Sarah gripped Simon's hand in a demonstration of support. He continued.

"We must accept Tarquin's words that the edicts from those scriptures have prevailed and served to help maintain a behavioural status quo of the world's populations. Although within the church's evolution, there have been dark and selfish periods; on the whole, we must respect the balance of behaviours which their guidance has created. I believe, we should not underestimate the power of the religions nor their influence which is present in all realms, including Between Worlds. Perceive power for what it is. It is neither negative nor positive, it merely propels change at a rate proportional to its magnitude and intent," said Simon, who then continued further.

"I have one last point. Both Christian and Muslim scriptures record the valuable teaching of David and Goliath. It was David, the courageous wise man whose wisdom strengthened both their causes as a result of his faith. My hope is that they do not forget to remember the message Goliath also brought, as they are now the Goliaths of the religious followings and yet they are not above the Collective's or God's judgement. We all need each other to harness the power in the same direction to rebalance this global mess. We need not, to fight amongst ourselves but use our own patience with each other to stand firm together," he said.

"Brother! Not one West Yorkshire eeeeee or than-os, in your delivery. Your eloquence improves daily. I agree with your wise words," I teased.

"James? How much time do we have left before we restart?" asked Simon.

"We have a few hours. Why?"

"Come fly with me," he requested.

We transformed and took off flying across the paddocks before accelerating quickly into the sky above. The day was clear, blue skies smattered with lazy clouds and a warm breeze carrying pleasing scents to us from afar. Simon's raptor form was a Martial eagle which I found a little strange. Although he matched my weight as a golden eagle, he had a larger wingspan and was grey in colour with a spotted under belly and chest.

The strange bit was that his breed was from sub-Saharan Africa. Unlike Alana and I, whose species reside in the Northern hemisphere. Both he and Sarah's breeds came from much farther afield and yet we shared a lifetime together in England. My guess was that the Harpy race must have scattered widely to escape persecution, or perhaps even before, when their spirit descendants evolved to or assumed localised raptor forms or disguises. It amazed me how as a race, we held such diversity within the limits of being the same.

Martials like their solitude, which mirrored Simon's character. He was not moody, but since his arrival in the after world, he would seek time to be on his own. The reason for this became clearer as we talked. Simon created a thermal to enable us to focus on our conversation without effort.

"Do you remember during that time when you and Alana came back to see me in Denby Dale, when you first met the governor?" asked Simon.

"Yes, I do, why?"

"You called me a warrior for how I fought to help others in Between Worlds and you said you could do with someone like me in your world. I asked you if you have to fight in heaven as well and you said 'not exactly, but there are things in so-called heaven, that need to change and we have to fight for them'. This is it, isn't it?" asked Simon.

"Yes, this is it. But you have been aware of the different conversations we have had about the problems the Earth is facing. What is it, Simon? I need you to speak your concerns rather than me read you."

"I can't fight anymore, James. I am tired and battle weary. I thought in coming here, I would adjust to life quickly, but I find myself wanting to hide from people. Back in Between Worlds, I was involved in combat nearly every day, always looking over my shoulder and ready to power up to defend."

"Do you have waking dreams about the things you went through?"

"Yes, and thoughts and flashbacks."

"Is this why you spend so much time flying?"

"Yes, but the freedom of flight does not free me from these feelings."

"What does Sarah say about this? She is the best person to help you through it. She is a powerful healer. However, I think I know what this is," I said.

"She calls it post-traumatic stress, but even with my levels of knowing and recollection of our lifetimes together, I can't shake this off and I feel ashamed of this weakness. I feel I will let her down, that I will let you all down."

"She needs to hear this. I take it you have been filtering most of these feelings from her?"

"Yes, I have shielded and I am afraid she will read my withdrawal as a sign that I do not want to be with her after our long separation. That is furthest from my truth," he said.

"I am going to ask her to join us up here. You are my family and friend and she is as well, to both of us."

"Sarah, can you come up and join us please?" I asked, connecting to her by mind link.

Just as Sarah's majestic bald eagle materialised on my wing tip, Simon disappeared and avoided my calls.

"I heard your conversation with him, James. I am worried about him but what is happening to him is nothing that he, I and the horses couldn't put right. When we first met, I told you he was stubborn, however, I think the symptoms of his PTSD are stopping him from accepting that he does need help. His sense of his own weakness only perpetuates his increasing feeling of failure."

"He has made his first step in telling me. I would suggest that he knew you would be listening and in so doing, indirectly told you. Wanting to be apart from you was farthest from his truth."

"I know you are right; it is just finding the right next step to unpick the magnitude of effects from centuries of combat and guilt. It is going to take some knowing. We will have to re-join the gathering soon. I suggest we leave Simon to his own devices and find him when we return. We are fortunate here that he cannot take the ultimate step, which is one relief and having lost him for all of that time, he better realise, I don't give up easily," said Sarah.

"I am more worried he will hide back in Between Worlds Sarah and stay there. Let's join the others," I said.

When we got back, the others also shared their concerns about Simon and having spoken about what was happening to him, naturally agreed to support him in whatever way possible. We had about an hour before we had to go back, which was experienced as being much shorter in spirit time passed, so I asked if there were any immediate concerns about the possible continuation of this morning's dialogue. It was Scout who answered.

"Like all of you here, I have also been hunted in my lifetimes and instinctually connect to my sense of free will and freedom of choice. I also recognise that we are masters of the transformative which has helped us in adapting to survive as long as our race did. I am also proud to be Harpy and I can also accept that security comes through familiarity. I think Matteo demonstrated his insecurity by saying what he did. Therefore, out of respect and in the spirit of forging positive relationships, I think we should all return to the meeting in human form."

"Is that possible for you, Scout?" replied Alana.

"I have been chatting with Audaz about this idea and yes, we partly feel we are falling in line to appease the insecurities of certain members' present. But, at the same time, we are choosing to support their comfort to focus constructively on what, as a group, we need to achieve."

"Is there an eloquence virus going around or something? You are all sounding like international diplomats all of a sudden." My observation was met with a loud fart from Scout.

"I stand corrected. Perhaps in some ways," I added.

"I keep telling you, it is a horse thing. Anyway, Audaz has shown me how he transforms from his Harpy eagle to his grey-haired man. I haven't tried this yet and I wouldn't know what an acceptable human looks like, so I would appreciate your thoughts or judgements for that matter," he said.

Scout's first stage of transformation was from Mustang to his Pegasus. There was something awe inspiring about his presence as he stood with wings spanning outstretched. As he attempted the process for a second time, rather than an instantaneous change, we were witnessing what was more like a horror movie inspired genesis of his form.

"Bear with me, just not sure of all the links in the process," he said.

Finally, he settled, albeit kind of midway through the full transformation.

"Definitely, definitely. Go like that, I would love to see their faces struggling with that reality," said Alana.

Scout stood as a spectacular Centaur, except he had managed to incorporate all three, horse, human and bird features into his form, as his wings still embraced his flanks. His torso and head were definitely human male. He was broad, muscled and square jawed. High cheekbones and deep-set brown eyes along with a thick mane of dark hair, complimented the rugged personality I had come to love and admire. Audaz flew to him, perched on his shoulder and leaned forward to whisper in his ear.

"Yes, okay, forgot about that. Thank you, my friend," he whispered back.

The next transformation was instantaneous. Scout stood tall at six foot six inches. His muscled legs sculpted to match those of his upper body, hands like shovels.

"Nice, definitely a perfectly passable human male. Although perhaps, a little more than average," commented Alana.

Scout beamed widely, rounding off the impression with a perfect set of teeth. I glanced at Alana and winked.

"Clothes might be an idea Scout," added Sarah. "We don't wish to add to the distractions, do we?"

"I am a horse, what do you expect?" Was his reply.

"Dignity and perhaps just a little reserve which you may find hiding somewhere in your overwhelming presence of free will. Here, what do you think of these?"

Sarah completed Scouts image with a pair of three-quarter length black trousers tucked into black riding boots and an open neck white shirt. A galloping mustang tattoo, adorned his right forearm.

"Well, the clothes, I am sure are fine, but I like that. It even looks like me."

"Let's go," I said.

System Thinking

The second half of the meeting was to take place at a different location. It had been communicated to us by Tarquin, just as we were about to travel. We rematerialized outside the perimeter of the meeting circle. Tarquin had selected a wooded landscape within which was a circular clearing. At its centre was a stone Dias, the width of about fourteen metres and constructed of what looked like ancient segments of granite all fitting precisely together. The sun's rays accentuated the crystals in the rock, sending splinters of its reflection in all directions.

At a tangent to the circle, a babbling stream sprang from an opening which could be described as like a stone serpent's mouth. The serpent's body circumnavigated the dias, its tail ending inside of its own mouth. Conveniently, it also served as a seat for all those attending to sit at ease upon.

I thought carefully about the symbolic Ouroboros snake message Tarquin was delivering to the aware in the group and whether or not it was intended for us as Harpies. Ouroboros, the circular serpent symbol, appears in many different cultures and in ancient alchemical texts. The alchemist's aim was to achieve individual self-perfection through physical transmutation and spiritual transcendence. As Harpies, we were able to transmute our appearance at will and our ability to develop links with knowing were strong. I linked into Tarquin to ask.

"James, the symbol is for everyone here to interpret and digest. The Ouroboros is a symbol for the integration and assimilation of the opposite, the shadow part of our nature, the unconscious," he said, before expanding his description.

Those striving to gain knowing, consume their own unconscious, the tail, in the circulatory pursuit of greater consciousness. The snake, as it grows, sheds its own skin, which is also a symbol of change in this respect. Our growing consciousness changes as we consume the shadow within ourselves and the image projected to those who encounter us, is also changed.

The paradox was that others would go around in a circle attempting to achieve the same, which would remain futile unless they overcame the fear of the shadow. The stream placed, which poured from the serpent's mouth, represented a new direction or tangent that we could choose to take as the result of greater joint understanding. It was the symbolism of the water, a supporter of life and the symbol for emotions and balance which added value to it.

"We must work to achieve unity in our tasks and wholeness in our decisions, if we are to make positive changes with the Earth and ensure the immortality of our worlds," he summed up.

"Sometimes, Tarquin, a response is unrequired," I said.

"Gosh, James, what no debate!"

I smiled back at him.

"I can see you have all been discussing what happened this morning and whilst Scout and Audaz' decision to fit in was unnecessary, I appreciate and respect their motive. That's if you call Scout's human form, fitting in!"

"Yes, perfect, isn't he? You are aware of Simon obviously?" I said.

"Yes, you and Sarah are right about battle fatigue. I take it you know he is in Between Worlds at the moment."

"I had not located him, but it doesn't surprise me. I am sure he will be all right."

"He will be. Catch you later," assured Tarquin.

I sat down with Alana and synchronising the split, enabling our consciousness's to locate Simon. We found him sitting on top of the viaduct in Dendy Dale watching a number of Leaves going about their business. We chose not to disturb him.

All of the members of this morning's group had arrived and were seated around the circle. Tarquin walked into the centre.

"Thank you to all for returning to our meeting," said Tarquin.

He drew everyone's attention to two new faces in the audience, identifying the tall mountain of a man as Scout and the elegant grey-haired gentleman as Audaz.

"They are from the Harpy group and appeared this morning in their natural form of a Mustang horse and a Harpy eagle," he said.

He explained in being able to transform, Harpies, as a race in the after world, chose to remain hidden and many at the gathering would not have encountered them before. Tarquin introduced us as an ancient line of spirit who lived on Earth as a peace-loving race of beautiful birdmen and women. Being hunted by humans out of fear for our difference, our race was sadly extinguished. Without an Earth born body to revolve or reincarnate into, we revolved as humans, horses and birds of prey.

"They are masters of transmutation and are able to shape shift into animal form as well as human, having powerful instinct, intellect and connection to harness knowing. They are here, not only for these reasons and that they can communicate with Earth bound animals, but also because they are extinct on Earth. They fought for centuries to avoid this catastrophe, a catastrophe now facing many humans," explained Tarquin. Matteo answered his introduction.

"I should like to repair or perhaps restore some level of equality following my label of 'deviant' I bestowed upon you all this morning. In dialogue with my colleagues during the break, it seems that your kind appear in scripture and stone inscription across many cultures and countries on Earth. I now know, you are a race which did in fact wish to live peacefully amongst humans. Rather than deviant, perhaps a description of extra-ordinary would be more fitting. Please accept my humble apologies again," said Matteo.

It was Scout who replied to Matteo's statement.

"I am Scout. Although I am of Harpy spirit, my ancestors chose to live on Earth as horses. I have served humans in my time and have met some who have a greater understanding of the natural world than others."

He explained he had chosen to return to the meeting in human form, not out of fear of judgement, but because he wished Matteo to be more comfortable and less fearing of our presence. It was God or the Collective who had enabled life in us to become who we are, as had been granted for all forms of life as they evolve. He knew this because he accepted it and accepted it, because he also knew it. Matteo concerned him this morning because he neither knew nor accepted us and he wondered for a moment about the value of his presence.

"I wonder of you, that in addition to your depth of knowledge about the world's religions and their beliefs of the after world, that others connected to you might benefit from your own insight into our value as placed at this meeting as well as in the worlds."

"Perhaps you can now see why all of Earth's life is important to us in addition to human kind?" added Alana.

"I see how your kind will be able to bridge the gap between animals and humans so that potentially all may have a voice in righting the errors of man. I also see that we have an opportunity to learn from each other as we work together," said Matteo.

"Unity and a common goal is the only way we will achieve this. In our process, we must accept that concepts and ideas may personally challenge us. However, let us hope that our shadows are consumed by the light of our growing consciousness. Let us get to work. Arthur?" said Tarquin straightening the course of the meeting.

"Thank you, Tarquin. I am going to talk about the energy production and surrender situation which a growing number of us guides and catchers believe to be a system. The system powers the entirety of the after world including Between Worlds. It also provides the necessary energy that the Collective modifies to create a new life spark for additional lives on Earth. Bearing in mind recent discussions, I realise this is a concept for debate."

Arthur proposed that conscious life on Earth, held the choice to develop awareness of Self and of others and in so doing through the will to affect positive change, wisdom and then knowing were accrued from these experiences. As knowing was accumulated during a lifetime, energy was also accrued.

On entering Realm Four after death, any excess energy required for individual existence was recovered by the Collective. The individual knowing accrued, although shared with the Collective, thus feeding its consciousness, was retained by the spirit person. Although knowing remained unconscious in future revolutions back to Earth and again during times in spirit between lives, what was gained was not lost. Having completed our revolutions, we were able to consciously access everything we had learned and experienced.

"That is unless you are a Harpy, who on return from subsequent Earth lifetimes, can awaken to the collective knowing accrued, as well as the experiences which happened during each of their Earth lifetimes and times in the after world between them," added Arthur.

There were looks from all of those present, in our direction. Arthur continued by comparing the system to earthly financial investments, where those who developed knowing energy from the same basic amount of life energy, were comparable to the same level of financial investment gaining interest over time.

The pursuit of Self-awareness was not an easy road to tread, in fact termed as 'being deep', it was avoided by many who pursued lighter or more leisure related forms of reflection. As with financial investments, if risk compared to efforts to invest in the truth of life, personal effort, leading to greater awareness and knowing, provided a greater return.

"However, there is a need for diversity and difference on Earth, as how else might we learn from each other as to not judge, but accept our differences. I think that the Collective has managed the investment portfolio effectively to date until now. The reason for change is due to human ignorance and greed creating global warming and pollution on Earth," said Arthur.

Arthur and his group believed that the Earth was moving towards a level of change which would result in high levels of human casualty and the Collective knew this. With the level of higher return individuals being in lesser number, the Collective was flooding the Earth with increased levels of population, attempting to maximise its return through numbers for when the Earth washed its decks, perhaps by another flood and many humans perished.

Although dramatic reductions in population levels, by catastrophe, would lead to a significant influx of energy into the system when they died and passed over to Realm Four, it may not be enough to sustain the system or the Collective until the world resettles and population numbers grow again.

The guide group's suggestion was to view the Collective as a system, not unlike a thermostatically controlled one, where the Collective sensed global climate change as a threat to world population. By it accelerating population growth to overpopulation levels, when catastrophe arrived, the system would have an even greater influx of energy which may sustain it until Earth recovery.

"Our concern is what affect this influx of Earth humans, in fact all life lost, will have on us in the after world and the whole process of revolution back to Earth for developing spirits. I appreciate that there are a lot of assumptions in this theory and it may not be received well in all quarters. However, taking a system's approach enables us to consider the effects on outputs by varying inputs, even when the black box or Collective is not truly understood," proposed Arthur.

I could see the religious group speaking amongst themselves and was picking up their concerns. A key difficulty was that God, having been perceived by humans on Earth as something which was capable of demonstrating power beyond human control and so given various titles denoting divine status and worship worthiness, maintained the overall right of choice and fate. I chose to speak.

"Forgive me for sharing your thoughts, however, there were no guards in place so all could hear. I hear and acknowledge fate always being left in God's or the Collective's hands. This is true and for thousands if not millions of years, fate has been managed in the pursuit of expanding knowing through the choice of all who act as the guardians of Earth. The guardians being the very dwellers who populate Earth. It was the Collective whose design, gave them this responsibility and the freedom of choice to manage their own progress. It is the act of choice by humans that the Collective needs, as it is this vehicle that produces life energy when directed to benefit Self or other's awareness of good or in right relation."

"This we accept as truth, as we serve him. Although, energy and deeds of compassion and love are interchangeable here, as God needs our love," replied Matteo and I continued.

"I am proposing that in granting us the free will to choose, out of his love and belief in us, the Collective did not anticipate the rapid onset of industrialisation starting in the 1800s, crude oil use from the 1880s and the onset of synthetic plastics from the early 20th century. In less than three hundred years, or ten generations, humans have created more choice for themselves by consuming resources that pollute and destroy the very world they live on. Unfortunately, those generations did not have the insight to see the implications of their growing desire to consume."

"It may all be God's plan. It is not as though we are going to die, is it?" said Matteo.

"That's true, but what if we were to cease to exist. What if the Collective was also to cease to exist? The question is, if there was a possibility that God might cease to exist and you had an opportunity to stop that happening or to ensure God's long-term survival, would you take it?" I asked.

"If I was able to accept that in his all-knowing, what is happening is not in his plans for us, yes I would. Yes, we would. My issue is whether to believe his actions are not his plan," summed up Matteo, then one of his group spoke.

"I have a tangent for this circle. I am Aarna. In our belief system, it is accepted that we reincarnate, not only as humans, but as animals also. If what you are proposing happens and a backlog of spirit people waiting to revolve occurs, could they be reincarnated to animal form, if only on a temporary basis? Then at least, some sort of experiential chain is maintained."

"What about the animal spirit?" asked Alana. "Should they be made to wait to benefit our needs?"

"Animal populations are reducing, as human populations grow," replied Aarna. "They are not the ones causing the climate issues. I am suggesting that if the Collective's focus could be redirected to inject life energy to create an influx of animal life instead of human life, that might slow human population growth and populate the planet with creatures not causing the problem. It would also allow existing animal life to revolve. Admittedly, in Arthur's terms, this would provide a smaller return per unit of life, however, animal life spans are shorter and they revolve more quickly, thus increasing, how would you put it? Cash flow."

"I think your idea is a good one, providing we could encourage the Collective to do so, but animal habitats are reducing. They would not be able to sustain themselves," replied Alana.

"There is one habitat that, due to global warming, is increasing in size."

"You mean the oceans?" said Alana.

"I do. There is no doubt that marine life is being hammered by human action, such as reefs being affected by temperature shifts, plastic pollution and migration patterns and breeding cycles of different species being affected. However, the oceans capabilities and potentials remain mostly unknown. I admit, global warming's impact on the conveyors would be catastrophic to ocean life, but as I say, we do not fully understand the oceans potential or resilience," said Aarna.

"Let's hope they are resilient, because after what you say, they don't sound in great shape either," said Alana.

"Am I right in thinking you are suggesting the process of jiva?" Injected Sarah. "Where the soul or jiva begins life in a very simple form inhabiting a very simple body. Then as the jiva grows and reincarnates from one life to the next, the body becoming increasingly more complex, until the soul finally revolves into a human body?"

"Yes, basically. The suggestion is the human restarts in a simple form and reincarnates or revolves back towards human form during the time it takes the Earth to recover. The honour would be great, for it is the smallest of creatures who support the entire marine animal structure, is it not?" replied Aarna.

I could hear Alana forming her thoughts involving a sanctuary in support of this idea.

"I have another tangent," proposed Simon.

Simon had rematerialized into the group and linked to Sarah and I, explaining that he had visited Between Worlds, the time during which, he had been able to think about what was happening to him whilst he watched the Leaves go about their lives.

It had struck him, that Between Worlds was their world, their type of heaven or hell, an existence that they chose to live in, albeit in their delusion based on many a judgement. What occurred to him was that in Between Worlds, Leaves, who currently trapped themselves, in fear of passing to the after world, held onto the energy they had accrued there and on Earth. This was an untapped source separated from the main after world.

He spoke into the group, explaining he had recently come back from Between Worlds, having spent four hundred years there, under the illusion that God would punish him for his part in the accidental death of his brother James. He turned to identify me. After transitioning, his process revealed his fate was not to be sent to a dark realm, confirming to him that religion does not always know the truth.

Over that time, in fact twelve generations, he had survived to enable him to address this meeting today. It had taken him that long to build his courage and with a lot of convincing support, accepted he would be judged truthfully.

He had helped other Leaves who had misjudged themselves, to see their truth and believe they would also be accepted into the after world without the harsh judgement they expected.

This had enabled him to build his own energy reserves. It had occurred to him that believing in someone or something requires trust. This he interpreted as a sort of divine will, an acceptance of an energy obtained from beyond other wills and an energy that allows us to accept the probable, as it transitions from possible. Simon continued, adding weight to his idea.

"Since coming over here, I have felt low and depleted and I have wondered if the cause is due to the change from being constantly alert and battle ready, as Between Worlds can be a hostile place. This I accept as part of it and it will pass. However, I now consider that over those many generations, I built up energy reserves which were taken from me or donated by me on entering Realm Four and my internal system is adjusting to the difference. When James, Alana and my Harpy friends came to free me, they also provided hope to other Leaves, enough hope to change their own belief in the system and pass with me. I wonder about the additional energy Leaves like me hold, compared to that generated by a soul living life in a 'by design' way of being, as they go through the process of birth, life, death and transition from Earth?" said Simon.

"Much more," injected Tarquin. "The energy accrued in trusting to overcome the fear to seek passage, is significant and something most come over with. To deny your own passage out of fear, then live in Between Worlds, requires a greater degree of trust to pass in the future and with it, so a larger amount of energy is gained. That is not including other energy they may have gained during their time there. For you, Simon, it was multiples of, not including that which was generated by helping those you did. For others, it will vary, but on average, about five times the usual Earth journey level."

"I am thinking then, that there is currently an untapped source of energy which may offset the energy the Collective is attempting to gain from overpopulating. If the guides and catchers were willing, their resource might be focussed on providing greater assurance to Leaves to accelerate their transition," proposed Simon.

"That would help. We estimate there are six hundred and fifty million Leaves scattered all over the Earth and the number of spirit deciding to remain Between Worlds increases daily. If we were to accept Arthur's theory of the Collective acting and reacting like a system, an energy influx from a consistent Leaf transition might slow down the Collective's need to create additional life on Earth," said Nevaeh.

"I have a tangent which may lay parallel to that of Simon's and along the same lines of untapped energy reserves," I suggested. "If energy is not recovered by the Collective until a spirit person enters Realm Four, that suggests that there is also a large reserve potential in Realms One, Two and Three. Am I right in thinking the energy created by the authentic Self-judgement system operating to free and transition spirit from these Dark Realms is also higher," I proposed.

"Yes. It is even greater than that of the Leaf transition," confirmed Tarquin.

"Then, if we were to invest in more support to help individuals in the Dark Realms to accept the truth and responsibility of their actions against themselves and others, we may be able to accelerate their transition. I think we need to look at what we are currently doing to support these individuals," I also proposed. Simon spoke again.

Simon felt we were fortunate in the after world as the system kept our darker realms, separate from our realms. As we all knew, there were humans on Earth who sought to manipulate others for gain by varying abusive means and it was also the same for Between Worlds.

There were many in Between Worlds, who if they passed over, would go into the darker realms in the after world and they were able to avoid this judgement by remaining where they were. They negatively impacted on others around them, but unfortunately and as he had experienced often, they also affected Earth dwellers. Simon explained.

"I am sure that all of you here have experienced fear and most, a fear of the unknown. There are Leaves who suffer, who are anxious, miserable, fearful and abandoned. They want to live again on Earth and some believe they can achieve this. In their desperation, they will stay close to the living and target the sensitive and vulnerable. This is not always out of malice; it is also out of a desperation for contact with the living. In doing this, they transfer what they feel onto the recipient who also feels the symptoms but without apparent cause. Hence the unknown. These entities spoil life, limit choices and create misery. Our guides and catchers know all about these and their quality to be limpet like in their quest," said Simon.

"We are increasingly having to defend ourselves against aggressive and malicious Leaves and we cannot be in all places at all times. It is apparent that their numbers are growing," said Steven one of the catchers.

"It is evident; the total numbers of Leaves continue to grow in Between Worlds as a whole. I wonder whether we have the resource to help these affected Leaves as well. The concern in my idea is if we accelerate the movement of less affected Leaves from Between Worlds to over here, this will upset the balance and could turn that world into a more hostile place," warned Simon.

"What do Leaves do? I mean the ones who are not the limpet affecting kind?" asked Haadee, a prominent member of the religions group.

"Not trust, is the main occupation. Over the past three generations, I have seen more and more who have lived by cause and effect. There are more humanistic Leaves as well as those who have lived on Earth motivated by fulfilling their own desires in the absence of belief. They are not unintelligent and continue to be experiential, exploring the Earth for interest and knowledge. Leaves are not organised, in that, there is no governing head or body, other than localised personalities who manipulate and threaten less dominant Leaves to help them gain territory to govern over. There are relationships between them, but nothing they can acquire such as possessions to project symbols of power," replied Simon.

"You were a Gatekeeper for all of those years without realising it and yet you continued to help spirit people cross over?" asked Haadee.

"Yes. Tarquin and I set myself this supposed one lifetime task all those years ago, but the trauma of killing my brother stopped me from awakening to it when I died. As I said, I stayed in Between Worlds out of the fear of judgement if I was to pass."

"In your view, if we focussed more attention on what might be called a 'missionary' resource to increase the number of converts and thus cross overs, do you believe it would be successful?" asked Haadee.

"I do. Although forgive me for focussing on your use of terminology, as 'conversion' would have to be achieved based on the truth of the after world. This includes the opportunity to revolve or reincarnate back to Earth. This is a doctrine which is not upheld by the religious faith of either your religion or Matteo's," replied Simon.

"Are you suggesting that we might use this opportunity to grow our numbers?" said Matteo. Sensing another potential for conflict, Tarquin responded.

"He is suggesting that if you were to offer 'missionary' forces from your numbers, lay guides, if you like, you would be faced by Leaves still loyal to your religions, who if encouraged to pass over, must do so knowing all truths of the after world. In providing those truths, it may create a challenge for your missionaries, as they would have to admit that one of your main doctrines of remaining in heaven after death was unfortunately incorrect. However, as the Leaves' main objective is to stay close to the Earth and magically become reborn into it, the truth about revolving, I feel, would offer a great incentive to pass," Tarquin continued.

"As for upsetting the balance Between Worlds, by freeing more of those who have misjudged themselves wrongly, I agree that would concentrate the numbers who would be candidates for the Dark Realms. This has the potential for creating a more miserable existence for those unaware souls newly entering Between Worlds."

"But that is their choice and reflects their own level of development. Perhaps upon realising the difficulty of this existence, they would be more open to guides or lay guides explaining the benefit of passing?" said Haadee.

"That is unless we police Between Worlds and separate the darker souls from the less aware, but lighter individuals. We must view a larger picture. Audaz, you were able to achieve this when your Harpy group freed Simon," asked Tarquin.

Audaz hesitated, looking around our group for support. I caught his eye and reassured him through a mind link.

"Yes. I used licence though, basing my action on the eye for an eye teaching. Meaning, I scared him, as he had scared and manipulated vulnerable others around him. In truth, if he had chosen to pass, he would have been a candidate for Realm Two and we did give him that option. Essentially we banished him to live away from others, with a little threat, which was, if he didn't, I would fly him to a place and on dropping him, he would fall for centuries."

I could see that Audaz spoke with a degree of sheepishness in his concern for our group being judged. It came anyway.

"Hardly a justifiable and compassionate form of behaviour we might expect from a dweller of Realm Four," jeered Matteo. "And from what I saw this morning, perhaps a little trigger happy?"

I sent the message immediately to our group to 'cool your jets', just as Alana sent me hers of, 'What is up with this guy'. Still mind linked to our group, I messaged, 'he sees us as mercenaries, because he is not sure how we fit into these proceedings. Remain calm, I will handle him'. Neveah intercepted my message and told me to stand down, as she would.

She thanked Matteo for his self-right-chosen gift, Tarquin quickly glancing in her direction with some concern and then smiling. Words which she assured herself were spoken so that we could learn from his affirmative experiences and views. She reminded him we were not talking about the behaviours of those in Realm Four, we were talking about Between Worlds.

Being occupied by dwellers not yet judged by the system, they were free to impact on all around them, negatively or positively. Both the Earth world and the after world, policed and segregated negative elements. In ours by the judgement system and segregated Darker Realms and on Earth by their judicial systems and prisons.

However, Between Worlds was a lawless state, occupied by those who remain lawful through compassion and by others, some of whom would kill the already deceased dwellers if they could, to achieve power. The Harpies, guides and catcher, who had been involved in that incident, had used the tools available to them and acted out of compassion for other more vulnerable Leaves and Earth humans. The individual who was 'scared' away, had remained apart from others, as the threat intended. She pointed out to clarify his misconceptions.

"And how was the fear created to make the threat real?" asked Aarna. "I ask this as within our group, there seems to be, not so much a fear of your kind, but an uncertainty of your potential."

"Not unlike how I feel about your group at present. Potentials include motives and I feel that even though we can read each other's minds, there is a degree of transparency we are not achieving, which is essential to this task," replied Audaz.

Using the Harpy channel, I linked into the group, including Nevaeh and then to Tarquin and asked the question concerning each of our feelings towards transforming to battledress. I felt that if any judgement might be placed, it should be on all of us and not just Audaz re-enacting the incident. Reminding all that this was not about pride or creating fear, it would however, probably widen the differences between our group and theirs. The response was unanimous.

In crouching position, it was the skin on our backs which tore first. There was no pain, just a feeling of internal movement and release. With wings emerging and growing, my legs contorted, snapping backwards into reversed avian position, as sharp talons extended, anchoring into the ground. My torso expanded and ribbed itself, amassing powerful pectoral muscles in compensation for the large deltoids and trapezius forming at the top of my back. Facial features lengthened and became more pointed, giving me a broad beak-like structure, with brows widening and eye sockets sinking. My skin, striated with tones of brown, was tough and flexible, stretching easily about my form. At nine feet, I stood as the monster of legends, powerful, frightening and awe inspiring. I was ready to battle any foe who threatened either my life of the lives of my kin.

All seven of us stood, some with wings outstretched, as members of the group watching, took paces back to increase their comfort. Alana and Sarah stood at ten feet tall and Nevaeh, almost eleven, their chests, shoulders and legs noticeably more defined and powerful and talons lengthier. Their faces were adorned with slightly finer features than the males in our group, providing some relief to the onlooker within the overall gruesome apparition.

We were all edged in blue and white light with the exception of Nevaeh, who glowed in pure white light. Audaz powered his huge wings, lifting himself to fifteen metres, where he hovered, creating a massive down draft.

"Good God, what are these creatures?" asked Matteo.

"Masters of the transmutable. What you see now, is the ancient form achieved as they went into battle against humankind to fight for their right to exist. It was not in their nature to kill and unfortunately, the fear they created, only motivated humans more, to exterminate them," said Tarquin.

"I think we would be forgiven for looking at their forms as those which may be described in ancient texts as devils," added Haadee.

We all transformed back to our natural evolved lines. I addressed the religious group, concerned that their terminology of our form as creatures, yet another label, suggested that we were once again, something far less than human. I confirmed we were not human, our ancestors being of another race, part human and part bird of prey in appearance. We did not consider ourselves to be better than humans, we evolved differently and could do things that humans were incapable of.

With the exception of Scout and Audaz, we had all lived many lifetimes in human forms and had lived as humans, mostly unaware of our heritage. I accepted Scout and Audaz as sharing the same Harpy spirit as us, knowing their forms were different, but nothing else. Both of our races, human and Harpy were given life powered by the Collective. In essence, we were all the same. In image, if I were to accept that God or the Collective had one, who was to say that we were not in fact created in its image and humans were the ones who evolved?

"I accept difference amongst my kind. Why is it that you experience difficulty in accepting all of God's kinds?" I said. It was Haadee who answered.

"Fear woven into our histories and teachings I suppose. Judgement and trust are heavy burdens to bare when the acceptance of other knowledge is forbidden or feared. Sometimes following what appears to be a true pathway, can create blind spots to the truth achieved by following other paths. My path, to me, is a path to the truth. I can see that yours has forced you to hide and fight to escape persecution by those in history who were denied the acceptance of the ultimate truth. That being, as you say, we are all of the same essence," said Haadee.

"If we were to become like an army, I can accept that each of us would have an invaluable roll to play. I also believe that fighting the good fight, shoulder to shoulder would enable greater understanding and acceptance between us all," suggested Matteo.

"We are agreed then, to accept differences and work towards exploring pathways to reverse or limit the damage of the current Earth truth?" asked Tarquin.

There was a unanimous 'we are' released at various volumes and the water gushing along its route. Tarquin summed up with a slightly adapted piece from Matteo's scriptures.

"Let us be fruitful and increase the number of our ideas and gains; lessen the burden upon the Earth and free it. Include the views of the fish of the sea and the birds of the air and every living creature that moves on the ground. Let us, in the eyes of the Collective, become the servants of us all," said Tarquin.

I could see Tarquin smiling warmly at Matteo. A smile escaped from the side of his mouth. He responded thoughtfully.

"A Mark of Genesis you mean?"

"There is truth in all. It is a matter of perspective," replied Tarquin.

"We all have ideas to convert to tasks. Nevaeh and I will connect into you all for further discussions to share additional ideas and progress. See you all soon," said Tarquin to all present.

Island Games

Alana touched my mind and suggested our group gather together to talk about how we were going to approach the ideas and tasks raised at the meeting. Instead of retreating to our Capri style home, she had decided we go to the island. This was a location we had created from virtual world many years ago. Virtual world was an imagination-based dimension from which imagined ideas could be created and actualised into the reality of Realm Four. Our design was based on Aogashima, an island which sits slightly more than three hundred and fifty kilometres south of Tokyo in the Philippine Sea.

The attraction was high steep cliffs and an outer rim with a volcanic, forested crater within which another raised crater nestled. Our island remained uninhabited with no dwellings, buildings or roads, other than our white washed abode. This, fringed with a wide veranda, was supported by stilts anchored into the rock face and tucked just below the crater rim.

The veranda provided beautiful views down into the crater and out to sea. Like the actual island, ours was surrounded by water as far as the eye could see, across which the winds blew creating a warm temperate climate. The other attraction was it was a great place to fly and then relax in warm water springs heated from hot spots below the volcanic rock surface.

On Earth, Aogashima was one of the closest islands to the Mariana trench, the deepest ocean trench on Earth. I knew from Alana's thoughts, she intended to investigate Aarna's ideas around revolving souls into creatures who could inhabit a world far removed from the climate change effects on the ocean surface.

Whilst it was very easy to cocoon yourself away from others, Alana and I liked to use our imaginations to create home like retreats based on our experiences whilst living on the Earth plain. Inspiration also came from those times we had visited different parts of the Earth when we were between lifetimes in the spirit or after world.

With travel being an instantaneous thought away, distance or dimension had no bearing on access or feasibilities. Locations were shared with friends or family who would come and go following a communication to locate where we were. Homes were furnished, usually in congruence with the setting or culture, however, imagination was the limit and our homes had been evolved throughout the ages. Everyone in our group accepted our invitation, with the exception of Nevaeh and on sharing the location, we transported in.

The gardens and surrounding landscape had been designed to reflect ornate Japanese water courses and ponds. Plants, trees and shrubs were carefully cultivated and manicured, with pebble pathways meandering to the contours of the grounds. Volcanic rocks of varying sizes punctuated walkways and lanterns swung from higher branches. Those lower supported bamboo wind chimes, which gently knocked to the sweetly scented breeze.

"Another nice place Joao, Alana. Why do you need so many places to live in?" asked Audaz.

"Choice and creative visual imagination. We like to create escapes. During so many Earth lifetimes, we had no peace. There were always people around and whilst interaction is important, there is also a desire for quietness and the space to reflect. We also like to share our spaces with our friends," I replied.

"Anyone up for a game of tag and mock aerial combat? After today's events of labelling and judgement, I just want to be me for a while. One of the good things about this island is its only nine square kilometres, has steep external sides to the crater and a forest to hide in, so you should be at home Audaz," suggested Alana.

"I do not need to hide Alana; I am a—"

"Harpy eagle, yes we all know Audaz. Well then?"

"We are in," said Sarah answering for herself and Simon.

"I know I will win, so I am happy to amuse you as you try," said Audaz.

"What about me," said Scout. "As a flying horse, I will be the slowest and a large and easy target."

"Scout, you asked for my help to enable you to transform to human form today. This you achieved admirably, therefore, there must be an eagle in you also," stated Audaz. "I will speak to you again in your mind, if you wish to have more of a chance by transforming?"

"I love surprises. I am excited to see who you are. Go on Scout, be your raptor," said Alana.

I could hear Audaz speaking the levels of transformation into Scout's mind and his acknowledgement of Audaz' instruction. It was clear that these two had become close friends and a great degree of trust had grown between them. I figured that this was because they were Harpies who had descended through animal lines rather than human, so instinctively they trusted each other on a different level. The transformation was instantaneous and surprising, Scout was a massive bird.

"Well, I have to sadly say that you are a double extinct," said Sarah.

All of the group were shocked by the size of Scout's bird. Although we all instinctively knew what breed of raptor Scout was, nobody had any expectation that he might be a Haast eagle. With a three-metre wingspan and talons three times the size of a human male's hand, he was a formidable predator.

"How long has your line followed the horse breed?" asked Simon.

"For as long as my preceding generations can remember, why?"

"Your raptor is a Haast eagle, the largest eagle to have ever existed. Your breed went extinct nearly several hundred years ago. It is a personal honour to meet one of our forefathers. Your history must have many fathoms, Scout."

"Can I fly like this and give you all a run for your money?" asked Scout.

"Most definitely, you are like an air tank, you could take down and lift a wolf. But we do not know your capabilities and I am looking forward to seeing you in flight," said Simon.

"Rules of engagement? No use of conventional weapons, agreed?" said Alana.

"Agreed," all answered.

"Reduced topplers only, targeted from the ajna. If you are hit, you will drop rapidly, but momentarily, only. All will know how many hits each of us has taken. If you are hit three times, you will automatically be transported back here to the veranda, where you are welcome to help yourself to a glass or two of lotus flower tune juice and watch the residual combat. If you wish to place bets, they can only be placed on others than yourself," she proposed.

"Not worth betting then," said Audaz grumpily.

"Don't worry, Audaz, I will bet on how many times I will blast your ass," said Alana.

"In your dreams, pretty bird."

"Smaller target, Audaz, your cost, my advantage," jibed Alana.

We all disappeared, with the exception of Scout, who on flapping his wings powerfully, launched himself over the ornate balustrade of the veranda and into the crater at high speed, before vanishing himself.

My first move was tactical. I chose to appear at six hundred metres above the centre of the island, giving me a panoramic view and the potential location of each of the team. I figured that most eagles spend their time when in the air looking down and I was right. Being a golden eagle provided me with a dive speed advantage and I intended to exploit it. I could see Simon and Sarah flying together towards the crater from the north as their Martial and Bald eagle raptors and guessed they could not bear the thought of shooting at each other.

"You are right, James, however, four eyes are better than two. Where are you?" linked Sarah.

I did not reply and mind blocked immediately before they were able to get a baring. A slight movement in the trees at the crater bottom gave Audaz' position away. He had double bluffed and was in fact hiding. Two shots rang out from his position impacting into Sarah and Simon, both falling twenty metres before they were able to recover.

I could feel the shock on the airwaves, followed by another shot and Audaz fell out of his tree. It was Alana. She had rematerialized back onto the veranda, a place no one assumed anyone would locate to for the game. I dived keeping Alana firmly in my sights. At four hundred metres, I took the shot, which knocked her backwards from the balustrade. She landed in a heap of feathers on the wooden floor.

"Oh, thank you, darling, I didn't see you up there. Probably because the sun is behind you and…oh, never mind."

"What? You do know I love you all the same, don't you?" I said.

Alana broke the mind link, just before I spotted a shadow growing on the crater floor. It seemed that the sun was not the only thing that was above and behind me. Scout had had the same idea and had been circling at eight hundred metres. He was now on a collision course with my position.

I stalled and span to face him, talons stretched forward and opened fire, however he had already launched his attack. The first toppler burst clipped my left-wing tip, the second impacting the side of my head. In compensation, my shot at Scout had met its mark. I dropped immediately, which was fortuitous, as Scout's flight path would have coincided with my last position and being struck by the mass of a Haast at that speed would have been painful. Well, if I had been alive and on Earth, it would. I could hear Alana chuckling.

"Oh, poor darling."

Her sympathy was short lived however, as she toppled me just after I had recovered from the fall and then blasted Scout, following the line of his recovering descent. With two shots in quick succession, she had exposed her position and had been targeted by Audaz. Miraculously, the shot curved away and missed her. I was now sitting back on the veranda watching the battle and detected what felt like an echo of magic shielding her in her efforts to evade Audaz' fire.

"That was lucky, wasn't it?" I said to her.

"I wasn't cheating. I was bending around it. The shot remained straight, the illusion was it looked like it bent around me," she replied.

"I believe you. You will have to show me that one."

Meanwhile, as Scout pumped his wings to gain height from the crater, he was intercepted by Sarah flying directly towards him. With such a wide wing span, his manoeuvrability was compromised. Without hesitation he opened fire, stalling her flight path and she dropped to reveal Simon flying directly behind her. As his form was revealed, he too opened fire and toppled Scout. Scout materialised on the veranda beside me.

"I should complain because I was outnumbered by a team, but they are my friends and it was good fun," he said.

"Well, I am not sure that being shot twice by the same adversary in quick succession, should count as part of the three hit knock out rule?" I complained.

"Ha, ha. You didn't expect that did you. I had connected to my Greek ancestry and had thought about Icarus," Scout replied.

"I am glad we thought alike. Like you, I also know of Icarus," I replied.

"Just to let you know, Sarah and I are retiring to the veranda. We have been working as one team and we have been toppled three times, so it's only fair we play equally," said Simon.

Sarah and Simon appeared on the veranda and joined Scout and I in watching the final conflict. Both Audaz and Alana had taken one hit each and the interest heightened. Audaz was one of the most powerful eagles in the world, a Harpy, with the strong grip. Although he had a slightly longer wing span than Alana, she had an 'M-shaped' wing construction and greater aerial agility.

The rainforest was his Earth hunting ground and his grey colour blended with the trunks of trees even in the crater forest. Alana as an Osprey, hunted for fish in open water. Her best chance was to draw him into the air to out manoeuvre him. There was silence and stillness for some time before either decided to declare their positions. It was Alana who broke cover first anticipating that Audaz was hiding somewhere in the forest. He remained in stealth and camouflaged, so none of us could determine his position. His voice projected from his hiding place behind her.

"As I said, we do not hide in the forests, we hunt in them."

The shot rang out and Alana toppled to the forest floor.

"That was a sneaky one Audaz. Let's see what you have got in the air?" she replied.

"I'll give you a head start as I fly a little faster than you," he said.

"Afraid to come out of the forest, are we? I thought you were a Harpy eagle not a chicken?" Alana delivering her insult, as she accelerated upwards.

"I know what a chicken is and that is not me," Audaz took off.

I knew from Alana's mind, that she was attempting to gain as much height as possible. I remembered when we first met Audaz, as he chased us across the canopy of his spirit world rainforest and wondered what she may do. She was restricting her thoughts and her plan was unclear.

She twisted and turned as he opened fire, nipping in her wings to reduce the target size as she spiralled upwards. After his third unsuccessful shot, she anticipated a short recovery time before he could fire the next and arrested her flight, turned and plummeted towards him at a forty-five-degree descent angle. Ospreys have a fifty mile an hour dive speed and in dive form, her target area was further diminished. He opened fire, missing his target. She returned fire making contact with Audaz' right wing. The impact spun him, spiralling as he dropped. Matching his descent, she locked her talons onto his and span with him.

"I could shoot you again now and win," she said.

"And I could shoot you too my friend, but the need comes with little desire."

"Draw?"

"Draw."

They both smashed into the treetops in fits of giggles as we applauded them from the veranda.

"Is the tune juice cooling, James?"

"Ready and waiting, darling."

Both joined the group and we relaxed and laughed about our game and our efforts to evade each other's sorties. The lotus tune juice was an apt refresher. The lotus a symbol for enlightenment was at the same time a symbol from moving from the darkness into the light. The task ahead would encompass both for all of us.

Tasking

"This is not a Jacuzzi, Scout, it's a hot spring," I pointed out.

Everyone was discretely shuffling away from him to provide safe distance. We had relocated from the stilted house, to one of the hot springs, both Audaz and Scout assuming human form, so that they could take part in the experience. The light water was warm and soothing.

"I have told you before, it is a horse thing. I don't even notice I am doing it."

"I wish we didn't!" I replied.

"Speaking of pollution, I heard on the guide waves recently that over eight million tonnes of plastic is finding its way into the oceans every year from Earth populations. What is up with them all? Can they not see the effects this is having on wildlife and habitats? They will turn our beautiful jewel into a wasteland literally," said Alana.

"Plastic is convenient, versatile, durable and cheap. It is so well ingrained in the consumer infrastructure that manufacturers and consumers have come to depend on it. It would take years to find replacements for all of its uses, not to mention new investment and research." I was playing devil's advocate and I knew Alana was aware of this and responded.

"I agree in part but a high level of major offending plastics come from consumer packaging and the micro debris they fracture into. In addition, large quantities of nurdles, the raw material, are spilled into the oceans from cargo ships on their way to becoming plastic products. In my view, it's the final consumer who has the power to change the chain. Perhaps by boycotting products which use it. Or by putting 'Earth warnings' on packaging: 'contains high levels of plastic, detrimental to your environment'," replied Alana.

"Can't they just burn them and use the heat to create electricity?" suggested Simon.

"That will just add to the greenhouse gases," said Sarah.

"People need to change their habits quickly. Otherwise, even the deepest parts of the oceans will become further affected. If they are, they may not prove to be a safe haven for revolving spirit creatures to take refuge in if Earth populations are reduced by climate change affects," said Alana.

"Is everyone okay if I steer the tasking?" I asked.

"Yep, that's fine by us, James," everyone agreed.

"Alana, I know you want to check out the Mariana trench as a possible safe haven, as per Aarna's idea?"

"Yes. I would like to take Audaz with me, if that's okay by him?"

"Do I have to be a fish now?" he asked sarcastically.

"Well, you could be a flying fish, if you like," she replied.

"No, I am happy to come with you. It will be an experience to encounter those in the water world," he confirmed.

"Sarah and I are going back to Between Worlds with Scout. I spoke with Tarquin after my last visit and he has shown me a way to ascertain the energy levels of dwellers there," proposed Simon.

"We are also going to visit the larger city environments. The Earth guide community has reported a growing number of attachments, where darker Leaves are attaching themselves to dark minded and vulnerable humans, in their ambitions to nurture violence and fear. We need to get an idea of how organised they have become. We also want to know if the tale of the between worlds border patrol has spread," said Sarah.

"That leaves me then. I am going into the darker realms. I want to see if we can change a few things to increase the pace of authentic transition into lighter levels, to release energy. I need to contact Arthur and see if we can recruit guides who are experienced at navigating in the dark. I don't need to say this, but let's all maintain contact and should we need a little extra help, be in a position to transport in at a moment's notice. I will let Tarquin and Nevaeh know what we are doing."

"There is one thing we haven't covered. Nobody has mentioned finding more of our kind who could help," said Simon.

"If you link in, you will see that there were Harpies who did attend meetings like ours organised by other high planers. It seems we are low in numbers, but that is probably because many of our race are either back living lives on Earth, are in the next realm up or who are remaining hidden," I responded.

"It's the ones currently on Earth that I am interested in. I am thinking whether it would be possible to wake them up, let them know who they are and help them to help Earth by giving them a direct link into us," said Simon.

"But we know, direct contact with Earth dwellers is forbidden, unless of course they are clairaudient or clairvoyant, like my grandma," I said.

"Yes, but these are testing times and we need all the help we can get. Harpies are a little more tuned in and with discretion, we may be able to generate some impact?"

"I don't know, Simon. It is something we would have to discuss with Nevaeh. But it is an idea. Good luck everyone, be mindful and take care."

Alana gave me a squeezy hug and a big kiss. "Beware the Stains, darling; they can darken your light suit."

Once again, the island became uninhabited.

A Drop in the Ocean

Alana and Audaz, now in Between Worlds, flew southwest from Japan in the direction of the Mariana trench. Between Worlds was a domain on Earth, undetectable to most Earth dwellers, with its inhabitants able to see and experience the Earth without being able to physically impact upon it.

They were looking for two types of whale, Sperm and the Cuvier's beaked whales. It was these two which dived the deepest and Alana's idea was to join them on their dives into the depths and gain a sense of life and climate in that part of the sunken world. Although neither breed was engineered to reach the bottom of the trench at thirty-six thousand feet, the beaked whale could reach depths of nearly ten thousand. It was Alana's intention to dive further deeper to ascertain the extent of life hidden there.

It was not long before we spotted a matriarchal pod of about fifteen Sperm whales with their young calves. Swimming close to them was a pod of dolphins, a few of which were playfully mingling with the whales. At ten metres above the waves, both Audaz and I transformed into dolphins and dived into the water. I knew that it was unlikely that they would be able to see us, but I was hoping the dolphins and whales would be able to detect our presence. Immediately, three dolphins split away from their group and began circling us, chattering to themselves.

"Do you know we are here?" I asked.

"We can hear you and see you in our minds, but you are here without being here. Your echoes are a bit like humans and yet you echo like birds also. Your form in my mind is in a shape like us but you are not of this world, I cannot taste you in the water," replied one of the dolphins.

"No, you cannot, as we are from a place beyond Earth and water, in a world of spirit," I replied.

"I have met spirit humans before. They come and swim with us from time to time. We cannot speak with them nor see them and they are not from another world. We have heard them say that they are of this world."

"Yes, it is possible they are Leaves. Humans who decide to stay on Earth after they have died to experience more of it or because they are scared to come to our world," I confirmed.

"Why scared?"

"Because of the things they have done in their lives, because of what they think they may have done or because they want to stay here."

"Your friend, the quiet one, is stronger with instinct, I read him as less human, although he has a part echo of one. You are strange creatures and yet I came across what you would call a blue, who had parts of his echo similar to yours."

"I am Audaz, this is Alana. You are right. My natural form is a Harpy eagle; I have lived on Earth as one for many lifetimes, but I can transform to human if I wish to. Do you mean a blue whale, one here in the oceans was like us?"

"I am Yahya, this is Chuchi and this is Orti and I am not sure if he is like you but there is something about you that reminds me of him."

Audaz and I linked minds. "Well, that's interesting, I wonder what the similarity is?" I said through the link.

"He is known as a guardian, they are interesting. There are other whale breeds who have the same echo, but there are not many, or so it is told."

"Did you just hear what I said about it being interesting?" I asked.

"Yes, we hear at many layers of upper and lower, you just changed the level."

"I am impressed," I said.

"We are sociable, we chatter and can understand and speak to many of our extended family, even Orcas, when they are in a good mood and not hungry. Are you here on a social visit?"

"Not exactly. We have come to visit the trench and see what's down there. We wish to see the difference between the surface and the depths and see what creatures live down there," said Audaz.

"Nothing can get that deep, well nothing that can live on the surface too. There is a whale that hunts squid, which looks a bit like us but much larger. We call them Beakers; they are the whales that can dive the deepest. You should talk to them," said Orti.

"We would like to but we did not spot any when we were flying in," I explained.

"The whales over there will be able to help you. They can speak into the distance further than we can and if the Beakers do not want to reply, there may be one of their kind, near a Beaker pod."

"If you could introduce us, that would be great?" I asked.

"Yes fine, I will tell them who you are and why you are here. Theirs is a thinking world as they mostly see into each other and will do the same with you as I have done. When they are in a sociable mood, they will click and whistle all day, if you are interested in the various tastes and varieties of squid, that is! I joke. They are easy to get on with, that's why we hang out with them. They know you are here anyway," offered Yahya.

Yahya swam back to the whale pod leaving Chuchi and Orti with us. I was remembering my time in Scotland with James when we met Sealgair the Earth golden eagle and fed the images to Audaz.

"Do you remember Audaz, when we were flying out of Denby Dale at the end of the battle, we were seen momentarily by Earth people?"

"Yes, I do, and judging from your Sealgair memory, I take it you want to become visible here."

"I do. I think it would help if others around us could see who we were in our chosen animal forms. You see, we are communicating with them from 'between worlds' and yet Sealgair was able to see us from her Earth world."

"Was it coming into contact with her that helped?" asked Audaz.

"Yes, by blending with her energy, but there is something else about perception. Remember when we were battling on the island and I managed to dodge your shot?"

"Yeah, Jaoh said you must have used some kind of magic?"

"Kind of, but since that encounter with Sealgair, I remember it occurring to me, how we had to slow down our vibrations or frequency to enable us to transform to eagles in Between Worlds for her to see us. I have been practicing since we got back as to how to vary the frequency levels and Yahya got me thinking when he said he could hear on many upper and lower levels. When you shot at me on the island, I had increased my frequency, but was projecting a slower one, so what you were shooting at, had already moved."

"Think it into my mind," said Audaz. "Yes, I see what you are saying. We have to project a slower version of ourselves along the same lines as how we slow down our communication, by imagining we are heard and understood."

"That's the magic. We imagine, they can imagine they are seeing us and plant the seed when physical contact is made."

"Orti? Yahya said he could sense where we are from our echo?" I enquired.

"And from your voice, I can see you in my mind from the echo, but I cannot see what you are like, like I can see Chuchi here."

"Would you help us bridge our two worlds, so you can see us?"

"I have never done that before but your presence has no threat so yes. How? What do we do?"

"We need to feel you, to sense your energy through touch. Let's make this fun. You two take off and we will try to catch you," I said.

"You will not catch Orti; he is the fastest in the pod. He is the one who keeps the shoals together when we hunt," said Chuchi.

"I am a Harpy eagle dolphin. Don't you worry, I will catch you."

Following some rapid chatter, the two of them took off at high speed. Audaz and I sped after them adjusting to the imagined water drag to make it a fair pursuit. At high speed, they would be energised with the vibrancy of anticipation, making touch electrifying.

When we caught them, the idea was to spiral our pursuit, so when we swam past them, they and we could sense our touch on both flanks, the dorsal and lower body surface. By energising the slow down transformation on the final touch, we would invite them to follow and end with a breach.

Trying to catch a dolphin was not as either of us anticipated. They were so obviously designed for speed and agility and twisted and turned avoiding us at all costs, even though they were reliant on echoes to judge our location. It was fantastic to experience them as the masters of their own habitat, playing with all of their advantage.

"I am increasing speed; I cannot match them," reported Audaz.

"Me too, they are too fast," I replied, with giggles and chatter reaching our minds.

Increasing speed in our light mode was easy and we closed the gap rapidly, however these dolphins could turn and tangent in a moment and anticipating their next direction was almost impossible.

"I would love to see these two in the air. If they could fly, they would make formidable opponents in one of our tag games," said Audaz.

"They are flying. This is amazing; their design is perfect for pursuit. We have no choice, synchronise with their next thought and mirror each movement. You go after Orti; I will catch up to Chuchi," I told Audaz.

In less than five seconds, we had caught up. Switching to spiral flight, we both shot past each of them, purposefully making contact in the four target areas. On the final touch, I saw Audaz flicker into this world. Widening the spiral both of us created vortex patterns as we powered towards the surface, slowing our outward visual projections.

"Follow us," invited Audaz.

As we broke the surface, our speed propelled us to a height of ten metres, within which Audaz managed three somersaults with twist. I gracefully piked and watched our new friends break through into synchronised longitudinal somersaults, before splashing tail first, back into the water. Yahya had returned from speaking with the whales and was excitedly breaching and chattering with his friends.

"We see you, we see you! You are shiny and you look like us!" said Orti.

Both of us chatter-laughed and thanked the dolphins for their help and the game. Our skins were silver and reflective; our forms edged in the familiar blue and white light.

"You feel different now. Your echoes are slower and yet fast at the same time. You are like star twinkles," observed Yahya.

"Yes, we have had to slow ourselves down. We exist at a much faster and complex echo or wavelength in the world we come from. We are Harpies and we are a mixture of animal and human forms. We can transform into any animal form, but here on Earth, it seems we need to make physical contact with an animal and reduce our frequency in order to appear in your world," said Audaz.

"I am keen to know something of you. Why do you breach?" asked Audaz.

There was a chatter amongst them, which was more them deciding who would answer. It was Orti who explained.

"For different reasons really. We can see really far both under and above the water, but for some reason what is above looks different in size under water. When we are travelling or hunting at speed, we use our echoes to sense what is in our paths, but we breach to check because we swim just under the surface. We also spot shoals in flight, communicate with each other and do it for fun. There is something happy about being totally in the air, then diving or splashing back down into the water. Everyone enjoys it."

"I can relate to that," I said, showing them an image of an Osprey, as it plummeted into the water to catch a fish.

"And we would love to be able to fly above the water," commented Orti.

"Cuchiq is calling. She is the head mother of the whale pod and the one I spoke to about you looking for the Beakers. Come on, I will introduce you," said Yahya.

As we approached her, the enormity of her size at nearly forty feet in length transported Audaz to a place of awe. Gentleness and wisdom exuded from her mind and with it, an overriding feeling of just wanting to be. Her purpose was to live her life enjoying the wonders of the oceans at peace with her kin.

Although skilled and veracious hunters, armed with an accurate low frequency stun gun for catching squid, they were sociable and loving beings, respected by many other species. I felt sad that over the centuries, so many had been hunted and taken at the hands of merciless and ruthless whalers.

"I listen between your thoughts and I hear that my ancestors were not the only ones who were hunted?" she said.

"Yes, you are correct. You will know I am called Alana and this is Audaz, our race did not make it past the human pursuit."

"We came close, but it seems that for the past thirty years, the humans have placed their interest in ending life elsewhere."

"Sadly, the hunting still goes on in some of the seas and oceans. If only your songs could be truly heard by them," I said meaningfully.

"Our songs are clear. It is their own voices of competition and power that deafen them to our one voice, calling to be left to be in peace," she replied.

"Thank you for agreeing to speak with us; it is a great honour and privilege to meet one of your kind. I understand you are aware of why we are here," said Audaz.

"I am and I sent out a message to the beaked whales, who have responded. There is a small pod about five hundred kilometres south of here. They are very interested to meet you as I have told them where you come from."

"Thank you. May I ask what has changed in your world that affects you most?" I asked.

"Noise. The ocean is becoming noisier. It affects our communications with our friends who live long distances away and at shorter distances if the noise is nearer. Sometimes we hear noise that does not happen often which is of a very low echo. It is almost like it is trying to speak with us, but the sound does not make sense. These are dangerous noises to us because if we are diving at greater depths, it feels like you lose yourself and can then panic. It seems to affect us less, but the Beakers cannot manage the affects as we can and there have been times when many have died by coming back to the surface too quickly."

"They call it sonar in the Earth world. The humans are trying to master echo location, something that your species does naturally," said Audaz.

"It has been present for more than my lifetime, but these sounds have arrived more recently. We have a chain system where wherever they happen in any of the oceans, the location is passed from whale to whale across them, so everyone is warned. The problem is in not just the effects, it makes us nervous about deep hunting, in case something goes wrong."

"Any other things?" I asked.

"We call them ghost floaters and we have all eaten them, apart from the very young ones. They taste of nothing but they hang in the water and when we are hunting in the dark, an echolocation of one of these things is similar to a squid. Even in lighter waters, if they are white in colour or you can see through them, they can fool you, into thinking they are food."

"This makes me so angry. This stuff is called plastic. It comes in all shapes and sizes. You must teach your friends and children to stay away from these things. If you eat enough, it will kill you," I warned her.

"Where does it come from?" asked Cuchiq.

"It comes from the things that humans throw away. Their food and drinks and all kinds of things they want is wrapped in this material. They are careless disposing of it, with large amounts getting into the seas and oceans," I said.

"It seems like they are trying to kill us off, but in a whole new and different way?"

"Sadly, Cuchiq, many of them have no idea of the dangers they create for animals and the environments and a whole lot more, don't even care," I frustratingly added.

"Are they the ones who are making the oceans warmer too?"

"Yes," said Audaz.

There was silence between us all, as Cuchiq averted her gaze to a young calf of about three years old. She nuzzled Cuchiq's flank, interpreting the sudden interest as an opportunity to latch on to a life-giving nipple. She sent an unintelligible signal and the youngster happily claimed her prize. Sighing in whale tones, she reconnected with me.

"We have a sense, which is that all will be well, but this sense diminishes. My fear is that the young calves like her will never know this sense."

"We are working in our world to try and slow this destruction and we are working at many levels. If this beautiful world is badly affected, it will damage our world as well. The humans do not know our world exists for laws state that they should not. We have to do what is within our powers and work to rebalance the ills."

"You need to work quickly," she replied.

"We know," confirmed Audaz.

"Before you leave the oceans, visit a guardian. There is a blue that is currently about seven hundred kilometres west of the largest land mass southeast of here. Reading your guesses, I think you would call it Australia. I will let him know about you, but I will not tell him of your ancestral line. There are parts of his vibration that have a striking resemblance to yours and Audaz'. You better get swimming; you have four days' hard push before you reach the Beakers."

"You are a special matriarch and I wish to thank you again. You have done nothing but help and welcome us and we are indebted to you," I said.

I swam around to the front of her head and kissed her on the nose. Audaz was chatting to and thanking the dolphins as I did this.

"Bye Cuchiq, bye boys, maybe we might see you again?" I said.

"Alana, Audaz, thank you for your visit and remember, if you are going to save the planet, start with the oceans first!"

We swam at high speed and breached, lifting to eight hundred metres after we had transformed to our raptors. At our cruising velocity of Mach 2, twice the speed of sound, we would be with the Beakers in about twenty minutes. This was not my idea, as we could have just transported there, however, I was persuaded by Audaz that this was on his Harpy eagle bucket list. I reminded him that he had already kicked that.

Between Worlds

It was a typical day in Denby Dale when Simon, Sarah and Scout, in his human form, materialised on the high street. The sun was shining and Earth dwellers were going about their business, buzzing between shops and cafes, running their errands oblivious to a few Leaves who mingled with them. Some followed the shoppers to re-experience day-to-day life as they had when living in the Earth world. Some were differently affected.

As we watched, there was an Earth dwelling man in his late thirties walking slowly along the pavement with his head lowered, as if carefully watching where he stepped. Two Leaves walked closely beside him, leaning forward occasionally to say something to the man. Each time they did, his chin would drop again, as if to avoid the content of their whispers.

The man looked drawn and tired. His apparel signalled to others not to engage, as his passage split the oncoming pedestrians, who purposefully avoided any kind of contact with him. No one acknowledged or spoke to the man, who it seemed was being placed in a world separate from others around him, even though he existed in their world.

"I have seen this before. There are many Earth dwellers who become trapped by their own minds and perceptions and their condition isolates them away from the world around them," I said.

"And we have worked with spirit who have come over, who have been in similar states, who carry a residual sense of not belonging." Sarah looked at Scout and gained acknowledgement.

"I used to call them Limpets because they cling tightly," I said.

"Why do they do this, Simon?" asked Scout.

I explained, they were not only drawn to the misery and anxiety of the person's condition, but also to the disconnection the person feels by alienating themselves from the world around them. Leaves were disconnected from the Earth world, not being able to experience it in the same way as when they were alive. An Earth person with a mental health condition can mirror the way they feel and almost becomes a bridge between the Leaf world and the Earth world.

Many Leaves were not as parasitically intense as Limpets, who would cling to Earth dwellers and other Leaves who were vulnerable. Their behaviour suggested they'd had their own issues whilst living on Earth, which they had retained even past death.

"If they feel they can in any way influence this man to act on their suggestion, they will not give up. It gives them power and they will drain that person, sometimes to a point where they will take their own lives. The added trauma being a bonus for them," I said.

"But, as you said, not all Leaves are like this, are they?" said Scout.

"You are looking at one that wasn't."

Scout smiled at Simon. "I am glad about that."

"Right! I have had enough of this. I am going to cage these two and hold them whilst we have a little chat. When we trap them Scout, you and I will take them to a quieter place. Perhaps you Sarah can—"

"I am with you. I will walk a while with our friend, share some light and try to lighten his load," responded Sarah.

The two Leaves were held to the spot as they watched their quarry walk away from them. The look of panic on their faces, signalling the uncertainty of their present situation. Materialising next to them, I spoke to them threateningly.

"You may not remember me, but I know your faces. We need to talk to you about what you are doing," I said.

Dematerialising, we took the two of them to a small copse on the outskirts of the village. Scout took over the transmission to hold the two, an anti-transitional energy that stopped them from transporting or using their weapons in retaliation.

"I know you. You are that Simon bloke who the border patrol messengers took back with them a while back. Why are you making our business, your business, this is a free country?"

"Because I am now part of that border patrol and you know what happened to the governor, you need to know that I have already messaged the tracking team with your images and vibrations."

"You mean that monster creature?" The two of them were suddenly focussed and agitated.

"Yes, that's the one. I am telling you, he and his kind will deal with you if you continue to trouble Earth dwellers."

"What happened to the governor anyway?"

"Let's just say he lives on his own in fear for himself now," said Scout.

"The problem is, we like what we do and once you have tasted, you want more. Personally, I'll take the risk. They can't track everyone."

"You think not?" I mind linked with Scout to spread his Harpy wings.

"You don't think I would come back here without one of his team, do you?" I said.

Scout crouched and with splitting the flesh longitudinally down his back, two huge skin covered wings emerged which he spread at full span. He growled and spoke intently:

"You…have…been…marked."

Tossing two hypnic topplers in between them, they fell to the ground immediately. Within a couple of minutes, they had recovered enough to hear my message.

"Your business is ours, as is others like you. I suggest you tell your Limpet friends to attach themselves to each other and not the Earth dwellers and speak to the guides coming here. You may just wake up enough to realise that a whole new world awaits you if you cross. You are wasting your time here."

"We get it, okay let us go."

Scout released their bonds and they disappeared.

"This is going to take some organising Scout. We can't keep threatening without some kind of back up action. Without it, these Leaves will catch on and resume their activities."

"We need more funding," said Scout.

"What? Where did that come from?" I replied laughing.

"I heard it from a newly passed spirit at Sarah's ranch. He said that crime was on the increase because the funding had been cut. This is like crime, so we need funding, whatever it is?"

"You know what, Scout, in a way you are right, we need resources and a way to manage these intrusive Leaves."

Sarah had been following the man for a short distance before he decided to sit down on a bench. She could detect a slight lift in his step following the departure of the two Limpets. A woman at the other end had shuffled hard up against the armrest, as he settled. He turned to her and half smiling gave a gentle nod. She huffed, got up and as she walked away, muttered 'loser'. Sarah could feel the momentary reprieve of his freedom fall from his heart into his stomach and a tear rolled down his cheek.

"I am not a loser; I'm just not well at the moment."

"Yes, not a loser, just a little lost to yourself," Sarah gently whispered.

"Yes, I'm just a little lost."

Sarah held the powers of a skilled healer and intuitively deciphered the complexities of the man's aura and vibration. Blending red, yellow and green light from her own chakras, she let the energy rise to her ajna and specifically coating it in indigo light, propelled it through the man's own insight energy centre. The light dissipated to the corresponding base, solar plexus and heart chakras which gently kick started each of them spinning again. She could tell that they had been shut down for some time. The man slowly raised himself to sit more upright and took a deep breath as if surfacing from water.

"Breath through your nose letting your stomach expand. Then blow out through your mouth. Be not afraid of your emotions, even though you may have been neglected in your growing years. Allow them, they will lead you to being well again," another whisper.

The man followed her lead and breathed as she had asked. Tears welled in his eyes and then he smiled to himself. He sniffed hard and wiped away the tears on his sleeve.

"I am loveable, aren't I?"

"You are loveable and you are who you are," Sarah replied.

The man rose from the bench. When he got to the pavement edge, he turned back.

"Thank you," he whispered.

"You are welcome. Can I ask, did you hear me?"

The man turned away and walked across the street without replying. He hesitated in front of a café, walked past, then retraced his steps to its door. Sarah watched him take a deep breath and walk inside.

She sat motionless for a while and wondered about how she could be sure that Earth people could hear her and whether she should be doing what she had just done. Sarah connected to Neveah and sent her the sequential mind and emotion images.

"Do what you do best. Do not concern yourself with whether you are breaking laws, Sarah. Listening creates affects at many levels and it is the nonverbal responses, such as the one where he followed your breathing request, which should provide the evidence you seek. Remember, don't strive, always allow," advised Nevaeh.

"Thank you. Have you heard from any of the others?"

"No, but I know they are all fine."

"Catch you later."

"Hi, Alana, how are you doing?"

"Travelling at Mach 2 at the moment across the Pacific Ocean on our way to visit a pod of beaked whales."

"Why didn't you just transport in?"

"Tell me about it! I am co-operating with a wish from Audaz. I tell you what though, you want to see some of these plastic waste fields floating on the surface, they are immense. This is madness. There is little life beneath them and the toxins that must be leaching out of them must be horrendous. If the Earth populations really knew what affect they were having, they would be treating them like oil slicks and cleaning them up. I am getting more concerned."

"Me too," said Sarah.

"How are you getting on?"

"Just a toe in the water so far. I've been healing Earth dwellers."

"Doing what you do best then?" said Alana supportively.

"That's what Nevaeh said. Catch you later, Alana, I have Simon coming in."

"See you."

Scout and I rematerialized beside Sarah and exchanged our experiences.

"Let's have a wander. I want to talk to some of the Leaves around here," I said.

We were approached by a group of three Leaves, one Scout recognised from the two left who disappeared after we had banished the governor.

"Hello, Simon, no hard feelings?"

"That depends on what you are up to now, Nigel?" I replied.

"Things are very different around here since that group of angel birds and the flying horse took you. We weren't sure if they had tricked you into going with them."

"No, I went willingly. I realise now, I wasted too many years in this place. Your friends who came with us are doing well and finally enjoying life in the after world. There is not one of them who regrets going over. This option is open to you also, there is nothing to fear, in fact there is more to fear here in Between Worlds."

"No, you are all right, Simon. I like it here. The fear feelings are similar to those I felt when I was alive. I manage them like I have always done. I have to say though; it is interesting meeting you again after all the years I knew of you when you were here."

"And why is that?"

"Because I can clearly see you have been brain washed into accepting non-reality."

I smiled at him. "I have accepted that reality to some is not reality to others. The difference is perception based on what is true to you and the purity of truth comes from knowing, not risking something is true."

"How do you know though; do you just suddenly believe it?"

"No. You wrestle with it until the point is reached when the reasons not to accept the change are outweighed by those that support it. Then you decide."

"Umm. But the decision is still a risk."

"Of course, but with less doubt in that risk and if you decide to change something and action it, you are defining who you are, as it is our actions which define us, not our thoughts about action. It's up to you. I am not here to convert you, well, convince you otherwise."

"Why are you here then?" asked Nigel.

"You said things were different around here. We wanted to know how they had changed?" asked Scout.

Nigel explained that news of the visit had travelled far and wide. That there was a group of unusual bird spirits and a flying horse, who came with a monster. They called themselves messengers from the after world who were some kind of border patrol. The governor had been well known and after he was banished, others like him either scaled down their activities or stopped them, fearing they would also be targeted. Since his departure, no one had taken his place and there had been less hostility as Leaves were no longer threatened or bullied into controlling others for him.

"We see more regular visitors from the after world come and go when they visit their families and yes, we still encourage the newly departed to stay. But on the whole, this place is more peaceful," he concluded.

"What about the Limpets?" asked Scout.

"Their neediness they brought over from their lives on Earth seems to get more severe here. They are fixated and they are always on the hunt. Most of us just deal with them and send them away. There are other more vulnerable Leaves who are manipulated by them and their lives are harder, as are certain Earth dwellers they attach themselves to," said Nigel.

Sarah had spotted another of these beings who had attached herself to a young Leaf woman walking hurriedly down the street. They turned left down a side road approaching an old mill and out of her view.

"Excuse me, gents, I need to be somewhere else," Sarah disappeared.

"Do you see them as the same as you, as Leaves I mean?" asked Scout.

"Yes, but it's almost like they live in another world or they are not in their right minds."

"Living in another reality you mean," I replied raising my eyebrows in question.

Nigel smiled out of the corner of his mouth. "Their actions are real enough; why they need to do it is based on their reality. Yes, okay, not mine."

"Maybe I will see you again one day, Nigel, it has been good to talk."

"And you, Simon, you appear well."

The group of three resumed their journey along the High Street. I linked into Sarah, knowing why she had disappeared. She told me she needed to handle this situation on her own. Respecting her wishes, I took Scout on a guided tour of the village to show him the Leaf hotspots in order to gather more information.

Sarah reappeared about a hundred metres from where the two were. Neither detected her presence as the young woman sat propped up against the mill wall with her face in her hands. The other woman was bent over her, poking her intently with her forefinger in an attempt to keep her attention. Fighting with her own true nature, Sarah overcame the doubt and purposely powered up each chakra focussing the mass of energy in her base. She then accelerated it upwards, directing it through her ajna and blasted the Limpet in the back of her head. She fell to the ground immobilised.

"Stay where you are. I am no threat to you. The woman who was harassing you will be disabled for a few minutes, then I will deal with her," she said to the young woman.

"Who are you and why did you do that."

"I am Sarah, part of the border patrol from the after world. It seems like this person has grown quite attached to you. I assume her attention is unwelcome?"

"She has not let me alone for two months now. Is this place hell or something?"

"No, there is no hell, only darker and colder places and they are a part of my world."

"I am Chloe," she said, lowering her gaze.

Chloe was about five, seven, with straggly strawberry blond hair, which fell about her shoulders. With a pale complexion and a drawn physique, she reflected the effects of her later life choices.

"I see you have some shame going on in that young mind of yours." Sarah had already read her mind and emotions and knew her story, however, let Chloe find her own voice.

"I'm not from around here, I come from Leeds. But I wanted to get away from the city, it is too dangerous. I did not realise I would get this kind of problem around here as well. I was only twenty-two when I died, that was three months ago," she said.

"Why didn't you go with the catcher when you died?" asked Sarah.

"Because I thought I would go to hell. I got mixed up with some bad people towards the end. This Leaf told me I would definitely go to hell and he would help me if I stayed. He was nowhere to be seen after about an hour and I was all on my own. I soon found out that my family could not hear me and I didn't know what to do or where to go."

"Have you seen anyone else from my world?"

"Yes. There is this man I see from time to time. I know he wants to talk to me, but there is much talk around here about not trusting the 'other worlders', so I just run away."

"You can trust him. He will not force you to do anything you do not want to. You are actually talking to me and I come from the same place."

"Yes, but you say you are part of the border patrol, the bird-people and I don't know why, but it feels like you are really genuine."

In the time since they had been talking, Sarah had been transmitting sky-blue light towards Chloe's throat chakra to enable her to speak from her feelings and a mixture of the same light and green light to create a bridge with her heart.

"Also, I know that the border patrol helped a lot of Leaves free themselves from this place and they symbolise some kind of hope beyond the mistrust. Are you a bird-woman?"

"I am."

"An eagle?"

"Yes. If you stay here and wait for me while I speak with this person, I will show you what I am, as you are showing me more of who you are."

"I am going nowhere!" Chloe said.

Chloe's unwelcome companion was beginning to come around and Sarah fixed her with the light sphere restricting her actions. She struggled in her heart again with a real sense of compassion for this person, whose needs had become so distorted that she had become blind to the needs and choices of others. Sarah knew that a message must be sent to those like her in an attempt to halt the kind of torture they administered on others. The woman was wild eyed and jittery.

"Enough of this. You must stop what you are doing," said Sarah.

"You can't hold me forever, bitch. Piss off, she's mine."

The transformation to her Bald Eagle was instantaneous. Sarah grasped the woman's feet in her talons and took off beating her powerful wings. Although she knew she could not physically hurt her, the woman screamed and cursed as she struggled still held by the sphere. Lifting her to about five hundred metres, Sarah invaded the woman's mind with her thoughts.

"Getting an idea of what it is like to be controlled by another? You have a choice in this."

"You are not going to drop me in this cage, are you?" the woman asked.

"That is up to you. All I am asking is for you to stay away from vulnerable Leaves like Chloe and Earth dwellers as well."

"She is a low life," cursed the woman.

Sarah dropped her, still caged and dived to match the velocity of her descent keeping eye contact with her and calmly speaking into her mind. She knew they had about twelve seconds before the woman hit the ground.

"You do know I can keep you in this state for centuries." Sarah was counting down the seconds out loud.

"So I have heard. Okay, okay. I will do what you say. Now let me go. Please."

Before releasing her, Sarah flooded the woman with violet light. There were too many chakras imbalanced for her to work on everything in the drop time. This light would offer her the opportunity to spiritually connect to her sense of Self if she chose to.

"Pleeease…!"

Sarah released the cage and the woman vanished. She flew back to where Chloe was stood watching and landed gracefully in front of her. Shaking her feathers, she transformed back.

"You are amazing. I can see why people call you angels. Thank you for helping me, I don't deserve it you know. I… I…was a drug dealer when I was alive."

"Why?" asked Sarah.

Chloe explained she was made homeless when her mum's new boyfriend and she could not get on. The truth was, he also had designs on her but her mum didn't believe her and still kicked her out. She had sofa surfed with friends and then acquaintances and benefits always got messed up and suspended, leaving her with no money. Being homeless was expensive because without a base she was reliant on takeaways and readymade foods in order to eat.

A 'friend' of hers, who she owed money to, persuaded her to sell weed as a way of settling her debts. She soon realised she could do this on her own, make money, plus users gave her a kind of respect. She rarely made a lot of money, but it got her by and she could stay under the benefits radar.

"I wasn't greedy or anything and just managed to plod along, if you call phone calls at all hours of the day and night and sealing deals, plodding. And then I met this guy, who I must admit, I fancied and he used to chase. I had never used heroin and did not intend to but it happened and I got a taste."

Chloe said that it wasn't long before she needed and so became a more regular user.

"I did some dirty things to get fixed that I am not proud of, but I never pushed it on anyone else. I always saw weed as fun and very different from harder drugs, after all it does grow naturally."

"So does hemlock," I said, my point not registering.

"Anyway, when you are stoned, it makes you think you are channelling wisdom, so after having a good giggle, my friends and I would put the world to rights."

"How did you pass over, Chloe?"

"I went to this sort of party with my boyfriend. Just a place to get wasted really. He left pretty soon after we got there and I was okay talking to this dealer. I was negotiating a hit and he told me he would give me two for a discount. He said he would be there all night so after I had taken the first hit, he would give me the second, which would keep me in for much longer. I had done this before and because I was now injecting, it wouldn't be a problem. My guess is he had to leave early and he gave me the second too soon. The next thing I knew, I was having an out of body experience watching myself rattling."

"Rattling?"

"Gurgling, having difficulty breathing."

"Who was with you?"

"No one I knew well. There were these two girls who hadn't been using long, who looked inside the room where I was, saw me and then shut the door. That's when I started to panic, but I was dead within two minutes. I thought I had gone straight to hell."

"Why did you think that?"

"I did not know at the time, obviously, but after a few minutes, there were five male Leaves in that room. All of them aggressive and barraging me, telling me I was a low life and that I was dead and should come with them, as I would not be going into heaven. Then this other guy showed up, he was a bit like you and tried to calm me down. He was followed by another guy less angry than the others. He took my hand and said 'don't trust him, darlin', he may come over nice, but he will take you straight to hell. I know his kind. Come with me, you look scared, I will look after you'. You know what happened next."

"Why did you leave the city?"

"Too many Leaves and so many of those Limpet kinds. They were on my back all the time. Also, I had to get away from what I had done."

When she used and dealt weed, she and her friends used to laugh at people who smoked and got paranoid, calling them lightweight. When she had died, she had gone back to her patch and seen that every one of the paranoid smokers both living and, in this world, had Limpets attached to them. It was as though the drug opened a link or channel for these things to get through. She could see they were suffering and knew she had caused this. It was the same story in the wider drug community.

"It's like the disease follows you past death. And now, I can't even kill myself to escape from them," said Chloe.

As Chloe spoke, Sarah linked to Tarquin who informed her of the likelihood that Chloe would go into Realm Three if she passed, the less harsh of the after world Dark Realms. She knew that Steve was the catcher who served this West Yorkshire area and linked to him to place him on standby.

"No that's right, you cannot kill yourself, but you can change something on another level. Do you trust me?" asked Sarah.

"I think so, why?"

"You have a choice. You can get out of this place and the fact that you have started to take responsibility and are regretful of what you have caused, is going to help you. True, you are not going to get into the part of heaven where I come from, but the place where you will go is not hell. It is a place that will help you to deal with the consequences of your life's path and the actions you have contributed towards others taking. I can tell you now, you will find more peace there than here."

"Like a prison you mean, because I have done wrong?"

"No, not a prison, you are not confined and there will be plenty of others around you to learn from and care for."

Chloe let out a long sigh.

"If I want to find the truth, there is no way around this, is there?"

"You could stay here."

"Will I ever get into heaven; after what I have done?"

"It is only you who will stop you from getting there."

Sarah stepped forward and wrapped her arms around her, drawing her close. As she released her, she could see that Chloe's eyes brimmed with tears and knew she had chosen.

"I am a bit scared," she confessed.

"If we trace our fears to their source in us, they show us more of who we are. Do not fear, fear itself, it is a signpost to knowing more."

"Thank you for finding me."

"This is Steve. He is a friend of mine and he is going to take you over. Trust him. Good bye for now, Chloe, come and find me when you have found your path."

Steve took her hand and led her into the mouth of a tunnel he had created through to the after world. She turned, smiled and waved as the entrance closed.

"Simon, it's Sarah. I think we need to get into the cities as soon as possible. The Leaf I have been talking to has described them as pretty desperate."

"We have been following your conversations with the young woman. Nice one by the way, you are so good at this darling, proud to be your mate. Let's go for London, might as well start with the biggest," I replied.

I tuned into Tony, James' last Earth guide to see if he could recommend and locate a guide who could lead us into one of the areas in London, most prevalent with Leaf activity. The plan was to get a feel for the Leaf sub culture of such an area, probably one which was most affected by crimes committed by Earth born dwellers.

Trauma was a great attraction to a lot of the Leaves who feared to pass over and where there was misery, there would always be Leaves. Within seconds, Tony had found someone willing to help and gave us the coordinates for a meeting. Linking together, all of us relocated.

Into the Dark

"Do you think the Collective operates like a system, James?" asked Arthur, my Earth guide friend.

"I think it is more than just a reactive system. I think lower order parts of it operate much like ours when reacting to temperature, thirst or hunger, responding to needs automatically. I don't believe the Earth is part of the Collective, nor did it create it, but it knows it intimately. I think it is now predicting as part of its consciousness or instinct, which is causing a lower order system to build energy reserves."

"You mean it feels insecure?"

"Yes, but more than insecure. I think it is afraid that if it cannot accumulate enough energy to maintain the balance on Earth and the realms, it then faces the unknown. Something that it strives to overcome through all of us generating knowing. If you think about it, certain animals on Earth will instinctively gather food stores before going into hibernation to combat the unknown," I said.

"Could the Collective be changing the Earth for some reason and with it, life on it?"

"I don't think the Collective has any influence over the way the Earth adjusts to changes caused by tectonics, weather or atmospheric pollution. It influences life, as we know, but not the template it exists on. Like you, I think it is responding to the potential for a threat to life and with life being its energy source, it is investing heavily by over populating to maximise a return if populations are dramatically reduced on Earth."

"But it must know it is making things worse, unless it has adopted an acceptable collateral damage approach," proposed Arthur.

"Again, I think it is much like us, Arthur. It must be because it is a collective consciousness and I reckon this is where the system bit or your thermostat idea comes in. If we are starving or dehydrated, for example, we become driven to satisfy the need, we become reactive more than proactive and focus on righting what is immediately threatening our survival, rather than the bigger picture. It may have a critical level of energy it must acquire to satisfy what will be needed to survive the level of catastrophe it is predicting. Potentially, over population will continue until that level is reached and the thermostat shuts down."

"But the Collective is supposedly all-knowing?"

"Maybe it hasn't faced this before. Maybe it sees over population as the only way to survive, even though it speeds up the demise of the Earth. This is why the high planers are attempting to become sounding boards for it and we are working to find possible ways of re-righting the system."

Arthur and I were at his lighthouse waiting for a guide called Thomas to arrive. He had spent many years working with those who resided in the Dark Realms. He and his team worked selflessly, encouraging residents to see themselves and others in the truth of their previous Earth lifetime and to take responsibility for actions against themselves and others. It was an occupation demanding patience, empathy and allowing. Although guide experience enabled them to see through behaviours to the truth, progress was only achieved by the authentic acceptance from the person involved.

Neither Arthur nor I had visited the Dark Realms previously and whilst Arthur knew of Thomas, it was Tarquin who had arranged for us to meet and work together. My first impressions of Thomas, when he materialised, were that he was a jolly looking man with a mop of fair hair, about five ten and robust in stature. His pale-blue eyes provided an intensity to his impression which seemed to be contra to the rest of his appearance.

"Hello, James, Arthur. Have you packed your sandwiches and a flash light?" Thomas greeted us warmly with a big grin. "Oh, and you will need your hiking boots if we are going into Realm One."

Both of us greeted him in return. I was pleased there would be the possibility of some humour on our trip to balance Arthur's intensity.

"Do you intend to take us into Realm One today?" asked Arthur.

"We will do a short visit to all three. It will give you an idea of the terrain and we will make time to meet some of the residents. I will make no apologies for the phrase; 'you will follow my lead and do what I say'. These are fear-based realms, especially one and two and you must remain guarded at all times. Some of the individuals you will come across have two priorities: create fear and control. They will take every opportunity to manipulate you in any way they can," said Thomas.

"Splendid. How dark is dark?" I asked.

"The lowest two have no sun or stars. Realm Two is lit by something like an aurora from time to time. It changes colour occasionally and we like to think it responds to the overall chakra emissions of the residents, depending on how they feel. The rest of the time there is a subdued glow. The terrain is like tundra with rocky outcrops and water expanses, like lakes. Rocks are a currency because shelters are built from them by residents and there are never enough rocks."

"Are there relationships between the residents?" I asked, attempting to gain an idea of collaboration and community.

"Relationships exist and are an indication of progress because of the trust indicators. You will see that mostly, they are forged out of co-dependency, thus perpetuating their conditions," Thomas replied.

"And what is One like?" asked Arthur. I could tell by his tone, he had reservations around this visit.

"In the main, it is gloomy, subdued and in some of the deeper places, it is almost pitch dark. Realm One is mountainous; we don't know why. Most of the inhabitants live on the mountains and the most affected live at the bottom of the valleys and in cracks and crevices."

"Crevices, how do they live there?" asked Arthur.

"Some of the evilest, a term I use for ease of description, choose to have no form. They can appear in the simplest of guises as a stain. When they are hunting, they will attach themselves to an unaware dweller in an attempt to manipulate them and draw energy from them. Unfortunately, many go unnoticed and they add to the suffering of the host."

"Can you communicate with a stain?" I asked, the thought difficult to comprehend.

"They have the same consciousness as us but rarely communicate out of it. They are difficult to support because their will and awareness are subdued, other than that employed to cause another to suffer. This is a hostile environment, made hostile by the inhabitants' own choices. Relationships are very rare; it is a case of every man and woman for themselves and isolation is usually the order of the day."

"How big are these realms?" asked Arthur.

"There appears to be no limit, but there are horizons suggesting a spherical construction. There are no pockets of separate mini universes within them and there is no virtual world facility in any of them either. Comfort is sparse and inhabitants are where they are through choice of action and so suffer as they dealt suffering to others on Earth," replied Thomas.

"What about their ability to use weapons," I asked.

"Most of the dwellers in Realm One are inactive. Meaning their chakras are shut down by their own choices. Therefore, they do not have the energy to project light-based emotion like we can. They will use creeper vortices and you might see the occasional solar plexus shot, but not much else other than a parasitic attachment used by the Stains. It's a different story in Realm Two and Three. However, weapons use is a choice and they are well aware that they will affect their progress if they use them to persecute. Not that, that stops them and some just don't give a damn, with other residents staying out of their way."

"Do you intervene in hostilities?" asked Arthur.

"No, these realms are here for people to contemplate their actions and take responsibility for what they have done. There is no reward here, other than that which they generate themselves by gaining Self-awareness. We continuously remind them they are the ones who can lighten their futures and it's up to them to adopt a way of being that frees them from the dark."

I asked what the residents thought and felt about guides coming in from the higher planes and Thomas explained they were received with a lot of contempt and suspicion. The realms had been in existence for thousands of years and were deemed by inhabitants as a prison. It appeared that many residents believed they were being held here against their will, that the justifications for their actions placing them, were unsound.

In knowing of the existence of higher realms, they would continue to profess their innocence, even though they had judged themselves and had sealed their own fate. It was the curse of denial that many were affected by and yet they were not alone, as denial was rife across all three of these realms, the Earth and continued to maintain a presence in Realm Four.

It made me think whether denial was purposely seeded into us by the Collective as something we were supposed to overcome with awareness and will, to generate the energy and knowing it required. After all, truth is the only thing that the Collective would really be interested in to widen its knowing. Yet, at the same time, there is truth underlying non-truth, which shrouded the reasons behind misdeeds, which people continue to deny. Back on Earth, nobody likes to be lied to and yet we have the ability to lie to ourselves and believe it, or somehow overlook it. Yet, without denial, there would be no opportunity for us or the Collective to grow.

It was as though we were being purposely handicapped to benefit the Collective, but this wasn't a system, this was more like cultivation to feed the system. I was thankful that as Harpies, we were more instinctual in our reasoning giving some reprieve. However, when reincarnated on Earth in human form, we seemed to be equally affected as humans. At this point, I wished I had been a horse. I could sense Arthur listening to my thoughts and he suggested that we were becoming more alike by the hour.

"What about Realm Three. What is that like?" I asked.

"This is a more pleasant place to work," said Thomas.

There was a sun which rose, but it is like a winter sun that barely ascended over the horizon, so the daylight was shorter. Again, there was no virtual world facility, so people could not imagine things and create them like we could in Realm Four. They were, however, able to transport themselves within this realm, unlike One and Two.

Over the millennia, inhabitants had built simple structures to live in, but in the absence of either virtual world or technology, the existence was medieval. Like the other two realms, there were no animals however in this one; there were trees and plant life, with a climate which was temperate but never warm. The terrain was mixed with mountainous regions, rolling countryside and coastal areas.

"It is pleasant but not beautiful," described Thomas.

"It sounds like a place, that hasn't quite got there yet, but shows promise," said Arthur.

"Exactly like the residents. Many know of the beauties of Earth and this hasn't quite got them. But that's the point because neither have they and it serves their reflection. It is a lot easier to work with the inhabitants there," confirmed Thomas, who continued to outline its impression.

There were relationships between people and a sense of community. The different Earth races tended not to mix and the tribal mentality persisted with some further issues caused. The important thing was it was like Earth but without the abundant beauty and sunshine.

Inhabitants knew that life was better and more rewarding in the higher realms and this gave them the opportunity to reflect on what was behind them in their histories and what was possible for them in the future. Minors could also be found in this realm, whereas they were not in Realms' One or Two. Many thought wrongly that Realm Three was an open prison. Again, the inhabitants held the keys to secure their freedom from it.

"Who lives here?" Arthur asked.

"There are inhabitants who have graduated from Realm Two, some from Realm One, but mostly and increasingly so, it is occupied by people coming directly from Earth. What a lot do not realise on Earth, is we have a responsibility to know our Selves and others. To build awareness and channel will to foster right relations, meaning not to seek power over another to satisfy some kind of inadequacy. So many cannot get this and denying instinctual right relation or using ignorance as an excuse for behaviour which impacts on others' lives, is not enough for them to escape a period of reflection in this realm."

"What kind of things are you working with?" I asked.

"Other than guiding them to reach and maintain a level of responsibility, we mostly work with issues such as guilt, shame, lack of empathy and denial. There are those who realise and accept what they have done and the impact they have caused, but self-forgiveness is harder to achieve. I am thankful we have the Self-judgement system, as orchestrated directly by the Collective and it is not left to us to decide whether they have reached a state of internal balance qualifying move on."

"Am I correct in thinking it is the same as the judgement agreement made between Earth dwellers and the Collective when they pass over to the after world from Earth?" I asked.

"Yes, except the dwellers here, know the outcome is a reality. They know that Realm Four or heaven exists," he confirmed.

As a rule of thumb for Earth dwellers, the degree of suffering created was the gauge for entry into Dark Realms. If there was a degree of consciousness, which motivated the individual to cause the intended suffering of another, an animal or the environment, you arrived at malicious intent. This would confirm your reservation as one of the Dark Realm guests on your departure from Earth.

"This free will has lot to answer for," I said.

"And free will, merely allows us to choose. But without it, our worlds would not exist."

"Will we start in Realm Three?" I asked.

"No, we are in the deep end first. Guards in place, we will start in the depths of One. Follow my lead and stay close. And by the way, they are attracted to light so we will have no shortage of inquisitive observers," said Thomas.

The first thing that hit me was the cold and then the dark. It was freezing and I adjusted my need for warmth. Although it was not totally pitch dark, it was difficult to see, however our light bodies emanated enough to make out shapes and forms in a five-metre radius. Beyond this, there was an overwhelming sense of being closed in, the blackness manipulating the senses and resurrecting earthly childlike fears of menace poised to strike from the shadows.

"Not somewhere you would choose for your holidays, hey boys, let alone live in," commented Thomas.

I linked to Arthur in an attempt to comfort the fears intensifying from the unknown and was met with a similarity in his perceptions. The old adage of safety in numbers was somehow defeated by the eeriness and intensity of the unexpected, which was placing me on edge.

Being guarded and being a Realm Four light spirit increased my courage as did my faith in Thomas who appeared relaxed and composed. I shook the feeling off and looking ahead, could see four sinister patches on the ground moving towards us. They slithered along, attempting to come as close as possible.

"It is hard to think that these were once humans living on Earth," I said.

"They could transform back to that form if they chose to. This is self-inflicted self-pity, plus it creates fear in the others living here, which is a bonus for them."

"So they are totally capable of hearing and responding to you?" asked Arthur.

"They are if they choose to respond, many do not," replied Thomas.

"Who are these people then?" I asked.

"To use the phrase, you are in luck, is the wrong description, but we have someone here in front of us who is well known on Earth, but few would consider his presence an honour. If this Stain was in human form, you might just recognise him. You will know his name for sure. This is Adolf," said Thomas.

"You are joking!" I replied.

I found myself fighting with the notion of stepping on him, but I wasn't sure how long it would take to scrape him off my shoe. The stain stopped in its tracks.

"Now James, my friend, just you stay there with that thought and feeling," said Thomas thoughtfully. "I want you to contemplate the idea of him having started on his road to awareness and regret where there were slight glimmers of hope in his resistance. Would you still step on him and crush any inkling of hope and trust he might have worked hard to gain? Or would you support him to move forward? Let's hypothesise and consider him being able to work on himself enough to even get past Realm Three and into Realm Four, where in ten years he decides to revolve. Back on Earth in his next lifetime, he would have no idea what he did in his previous one and neither would anyone else around him. He could even revolve to become a care giver or a midwife, someone respected and admired for their dedication to serving others."

What Thomas said connected and sparked my sense of compassion. Who was I to take away the opportunity of another finding their way through to the light.

"I see what you mean; all should have an opportunity to redeem their actions, whatever the magnitude." The words coming from my mouth slowed by my contemplation of the sheer horror of his actions.

"And the Collective allows that opportunity. I wonder about how many, if standing face to face with the Collective would challenge its decision to do so?" said Thomas.

I looked at Arthur, who had suddenly mind blocked. He took five paces forward and stamped on the Stain, grinding his foot into the dirt.

"No!" shouted Thomas.

It was immediately apparent, Thomas was not concerned for the Stain, which had now attached itself to Arthur's leg and was pulsating slowly, as if suckling from his light form. Arthur, having fallen to the ground held a look of a person caught in quicksand, one where all hope is lost.

"Blast it, blast it off!" I shouted.

"No. Hold your fire, that is exactly what he wants you to do. These beings feed off negative energy and conventional weapons which are designed to create anxiety and foreboding add to the negativity they already possess. If you did, it would increase his ability to cause fear. Don't work against me, I know what I am doing," stressed Thomas.

Thomas created a dome shield around all of us including the Stain to ensure the others could not approach further towards us. I was more than a little concerned that this thing was now inside it with us and could not get out even if it wanted to. Arthur was slowly losing his luminescence, eyes closed and teeth clenched.

Thomas instructed me to generate a golden-yellow cord projecting out from and still connected to my solar plexus chakra. He intertwined it with a green cord projected from his own heart. Conducting the combined threads, he bound them around the Stain attached to Arthur's leg.

"Flood your cord, it will reduce the effects of anxiety and fear and lift optimism."

I did what he asked and increased the rotational speed of this energy centre to maximise its output. Thomas energised his heart, transmitting unconditional love, empathy and compassion. The binding glowed as the Stain fought to increase the veracity of its draining task, then slid from Arthur's leg onto the ground still bound.

"I will hold him; Arthur will be all right for a while," said Thomas.

Thomas caged the being with a sphere of golden light and shrunk the dome to protect Arthur only, whilst we further energised our own guards. He filled the dome with violet light.

"What now? Will you speak with him?" I asked.

"I have never heard him utter a word in all the years I have known of him. But I have never bound him before and the effects of the cords might evoke something," said Thomas.

Suddenly, the stain metamorphosed into human form and broke the cords with a downward thrash of his right arm. He stood there, chin raised inspecting us with a look of contempt. Being in close proximity to a man who had directed and sanctioned the suffering and death of millions of people on Earth was surreal.

My mind could not clear and vibrated in on itself as it struggled with anchoring the enormity of his actions to whatever his truth was behind what had driven him. I accepted that power begets power, but the motive behind the need for power is always based on insecurity or dis-ease. I linked to Thomas and asked him to trust me as I had done him. He nervously agreed, then caught my train of thought.

"This could be interesting!" said Thomas.

I addressed the Stain. "I guess you needed to do what you just did and I guess that is because you believe you must remain in control?" There was no reply or gesture to acknowledge my question.

"I am not a guide for this world, but I come in the spirit of Gebo," I said.

The single word and symbol taken from a language I knew would be elusive to many, connected to something central to him. He diverted his eyes towards mine. As he did this, I transformed into my eagle and spread my wings horizontally. His raised eyebrows were an obvious gesture of his surprise. He fixed a look of scrutiny on me, holding my eyes and muttered three words:

"Reich or Odin?"

"Neither. I am Harpy."

"Myth!"

"Extinct. We were hunted and exterminated. Too different it seems."

"Here to remind me, it seems." His eyes narrowed.

"No, to offer insight in the form of symbolism which may connect to your creative interest in the occult. Its power is in your reach. My guess is meaning may evade you presently but, if you choose to connect to what you know, you may reveal it once more," I said.

I folded my wings and spoke. His interest remained with me as I delivered the words. I told him that although Hagalaz and Laguz surrounded him as a consequence of his actions, Raido was possible by becoming aware of who he truly was. He would need to draw from Uraz at the same time to build a greater connection to Eihwaz.

Imagining the rays of Sowilo penetrating him and supporting each of his successes would allow him to know more. Tiwus could be his, but his journey would be painful. By drawing on Berkana, he would continue to grow and be sustained. The journey's companion would of course be Thurisaz; however, Jera would come into view if he remained true to himself.

"I can hear and understand you. But the path is not possible without the power of Dagaz and I dare not even contemplate asking," he replied, his eyes never wavering from mine.

The green and yellow glimmer had almost dissipated from his form and I could sense him shift back towards his darkness again. Thomas removed the cage, but he did not move.

"I am confused as to why you people come here. Why would anyone want us out of here?" he asked.

"Because we always work with the spirit of Mannaz," I answered.

"Something else I dare not ask for. However, in the name of my sanity, not all of you do, as that man lying there obviously doesn't. Sieg heil." Adolf dissolved his form and slithered away into the shadows as I transformed back.

"Now let's get Arthur out of here," said Thomas.

We stayed within the realm but transported to a mountaintop where it was a little lighter. Thomas set the dome shield again as we tended to Arthur. After administering further violet light, Arthur started to come around, then connected to me to orientate and update himself. While connecting, I discovered he was a victim of a Nazi death camp in his last but one lifetime, incarnated as a woman.

"I was overwhelmed by hatred and disgust; feelings I have not felt for years since being in the after world. I am sorry and not sorry for what I just did James."

"It's okay, Arthur, you had your reasons." The words designed to comfort.

"They made us strip, then we were herded into a large box like tank. The guards told us they were showers so we could get clean after our long train journey. We had no idea where we were or what was happening. We had been separated on our arrival from our families and children, being told we would see them later. So much fear of the unknown. As the doors closed against our crowded bodies, voices were rising and other women were crying. There were three clanks as the Zyklon B canisters were dropped from above, then nothing but screaming, terror, burning and so much pain."

"It's all right, Arthur, I can see this awful history in your thoughts and feelings," I spoke gently, as I tried to sooth him. Arthur was intent on continuing with the horror of his experience.

"No, I want to speak it, James. The moment we were all dead, so many catchers suddenly appeared, opening tunnels into the tank walls in all directions as they moved to swiftly transport us from that death trap. Many women were still hysterical or locked with fear having no idea who these light beings were and whether or not they could be trusted. The sudden brightness of light caused so much confusion, until they individually calmed us. As the terror and horror subsided, they worked effectively, to escort us all upon our journeys before the doors opened again. I was told by my catcher that this was done to avoid a panic and people running to escape in all directions, not knowing what had happened. He was kind and so warm. I remember he said, if I didn't like the look of heaven, I could always return to Earth one day."

There were no tears from Arthur that followed, just quiet reflection until two loud thumps echoed inside the dome. I looked up to see that we had present company consisting of about twenty dwellers. Two were lying on the ground, having thrown themselves against its walls in an attempt to breach our defences, intent on feeding from our light.

"Time to beat a retreat gentleman," advised Thomas.

"Give us a minute, Thomas, please. You have his vibration I take it, Arthur?"

"Adolf's you mean? Yes, it is one I shall never forget. Why?"

"Before we leave, send him the pictures and narrative of the experience you just described to me. I have a feeling he has not had insight from a surviving victim."

"But I didn't survive," Arthur said.

"And who might you be then, Arthur?" I asked with a wink and a smile.

He smiled back, closed his eyes, linked and transmitted.

"Right, Thomas, let's go and I promise to be careful what I tread in in Realm Two," said Arthur.

We smiled and waved to our audience, apologising for having to leave without engaging; the endings of the abuse and curses suddenly inaudible as we disappeared.

Entrenched

On their approach, Audaz and Alana decelerated, dropping into the water again as dolphins, a short distance from the Culviers. Five individuals made up the small pod. Two younger whales were playing by themselves, as the older ones remained on the surface, two of them breathing in and pushing air from their blow holes. Although the younger members were smooth flanked, the adults were all scarred by oval shaped pit marks and one with what looked like a lash mark.

"You arrived quickly; you must be blessed by speed. Cuchiq said you were strange creatures and I can now see why. I am Mahdee."

I thought she must be referring to our luminescence. Mahdee was the largest of the group at six metres, about two thousand kilograms and dark grey in colour. We introduced ourselves and said we were pleased that they had agreed to meet with us and we wished to dive with them if that was possible. I noticed that one of the oval marks was still a fresh wound on her right flank and remarked on it.

"We are not the only hunters down there in the depths. These wounds are made by small sharks, which suck onto your flesh before taking a chunk out of you. We are all aware of the sucking sensation and the momentary pause, followed by the sheering pain as they cut into you. The lash mark you can see on Lanee's side was caused by a fishing net, she very nearly did not escape from."

"Are there many abandoned nets?" asked Audaz.

"There are many of these traps. We see all kinds of ocean creatures caught in them and there is little we can do to help them. That is one of the reasons why we dive the depths in open waters, as there are fewer here," said Lanee, a slightly smaller female.

"So why is it you seek us?" asked Mahdee.

"One of the biggest mysteries on Earth is the potential of the deepest of oceans. This by large remains a mystery even in the after world where we come from. In fact, only a small part of the Earth's oceans has been explored by humans," I said.

"Why do you term it as a potential?" asked Mahdee, a slight scrutiny in her thought tone.

"There is an idea that the water world at the bottom of the ocean's trenches remain largely unaffected by what happens at the surface. Almost as though this environment is protected. Not only by the volume of water above it, but also the pressure, which prevents many sea creatures and humans being able to reach such depths," explained Audaz.

"We cannot dive to the bottom of the waters here, so we do not know what the world is like down there. With our echoes, we know that the bottom is over three times the maximum depth we can dive. There are no others of our kind who can go deeper, so no one knows. But why would those in the worlds of spirit want to know if it was a place safely apart from the world up here?" said Lanee.

I explained we were able to dive to those depths as we were not affected by pressure and we did not need to breathe. Our plan was to see what life lived down there.

"This is complicated, but the humans are changing the planet to such an extent that many of them may not survive those changes. Whilst this will slow down, if not put a stop to the causes of these changes, it means our after world will become over populated. We can accommodate everyone but the problem occurs when they want to return to Earth to live their next life. With less humans remaining on Earth, fewer will be born from them which will cause a bottle neck for those driven to be reborn," I explained.

There was a noticeable pause, punctuated by a number of clicks.

"That's their problem, not ours. Our kind and others have suffered at the hands of humans far into the distant past. Are you suggesting there could be large numbers of spirit people like you who will come to live among us in the oceans, because there would then be no escape for us?" said Lanee.

I told her that I was sorry she felt that way and all fair-minded humans would agree with her about it not being their problem. But that was not the idea. When all creatures passed from this world to ours, there came a time when they needed to be reborn to further experience themselves in this world. Because of the damage to the climate and shrinking wild animal habitats on Earth, it may not be safe or possible for those creatures or humans to be brought back onto the land.

"We are looking at the possibility and the potential of the oceans accommodating spirit in simple life forms in an environment of relative safety, until the Earth and human populations recover," I explained.

"So we get to eat human squid so to speak?" said Lanee.

"Sort of yes," I said.

"We know the oceans are changing. Temperatures are increasing, they are becoming noisier and this is affecting sea animal movements and behaviours. We also know that there are more floating ghosts than ever before and we assume these come from the land. How do you know that the oceans will not be affected badly by the changes in climate, because in some places, the guardians have reported they have been?" said Mahdee with genuine concern.

"We don't. We are looking for the existence of safe havens, where all kinds of creatures could live and take refuge, if that is possible. I assume the guardians facilitate communication across the oceans to keep you informed?" asked Audaz.

"The guardians have been amongst us for over a thousand years. All of my ancestors knew of them and they broadcast across huge distances for others to know what is happening. Like Cuchiq, I also sense that you have a similar echo to them, which is why we agreed to meet you," said Mahdee.

"These are difficult times and we must explore ways in which we can all live together peacefully. As a species, humans compete and they haven't quite worked it out yet, that life's actually about cooperation and acceptance," I said.

"Then maybe what's coming for them, is just what they need in order to learn that," said Lanee, her thoughts tinged with resentment.

"That is a hard lesson to learn and in the spirit world, we are working to try to prevent it getting to that point. If we can, we also hope what we achieve, will have a positive effect on the Earth's climate. I know that whales as a whole have suffered at the hands of humans and Audaz and my kind can empathise with your suffering, but not all humans are the same. Many wish to preserve the beauty of the oceans and the peaceful life of their many inhabitants. We are concerned for the future of all worlds and we must plan to weather the worst," I said.

"I remember the words of my grandmother as she basked in the sunshine floating on the surface with a full belly of squid. She'd say, 'all will be well, Mahdee'. We hope it will be."

"Cuchiq shares this saying, with you. We hope it will be too," I said.

"If you are to dive with us with the light that shines from you, it should be a good hunt. We were almost ready, when you arrived. Give us a little while to take more breath and we will go," said Lanee.

Audaz and I joined the others in the group to listen to their stories. The younger beakers were excited to be near our glow and wanted to know where we had come from and whether we were real. I thought it sad that humans and whales could not communicate across their divide. Like humans, whales and dolphins communicate with each other and have a brain capacity which grants them intelligence and emotional expression. Like them, Harpies are able to communicate instinctually and via a deeper sense.

Humans were unable to decipher the intricacies of a language blended with these qualities and the levels of communication and perception, all happening simultaneously. To describe it, it was like, if your sense was instinctual and told you that you could trust without doubt, your communication would not be needlessly interrupted by thoughts questioning its authenticity. You would clearly hear and understand.

I had thought about James from time to time and knew he would be in the Dark Realms. I thought into his mind.

"Oh, hello darling; how's the surf?" he asked.

"It's good to be in the water again and we have plenty of company. We've managed to appear to the whales like we did with Sealgair in Scotland, so they can gain a better sense of us."

"Nice one. We've just landed in Realm Two having just left one. You'll never guess who I have just had a conversation with?"

"I can see it, James. Saving the universe is one thing but you are not going to try and free Adolf Hitler, are you?"

"That's up to him, Alana. My sense is he has a long road in front of him and his arrogance shields him from even being able to come near to admitting what he has done, let alone feeling responsible. Arthur was badly affected by him."

"I can see. Poor Arthur, we think we had it tough. I miss you, my darling, and will check in again soon. We are about to dive with the Culviers', catch you later."

"Be nice to the squid!"

"I know. I have a feeling we are going to be the bait."

Our two diving companions had ventilated to a level they were confident they could reach their deepest dive and exhaled to complete the process. Whilst the remaining adult and two youngsters stayed on the surface, the four of us commenced our dive. I assured Mahdee and Lanee that we would be able to keep pace with them and marvelled at their streamlined forms and powerful flukes which enabled them to descend with less effort towards the darkened depths. Swimming together, there were regular knocks against each other, done as a way of maintaining reassurance between them.

Our plan was to leave them at their maximum diving depth and continue into the trench to further explore. Before this point, they had requested that we match their descent speed and swim ahead of them, not only to illuminate their path, but to act as lures to curious squid attracted to the blue and white light we emitted. The distance between us enabled both of them to detect squid by sonar and catch a glimpse of the incoming trajectories in order to synchronise capture.

Swimming down into the cold darkness reminded me of James and his choice of assignment into the dark. Although Audaz and I were not afraid in our spirit form, there were memories which re-emerged of what may lurk in the dark and the slightly unnerving unknown feeling which tainted the sense of anticipation.

We were now approaching twelve hundred metres. Although Mahdee and Lanee had been clicking during the descent, the clicks now became mechanised and regular. Suddenly, several forms appeared from the periphery of our illuminated field, propelling themselves straight towards us and followed by many others. We were overtaken immediately by the two Culviers, darting to intercept the squid before they could jet away in different directions. The ferocity of the clicks honed the precision of their movements to catch their prey, their agility and speed enabling the interception of many.

Feelings of their delight and satisfaction met my mind as they returned to our sides following their sortie.

"We must rest for a short while to allow our bodies to resettle before we move on," said Mahdee.

"To take the ache away you mean?" I said.

"Yes. Otherwise, our muscles will tighten. On the surface, we can breathe and it would clear quickly. Down here, we must allow the air we have taken in before diving to do its work and take with it any pain."

"I understand," I said.

The lactic acid formed in their muscles was ordinarily cleared during breathing and rest. In the absence of breathing and relying on oxygen reserves, the clearing process needed to be managed. Culviers were better adapted to internally balance at depth out of all the whale species.

As we paused, further sea life approached our light source. Squid were joined by frilled sharks and luminescent hatchet fish, all inquisitive to see the source of our glow. We were not sure if they could see us, or if it was just the light which attracted them. We guessed we must be invisible to them, as mimicking a dolphin form would have surely alarmed them.

Having recovered, our two Culviers recommenced the dive and at a steady pace, we descended further into the velvety blackness until we reached the extent of their ability to go further. At nearly three thousand metres, this world felt far removed from the sunshine above. Although we could not feel the pressure as the Culviers were experiencing, we sensed the feeling of being closed in and isolated.

"We must return now, our heads start to ache more than we can stand and we must take our time on the way up. We can hunt on the way to the surface also. As the light starts to increase, we can see silhouettes of fish and squid and as many are not looking downwards, we have the element of surprise. Farewell down there. I know you are safe and we wish you well with your exploration," said Mahdee.

"Thank you both for your company. We wish you well and your family up top. Goodbye."

Lanee and Mahdee turned and swam upwards and out of view.

"How are we going to do this? The trench is over two and a half thousand kilometres long, seventy kilometres wide and the deepest part is a further eight thousand metres below where we are now," asked Audaz.

"Look at this," I invited.

I sent Audaz a picture of a double helix conjoined with spindles, representing a construction of a DNA molecule.

"If we imagine this model running through a thousand kilometres of the deepest parts of the trench, as it rotates, the spindles will point to varying locations at different elevations on both sides and the bottom. Ignoring the spindles that point up to the surface and spacing the spindles at five-kilometre intervals, there will be approximately three hundred locations to explore. If we spend no more than a few minutes at each location, we should complete the survey in about five hours."

"Five hours! I borrow one of Joao's expressions: good grief! I take it, we will not be swimming," he asked.

"No Audaz, we will transport from one point to the next and save Challenger Deep, the deepest part of the trench until last," I replied.

"Remind me what we are looking for please, other than life down here?"

"We are trying to get an idea of whether the environment could sustain an increase in life forms, the same as current species. We are also looking for the isolation effect, of whether in our view, this environment is safe from impacts from the world above. Connected to this, we are looking for evidence of pollution. Let's work thoroughly but quickly, as the dark is starting to make me feel contained."

The next five hours passed quickly as we located, surveyed and rematerialized to the different points identified by the helix spindles fixed in our mind's eye. Life varied at the different depths. Whilst there is beauty in all creatures and animals, the depth, pressure and darkness appeared to have taken its toll on this and created more demonic life forms adapting to their surroundings.

Both dragon and angler fish, the visions of aquatic nightmares, used light to lure the intrigued and at greater depths and perhaps related, fang tooth fish displayed their toothy grins of no escape. Amphipods, shrimp-like creatures appeared common and successful and were found at varying depths.

The top of the trench was slightly over three thousand metres below the surface with the deepest most point just short of eleven thousand metres. These depths were the quietist, the darkest and the most foreboding. When we finally arrived in Challenger Deep, my impressions were that the trench was a harsh environment.

Whilst life was evident, even at these depths in the form of amphipods, snail and grenadier fish and eel species, I found it hard to believe that a large influx of life could be supported and take refuge successfully in this habitat. This I based on the frequency and diversity of species numbers, indicating a lack of sustenance at the bottom of the food chain in the trench.

"I do not think I could live down here, Alana. This is a really strange place."

"It is, that is not a doubt, but if you knew no different Audaz, this would be your world and it is far from the world above, even though in metres, it is a short distance away. However, I don't think this place would be suitable or viable for an Earth spirit refuge when and if they revolved to localised life forms. If the

Mariana is representative of other trench environments, I think Aarna's idea of ocean havens, although a good one is a nonstarter."

"It is pleasing not to see vast amounts of plastic down here," said Audaz.

"There is enough, but not as high as I thought. There is something else here though, which is not quite right and it makes me wonder whether this trench is the deepest of drains for those unwanted chemicals which should not have been manufactured in the first place." I quietly despaired over the easy fix motives behind the 'out of sight, out of mind' decisions of the offenders.

"Good job we don't have to decompress on the way up. I am not swimming," said Audaz.

"Me neither, let's get out of here," I said.

We rematerialized in raptor form in mid-air and spent the next ten minutes airing our wings and enjoying the sunlight. It was like being freed from a dark prison. Worth investigating but sadly, not the solution.

"Come on, Audaz, we have a guardian to find."

"I am looking forward to this. But a whale with wings is hard to imagine, if it is like us."

"They have them already, they just fly in the water and not the air. Let's head for the west of Australia and see if we can pick up a vibration similar to our own."

"A vibration similar to ours in a vast ocean? I think we will need some help," he replied.

"Ummm. You have a point. No Mach two, we are just going, okay?"

"I have done that now, I am happy. Let's go find the blue!" said Audaz.

Autumn in Spring

Scout, Sarah and Simon had arrived on a top of a tower block as the evening was setting in. There were impressive views across London in all directions. Whilst Sarah and Scout admired the skyline, I awaited the arrival of our London guide Tony had arranged for us.

"*Waa gwaan breden*," was the greeting made by our host, as he appeared.

"*Mid deh yah*," I replied with a broad smile.

He laughed and introduced himself as Nesta, a Jamaican national who had lived many lifetimes in the islands before choosing to guide. He was about six, three, heavily built, warm and oozed the mellowness of wisdom within his words. We introduced ourselves and to save dialogue, I let him read the reasons why we were here from my memories. He already knew of our identities from Tony.

"Dese be worrying time. I know of the meetings that are happening to look into ways we can rebalance the energy. I am looking forward to helping in those changes, once we have a plan. I am guessing by the size of you Scout, that you are the famous winged horse. Your name kind of gives it away too."

"Yes, that's me and by your looks, if you were a horse, you would make a powerful stallion yourself," he replied.

"Has word of our actions in West Yorkshire reached this city?" asked Sarah.

"They are just rumours at the moment. Many Leaves think your border patrol is a story made up to unnerve the more powerful amongst them. We have spread the word, but not many believe us either," he replied.

"Where are we anyway, Nesta?" I asked.

Nesta explained that we were in Bermondsey, Southwark, an area of South East London and very close to the Old Kent Road. To the north, he pointed out the Thames, The City of London and the Shard. To the west was Westminster, the east, the Isle of Dogs, then Camberwell, Peckham and Brixton to the South.

Southwark represented one of the highest crime rate areas of London and rife with Leaf activity. Within it and the surrounding areas just identified by him, were twenty-four organised street gangs of young people who fought to maintain dominance over their territory.

In the current times, it was not so much about territorial pride and street presence. It was more about protecting a territory which could provide a lucrative drugs business. That and maximising 'likes' and followers on social media apps. The increase in social media use had seen a semi withdrawal of numbers from the streets, its use creating large followings for individuals whose activities and notoriety were now publicised digitally.

It was these individuals or 'wanna be' controllers who elevated their status in an attempt to become the most talked about and feared. They drew attention to themselves as potential targets to rival gangs, as part of their showmanship bravado. Respect in their world was far from the meaning of respect in ours. The attacks and violence increasingly seen, were usually planned and communicated before the event and although being premeditated in the background, they could appear random and impulsive to investigators.

"We know differently of course," said Nesta.

"Are the Leaves organised as well?" I asked.

Nesta smiled at me as if to say 'what do you think?'

"You know that Leaves get drawn to all kinds of negative behaviour and trauma. In fact, anything that has the potential for suffering connected to it. Being involved in gangs increases the likelihood of young people becoming either a victim or a perpetrator of violence, or a dealer of the kind of stuff that creates misery, meaning drugs. Gangs are organised to deal in creating all these and the Leaves run with them," he replied.

"When I was in Denby Dale, there was a self-elected head of the local Leaves and he would manipulate and control to maintain his territory. But it was the pride and notoriety he wanted for himself. There must be others like him in cities and we would like to know what their motives are and how they organise others," I asked.

"As I said, Leaves follow distress from all sources, not just the gangs, but the gangs are a productive source of trauma which is more predictable. Leaves and gangs are together. Where you find one, you will find the other," said Nesta.

Nesta described a symbiotic existence where every gang member would have Leaves attached to them. Being young people, they were more susceptible to psychic attacks in the form of Leaf presence and negative influences. Drug use increased their openness to the feelings of fear, paranoia and suggestion. The Leaf Commanders, those who were at the top of the hierarchical structure, would control a number of Leaf lieutenants, who managed the day-to-day information streams and decided which of the lesser Leaves attached to which gang member.

Significant Earth gang members or gang whips would have Limpet Leaves purposefully attached to them by order of the Commander. Their neediness and constant and persistent negative transmission to the hosts had an increased chance of inciting fear, control and suffering in others. In most cases, two or more Limpets were deployed.

Although Limpets were naturally single minded in seeking the hosts they chose, the Commanders knew how powerful their influence could be. In controlling them, whilst allowing them the richest pickings, Commanders knew they were more likely to get the best results. These assigned Limpets answered directly to the Commanders and fed back potential trauma plans being made. For this, they were protected from other Leaves attacking them to gain a piece of the action.

The motive of the head Commanders was to manage territories which produced the most trauma and misery. If Leaves came in from other areas, they were attacked on sight, and threatened, to deter them from returning. Less important lieutenants were assigned the management and information streams back to the Commander for non-gang related activity.

The Commander, in effect, replicated the behaviour of the gangs, which was to create no go areas for other off-territory Leaves. The benefit of being in charge was they were always in the know as to the next event. They controlled and manipulated the Leaves beneath them to maintain their influence under threat of attack or banishment and they were ruthless and purposefully indiscriminate in making examples. The other benefit was they could cross-territory lines.

"What do you mean, they can cross territory lines?" asked Scout.

"There is a kind of network going on between territories, in the form of a cautious mutual respect between Commanders. They will visit other territories by invitation, should there be strong likelihood of a significant negative event occurring. They are invited to view it and the favour is returned in the future."

"Like a night out at the movies you mean?" said Sarah, sarcastically.

"To watch horror only, I am afraid," replied Nesta, shaking his head.

The other benefit for the Commanders was in being aware of potential killings. These represented recruitment opportunities and gang members, especially the leaders and whips were intercepted quickly and persuaded their only possible future was to serve or face the consequences of their refusal in the form of banishment from the area.

"This must make your work as a guide incredibly difficult?" I said.

"It's a nightmare. I spend a good amount of my time immobilising Limpets, so I can attempt to positively influence my charges or seed positive thought and emotion. As you know, guides have multiple charges and yet everyone has either a negative Leaf or Limpet attached to them. It feels like we are fighting a losing battle. If only I could be in more than one place at a time," he replied woefully.

"What about attacks on you?" asked Sarah.

"Every day. I spend most of my time guarded. This is an inner-city battleground. The other guides, catchers and I are always on high alert. It's a good job we don't get tired."

"Don't you get tired of the job though?" asked Sarah.

"Not the job. I know it's tough, but like Simon here, I was a Leaf in the past and knowing the score, I have compassion for them. It's the energy suckers I have less for though and I know I should not say that."

"The Limpets have been badly affected in their previous lifetime."

"I know that, Sarah, but most are so difficult to get through to and for some reason are disconnected from compassion for others. They take from and manipulate in their task without the slightest regret," replied Nesta.

"Perhaps because they were never shown compassion in their lifetime and so, do not feel the sense," said Sarah.

"Umm, pain in my arse though," he muttered under his breath, as he looked towards Camden and the south-west horizon.

"Right, we have an opportunity to show you what is happening, follow my lead," he said.

We rematerialized on a rooftop overlooking a street along which two young men we running. Fifteen or more Leaves were in hot pursuit. A Leaf at the front of their group was shouting at the rest to stay close. At the top of the road, the two men slowed down, turned a corner and came face to face with another individual, leaning against a wall, seemingly minding his own business. The Leaves crowded around the group intently. When it became apparent, it was nothing but a drug deal, the Leaves disbanded, drifting off in different directions in obvious disappointment.

"Knifings always draw a large crowd; I guess they weren't in luck this evening. Just pushers making ready to serve passage to the dark side for their regulars," said Nesta.

"There must have been about twenty of them in close pursuit," I said.

"It's the same old-fashioned idea of reporters following ambulances. They are hoping to get lucky with an interesting story. We see a lot of that behaviour around here," said Nesta.

"How do you ever manage to guide people with this gang scenario going on?" said Sarah.

"In a lot of cases where Leaves are attached, I go in and don't even bother with pleasantries, I just open fire and immobilise the Leaf or Limpet. I place a dome shield over the charge and myself and then I can get to work. I really wish the gang charges could hear me and see what effects they are having on others, their families and actually see how the Leaves work. There is so much emphasis placed on protection, on attempting to feel safe as part of a group where they can belong. Yet in doing what they do, they make themselves vulnerable to these Leaves and Limpets, who do nothing but drain their energy and incite less safety through increased fear."

"It's out of control, isn't it?" I said.

Nesta lowered his chin and a crystal tear fell from his eyelid, rolling down his cheek. The guide consensus was something needed to be done. The Earth police did not have the same resources as they did in terms of information. They were not only fighting to control crime in the Earth world, they were up against an organised force which unbeknown to them, strived to motivate the very crimes they were dealing with.

These were unseen influences and even if the police categorically knew about them, they were powerless to control or take action against them. In Nesta's view, Between Worlds was a realm in itself, however, it was not governed by the same laws as the others.

He was not alone in thinking that the Collective needed to manage this place more effectively. Leaves were able to suggest, drain energy and unconsciously affect the Earth born and we were now in a situation where they had adopted a systematic approach to exploit them for their gain. We were in agreement with him, but pointed out we are not sure what the intervention would look like yet.

"Segregate them, Simon. Separate the powerful Leaf Commanders and key lieutenants from the other Leaves, thus eradicating their influence. Those lower down in the hierarchy would be put off from taking over from them, just by doing that. I would take the Limpets out of the equation too," explained Nesta.

"A bit like what we did in Denby Dale, you mean?" said Scout.

"Yes, but I understand you threatened him and told him he would be tracked, if he did not stay away from others? But is he? How many of these kinds of Leaves could be tracked? And how long would it be before they took the risk to reassume their previous activities?"

"You mean create a more permanent solution, but who judges and takes the decision to exclude these Leaves, if they could be?" said Sarah.

"The judgement is beyond me. Having said that, we are all able to ascertain the level of malicious intention and historical action individuals have taken, just by reading them. So we could do it as guides. After all, they have a judicial system on Earth designed to exclude negative elements. The question is, where do you put them?" said Nesta, excited by his idea.

"To be honest, Nesta, I cannot see the high planers in Six or Seven, or the Collective granting judgement rights to guides. That is not to detract from the importance of your role, but to negate situations of misjudgement based on personality. There would have to be a referral system to a higher authority able to make those kinds of decisions," said Sarah in an attempt to make the process more procedural.

We had no right to judge and exclude the Governor in Denby Dale and yet we did it for the sake of others affected by him. The fact that we used licence and the threats were empty in that there wasn't any organised surveillance, served as a temporary measure to eradicate his impact at the time.

However, because Between Worlds was not a realm in itself and individuals could remain in it to avoid judgement, why should individuals be allowed to overlord negatively upon others without some form of judgement and exclusion served on them.

After all, Leaves chose to remain on Earth, so therefore, they should be governed by Earth type rules, but administered and policed by the after world. I felt that up until now a suggestive balance was maintained where guides supported Earth dwellers and Leaves negatively affected them. But with the Leaves becoming more organised and being governed by no laws, the suggestive balance was being tipped in their favour.

"It's almost as though Between Worlds was an oversight by the Collective," said Nesta.

In my view and taking my own history into account, I now saw Between Worlds as a buffer providing a time for reflection before going to the after world. But with religions losing their influence to consumerism and experiential pursuits and without a belief in 'you will be judged by your actions after death', people were becoming more focussed on serving themselves. Numbers were growing as Between Worlds was now seen as an alternative to the after world. I gave Nesta my view on it.

"I don't think the Collective predicted the speed that this was going to happen. Neither did it see Between Worlds increasingly becoming a refuge for the malicious, or the degree Leaves could impact on the Earth dwellers. The problem now is, the more you live a life of cause and effect in the absence of a robust moral code on Earth, the more vulnerable and susceptible you become to the negative suggestion of Leaves," I concluded.

"Where would you put them Nesta?" asked Scout.

"Alcatraz comes to mind."

"An island fortress, you mean. Far away from anyone or anything. But they could transport out. How would you hold them?" replied Scout.

"If you could cage the island in a holding sphere, that would be good," said Sarah.

I didn't think we could do that on our own and I didn't know how long a holding sphere could be kept in place. I would have to talk with Tarquin and Nevaeh. We also needed some input into whom we would refer to for judgement if that was at all possible. In terms of possible locations, James had told me about his Scottish trip to the highlands and how remote the area was. I had an idea.

"Give me a few minutes, I want to check something out," I said.

Visualising the area, I transported as a Martial eagle and from a high vantage point scanned the Scottish Highlands coastline for potential islands. On the horizon, a small group of islands, more like large rocks, presented themselves and transporting to them, I felt we may have found a potential home. Honing in on Sarah's vibration, I returned back to our group.

"I have just done a search and there is an uninhabited island called Boreray not far from Hirta Island, about eighty kilometres off the North West coast of Scotland. It's worth a try talking to the high planers to get their view," I said.

I group linked into Tarquin and Nevaeh and was told they had been making headway with their own dialogues with those in Realm Six. It appeared that there were longer-term proposals for managing Between Worlds, which I could not be party to at this stage, but they were aware short-term measures needed to be put in place.

Astonishingly, I was granted judgement rights based on my own personal experience of and time I had spent in Between Worlds. However, my actions would be policed in the short term by Tarquin, after I had made the judgement. He informed me that he would instigate release, should it be necessary, but he did not doubt my authority in these matters.

As for the island fortress idea, he took the coordinates and said it would take a short while to get this approved. Evidently, the energy required for the holding was accessible from sources he could not discuss. He also said he would speak to the guides to ensure that they were aware of any action taken against Leaves and to continue their contact with them, wherever they ended up.

"You are giving us a green light!" I said to him.

"We are. Use it with compassion and use it well. I will be in touch," said Tarquin.

I broadcast the conversation to the others.

"Bloody hell, that was worth the try. You have a direct line into the high planers. He must hold you in high regard?" said Nesta.

"We go back centuries; he knows me as well as I do and it is because of who we are, that he holds us close," replied Simon.

"Who you are. You mean Harpies?" asked Nesta.

"He fought tooth and nail to stop our race going extinct on the Earth and watched in distress as the remaining few took their last breaths, as it was at the hands of his kind that we met our end. Tarquin is a spirit of justice and compassion and it gives him great pain when races and species are extinguished through ignorance and fear," I said.

"Uncle Simon, Scottish Island Tours here. Your reservation has been confirmed and guests can arrive at your convenience. Say hi to Aunt Sarah and catch you later," interrupted Nevaeh.

"Nevaeh is your niece!" exclaimed Nesta, the connections of his new companions cementing his respect.

There were a few moments of silence as each of us contemplated what had just happened and then the plans took shape. We decided to hit hard and fast.

Nesta located the Southwark Commander through the guide channel and confirmed his vibration. Like Nesta, he was also from the islands and went by the nickname Dreads. A name chosen, not only to reflect his mane, but also to speak of what he brought to others. Nesta described him with one word, 'cold', then added ruthless to confirm the impression.

Rather than walking through the front door as we had in Denby Dale, the idea was to 'split' and view the situation from a distance undetected. We needed to reconnoitre their location and ascertain whether he was alone or not.

Splitting was a technique of extending your consciousness to any distance whilst anchoring your light body in its current location. A cord of silver light connected one to the other. The projected consciousness was able to observe a scene without being detected by others present and the light body could then be drawn towards the consciousness in order to effect a materialisation.

The hope was that others would be with him as we were looking for maximum publicity. Once the reconnaissance was done and tactics agreed, we would follow the split cords to their location and immobilise as many as possible in the vicinity before commencing 'friendly' dialogue.

Dread's vibration pinpointed him in a derelict building on the Old Kent Road. On initiating the split, we found ourselves viewing a large, shadowy and decaying room. The smell of damp and rotting timber overpowered the night air. Plaster had fallen from the walls in places, some still held precariously by tasteless seventies wallpaper. Floorboards were patch-worked, not only by fallen pieces of plasterboard from the ceiling but with gaps revealing the void of the room beneath.

Dreads, sat in the far corner on the remnants of an old armchair. He was cursing and swearing at three Leaves in front of him, who with heads bowed, shuffled nervously. Another two Leaves looked on, smiling their pleasure at the barrage the three were receiving. A young woman stood apart from the rest, partly obscured by the shadows. Her anxiety was obvious to the reader, given away in her stature and how she nervously wrung her hands together. She was the only Limpet in the room and I could tell how desperately she wished to be somewhere else. She was also the only one who was guarded.

I mind linked with the rest of the group.

"When we arrive there, we need to work swiftly and surgically. Sarah, as the young woman is guarded, can you cage her. Like you, I am picking up something that's not quite right with her and I think it would be beneficial having a chat to ascertain why. Scout, you take out the three who are getting a roasting. I am sure you can handle the rapid fire. Nesta, you immobilise our two smug friends and I will blast the crap out of Dread's ass. When they are down, cage them, so we can exchange pleasantries. We want no one escaping," I ordered.

"I am not so comfortable with this Simon. I am a guide, not a soldier," said Nesta.

"Think of it as a way of freeing others, of creating opportunities for you and other guides to start to make more of a difference on your patch," I said. "We can't delay further, transform to raptors as you exit the cords. On my mark…go!"

Bright red flashes filled the room as head shots blasted into the Leaves from different directions. The expression on many of their faces was shock, fear and confusion. Sarah having caged the young woman was scanning the scene of conflict and found Nesta hesitating to fire on his second mark. She took the shot and he fell to the ground.

Scout had somehow confused the raptor order and had filled the room in his white Pegasus form. His three targets had spun quickly on our entrance and then appeared to freeze, not able to comprehend what stood before them. He opened fire, cutting each of them to the ground in quick succession.

Dreads had managed to stand up from his chair but because of what was happening around him, his reaction to transporting out was slow and my head shot caught him squarely on his left temple. With all Leaves down and unconscious, the red fire haze dissipated, revealing a Martial and Bald eagle, a Pegasus and a Jamaican spirit guide, standing in a battle scene littered with fallen Leaves. I knew we had a few minutes before they started to recover but caged them to hold them where they lay.

I looked at Scout and laughed.

"Which part of raptor didn't you hear?"

Scout let off an enormous fart.

"Ohahh! I've been wanting to do that for ages. Look, I haven't quite mastered split-second transformation. I am a horse. I did my best," he replied.

"It's fine by me, Scout, and it's good to see you again, my friend," I said.

The young woman chuckled and we all turned to face her. The acute level of her anxiety had somewhat reduced.

"What are you laughing at?" asked Scout.

"You are not only a horse with wings; you are a farting horse with wings, who can talk. This is mad; it's like an LSD trip. I didn't think the rumours were true," she said.

Sarah linked to my mind and added weight to my suspicions that this woman was not a typical Limpet and was in fact a sensitive. Sarah transformed back to her human form and asked the woman's name.

"Ruby."

"I am Sarah, Ruby. This is Simon, Scout and this is Nesta. We are here from the after world."

"I have seen Nesta before; I know he is a guide who works around here. I enjoy the feeling he brings, that's when I have been close enough to sense it," she said.

"We were watching you before we arrived and you were very anxious. And yet now, you seem to be a lot calmer. What's changed?" asked Sarah.

"I feel things; I did so even when I was alive. I sense your energy Sarah, it is warm and strong and sort of holding. You all have this energy, but yours is the strongest Sarah."

"Why are you involved with these people?" asked Sarah.

"It's a long story," she replied.

The captured Leaves were starting to stir from their unconsciousness.

"I am sensing that you are picking up energy from us. Is the feeling it brings more in tune with your true feelings or nature?" asked Sarah.

"I am not sure about my true nature. There has been another side of me which has been dark," she replied looking downwards in sadness.

Sarah mind linked to me and the others and said she was going to find somewhere she and Ruby could continue to talk, before any of the others recovered and threatened her.

"If you are this sensitive and you see who I truly am, would you take me to a place we can be alone and talk. I would like to try and help you."

Ruby hesitated and Sarah registered the threat she was under.

"Yes okay, but I cannot be gone long. I think you know I can trust you, so follow my link," said Ruby.

Sarah released the cage and both of them disappeared, just before Dreads hit consciousness.

"You dare to crash my turf, uno bumbaclaat," Dreads asserted.

"Hello Dreads, I am Simon, the big flying horse is Scout and this is Nesta. Pleasant evening for a gun fight, sorry you lost. Shame really, we should have given you notice and you could have invited one or two of your Commander friends over to watch us blast your ass! It is you who is the douchebag in this room," I said with all due contempt.

"So, I suppose you are going to tell me to stop my activities or I won't get into heaven. I've heard that all my life. Do you think I care? This place may not be Earth, but it's good enough, although I would kill for a reefer," he sneered.

There was muffled laughter from his colleagues in support.

"This is not about you getting into heaven, nor you stopping your activities," I said.

We transformed back into our human form. There was a slight look of confusion on his face, blended with a flutter of uncertainty.

"I know; you are going to tell me to stay away from others, like I heard your so-called border patrol told that guy up north. That's if you are that group of do gooders?"

"No. I am not going to tell you to do that." I shook my head, with an expression that I knew something that he didn't.

"Then what the hell do you want dick head, stop wasting my frigging time!" Dreads spat towards my feet.

"You are going somewhere you can no longer harm others and spread your venomous control," I said.

"You can't do that. I have to choose to pass to the other side. You can't touch me or make me do anything," he replied contemptuously.

I mind linked to Nesta to expect the unexpected, to not be afraid and to continue to hold the three Leaves caged. Scout knew exactly what my plan was and synchronised with the coordinates in my mind.

"I am not going to make you do anything," I concluded to Dreads.

I turned to the three Leaves who had been at the sharp end of Dread's tongue and asked them if they thought I was capable of dealing with their commander and whether I should let him go. They all looked at me, not daring to say anything and shrugging their shoulders.

"Say your goodbyes to them. Your two lieutenants and you, Dreads, are coming with us."

This was the cue to Scout to transform with me to battledress and within moments, the room was filled with our huge, monstrous Harpy forms. With screams still sounding, Scout grabbed the feet of the two Lieutenants in his talons as I grasped those of Dreads. Still being caged, they were incapable of transporting away from us or launching an attack.

We both vanished with our quarry and rematerialized on the uninhabitable rock in the North Sea. We released the cages, I must admit, with fingers crossed and each Leaf immediately attempted to transport with no effect as we transformed back to human form.

"What is this place?" exclaimed Dreads.

"Home. You are free to do what you like here. Be nice to each other and, oh, you will get visits from guides from time to time, who will help you consider how you have treated others," I said politely.

We both disappeared and rematerialized back into the grimy room where Nesta was still holding the three remaining Leaves.

"You will never see them again. Do you understand?" I said. All three nodded.

"We want this operation disbanded with immediate effect. If it isn't, you and many of your colleagues will be joining them." I pointed my finger at them to exaggerate the point.

Nesta released the cages and all three Leaves disappeared.

"You don't muck about, do you?" said Nesta.

"No, we don't," replied Scout.

Bound to Dread

Ruby and Sarah had left the room and her link had taken them to the top of a modern glass building overlooking the waters of the Thames. The unmistakable structure of Tower Bridge spanned the river to their right.

As Ruby and I sat and scanned the view, the night air met us with its tepid embrace. Although the skies were clear, the hue of the many city lights created an orange tinted glow above the buildings, obscuring the stars. Sitting beside me was a young woman of about nineteen. She was dressed in black combats which made her already pale complexion more pale. Her short mousy coloured hair framed her freckled face, drawn cheeks and a thin nose, accentuating her dark deep set brown eyes.

"Why here?" I asked.

"You can read me, can't you? So is there much point in me saying anything?" replied Ruby.

"And lose the opportunity of experiencing the poetry of your words?"

She looked away smiling.

"It's nice to be seen once in a while. I come here so I can lose my head. Not like those who lost theirs across the water there, but to cope with my worries by slipping into the calm space between things and between ages. Although we are sitting on something really modern, it's also designed to be reflective and I reflect on the history and sadness of the innocent people who made their final journey up from traitor's gate, to meet their death in the tower," explained Ruby.

"So you are drawn to an ancient form of misery and trauma?" I said.

"You read badly. I said sadness!" she replied.

"I apologise, Ruby. I know you have been used by Dreads as a Limpet. I am trying to gain more of a sense of who you really are from your story and why you are involved with his exploits?"

"I don't have a choice; I am bound to him."

"What do you mean bound?" I said.

Ruby explained that the dark part of her she mentioned previously was to do with her involvement in occult practices when she was alive. She had been affected by unseen forces since she was a child, although she knew nothing more of them then, other than feelings and sensations. When older, although she was aware that not all occult practices were fear inducing, her interest led her to ride the edge between what she felt was the dark and the light.

She and her friends would get together whilst her mum worked at night, drink a bottle of vodka and try and make contact with the spirit world. Being a bit of a laugh at first, they were able to read random names coming from the board's indicator. She had constructed the board herself and decorated it with symbols she had found on the net. The idea was they would induce some kind of contact.

"One night, I asked if anyone wanted to speak to me. The indicator spelt out 'dread'. We closed it up straight away and my feeling was we had possibly opened something which may bring us just that."

Some weeks passed and she and her friends were together again and being fairly drunk, the board came out. Rather than inciting one to one contact, she asked if there was a message the spirits might have. This time, the indicator spelt out 'bound to dread'. She felt then and realised now, they were channelling something dark, so she thanked it for coming through and wished it well, asking it to move into the light. It then spelt out 'dark' and they shut the board.

"What did you think bound to dread meant?"

"Exactly that. That we were bound to dread something or something dreadful was bound to happen. Like a warning. Three weeks later, I was dead," she replied.

"Good grief, Ruby, how did it happen?"

"We rented two adjoining rooms in this old building in Peckham. It was a pit, not looked after by the landlord and cold and damp. I used to sleep in the room which was a lounge/kitchen and kept the gas fire on low at night to take the edge off the cold. We had no detectors and it had not been serviced for years," she said.

"You mean carbon monoxide killed you?"

"Not just me. My little brother as well, who was asleep in the other room."

"What happened when you realised you were dead and why didn't a catcher take you over?" I asked.

Ruby told me that there were three men in the room with her when she passed the death point, although she did not realise she was at that time. One with locks held the hand of her eight-year-old brother. He was wide-eyed and petrified and had died a few moments before Ruby. She knew not to scream and was quiet while she thought about how she and her brother could get away from them.

"He told me that he knew I had been practicing the dark arts and it was him that I had summoned. That I should recognise the words 'bound to dread'. He told me his name was Dreads and I was now bound to him as I had chosen my fate and sealed my pact with darkness. I was so afraid and could not think."

"What about the catcher?"

"There was a fourth man lying still on the floor. I thought he was dead, really dead. I know now that it was him. Dreads made us go with them and the nightmare grew."

Ruby's story unfolded and she realised she was still alive as such, but in some twilight dimension still on Earth but disconnected from it. She came to know about after world guides and catchers, but assumed they would not help her because of what she had done. The message from other Leaves was they would take her straight to hell if she approached them.

"I could not get away even if I had tried. Dreads had a close watch kept over Corey, my brother, and he told me he would not come to any harm, provided I worked for him and did as I was told," she explained.

"What did he tell you to do?"

A Limpet, a young man, had been assigned to her, who was very nervous and needy. She had to go with him and visit Earth people and would stay with them sometimes for days on end. He showed her how to suggest negative things and use their personalities to try and get through to them to do awful things. He would also show her how to project fear and make them feel as though something was in the room with them. She would watch him take energy from their auras and disrupt their mental and emotional balance.

"I knew I was sensitive and found it easy to read people and gather information. I hated doing it and after I had completed my training, I was told to visit my own Earth dwellers, who Dreads selected. I minimised the negative input, chose not to drain their energy and purely gathered information. This was the main thing Dreads was after. He's given me the gang whips to visit now, because he knows I can see and read more than others and for this, allows me to see Corey occasionally."

"Where's your mum?" I asked.

"Living in one of the tower blocks. She hasn't worked since she lost me and Corey and blames herself for our deaths by making us live in an unsafe home. She is so sad, but I can't get through to her."

"What is your dream, Ruby?"

"Why? Are you going to grant me three wishes like a fairy god mother?" She looked at me, doubting I could help her.

"I'll do my best! First one?"

"All right, get your wand out. Get rid of Dreads, so he can't control me, Corey or anyone else for that matter."

"Done. Second one?"

"How do you mean done?"

I knew Ruby could not split under her own power, so I took her in my mind to Boreray and let her see Dreads and the two lieutenants marooned on the island. I drew us back to the rooftop. She was smiling widely.

"Second?" I could see the tears starting to form in her eyes before she spoke.

"I want Corey with me."

I read into Ruby's mind and replicated Corey's vibration into mine, then pinpointed his location.

"Do you know how to speak with Corey through your minds?"

"Yes. I talk to him every day."

"Speak to him now and tell him to trust the eagle, she will not hurt him and tell him not to be afraid. Tell him the eagle is your friend."

I transformed rising into the air, engaged the coordinates and vanished from her view. Corey's location was a bedsit in Camberwell. I materialised in eagle form, meaning to be purposefully witnessed and opened fire at the Leaf left to watch over Corey and keep him caged. He hit the deck stunned, with a priceless expression on his face.

"I guess you are Corey? I am Sarah. Going to come with me?" I asked.

Corey nodded and wrapping a wing around him, I told him to keep Ruby firmly in his mind and hold onto a feather. We disappeared, reappearing on the rooftop by the Thames, where I transformed back. There were hugs, kisses, more hugs and kisses and tears. The love that had helped them both through their ordeals was strong and evident. Ruby looked at me with tears in her eyes, her hand tightly grasping Corey's.

"I don't think you can grant me my third wish."

"You think not. Give me a moment."

I did not have to refer into Tarquin or Nevaeh to ask them where Ruby and Corey would reside, I knew. I linked quickly into Nesta and ascertained the name and vibration for the catcher originally assigned to meet Ruby and her brother. This confirmed I asked him to meet us if possible at our current location. He arrived in seconds.

"This is Ryan, Ruby."

"I recognise your face. You were the man lying on the floor at our flat when we died."

"That was me and I am sorry I was not able to help you then. It has been impossible to get near you since. I am glad Sarah has been able to help you."

I held my palm to the side of my head playfully and looked at Ruby.

"I have a message coming in from the spirit world, the vibration is getting stronger. Let me see, do you know a Margaret?" Ruby looked at me blankly.

"No? Let me see. Is it Melanie?"

Both Ruby and Corey's eyes lit up. I knew exactly who she was to them.

"It's grandma!" shouted Corey.

"She is waiting for you. Now go with Ryan, you can trust him totally."

Ruby placed her arms around my neck and hugged me tightly.

"Thank you for seeing who I am, fairy godmother."

"It is easier to see those who keep a true sight of themselves. Your reward is mine too."

"Can I have one of your feathers?" asked Corey.

"Certainly not, cheeky monkey." I bent down and gave him a kiss on his cheek.

"Thank you for helping us, I like eagles," he said.

"What else do you like, Corey?" asked Ryan.

"Rainbows!"

Ryan created a rainbow entrance to the tunnel through to Realm Four and all three stepped into it.

"Keep wishing, Ruby," I said.

"You know I will. Thank you."

The tunnel closed and I thanked the Collective for its guidance.

One Step Forward

As Thomas, Arthur and I arrived in Realm Two, we found ourselves beside a large lake. A short distance from the pebbled shore, a thick mist shrouded the rest of its expanse. It slowly and continuously rolled towards us, then dissipated before reaching the beach. The water was unmoving, inert and lifeless, matching the status of the dry and dead tundra surrounding it. Whilst a little warmer than Realm One, the cold bit into fingers and cheeks. Like Thomas had explained, there was a subdued glow of yellow light, almost twilight, circumnavigating the horizon in every direction, making terrain and objects in the distance almost visible.

Looking back towards the lake, my imagination conjured images of a ghost ship arriving out of the mists delivering a band of marauding spectres intent on plundering homesteads near to the shoreline.

"Spooky, isn't it?" I said.

"Unnerving," said Arthur.

"How are you feeling?" I asked.

"Yes, much better thanks to you and Thomas."

I could hear Alana coming in and gave her a quick update on what had just happened and whom we had met. Her words of 'you are not going to try and free Adolf Hitler, are you?' resonated for a short time after she had disconnected. I felt Thomas move into my thoughts.

"Can you imagine being someone who has done something so awful that no one would ever be able to forgive you for it? I mean ever? Even if you were able to feel even the slightest regret, the fact is you can never escape from the actions you have taken. Even after death, those actions would keep you in that place of 'what's the point of even trying'. I believe that even though the Collective provides an opportunity for everyone to redeem themselves, there are some who would choose never to take that one step forward."

"If you read me, Thomas, you will know that it is not my intention to even attempt to help him free himself."

"And yet you were able to hold his attention and he also responded to your Runic message?"

"He said that he understood the journey I was describing, but dare not ask for Dagaz, which is hope, happiness and being reborn into the light. He also said he dare not ask for Mannaz either, which is trust, faith and companionship. Dare not perhaps, because after what he has done, he cannot contemplate a power existing in the universe which would grant him a new beginning? It's a dilemma, isn't it?" I said.

"Welcome to my world. There is a lot of one step forward, then two steps back."

Whilst Thomas and I talked, I could hear Arthur's mind struggling in aberration, where abhorrence wrestled with his sense of compassion. I felt his mind flatten and rest in nothingness to ease the disquiet. Thomas was listening to him.

"Now, is that denial, Arthur?" asked Thomas.

"It's a nowhere place, somewhere to seek solace and refuge away from the torment. It is somewhere that does not connect to anything," he replied.

"It's detachment. Where there seems there is no escape from something we are caught in, we seek to detach from it. It is a stepping-stone into denial to avoid the dilemma and pain it comes with. Gosh, you gents are getting the full experiential, serendipitous tour today. This is what happens here," said Thomas.

Because there was no comfort in the dark, dwellers created their own in their own minds. So many were detached from the reality of why they were here and failed to connect to the justification for ending up in the dark, because it was too painful to contemplate. The guide's job was to help lead them into that difficult place, to face up to the implications of their actions. Many just didn't want to look or occupied themselves in endless pursuits leading to little gain. I felt many Earth residents were not dissimilar in this respect.

Something else that had struck me, was the lack of activity or presence of people in this area of the realm. Then a woman ran past us about two hundred metres away. She was carrying a rock. She seemed not to notice us, intent on her mission. I could make out another woman in the distance but running on a different pathway, in the opposite direction and again carrying a rock.

The first woman arrived at her destination which was like a livestock shelter constructed out of similar stones to the one she had carried. The roof, made out of bushels of sedges bound with dry grass would offer little if any protection from the elements. She placed the rock into the wall, adjusted the makeshift thatch and ran off again in the direction from which she had come. The second woman, on reaching her small homestead, placed her rock inside the shelter and also ran back in the direction from whence she came.

After a short while, it became apparent they were removing rocks from each other's abodes to fortify their own. It made me think of Adelie penguins in Antarctica stealing stones from each other's nests.

"Are you aware of how long they have been doing this?" asked Arthur.

"Yes, about five years," said Thomas.

"Don't they ever bump into each other?" I asked.

"Occasionally. They are, reasonably polite, say something like 'there's never enough rocks' and carry on. They are trying to build homes for their children, so they can all feel safe and secure," said Thomas.

"But I thought you said there were no minors in this realm?" I said.

"There aren't, but in their minds, their children are going to come home shortly. They think that home should be the safest place and that is what they must build. But it never becomes safe enough because there are not enough rocks."

"What happened?" asked Arthur.

The first woman we had seen was Andrea. She was found running through a park screaming that her child had fallen into the boating lake. The pushchair had just rolled away from her when her back was turned. The CCTV had shown otherwise. She had unemotionally pushed the buggy off the edge of the quay and calmly watched the child struggle as it drowned beneath the surface.

There had been no mental illness diagnosed afterwards and her truth was, she had become fixated on a man she wanted a relationship with. Sadly, he had not wanted to be involved with a woman who had a child. She had killed herself in prison six months later, not able to cope with the constant taunts of 'child killer' and the daily death threats.

"Good grief, what about the other woman?" I asked.

Thomas explained the other woman Nicola, was living a life far below her expectations having been left by her husband two years previously. She wanted more for herself and felt tied by her children. Her husband had met someone else and was enjoying his new life which she felt, was unfair. As there was equity in the property and her ex-husband had kept up the insurance payments, she hatched a plan to clean her slate.

She had pushed a petrol-soaked rag through the letterbox, followed by a lighted match, then let herself in through the back door. After opening the doors to the children's bedrooms, she waited upstairs for the fire to reach the landing, before she jumped from a back bedroom window to the lawn below breaking her leg. Although in pain, she calculated enough time to allow her children to suffocate in their sleep and then raised the alarm.

"That was in 1952," said Thomas. "She got her pay out and was convincing enough to cover up her crime. She did marry again to a sympathetic widowed man who had two children of his own and led a life of denial until her seventies when she died of cancer. She came here when she judged herself and it didn't take long, before she had 'forgotten' what she had done because 'it was a long time ago'. Now she is preoccupied with building a secure house and refuses to accept her responsibility."

"It seems ironic that these two women have committed similar crimes and end up together, locked into a scenario of continually going around in circles, trying to feel secure by stealing each other's rocks," I said.

"A fate designed by the Collective? We are never sure. I am hoping one day they will talk to each other and face the truth with each other's help. After all, they cannot judge each other, as the nature of their crimes was the same."

"Can't you divert them?" I asked.

"I have tried, but they are both so intent on their task, I cannot keep their attention," said Thomas.

"Why not give them enough rocks to build something that they might feel safe in. Once one task is achieved, it leaves a void for the next to be filled," I said.

"But that is gifting them. Rocks are a currency, a means to an ends," he explained.

"They may be a currency here, but the gift is compassionate. Rocks may be tangible, but they facilitate the intangible, a feeling of security. Is guiding not about helping others to feel safe enough to evoke a positive risk to change something?" I said.

"We guide with words and encouragement. I cannot be seen to do that," said Thomas.

"Why? Are not rocks the same as words and encouragement to hopefully motivate that change. I think if you gave them some rocks, you might get a result," I said.

"The model in the dark is simple. We allow people to find their own way, whilst providing guidance, we don't give them what they want. That would open us up to all kinds of jealousy and conflict in our relationships with individuals. Why should I risk making them feel better by giving them a few rocks?" said Thomas.

I was now bouncing against my frustration threshold.

"Do you have a therapeutic relationship with these two women, who have maintained this behaviour for five years? Wake up Thomas. One size does not fit all. Relationships are person centred and specific and you have the power to change this by facilitating what they need. I feel the 'need' may have just disguised itself as a 'want' to you," I said directly.

"Do you want my job? I am not naïve enough to know that 'one to one' tailor made support and guidance isn't the way forward. There are too few of us in this role to manage what you are suggesting," said Thomas defensively.

"Do you think the Collective wants the Dark Realms to continue to fill and become stagnant with little movement? No, I don't think so. You need to start to manage upwards and increase your resources, otherwise you will end up like the rest of them here, denying the truth," I said.

Thomas looked down, then raised his line of sight towards me through his fringe.

"I know you are right, bird boy," he said smiling.

"And I know, you want to do what's right, mop head. Come on, this is a JFDI," I smiled back.

Meanwhile, Arthur had been following the exchange and a thought had gone through his mind that one of us might get blasted.

A plan was agreed, with me taking full responsibility, to provide Andrea and Nicola with fifty rocks apiece. Each of us spending time travelling and returning with the items. I hasten to add, these were not taken from other resident's shelters, but from a remote source Thomas was aware of.

Once we had them all, they were divided and transported to the front of each dwelling whilst both women were running between them. We sat back and watched. There was no sense of surprise from either of them when the new stocks were discovered and each woman turned to continue with their rock collecting missions. This time, however, both returned with two rocks from each other's piles.

"There's never ever enough rocks," said Arthur.

Then something changed. Although they both started to recommence their journeys, a few paces taken, was then followed by a reflective look back at their new resource and both started to build up their dwellings. After about an hour, Andrea sat down, whilst Nicola swept the inside floor with some brush, before also sitting. We gradually approached Nicola, who was nervous about our presence.

"It's all right, Nicola, I think you have seen me before. These are my friends James and Arthur; we mean you no harm. You have made a good job with your house; it looks very sturdy and secure," said Thomas.

"Thank you yes, there have been more rocks today. I am waiting for my children. I seem to have lost them," she said, unsure of what she was saying.

"There is another woman who lives yonder; she seems to have lost her child also. Have you met her?" I asked.

"Seen her, but not met her. She is always running somewhere," she replied.

"Now that your house is safe and secure, would you like to meet her? I am sure she would welcome some company," said Thomas.

"Company?" Nicola seemed to struggle with the meaning of the word. "Is her house as nice as mine?"

"Hers is just as safe and secure. You would like it," I said.

"I am not sure if I am supposed to keep company. I have done something awful, I cannot quite remember and I am in this place to be punished. Why would you want me to do something that I might enjoy?" she asked.

"We are not here to put a stop to what small pleasures there may be, but more importantly, you may be able to help each other find your children and with this, you will have something in common. What do you think?" said Thomas.

"All right, I will meet her, but only for a short while," said Nicola.

Whilst Thomas left us to suggest the idea to Andrea, we sat and spoke to Nicola who told us of her life on the Earth plain and it being a shock to end up here after she had died. She was a church goer in her early life, but had somehow lost all of her faith later. She knew she must have done something bad because this could not be heaven, but it was unclear and she did not know what to expect when she had died. I told her that Arthur and I came from another realm which was beautiful and sunny and if she helped herself, she might live there one day.

"How can I help myself?" she asked.

"Start with Andrea. Perhaps you can help her find out what happened to her child and ask her to do the same for you. Your houses are secure now. You need not spend more time on them, when time is better spent on understanding why you might be here," I said.

Thomas was returning with Andrea, who had a rock in her hands. I was concerned as to what its purpose served, until I caught her thoughts. Thomas introduced us and both women searched each other's faces for signs of intent before Andrea broke the ice.

"This rock is yours. There was a day when I could not find any and I am sorry but I took this rock from your house as I was desperate," Andrea said to Nicola.

"Thank you but please keep it. As you can see, I have enough. In truth, I took a rock from your house one day myself as I also was desperate and I am sorry for that," she replied.

The tiny truth shone through the huge lie and I watched a glimmer of relationship grow as the first hurdle of judgement and guilt was precariously overcome. After a short while during which the women adapted their scrutiny of each other to mild interest, we bid our farewells and left them to endeavour to find paths for each other in the gloominess, next to a dead lake.

Kept in the Dark

Having left the two women, we relocated to a hilltop, overlooking a tundra plain. Instead of small hamlets, individual ramshackle dwellings were scattered across the terrain. Judging by the distance between them, their positions were an obvious mark of the inhabitant's non-trust of each other and fear of relationship.

"I wonder, James. Might you arrange a massive shipment of rocks from Realm Four for me?" asked Thomas with surreptitious humour.

"Consider it done, my friend. Looking at the buildings down there, they could do with some too."

In all seriousness, I said he needed something in addition to rocks. My concern was without effective resource a holding tank was being created. If we were going to generate a sustainable energy flow for the Collective from the dark, we needed guides who could act intuitively. Guides who were not afraid that provision for residents would be misinterpreted as satisfying 'wants' when they were justifiable and authentic 'needs'.

"It's Gerald Sentinel who watches over the running of the Dark Realms, isn't it?" I said.

"Oh, Gerry, yes I have heard of him," interrupted Arthur. "Bit of a traditionalist our Gerry."

"A traditionalist is one way of putting it. He is not one who embraces change comfortably and truth be known, the majority see him as reactionary," added Thomas.

"In my experience of Realm Fivers', I find them to be wise, knowing and thoughtful. How can he still be in post?" I said.

"Bloody hell, James, it's a good job we don't have thought police in these realms. Perhaps other fives don't want the shitty end of the stick to hold?" replied Thomas.

"You mean running the Dark Realms is not an enviable task?" I said.

"Frustrating, slow moving and not too fruitful," he replied.

I saw the role and the responsibility it came with as crucially important. The Dark Realms accommodated people who held the potential to make the most dramatic of changes. In addition, it was these residents who released vast amounts of energy once they had redeemed themselves with the Collective.

I knew that Andrea and Nicola for example, on self-release, held a potential energy between them equating to nearly a hundred lifetimes of an average Earth person living their life in quiet desperation, then passing over from Earth.

Following a thoughtful pause between us, Arthur suggested a scenario possibly explaining the slow movement based on a devil's advocate viewpoint. A view suggesting a design.

In his job as an Earth guide, he was well aware of the expression 'not on my doorstep', meaning Earth people knew of ex-offenders and criminal practices in their communities or wider afield, but did not want them close to their location.

On Earth, even if a person has served time for a crime and paid their dues to society, they were still thought of or labelled, denoting the crime they committed, such as a thief. In judging eyes, the threat still persisted because the person had actually committed the crime and therefore had a greater potential to reoffend, than someone who had not.

Like the two women who needed to build security around them, generally, as human beings, security is a basic motivator to enable them to face and achieve even the ordinary challenges that life presents. If a potential threat becomes present, people will instinctively judge, assume the worst, then factor the risk. This would either result in a diminished sense of security they could either choose to live with, or take action to alleviate.

Although existence is different in the after world and not all crimes are literally possible, spirit people still retain the ability to judge a person by their history and previous character. This is because on passing, they retained their personality traits and societal norms, taboos and beliefs they had held on the Earth world.

"I think what you are suggesting is that the system is being managed to minimise the number of ex-offenders getting into Realm Four? Perhaps to preserve the archetypal vision and experience of what heaven is supposed to be like," I suggested.

"It could be," replied Arthur, shrugging his shoulders.

"What's your view, Thomas?" I asked.

"Three realms dedicated to 'processing' the goodness back into them? An individual could spend hundreds of years or more moving through them before getting into Four," he replied, adding weight to the operation of some kind of design.

"And without the proper support, this would easily be maintained. As without it, residents go around in circles, attempting to find enough rocks to build a solid foundation from which to rebuild a sense of their true Selves," I suggested.

"You must also look at the process though, as designed by the Collective and the undoubtable final reality of committing such crimes. The ultimate message, it seems, is don't commit the crime in the first place," said Thomas.

In Thomas's view and experience, forgiveness wasn't an action, it was an acceptance and was hard won. In order for another to forgive a perpetrator and for the perpetrator to forgive themselves, they must suspend judgement and replace it with compassionate acceptance that the debt had been repaid and responsibility fully embraced.

For those committing crimes, to achieve true and open relationship with others, they were reliant on the forgiveness of others who, themselves relied on societal and cultural norms and doctrine to guide them. Even if self-forgiveness had been achieved by overcoming denial, we could not forget what we had done and were always reminded by our own memories. This was a simple inherent internal system, set up to give us insight because if we cannot remember, we do not learn how to choose not to make the same mistakes.

The only way to escape this was to revolve back to Earth in a new life, but it is only that lifetime and subsequent Earth lifetimes we are freed from the torment. The big prize having successively come back to the spirit world having completed our revolutions, was to achieve access to previous life experiences.

However, by doing this, we were once again reminded of what we had done. It seemed that being damned to suffer in hell for eternity for a crime causing suffering to others, did not necessarily mean we would remain in hell. It meant we could not escape our actions for an eternity. This suggested, there was no such thing as a clean slate, unless of course, the slate wasn't dirtied in the first place.

I checked my own indiscretions from my previous lifetimes and I could remember them all, although they were not great in a magnitude of suffering.

"But we hold the choice to move on from them," I said.

"But you haven't forgotten them. That is the wrestle the Collective has provided for us. The wrestle between moving on by the degree of forgiveness for yourself, verses never forgetting what you have done," replied Thomas.

"I hear you saying, there is no forgiveness from the Collective, only momentary reprieve by revolving?" I said. Thomas looked back at me with an expression of irony.

"Who is responsible for a crime? You are. Therefore, the Collective hands back the responsibility to us to find forgiveness ourselves. You are the one that chose to commit it and only you can free yourself from the destructive power of the memory of the crime. The Collective's part in it is to provide systems like the Dark Realms where you can achieve self-forgiveness and move on. Having moved on, it is never going to let you forget though, ever."

"For some reason, I had this notion of forgive and forget. But when I thought about my own experiences, I could see it was more about building resilience through forgiveness, so memories impacted less upon me."

"Why do you think Tune Juice is so popular over here?" said Thomas, raising his eyebrows. "No, joking aside, rather than 'forgive and forget'. I think 'forgive and accept' is more the reality."

Thomas explained that present company accepted we were human and we all had Cerberus, the three-headed dog, in our makeup. One head looked to the present, one to the future and the other to the past. In Greek mythology, Cerberus let souls into hell, but never let them out. The past head never let us forget our past actions. It also acted as a reminder to those who have not committed hellish deeds, that they will not be forgotten or forgiven if they ever commit them. The Cerberus awareness was one entwined into the connection between the Collective and all conscious life.

The state of self-forgiveness was hard for all to truly achieve. It was a fine balance attained by the wrestle between accepting our own forgiveness and being reminded. For that reason, once in the dark, it's hard to find your way out.

I thanked Thomas for his insights, as I had not been aware of the complexity of how systems and directives intertwined with each other. I understood the difficulty in achieving that state to move on and from discussion previously, the danger of ex-offenders from the dark being ostracised by those in Realm Four should they get there. However, I needed him to commit to two straightforward questions.

"Do you feel that being under resourced is negatively affecting the progress of those in the dark and do you feel the pace of throughput is purposefully designed to minimise it?" I knew I was asking for a huge commitment.

"Yes, to the first and with both questions being linked in my view, it suggests the second is also correct," said Thomas with some hesitation.

"I don't want your job, Thomas; you must have the patience of a saint. Thank you for your support and guidance, I see a little more clearly now."

"I could do with a bit of light shining on the subject, can we move onto three now?" asked Arthur.

"Yes, we will go there shortly," said Thomas.

As the two of them chatted, I linked into Tarquin and enabled him to see the content of Thomas and my recent conversation. It appeared that Gerry was an old school Realm Five high planer, who had been given the responsibility for overseeing the Dark Realms some centuries previously. He was in fact the oldest serving in Realm Five, as he had never made the transition to six. As Gerry could be quite aloof, he was also guarded with his thoughts.

For this reason, Tarquin said it was difficult to know whether he had chosen to remain in five, having been allowed to transition, or had not achieved a more progressed knowing to make it happen. It was felt that those in six had enabled this vocation due to his length of service, rather than basing it on his abilities.

Tarquin confirmed that those with a reactionary way of being, continued to strive to maintain the ancient ideals of the system. The most ideal being reward, security and peace of mind during a person's time in Realm Four before returning to Earth.

"But the system is set up to ensure that those coming out of the dark judge themselves in the reflection of the Collective and therefore present no risk to those in four?" I said.

"Realm Four is full of people in part way to achieving Self-awareness, who judge as part of their everyday lives. The idealist state is a world without judgement, but if that existed on Earth, we would not grow in awareness. Heaven and in particular Realm Four is a reward, where judgement, I believe, is purposefully minimised so people can rest between Earth lifetimes. Hence the saying, rest in peace, spoken when a person passes over, although many on Earth believe they will rest for eternity," said Tarquin.

"What's your view?" I asked.

"Because many of the crimes committed on Earth are not practically possible and therefore no threat in the after world, I see the main issue being the discomfort of the one who is judging another's history and as Arthur said, 'not on my doorstep'. However, by letting more into four from the dark, an opportunity would present itself whereby people could learn to forgive, without fear."

"An ideal replaced by another ideal, you mean, plus, your doorstep is wherever you put it in Realm Four anyway."

"Yes. However, in order to change what you think might be currently going on, you must be prepared to debate with some of the inflexible powers who control the ways things have always been."

"But why does the Collective allow such practices to be maintained, when it must know they are not the best?" I said.

"Why doesn't it directly interfere with the evolution of consciousness on Earth? It is the same principle in the after world. It allows us to evolve. Perfection is awe-inspiring and awe has a catatonic quality. I believe the Collective does not seek controlled perfection, as there is no growth in it."

"Only rest? Hence the current ways in managing Realm Four? It appears that others have decided they prefer perfection," I said. I could hear Alana attempting to connect.

"The key to a resolution is in understanding both sides of an argument. However, our hands are being forced by what is happening on Earth which is why we search for energy sources to right the balance. Those who are traditionalist must be helped to understand it is not our intention to pollute the system, which is how it may be seen. It is our objective to manage a lucrative renewable energy source, which will benefit all, including those at rest."

"Catch you later, I must go, I have Alana on the other line. Thanks, Tarquin."

"Before you go, you do realise, you are being watched."

"I had a feeling. I hope they are selling tickets because my intension is to provide value for money."

"I will look into what your conversations have revealed. Have fun, James, thanks for coming in."

As soon as Tarquin had disconnected, Alana linked in asking me for my help. I explained to both Thomas and Arthur, I needed about an hour, so would meet them in Realm Three when I had finished. They were both fine with this, so I honed into Alana's vibration, transported and transformed on route.

Ocean Guardian

Alana and Audaz' attempts to look for a blue whale in a vast area of the Indian ocean was like trying to find the proverbial needle in a haystack. Although now accustomed to whale vibrations, they knew where whales were but did not know the vibration of blue whales. Alana thought she would take the easy route and contact Nevaeh.

"Hi, Mum, mastered the backstroke yet?"

"Perfectly and having a whale of a time. Can I ask a favour?"

"Yeah, sure, reading you loud and clear. The vibration is unique from other whales; well, they all are actually. I'm sending it now. How's Audaz?"

"Thanks, Nevaeh. He's fine, enjoying the experience and wishes he had been born a fish." I was joking because I knew Audaz was listening in.

"She does not tell the truth, Nevaeh. I do not wish to be a fish; I am a—"

"We know, Harpy eagle." Both Nevaeh and I filled in the gap.

"You think you know me so well. I was going to say, a little fed up with all this swimming, but the flying over the oceans is magical. My great, great uncle Ronaldo was an Albatross. He used to tell me wondrous stories about his adventures over the seas," said Audaz.

"How is that possible? Your family line is of Harpy eagles," I said.

"Exactly, like me! A fish is the last thing I would choose to be," Audaz replied grumpily.

I mind blocked and told Neveah, I thought he was missing his forest, although what we were doing was a lot less boring than chasing Macaws. I thanked her again and checked out.

Sharing the vibration with Audaz, I suggested we transport to three thousand metres which would give us a much greater visual scan limit in every direction. Although having the vibration would enable us to scan further afield, being that high, with the eyes of eagle would help us pinpoint our whale.

I imagined him or her to be swimming alone rather than with others, so we scanned for single whales. The majority of echoes came from the south, with only one located off the northwest coast.

"I think that's our whale, Audaz, and it's a he," I announced.

We hit the water as dolphins at over 50 kilometres an hour, about three hundred metres behind him. Rather than, accelerate away, he stopped and let us catch up. He was massive, much larger than the species information Nevaeh gave me as part of her link. He was about thirty-five metres long weighing possibly 215 tonnes.

Although you could not call him blue, his colouration was a blue-grey, mottled with light grey patches and a dark fluke underside. I could sense Audaz' wonder, which matched my own as we swam along his flank towards his head. This was not all we sensed, as his vibration resonated with transitional will energy, albeit latent.

"Should I call you 'your highness'?" I asked.

The whale laughed into my mind.

"You know, don't you?" said the whale.

"Yes. There have been many lifetimes," I replied.

"My name is Theseus and in Earth terms, I am one hundred and twelve years old."

"From what I know, your mythical father was also a sea farer," I teased.

He smiled through his eyes and told us he knew of us, curtesy of Cuchiq, to be Alana and Audaz, visitors from the spirit world. Evidently, we had caused quite a stir in the whale and dolphin communities by us being able to appear to them and then intrigue, because they had said our echoes were similar to his.

What intrigues me is why they think we all have a similar echo? wondered Audaz.

"That is probably because although you are dolphins, you are really an eagle Audaz with a slight murmur of human and you Alana, are a mixture of human and Osprey. And I am a whale."

Audaz and I looked at each other, astonished that he could know of our true identities, as he was an Earth born creature.

"You are not an ordinary whale obviously," I said.

"Are any whales ordinary, Alana?" he replied with the enormity of his presence.

"No, forgive me, I mean you have incredible insight, plus you are on the Earth plane and the sense you have just demonstrated is highly perceptive."

"I will give you a clue. I have wings and I fly, but my medium for flight is water. Other than the last two centuries, humans have not presented as a threat in our domain. A domain purposely chosen to evade contact with them."

"Like a rainforest you mean?" said Audaz.

"Like a rainforest, my friend."

"You are a Harpy, like us?" I said, tingling with heightened awareness.

"Sadly, I am. Sadly, because our ancestors would have walked the Earth and flown in the skies and now on Earth, we have had to become something else and not through our natural choice."

Both Audaz and I simultaneously nudged his head with our beaks in an expression of separated family coming back together. I told him that although we were aware of the three lines Harpies assumed after extinction, we had no idea of a Harpy Whale line. Even those in a more advanced realm had no knowledge of it.

"You mean those in Realm Five?" enquired Theseus.

"How do you know this? None of my Harpy friends whilst on Earth had a clear picture of the after world, only glimpses and unclear memories."

"It's because I am a guardian and guardian whales report directly into Realm Six."

Both Audaz and I were shocked beyond comprehension.

Theseus explained that when the Harpies were being reduced in number making it difficult to revolve back to Earth, his ancestors also faced the choice of the three known lines as they waited in Realm Four. Having been persecuted by humans they were not sure whether they wanted to revolve as them but were concerned about the shortness of Earth lifetime of the other two options.

The time came when the urge to return was becoming harder to deny and his ancestors in their small tribe of about thirty souls, were becoming increasingly restless. A meeting was called between them to decide which Earth vessel to choose and no one was convinced that any choice was the right one.

As legend says a powerful spirit whose name was Thaddeus, appeared in their midst and offered a fourth option which was to become whales in the oceans. He offered a life in an environment free from humans, one where they would have little threat being at the top of the food chain and would live long and happy lives.

For this option, he requested that Harpy whales became the guardians of the oceans. It would become their role to operate a communication network across over two thirds of the Earth's surface, with information disseminated to and collected from local whale and dolphin populations. It was agreed that the guardians would report to Thaddeus and provide information on changes to our environment including human activity.

Thaddeus had always been aware of the importance of the oceans and how they were in balance with the land. The majority of the other high planers were occupied with land matters, as this was the human and land animal habitat. Another request was that their identities be shielded from other Harpies and other high planers.

"When we die, we rest in Realm Four oceans and revolve back as a natural course of events. It is only Thaddeus and our tribe who know our identity."

"So you revolve with full awareness of who you are?" asked Audaz.

"Not quite. There are inclinations when we are young, followed by an awakening at the age of about ten," said Theseus.

"Why are you telling us this if no one in Realm Four or Five knows about this?" I asked.

"Thaddeus knows you are here and what you are doing. All of the guardians are aware of the increase in threat to our environment and the time has come to work together across realms to manage this threat."

"I take it you are aware of the Japanese hunting again?" I asked.

"Yes, Thaddeus told me. When it happened, I sent out communications to filter down to Beaked and Minke whales in the North Pacific. My main concern is with the Minkes'. One because they are more difficult to contact because they are loners or in small pods and second they are young at heart and like to swim near ships because they are inquisitive. You have to understand, whales are instinctually motivated more than intellectually guided, although they have this capacity. Therefore, they are drawn to environmental and species custom familiarity and do not think in terms of potential danger. Why are they hunting again anyway?" said Theseus.

"Species custom familiarity. Although it's more to do with cultural tastes and profit," I said.

It was also the Minkes who were hardest hit in the North Atlantic by whalers. The guardians had great concerns for that area especially the arctic. The temperature and water density changes there, were badly affecting the feeding grounds. The Greys had always been known to travel vast distances from feeding in the Arctic to where they breed off the Mexican coast.

The warmer water in the arctic had reduced their food source. In the past, they would take on great quantities, not feeding again until they returned in the late summer with their young. Now they were staying longer in the Arctic, being forced to find alternative food sources and had to travel south without enough fat supplies to get them back up north again.

There had been fewer calves born and more and more whales were not sustained enough to make it back to feed, so perished on route. The change in water temperature was affecting not just whales but all kinds of ocean life.

"How do you get your information?" asked Audaz.

Theseus explained there were now two hundred guardians in total, each responsible for a specific area of the oceans and spread around the planet. He was responsible for the area north of Australia, stretching past Indonesia and the Philippines and up to Japan.

Not restricted to just blue whales, guardians were comprised of different whale species, giving the guardians a broad knowledge of language and character differences. Information on different events, whether that be on temperature changes or food issues were sung across vast distances between whales who passed it on as part of a chain. Messages could be relayed across the world in a matter of a few hours.

Their role was to monitor a range of issues which were determined by Thaddeus. Of particular importance were changes at the poles. Guardians in the Arctic and Antarctic particularly monitored water temperature, density or saltiness and water movement, in particular the ocean conveyers. Factors such as ice melt and surface ice regression, the resultant effects on the food sources, migration and migration abnormalities, were also watched.

For those outside those particular hot spots, other factors were also monitored. These included water quality, noise, pollution, human activity, in the form of shipping and fishing, including whale hunting, circulation and effects on marine habitats like reefs.

"We also keep an eye on fish stocks, whale and dolphin numbers and abnormal behaviours or events, such as the grey whale casualties," said Theseus.

"And you report all of this into, Thaddeus?" I asked.

"About once a month, unless there is something extraordinary and then as and when."

"And then there is plastic," said Audaz.

"The not so tasty killer, you mean? They just don't care do they? Their attitude towards and responsibility for destroying things or other life has not changed in the near one thousand years since they killed our Harpy race off," said Theseus.

"I think it's unfair to say that, Theseus. Many humans are passionate about the Earth's climate balance and preserving its wildlife. They have started to create ocean sanctuaries for example," I defended.

"I am aware but they need to make much more of the oceans a sanctuary and not just restrict them to coastal waters. You say many humans care, then why is all of this happening. Why don't the ones who care, make the ones who don't, change their behaviour. The evidence is all around you. The ones that care, don't care enough do they!" said Theseus, responding passionately.

I told him he reminded me of my mate, James, as his passion seemed to give him what he thinks is a clear line of fire too.

I explained to him his 'care' points were not as clear cut as that, as I had witnessed, having spent many lifetimes living amongst humans as part of my chosen Harpy line. Many humans were led by their own sense of domestic security, concerned about immediate relationships and emotional wellbeing. The impact of their consumption behaviour had been less important or their awareness not far reaching enough to think about long term affects.

In the past, information had either not been available or purposely hidden by those who stood to gain from environmental impacting consumerism. The problem we had now was, those practices and consumption needs, which produced the by-product which increases climate change, were well entrenched. Entrenched in the infrastructure of nation's economies and cultures, therefore the task of replacing them for lower risk alternatives had become almost too complicated to change quickly on a global level.

We all knew in the after-world change had to happen but the desperate thing standing in those on Earth's way was their history, where nations do not collectively consider themselves as part of a global society founded on instinctive trust.

"They are supposed to be socially intelligent. I don't understand why they are so preoccupied with competing, rather than cooperating. I am worried there is going to be a disaster and frustrated that we can do little but be affected by a totally selfish and short-sighted race of greedy incompetents!" irked Theseus.

"I am with you. They cut down our forests for the same reasons. It is almost as though they have lost their ability to live peacefully with the rest of the Earth and its inhabitants. They seem to think their 'intelligence' gives them a right to decide what they can do to benefit themselves, regardless of the cost to the planet," agreed Audaz. I aired my view.

"I have no doubt there is a disaster on its way. How many will be affected, human or Earth animal species is incomprehensible until it happens. This will have the potential to reset human consumption needs, however, it is not guaranteed they will not continue to use the same energy resources, after it, which caused the problem in the first place. Their attitude maybe one of 'we are consuming less, so polluting less'. Current resource use may persist if current systems can be brought back into action faster after a disaster, to provide the energy they want," I said.

For Theseus, if he had his way, he would send spirit delegates to visit all governments in the world simultaneously. Not to advise but to tell them to drastically cut all practices which produce greenhouse gases and invest hard in renewable energy systems with immediate effect. If they knew what they were doing was affecting their future in the next world, as well causing massive damage to and great loss of life on Earth, he was sure they would listen.

I felt dubious of this for different reasons. The first was, humans would probably not believe where the delegates had come from. Rather than believing they were 'dead' people, because that's just fantasy, they were more likely to think it was some organised extra-terrestrial invasion, with a motive to take control of the planet.

Any evidence that spirit might produce would be accounted for by vastly superior telepathic, transportation and information technologies. World leaders would want to know whose orders they were acting on and then demand they speak with who was in charge. I felt that sadly, miracles were no longer believed and in the name of science, everything had to be explained and evidence provided.

The second reason and if they did believe our delegates, it would fundamentally change the conscious relationship with mortality and with it the whole spiritual energy and knowing production system. As energy was produced by Earth dwellers through positive choice and growing awareness, introducing immortality and transparency of the after world, could act as a deterrent to people making negative self-centred decisions and related behaviours.

"But that is what we want them to do. To become aware of the impact they are having by thinking they are in control, when they are not," said Theseus.

"It's about balance, Theseus. If you take away risk, you also take away choice. Without risk and people behaving in a way to cause harm to themselves, others, animals or the environment, there is no way to learn from mistakes. In fact, there would be no lessons to learn for others either, who learn by judgement. Spiritual energy production would be irreversibly changed for the worse. We just need them to evolve and take action quickly, without our direct intervention," I said, attempting to widen the perspective.

"Then it is about time, the powers that be in the after world did the same as the Earth powers need to do, relook at the energy systems." Theseus passionately made his point.

"You definitely need to meet James, Theseus," suggested Audaz.

"I agree; he would love you," I confirmed.

"If he believes we should have greater transparency across all worlds, I would be interested to meet him too," said Theseus.

I connected into James, who said he was about to go into Realm Three and I asked if he could spare us an hour to talk with a blue whale who had some interesting thoughts on increasing the transparency between worlds and devising alternative spiritual energy systems.

"He sounds like a pretty clued-up whale for an Earth born. I'm reading more from you, he's a Harpy like us. That is incredible," said James.

"That's not all, darling. He and his kin, totalling two hundred Harpy whale guardians situated around the world, report directly into Realm Six. Nobody else knew about them, until now."

"I am on my way. Let me speak to Thomas and Arthur. I will be with you shortly."

Knocked for Six

I had explained to Theseus that James would be on his way shortly and asked if he had a mate.

"Her name is Selene and we have travelled through all of our lifetimes."

"Do you see her?" asked Audaz.

"Her territory stretches north of Japan, along the north eastern Russian coast and right around, including the Bering Sea and straits. She also monitors Alaska and north Canada. We do meet up in deep water in the northern pacific and spend time with each other every couple of months."

"Children?" I asked.

"Only one sadly and she was a member of our original tribe who revolved; however, the bond is strong between the three of us and we all talk regularly."

"Sounds strangely familiar. James and I only have one daughter too."

I could feel his senses immediately heighten. Suddenly, less than fifty metres away a huge blue whale outlined in blue-white light, breached the surface and splashed back down beneath the waves.

"Show off," I said.

"Well, you didn't say you were in dolphin form, whilst in Rome and all that. Hello, darling."

"Theseus, this is James."

"Pleased to meet you, Theseus. Good afternoon, Audaz."

"Greetings, Joao, my friend," replied Audaz.

"I am pleased to meet you as well, James. How is it that you can transform into something the size of me? And was that you who bumped into me a few moments before," he asked.

"Yes, that was me. I needed to get a feel from you, before I made my entrance. The size is just light projection from my core. We can transform into any animal species but my core is that of—"

"A golden eagle?" asked Theseus.

"Yes. Tell me, when you are back in the after world between Earth lifetimes, don't you transform back to your core raptor?"

"No, no one speaks of doing this. There are only two hundred of us; therefore, it is rare that more than one of us is back in the spirit world at the same time. We wait in the spirit oceans until the next time we revolve, which is always less than one Earth year," replied Theseus.

"Do you know of your Harpy tribe history? Did you keep yourselves hidden from other Harpies on Earth?" asked James.

"Not hidden but we chose to remain at a distance, which was upheld by the elders, for they believed we had more chance at survival if we were isolated. We were of the last few Harpies to remain alive before our race was exterminated."

"You do know you have a core raptor, as do all Harpies?" said James.

"I know that the sense of flying is strong with me. I do dream that I can fly in the air, but I have never connected to my core. Do you know of my core?"

James explained to Theseus that he thought he would need to be in the after world in order to effect a transformation.

"That is not exactly true, is it, James? Do you remember our first lifetime, when I was able to cross from the Earth plane into Between Worlds in order to meet you and we would fly?" I reminded him.

"How easy would it be, Alana, to show Theseus how to cross the veil? After that, you, Audaz and I could help him effect a transformation. That is of course if Theseus wished to fly for a while and we could continue to talk up top," said James.

"I want to reconnect to who I am. I have never had the opportunity to be with my extended kin. And if I get the chance to fly as well, it would be a pleasure of dreams realised."

"I know we can do it. Let me come into your mind Theseus," I asked.

I showed Theseus how to breathe and disidentify from himself, letting the resultant quietness within, settle to a place of expectation without anticipation. Allowing his perception to move forward, he was able to catch glimpses of another world coming into his mind even with eyes closed. I told him to focus and gently hold one of these images in his mind's eye and let that eye be drawn forward to the brink of the veil. The veil was like a screen, where without focussing upon it, he would start to see movement beyond it. Here he would sense a feeling similar to the ebb and flow of tidal water which drew and pushed him gently.

I reassured him that any need for fear was unnecessary as we would hold and guide him once he had crossed. At this point, he needed to time the tidal movement in his mind and allow his whole sense to be drawn forward as the tide pulled him and at the same time, surrender all will other than the will to allow passage.

With the draw forwards, he would find his physical body elongate as it stretched across the veil and on crossing into Between Worlds, the rest of his body would re-join to its natural form. I showed and demonstrated all of the sensations, thoughts, emotions and cusps he would experience and left his mind. We floated quietly, allowing him to breathe and relax and then he disappeared.

"He's gone, lock onto his vibration, let's join him. You are a master, darling!" said James.

"No, just your average common or garden witch," I replied.

We switched from the Earth plain boundary into Between Worlds to find Theseus wide-eyed and slightly nervous. His first words were concern as to whether he could get back. After reassuring him, all three of us transmitted transitional energy into him with a download of how to transform.

The transformation was almost immediate and before our eyes, flapping in the water was a Steller's fish eagle. I linked into him and all three of us lifted him to five hundred metres, with Audaz and James supporting his outstretched two and a half metre wingspan as he adjusted to the air.

"What am I?" asked Theseus.

"You are one of the heaviest, if not the most powerful eagle in the world today. You are a Steller's fish eagle. Pretty rare," said James.

Theseus's eagle was a solid and powerful raptor. He had a large body perhaps the size of a Harpy eagle, with a black body feathers, white shoulders and front wing edges, a white wedge-shaped tail and white leggings. His talons and beak were yellow in colour and equally as powerful as his overall persona.

"I always find it strange how our histories reflect the type of core raptor we are. Steller's do not mix with other birds, preferring to be isolated with their kind. They fly at high altitude and are rare with a limited geographic spread. A bit like your Harpy tribe," I suggested.

"This is strange, yet extremely familiar. I have been flying in the oceans for centuries but this feels like how I am supposed to be, like whom I really am. Please let me go," requested Theseus, keen to support himself on his own.

James and Audaz gently eased away and let Theseus fly under his own power. I could read from James's mind, a feeling of unsettlement, as he watched Theseus administer his first dive at speed. He followed him closely, as he became accustomed to the lightness of movement which altered his direction.

"What is it, James? I can see you have not formed your thoughts as yet. What troubles you?" I asked. James mind blocked whilst maintaining our link.

"Always revolving within a year; having full awareness of his lifetimes, thus becoming an expert in his role and environment; never being connected to his core raptor? Or it not being allowed, or it being purposefully hidden from him and then reporting directly to Thaddeus in Realm Six? Something is not quite right. I totally see the importance of setting up a guardian network in the oceans. And how the information would provide valuable insights for high planers to monitor global changes and evolution. However, these Harpy whales are on a treadmill and they have no idea of their true identities. Are they choosing to work for this guy, or is he ensuring they continue to work for him?" James said with suspicion.

"He's controlling them; you mean?" I said.

"Maybe the power that these Realm Sixers wield, enables them to manipulate the system?" James speculated.

"And we have just freed him. What kind of affect is that going to have on things?" I pondered.

"All we have done is give him a choice. It is up to him to decide what he will do, from negotiating better terms to freeing himself and his kin from this duty in order to live more freely," said James.

We caught up with Audaz who was enjoying the new sensations of freedom he was experiencing through Theseus.

As we approached his wingtips, we were all suddenly arrested in mid-flight by a red coloured light sphere which encapsulated us, making it impossible to escape from. A voice boomed out from within the sphere.

"What the hell do you think you are doing, Theseus?" It was obvious who the presence was.

The change in Theseus's mood was instantaneous, as he cowered within himself.

"Careful, darling," cautioned James, reading my mind.

"No, James." My hackles were already raised and I was ready for him, sixth planer or not.

"Should we have reason to fear you, Thaddeus, with all of your accumulated knowing and compassion. As one amongst us displays elements of concern in the face of your direct question?" My eloquence chosen to sweeten that of my own directness.

"My question was not directed towards you, Alana, nor any of your interfering brethren," he replied.

"To interfere suggests, we have become involved in, if not altered, a course of action, which for some reason you wish not to be disturbed. Theseus is one of our race and it seems his heritage and the qualities which accompany it have been, let's say, obscured from enabling him to be his true Self. That concerns me in both of its contexts," I pointed out to him.

"I see that Tarquin does not encourage respect amongst his…staff."

"Staff? As I remember, the Earthbound term identifies one or others who work for an authority who decides the degree of transparency of motive of the task. And who provides enough information to ensure that motive is achieved? We don't work for Tarquin, we work with him and being who you are, you can easily see the difference between our relationship with him and your relationship to Theseus and the other Harpy whale guardians. Rather than see, I know."

"You use the term 'know'. Let me point out that knowing is what separates our abilities. You are treading in my territory."

"That is a familiar term of reference, I have heard before, especially as we are currently in Between Worlds. It sounds like you are warning me? I could not call it a threat because that propensity is well below the level of knowing accumulated by one as powerful and reverent as you," I said.

There was a significant pause before he responded.

"There are motives and aims that are withheld from your knowing, which are part of the orchestration of the system. They are, let's say, above your pay grade. It is for those in the know to decide how they are achieved," he responded.

"Just so long as those methods do not contravene the Collective's aim of all beings achieving a 'know thyself' status and those who stop them, to have the opportunity to learn from their behaviour causing the denial of that."

"You have much to learn, Alana."

"And high on my agenda is how to learn to work with you for the benefit of all life within the system."

"As I said, you have much to learn. Now please return Theseus to the ocean and let us forget this little episode. I see little need to trouble Tarquin with this matter, if you get my point."

"I am warning you that I am about to be disrespectful. I will be talking to Tarquin, that is my choice."

Suddenly, the diameter of the sphere shrunk in size enough to create a sense of pressure on us which remained for less than two seconds. Its discomfort was felt by all.

"Tiresome, but do as you feel will most benefit you and those close to you. As I have said, please put Theseus back where you found him."

The sphere disappeared and with it, Thaddeus's voice. We all immediately dropped, having to recover our flight paths. We looked at each other with a sense of shock and disbelief, apart from Theseus, who with head down felt very small for once in his lifetimes.

"Nicely informative, Alana. I think he got the message once you had put the squeeze on him," said James.

"It's an eye for an eye in his world. I did not enjoy the squeeze he put on us though. I thought this was supposed to be heaven. What with him and that fifth planer Gerry, we have some choice high planers amongst the steering committee," I said with a sense of disbelief.

"We are in Between Worlds at the moment, Alana, not heaven," said James.

"Are you all right, Theseus?" I asked.

"I feel told off and threatened Alana. I have done as he has said for twelve lifetimes, almost eleven hundred years and there has never been reason for him to act the way he did today. I am not blaming you three for these events. It was my choice and you have opened my eyes, not only to a part of who I am, but this has also placed me in a position of doubt as to his true nature and motives. I am now worried about what I will tell the other guardians," said Theseus.

"Follow your heart and be true unto yourself. Do not feel threatened by him, Theseus, I believe and have faith that his actions will not go uncorrected," said James.

"You don't know that though, James. In the same way, we don't know the full extent of the power those in realm five and above weald. I will decide what I will do," added Theseus.

I entered his mind and guided him through the reverse process of returning through the veil to the Earth plane. Although I soothed him as best I could, I knew that he was disturbed by what had happened and for the future of the guardians.

I could not help but think that James and I had lived nine and eight lifetimes compared to his and his kin's twelve and that a blue's natural lifetime could reach ninety years. He had obviously surpassed an age where in my book; he had done his time on Earth. My feeling was one of manipulation, but the motive was elusive. Once we were all back in the water, Theseus relaxed into himself.

"We will support you, whatever you decide. You are one of us and what happens to you and all of your tribe, also matters to us," I said.

"I am a blue whale, the largest and most powerful mammal on Earth and whilst I am mortal in this current form, I come with twelve lifetimes of knowing I am immortal and a belief that the Collective is the only one who truly guides me. I will let it do so in this matter and let you know what is happening when I decide. It has been a pleasure to have met you all and I am grateful for your love and guidance and especially helping me connect to my eagle. Farewell for now, my friends."

Our goodbyes followed him as he dived beneath the waves.

"Do we wait for him to decide or talk to Tarquin in the meantime?" asked Audaz.

"I think we let Tarquin know of the situation and our concerns. Let's let him guide us on what we might do and he can decide how he's going to handle things at his level and above," suggested James.

We all agreed and also agreed that Audaz and I would speak to Tarquin and Nevaeh as James had to complete his tour in the dark and we were now finished in the oceans. After that, the others should have also completed their investigations Between Worlds and so we could all get together and discuss our findings and bring everyone up to date on events.

"See you soon, darling; you won't need your torch in this next one. I hear it is a bit lighter. Thank you for coming over, I love you lots." I kissed James on his big whale's nose.

"My pleasure and never a dull moment spent with you, my love. You are formidable in your eloquence and I love you too," said James.

"Oh please, I am suddenly feeling sea sick. Might I remind you that some of us have partners still on…" Audaz' colour suddenly changed.

"What's wrong, what is it, Audaz?"

"Conchita, my mate; she has just been killed. I must go to her," Audaz disappeared.

"Oh no. Poor Audaz," I said.

"Alana, you have been on Earth too long. This is great news; it means they will be together again. With a bit of luck, she will decide to join us, which will be good for Audaz."

"You are right. I was caught by the death and endings thing for a moment. What was I thinking?"

"Like a dolphin? Come on, Flipperina, we must get going. I will see you shortly."

Like synchronised swimmers, we timed our joint departure in perfect unison.

Special Forces

Back in London, once Sarah had re-joined Scout and Simon and shared her experiences with Ruby and Corey, they took Nesta back to the ranch in Realm Four to discuss and agree on the next steps. Once back, Scout transformed to his usual Mustang horse self to check on his herd. Sarah, Nesta and I relaxed on the porch, giving Nesta an opportunity to get to know us more.

"Simon, doesn't it get a bit confusing all this changing from humans to raptors, horses and monster-like creatures?" asked Nesta.

"No not really, it's who we are. Our core identities are our raptor forms, but as you may know, as a Harpy race we were both humanoid and raptor," I explained.

"Do you ever assume that form, the one I haven't seen?" asked Nesta.

"It is something we don't really do. Probably because of what happened to us on Earth and now it is a part of us which remains hidden. It is rare we transform to the image of our race even amongst our own kind," said Sarah.

"I have lived my lifetimes as a human, as that is what I am. I wasn't aware of the myths and legends concerning Harpies as I grew up. Even now, having met you and in getting to know you, I find it amazing that you could have existed as a separate race on Earth and sad about what happened to you. As humans on Earth, we tend to assume we are the master race and woe betide anything that threatens us," said Nesta.

"We didn't threaten anybody; we were just different. Where is this going Nesta?" I asked.

"I am just sad that ignorance, fear and control, popular traits inherent in humans resulted in the loss on Earth of a race we could have learned a lot from. I think we also could have avoided the current damage on Earth, by way of your instinctive affinity to the natural part of it. Also, I am very pleased I have had the opportunity to be working with you," he replied.

"We think you are very nice too Nesta and I imagine you have been on the receiving end of ignorance, fear and control, yourself, so you can go part way to understanding our lives," said Sarah.

"I would be lying if I said not and I think that is what I am trying to acknowledge and connect with," he said.

"Well, we have a job in front of us to help those currently under the control of those creating fear. Having just achieved what we did today, I suggest we target the higher crime rate areas in London, as that is where the Commanders will be located. Nesta, can you tap into the guide network and get a list of the key areas and corresponding Commanders?" I said.

"Yes, I'll get right on it."

Whilst Nesta completed his task, Sarah and I had an opportunity to talk about our experiences. Although we could read each other's minds, sometimes it was the little expressions and tones during dialogue which completed the picture of impressions and feelings.

There was no doubt her key passion was to help people like Chloe, Ruby and Corey directly, whereas being involved in gun battles was not her forte. She accepted that it was necessary, as and when but her preference was to skip that part of it. As for me, my energy levels were increasing and seemed to grow in strength, the more people we helped in Between Worlds. Interestingly, energy accrual was happening as it did during my time in Between Worlds previously, although I didn't realise it at the time and I felt better for it.

"Right, I think we have what we need. I have been given a few Commander vibrations already. The remainder will follow shortly," said Nesta.

"How many areas?" I asked.

Scout had re-joined us having caught up with his herd and spoken to his two flying buddies.

Nesta had gathered information which showed that Commanders used the borough boundaries to define their territories. Excluding Southwark, he had identified a further nine boroughs which made up the worst crime areas in London. These included, Croydon, Brent, Hackney, Haringey, Tower Hamlets, Lambeth, Westminster, Newham and Camden. The majority of Leaves in all of these areas were controlled by Commanders of varying power. It appeared that in one area there had been a recent take over which meant that one Commander now controlled both Tower Hamlets and Hackney together.

"Nine in total is too many to hit at one time. I suggest we focus on a further four including this new combined borough," I said.

The plan was we should visit Lambeth first because it was a next-door neighbour to the Southwark borough we had just exiled Dreads from and would be vulnerable to take over. News would have travelled to this area quickly, so we could expect them to be on guard. We would then move over to the East end, take Newham and leave Hackney and Tower Hamlets until last. I was anticipating this Commander was going to be a strong opponent.

"I am getting guide requests from all over. They all want their borough's cleared. News is travelling really fast! I have even had requests in from Birmingham, Manchester and Leeds. There is much excitement in the guide community," said Nesta.

"Put a stop on all communication about our missions on the guide network with immediate effect. We cannot afford guide bravado and information spilling to Leaves in the areas we intend to hit. We allow the PR to go into action after we have taken the Commanders down in the next four London boroughs," I said this with an assertion which made Nesta jump to it.

"Yes, Simon," Nesta left us to complete his task.

"Shall we call you General, darling?" asked Sarah. "You and James are so similar in some ways."

"Well, he is my brother but in all seriousness, I should have thought about this before. We need to maintain an element of surprise."

"You are doing fine, Simon. We will track them down and send them on their island holidays." Sarah cupped my cheeks and kissed my lips.

"Thank you, Sarah. After four hundred years of dealing with village bumkin Leaves, I suddenly find myself in the big league and there is much more to consider."

From what I had read from Nesta, the Leaves in these other London boroughs were organised in the same way as they were under Dreads in Southwark. I was sure the other Commanders would know Dreads had disappeared, but I was hoping that they would be defiant enough to stand their ground. They had no idea what we had actually done with him and possibly thought we had warned him to stay away from others, as we had done to the Governor in Denby Dale.

My immediate concern was about Nesta, where in the midst of our raid, he had hesitated taking a shot. We could not afford to have that happen again.

"Job done. All is now quiet."

"Thanks, Nesta. There is something we must talk about," I said.

"It's all right, Simon, I know what you are thinking and you are right. Fear is a strange thing, even when I know I cannot pay the ultimate price. However, I am a guide with a big heart and I cannot pretend to be a soldier," he admitted.

Based on this premise, he informed us he had already found us a replacement. The potential recruit also operated as a guide in London, knew the boroughs and would be honoured to serve with us. His name was Greg Nielson and had spent his last tour and lifetime in Iraq, with the SAS.

"We find him to be a very private and covert individual, you know, keeps himself to himself but he is a good man. Funny, he has an interest in birds of prey, so you should all get along fine. He will be with you shortly," said Nesta.

"Nesta, there is no offence meant," I said.

"And none is taken. It has been an eye opener working with you all."

We all gave Nesta a hug, thanked him and wished him well. In that moment after he left, we were a little subdued. It was hard making such a decision, but we were facing tough odds and we needed to be a team who instinctively knew how to watch each other's backs and make combat decisions effectively. Although Sarah, Scout and I were not soldiers, we were instinctive warriors, with a passion to fight on the side of the vulnerable.

A tall and lean looking man, with short dark hair suddenly appeared by the paddock and walked over to where we were sitting.

"Greg Nielson, reporting for duty, sir!"

"At ease, soldier. Apologies, I have always wanted to say that. What I mean is I am pleased to meet you." I smiled warmly and shook his hand firmly before letting him introduce himself to Sarah and Scout.

"The guide channels have been buzzing since your visit to West Yorkshire and have been going wild since last night," said Greg.

"Yes, my mistake. I should have gone covert," I said.

"No, you will have scared the lower Leaf ranks which will affect their focus and I think you will find the Commanders are sitting tight, albeit perhaps a little more defended. I think it was right to shake them up. Can I make a suggestion; I have read into your plan?"

"Please do, of course," I said.

"You could create decoys in the different boroughs except in the one you are really about to visit. If each of us were to put in an appearance and become visible to local Leaves in the target boroughs, word would travel fast we were in that area. The Commanders will be speaking to each other anyway to keep themselves updated," said Greg.

"Surely, you are going to put them all on guard, it is hardly covert?" I said.

"They are anyway. It is the opposite of covert; we need them to panic, because they know we are dealing in retribution and for that reason, they will be afraid. People who panic have lost the fight before it has started. Plus, it may just disrupt their current activities," said Greg.

"You said 'if we were each to put in an appearance'. How do you factor in the preview?" asked Sarah.

"In my soldiering world, you don't show your hand in the game of bluff. Nor do you draw attention to yourself unless absolutely necessary. I have just drawn attention to myself in the guide community by opting to help you and I have decided it is time to stop hiding and to be who I am," said Greg.

"We know you are ex-SAS if that's what you mean?" said Scout.

"It has taken me lifetimes to subtly alter my vibration at will and the ability did serve me well in the SAS on Earth to remain covert, even as a human. Even you cannot see, which I have to say, I am quite pleased about."

"Greg, I am sorry, we are all a bit confused," I said.

Greg transformed into a Black Eagle and in quick response, we transformed instinctively to our raptors, arming ourselves as his true projection in human form was obscured.

"Balance your vibration now! No games," I ordered.

"I am Harpy, just like you. Power down!" he responded assertively.

"Maybe, but a little too much on the dark side for comfort. Why so covert, we should have been able to pick up on your vibration easily?" I said.

Greg explained that he was descended from a tribe of Harpies which came from Abyssinia, before being exterminated by hunters from Yemen. Although he had revolved as human to various parts of the world, the message which came from his tribe was to remain hidden. Even when he came back to Realm Four between lives, he obeyed the message and did not until much later lifetimes, transform to his raptor.

By learning to project logic in place of instinct, he had been able to conceal the transformational aspect of his being. During Earth lifetimes, although not aware of his heritage, he was able to fully use his instinctual talents in the occupations he chose. There had been much soldiering, which finally led him into the SAS in his last lifetime, one of the most covert and specialist hunting forces in military operation. An Iraqi bomb had killed him and two of his regiment on his last mission and lifetime revolution in the Gulf.

He was aware that he had taken life during his lifetimes, even though he had been fighting under orders which were based on achieving the so called greater good. Most of his soldiering was not done out of choice. However, on his final judgement, he chose to spend time in Realm Three to reflect on his choice to become part of the SAS and so to kill. He also reflected on the lives he had taken in his previous lifetimes.

"Why choose to go to three, when you cleared yourself for four?" I asked, having a great deal of insight into his decision based on my history.

"When you kill someone in combat, you choose to end that person's life. You could always choose to miss, but you are motivated to reduce the threat of you or your comrades being killed by the enemy. I chose to rise through the ranks to become an SAS officer and so purposely put myself in a position where it was likely I would kill others and order my men to do the same. Although in previous lifetimes, I judged myself and always ended up in four, on the final judgement, I chose to go to three, to reflect on the reason why I chose to end other's lives in my last lifetime. I could have been a postman."

"How long were you there and what was your answer?" asked Sarah.

Greg told us he had served two years in there. His overwhelming feeling when he got there was, he felt hunted and should always remain hidden. What plagued him was something to do with him serving as an SAS soldier. His mate was not in that realm, so he was not awake to his lifetime's history.

The truth was, when he had forgiven himself, even in the face of this obscurity and left Realm Three to be found by his mate, she had helped him to reveal the early history of their tribe. It then became apparent; he had chosen to live a lifetime, where he was the hunter, in an attempt to deal with the obscure feelings of always feeling hunted. He had also gone looking for combat, which was far removed from hiding.

"It makes me wonder, though, whether by being a soldier, I was satisfying an unconscious desire to kill humans, the race responsible for exterminating our tribe," he explained.

"You mean, getting your own back in a legitimate way, for the supposed greater good?" said Scout.

"I now understand, that combat is in the moment. It is about survival. Causes or reasons are not always clear and do not matter in that moment. It is kill or be killed, immobilise or be immobilised. It is clear to me what you as a group are fighting for. It is not for Harpy ambitions, it is for the greater good of all races and life and I feel I have skills which may be useful to you?"

"If you were to work with us, you would have to keep your vibration clear to us at all times. We have to work with authentic intentions, so that we know," I said.

"You are my own kind, so I can be more of who I am. There will be no covert agendas," said Greg honestly.

We could see through to his true values and all of us agreed he should become one of us. Our newest member, was an eagle native to Africa, had black plumage with a white back and V shape on the shoulders and white cuffs fringed by black feathered wing tips. His ceres, eyebrows and feet were yellow, with a dark-brown beak and eyes. With more than a two-metre wingspan and weighing about five kilos, he was a large eagle with poise and a quality of grace.

"Let's get going and do these pre-visits. Greg, you take Camden, I'll do Newham and Scout you visit Tower Hamlets. No longer than five minutes in those areas. I suggest we fly in as raptors; perhaps a shot or two may serve the purpose of drawing their attention? Stay guarded and expect to draw fire," I said.

"Good luck, boys, have fun," added Sarah.

Greg downloaded the Leaf hotspots in each borough to both of us and we disappeared. Five minutes later, we were back at the ranch. Panic was the desired outcome. Each of us reported Leaves running in all directions and disappearing with minimum return of fire. However, there were many who remained at safe distances and watched, not quite sure whether the rumours were confirming themselves.

"Well, that stirred them up. Did you manage the raptor Scout, or was it the flying trot?" I asked.

"I could have flown in as a raptor, but if you had the choice to maximise your views, what would you do?" he replied proudly.

"I'd do the flying horsey thing," I said.

"Well, then!" He smiled broadly then farted.

"That would certainly give your position away if you were in the field," chuckled Greg, having not experienced the delights of Scouts more charming qualities.

"I am not in the SAS. I am a member of the FAHD and farting in fields is what I am best at."

"FAHD?" Greg looked at him quizzically.

"The farting air-born horse division." He then snarted to covertly cover his next deed.

Nesta had passed on the Commander names and vibrations to me before he left and Greg scanned Lambeth for the location of its Commander called Kingsley. Another islands descendent, he was Jamaican born, but formed his character in London, adding two murders and countless assaults on men and women to his name. Greg located him in a vacant flat at the centre of the Angell Town estate in Brixton.

Having already split, he had ascertained he was with, what looked like three lieutenants and four other Leaves. Our plan was to capture them and take them to the outside of the tube station on Brixton Road, albeit riskily, but as Greg suggested, to publicly announce our presence.

The station was suggested by Greg, as a lot of Leaves congregated here and attached themselves to young people, especially those from out of area, whose persona indicated drugs or violence. There were usually two or more senior Leaves present, who coordinated the Leaf queue, allocating lesser Leaves to travellers.

Once outside the station, we would place a dome shield over all of us and invite comment, whilst keeping our captured Leaves caged inside. Sarah would remain at the ranch tracking our actions, ready to transport in at a moment's notice. Scout, Greg and I split to reconnoitre the flat layout and target positions, before returning.

"We have eight targets and there are only three of us," noted Scout.

"Would you prefer that I come?" asked Sarah.

"No need, Sarah. I respect you are the commanding officer in these operations Simon, however, in light of my training, would you be prepared to let me lead individual sorties?" asked Greg.

"Most happy. We need you to do what you do best," I replied.

"Scout?" enquired Greg.

"Fine by me," he responded.

"In that case, I will take four of them. Scout, if you take the two standing against the right-hand wall and Simon, you take the Commander and the guy next to him on the left. Shoot Kingsley first at the moment we arrive. All their eyes will be diverted towards him, then open fire on the others. No cues, just execute," instructed Greg.

"Yes, sir!" I responded.

"Ready? Now," ordered Greg.

I had already powered up and at the moment, we arrived in raptor form, I opened fire at Kingsley, knocking him to the ground. The following fire was rapid. By the time Scout and I had secured our second targets, all of Greg's were falling backwards towards the floor.

Without time to comment, two Leaves came running through the door to the flat firing wildly. Greg span, crouched and fired twice. There was no bang when the shots went off, just two quick thuds and the Leaves fell. He ran through the door and outside to check if more company was about to join us. With the coast clear, he returned to the room and caged the late arrivals as we had done with the others.

"That was bloody impressive, just like clockwork. I notice you didn't change to your eagle as we came in and you shoot through your arm, instead of your Ajna or solar plexus. And you can get multiple shots off rapidly, like one after the other and it sounds like you are using a silencer," enthused Scout.

"Tools of the trade, my friends. Adapting my vibration is not the only thing I have honed during rest times between lifetimes," he replied.

"But what's the process. How do you do this?" asked Scout.

Greg had been trained how to use many weapons, but close quarter small arms fire was what he was most adept at. During rest in peace times in Realm Four, he would apply his transitional will energy to modifying basic light weaponry. His view was, 'you didn't use a rocket launcher to hunt rabbits', so why use a head shot, when a lesser charge would immobilise an adversary, just as well.

He had learned to split a chakra-loaded head shot into five consecutive segments of energy. In combat on Earth, he was used to holding a handgun whilst supporting the wrist with his other hand, then resting his cheek on his right shoulder, to sight a line of fire. Instead of using the ajna to emit the shot, he was able to channel the energy segments through his shoulder and arm and fire them from his fingers, as a child would, playing at cowboys.

"When I split the energy, it flows rapidly and repeatedly and the 'bang' of the head shot is subdued into thuds as they are emitted. It is extremely useful when you need to see one of your Charges and have to immobilise Leaves present, without drawing attention to yourself."

"Got anything else?" asked Scout.

"An intergalactic realm wobbler," said Greg holding a straight face.

"A what?" said Scout.

"Not really," he said smiling. "But I have a few options up my sleeve, which I am sure you will see as time and occasions demand their use. And yes, I will show you how to use them," he replied.

"Thank you, that's great. I have never had a need to use weapons before we started going on these missions and the feeling of being well defended, certainly boosts the confidence," said Scout, impressed with his new colleague.

The Leaves were beginning to stir and Scout and I changed to human form. News had obviously travelled since the Southwark raid and all ten Leaves included the Commander were obviously worried about what might happen to them. Each of them watched us intently until I spoke directly to Kingsley.

"Do you know why we are clearing out London, and you with it?" I asked him as he retained a fixed gaze into my eyes, with no comment.

"I'll make it clear. Whilst you have decided to remain Between Worlds, to avoid the consequences of your actions against others on Earth, you are not choosing to change your ways. You continue to cause harm, incite violence and create misery and suffering for not only your own Leaf kind, but amongst Earth dwellers too. Many of these are just young people who find themselves trapped by circumstances. You take advantage of them and increase their vulnerability and resentment towards others."

"Getting past mi worries made me chrang. Honing mi resentment gave me the power to kill mi own fada, who took his drunken anga out on me, mi sistas and mi mada," he replied.

"I am sorry you had to suffer that way as a youngster but since then, you have chosen to foster your anger and resentment and have killed a further two times."

"Be unu a judge and jury den?"

"Yes, we have the power and as a border patrol we are shutting down all operations like yours. Please tell me, if you are so attracted to misery and suffering, why don't you take your rightful place in the Dark Realms?" I asked.

"You cannot take me to hell. I know my rights of passage to the other realms. I have to choose to go and I am not going," said Kingsley confidently.

"You are right. We cannot make you go, but I can send you to the islands to be amongst your friends." I mind linked to Greg and Scout to get ready to transport all ten of them to Brixton Road tube arriving in human form.

"The Caribbean?"

"Not quite and we have a slight detour to make first," I said.

We all relocated right in front of the tube station entrance, highly visible to all Leaf onlookers in the vicinity. Many stopped in their tracks, as they started to recognise the party of Leaves we had with us. Our guests could do nothing but shout for help to others around them. Changing back to our raptors, caused many to step back, then the more senior Leaves amongst the crowd opened fire, with others following suit from all directions.

The light energy bounced harmlessly away from the surface of the shield. My feeling was they knew their shots would not penetrate the dome and impact their friends or us, however, it was a demonstration of intimidation and contempt.

"I have got something that will sort this out, because we really need to get our message across," said Greg.

He flew upwards, transversing the top surface of the dome and continued skywards at high speed. Barrel rolling, he dived, surgically targeting the more senior within the mob. Shot after shot rang out, thumping into their targets and knocking them to the ground. He flew upwards again drawing fire, before turning sharply and heading back towards the crowd.

"I'm going in. Can you hold the dome and keep them all caged, Simon?" said Scout.

"Yes. Go for it!" I replied.

"Greg? Got any machine gun type light weapons. I have to pause when rapid firing and I cannot shield when I am doing it?" linked Scout.

"No, not more than five rounds at a time. Use what I was telling you about earlier, you can cut the delay to a two second pause between bursts. You can shield as well, link in and take what you need," replied Greg.

Scout shot out of the top of the dome as a Haast eagle and flew to about twenty metres before turning to face those on the ground. He transformed to his brilliant white Pegasus, hovered and blasted into them, twisting slowly to create an arc of rapid fire. More Leaves were arriving on the scene, many standing at a safe distance watching the battle.

As shots impacted Scout's shield, they dissipated and created a red halo surrounding his form, accentuating his whiteness and blue and white light auric field. Some of the Leaf fire subsided, possibly because they were not sure whether what they were firing at, was some type of angel.

"Simon, Scout? We need to flatten this. Street fights can go on indefinitely and that is not our objective. I have a type of stun weapon, like an aerial mine. It will stun them for a couple of minutes causing slight disorientation, but they will be able to hear what we say and remember it. However, you need to get back inside the dome now Scout. I will follow."

With Scout safely inside, Greg flew and hovered above the dome, created the mine and dropped inside. The mine rested on its top surface, then exploded, making the dome shudder under its force. Wave after concentric wave of dark red and purple light pulsed in every direction, flattening all the Leaves standing within a hundred metre radius. The calm after the storm was as eerie as the silence which befell an Earth plain battlefield the day after the fight.

"Who are you people, creatures? You have powerful weapons. I did not think they would have allowed weapons in heaven. Are you from another place?" asked Kingsley. All Leaves inside the dome were quiet.

"We are Harpies, messengers from heaven and heaven does have its weapons, but we are only allowed to shoot at people like you and back at those who shoot at us. We are here to rid this world of those who do what you and your lieutenants do. And as you can see and will do again shortly, we have the power to do it and we do it to protect the vulnerable who your kind exploit," I said.

"They all heard you, Simon. The dome projected your voice to all around," said Greg.

"Greg, get on the guide waves. I want at least twenty guides and catchers here ASAP. Tell them to stay out of sight until we have left. I have a hunch there will be a few defectors. When I have finished what I will say, we transport to the island immediately. We have four definite passengers, but we will take a fifth. We will have to leave behind the Leaf seniors in the crowd for another day. I know what I am doing," I said via a mind link to him and Scout.

"On it," Greg replied.

I turned to face the tube entrance and spoke clearly to the crowd. I told them the voice they now heard belonged to a Leaf who had lived Between Worlds for four hundred years fearing to go to the after world. This was because I had judged myself and been judged by others wrongly. Many of those years were spent being bullied and threatened by others like Kingsley and Dreads from Southwark. Threatened, because I was a compassionate man and chose to fight for justice for the vulnerable. Now, as a member of the new after world border patrol, I had chosen to continue this fight.

As Leaves, we were all vulnerable, but if those amongst them chose to take power over others including the Earth born in denial of their own vulnerability, they would place themselves in the same position as these men here. Men, who we took action against with full justification.

"There will be others, guides and catchers who will be among you shortly. If you speak your truth and tell them your fears of passing, they will speak truth in return. I can see there are many of you who need not be living here, who could be with loved ones and enjoying a better life. Choose wisely, we are not your enemy."

We transported the five Leaves and ourselves to the island from inside the dome. As the dome dissolved, the other five Leaves were left standing in the open space. Once on Boreray, I turned to Kingsley.

"As I said Kingsley, you have friends here and you cannot leave. This has been your choice," I said.

We disappeared and headed back to the ranch, before he could reply.

A Lighter Hearted Realm

On arriving to meet up with Thomas and Arthur from the oceans, my mind was now concerning itself with the presence in the higher realms of individuals who seemed to be operating at tangents to the fundamental ethos of the Collective. As Tarquin had said, the Collective allowed for evolution of awareness in the realms as well as on Earth, however, both Gerry and the Realm Sixer, Thaddeus, seemed to use control reminiscent of perhaps more feudal after world system.

Whilst having no reason to distrust Tarquin's beliefs, I could not quell the thoughts of the Collective itself, allowing high planers to behave in such ways. Surely, at that level, there was the greater likelihood of direct intervention or supervision. On this premise, was Arthur's theory of the Collective being a system, more likely?

In Realm Three, the wintery sun was approaching the horizon, having been on its skyward journey for its usual seven hours. Following Thomas's vibration, I found myself in a hamlet of about thirty dwellings. These were constructed with rudimentary clay or mud bricks with twig or grass rooves. I expected to see plumes of wood or peat smoke rising from them, but the air was clear. The hamlet nestled in a shallow valley carpeted with meadow grasses, bracken and occasional wild flowers.

On its outskirts, there were small patches of cultivated ground, either bare of covering or showing evidence of flowers which were broken or trampled. In the chilling damp air, groups of people huddled together, unable to thermally regulate themselves as we could in Realm Four. In their midst, Thomas and Arthur sat on two boulders listening to a man who was holding his audience's attention, as he complained loudly to both of them. I walked toward them and the man turned to face me.

"And how are you going to make our lives more miserable? I suppose you are here with these two are you, just visiting and passing through? Are we fun for you to look at, not enough going on in your own realm?" said the man, his words delivered sarcastically.

He turned to address his audience. "You watch; it will be coach parties next. We will have to provide them with picnic tables and public toilets!" He turned again to face me.

"Why don't you and your kind leave us alone; we know why we are here. We don't need you to make it even more shitty for us with your self-righteous guidance and speeches."

"I am not a guide. Thomas is and Arthur guides those still living on the Earth plane. We are not here to make your lives more miserable. It sounds however, that some of your visitors do? What shit? What are you so pissed off about anyway?" I genuinely asked.

On reading him, I could tell my choice of language resonated with his own chosen vocabulary and knew I had sparked his intrigue. I could read from his mind what was presently bugging him.

"Who are you anyway?" Tinging his words with strands of nonchalance.

"My name is James and I am here from Realm Four. As I said, I am not a guide; I am a—"

"Spy," said the man turning to the others and saying, "look, it gets worse, they are now sending spies to watch us."

"I am not a spy. I work with those in the higher realms. I am taking a look at the Dark Realms and this one to see what's pissing people off and stopping them from joining us in Realm Four, sooner rather than later," I said.

"Didn't you know, it's our lack of consciousness around ourselves and others and that elusive forgiveness stuff. But we are working it out slowly, aren't we, folks? Just busying ourselves trying to reflect and freezing our nuts off in the process. Well, those who do have nuts and those who don't, I wager, are decidedly chilly as well. My guess is we haven't worked it out yet, that's what stops us. Because if we had, we wouldn't be here, would we?"

"But I get the impression some of the people visiting here make it harder for you?" I said.

"My name is Bill, by the way," said the man, his interest in me building.

He turned again to the small group of people and introduced them all. It appeared we were being joined by others standing on the margins.

"Are we in agreement we should tell him, folks? The very recent piss off, by way of example?" Bill asked the group.

There was a short discussion between them and the majority agreed. The small patches of ground on the outside of the hamlet were their gardens. Flowers were rare in this realm and much time and effort was spent painstakingly searching far afield for different kinds of the small-headed wild flowers. These were then carefully transplanting into their gardens.

Each garden grew a particular type of flower. On discovering the gardens, two guides had told them they could not do this and must leave the flowers to grow wild. Between them, the guides had trampled and destroyed all of the flower gardens.

"Why do you plant the gardens?" I asked, knowing exactly why.

"Because they are pretty, they draw the bees and we like them. It also gives us something to do when we are taking a break from our reflection. Doesn't it, folks?" Bill replied, encouraging audience participation.

There were muffled laughs from those gathered around.

"You don't strike me as someone who does pretty, Bill?" I said. "Did you tell the two guides the real reason? You have a choice right now to level with me."

"All right, because we like the bloody tunes their nectar makes when you sniff or sip it. That's why," he replied.

"Sniff it?"

Bill looked down, with a guilty smile on his face. His history revealing a cocaine addiction whilst on Earth. I had never thought of snorting tune juice, but could understand it would have a similar effect.

"Call it force of habit. Anyway, what's criminal or wrong with doing what we are doing? It's just a little bit of pleasure and what's more, sometimes the music links to a melody I can remember from the Earth plane. I then reflect on the memories whether they be good or bad. But they take it away from us saying, we are not here for pleasure, we are here to reflect," he said, shaking his head at the contradiction.

I looked at Thomas. The shrug of his shoulders said it all.

"Well, that's a load of old shit, isn't it?" Emphasising the obviousness of my comment.

Bill looked at me with a surprised expression then burst out laughing. So I told him he better shut up quickly or they might come and take me away too. This perpetuated his laughter even more and the joke resonated around the circle. Before long the whole of the hamlet's inhabitants were chuckling with us.

"Why can't you work with us? Why can't there be more people like you?" shouted a young woman, whose voice was supported by others around her.

"Thank you for that. I really appreciate your voice and it is nice to see you step into a place of faith. It has been a long time, hasn't it?" I asked her.

The young woman, Kathy, nodded her head and burst into tears. She was comforted instinctively by an older woman standing next to her. I caught the older woman's attention.

"And I see you have held your compassion harshly for a while also. Your name is Marjorie, isn't it?"

The older woman also nodded and looked down to evade my eyes, but kept hold of Kathy. She then looked up.

"You know us don't you. You know into us?" Marjorie spoke softly and I nodded, smiling authentically at her.

"If we had guides who knew us and helped us to know more of ourselves like you have just done in a very short time, that would help us more. Just being listened to with sometimes what can be a self-righteous response, only makes me feel misunderstood and angry. If I do get angry, I am told to master my anger before the next visit, which may be weeks away. I am getting nowhere quickly," she said.

"What's heaven like?" asked a young boy called Carl. He was about twelve, sharp featured, with dark hair. Within his shadow resided many deeds of cruelty towards animals, in particular to his own dog, a Jack Russel called Ben. The dog's vibration was imprinted strongly in his mind.

"What do the guides tell you?" I asked.

As he responded, I linked into my dog Tinker and no questions asked, requested he track Ben who may be in spirit. He was and was prepared to trust my idea. I thanked Tinker and broke the link. Carl answered the question,

"That it is nice, sunny all of the time, has nice people there, relatives, you know and that's about it. They never tell us what you can do, or if there is any special stuff going on or beautiful things we have never seen before," he replied.

"Special stuff? Like animals being able to talk to you, if you are lucky enough to hear them and deserve their respect," I said.

Carl covered his face in his shame and I linked to Ben, bringing him to me. He sat behind my feet looking around my ankles towards the young boy in front of me. There were stirrings in the crowd and cries of 'it's a dog', he's got a dog'.

Carl looked up and the expression on his face shifted between the extremes of guilt and shame and joy. Ben walked in front of me and sat on my feet. I mind linked to him and he assured me he could handle this. I told him I would facilitate him being able to be heard with his thoughts being projected audibly.

"Aren't you going to talk to him, you know who he is?" I said. You could hear a pin drop.

"I know who he is, but everything is crashing around in my head and stomach. I don't know where to begin," said Carl.

"Then I will speak first," said Ben. "You hurt me and all I did was keep trying to show you love and loyalty."

Carl's attention was immediately focussed on Ben's eyes.

"I am sorry, Ben. I hurt you and others because I was being hurt too," he replied.

"Do you think that makes it all right then? Shall I roll over now and let you tickle my tummy?" asked Ben.

"No, it doesn't, I am really sorry."

"It gave you some sort of power, didn't it? You liked that power, didn't you?" said Ben.

"At the time, I did. I was powerless myself and I felt the only way to control that feeling was to do what I did. I used to think about hurting you when I was being beaten, but I was sad for both of us. I did not want either of us to be hurt. I chose wrongly. I feel ashamed and guilty because you were my friend and I made you suffer," said Carl, his eyes lowered to meet the ground.

"You are missing out being here, but you have work to do. When and if you come to Realm Four, we will be friends again. Think long and hard about choosing to pass on your suffering to others, including a dog who cannot say anything in his defence," summed up Ben.

Ben walked over to Carl and sitting in front of him, held up his paw. Carl held it and shook it. He then attempted to pat him on the head. Ben snarled and he withdrew his hand quickly.

"Forgiveness comes after acceptance. Our future friendship is in your hands," he said to him.

Ben looked at me and I told him he had been nothing but authentic, based on Carl's current reality and thanked him.

"Sad though, he used to be a nice kid," he said, then disappeared.

Carl stood there holding his pride, but struggling in the intensity of all his mixed emotions.

"We make our own miracles, Carl. Work firstly on your pride and justification behind it." I looked out to all of the people surrounding us.

"Anybody out there who can understand Carl's situation, but has made a little more progress?" I asked.

A young man in his early twenties raised his hand and agreed to help him. I thanked him and reminded those present about what Marjorie had said about it being better if the guides knew them. Inviting them to help each other, I said they may not be experts, but sharing and understanding difficulties could help to overcome judgement and reveal the true motives behind actions. Once they were revealed, the work was to accept their responsibilities and start to forgive themselves.

"It's not easy to know true intentions and authentic support here. A lot of us are still in de-Nile with the dead donkeys swimming upstream. This makes trust difficult and truth is manipulated. It keeps you on guard most of the time," explained Marjorie.

"But it's the same as the Earth plain. You never truly understand motive until you trust and behaviour confirms you were right to," I proposed.

"Yes but, we are all here because we didn't trust or took action against others breaking theirs. On the whole, there were more trusting people on Earth, but not here," she said.

I said I felt that this was the key to their development here. The Collective was not going to make it easy for them to gain trust. Trust led to forgiveness, because if you could trust that, you would no longer repeat a behaviour, you could then start to forgive yourself. Without it, you or others would have no grounds to believe you would not behave similarly in the future. That was because you were capable of behaving in a certain way, as you had done it before. I attempted to clarify the purpose of this realm.

"This is a reflection realm and you have a choice to look at yourself and accept what you have done and take responsibility for it. Denying, as the other choice, takes you in the opposite direction to truth and trust and you will never forget what you have done for good reason, because that gives you a choice not to repeat it again."

Development was hard won in this realm, but at least it is just themselves and the Collective who judged their Self-development and not some self-righteous guide who jumped up and down all over their flowers.

"Why can't they just wipe us clean, so we get a fresh start?" asked a man in his fifties.

"Because you would not learn from your experiences and the Collective needs you to learn for yourselves. It needs you to choose a way of living that not only benefits you, but others at the same time. You will get a fresh start when you go back to Earth, but not from here. You can only do it from Realm Four," I said.

This line created shock and surprise amongst all of them. Thomas linked in and told me people were not made aware of this in the lower realms. My thought reverberated back to Thomas asking: 'What the hell are they doing here?' His response was, 'keeping them in the dark'. I thought hard before choosing to add to the disclosure. I chose wisely, which in my view, was for their benefit, if not for my own. I strongly disagreed with this policy and the authority enforcing it.

By this time, it was getting dark and voices were arriving from the shadows. Although I could see whom and where they were coming from, for others, they were forced to relate to just the voice and not the person, unless they were standing right next to each other.

"Before I talk to you about being able to go back to Earth, is there something else which would help you reflect, which is currently denied?" I asked.

There were rumblings and conversations in the crowd and people shouted out a number of things including animals, television and even one call for a slot machine. The majority wanted the ability to make fire. The most obvious reason for this was to have warmth and some comfort. However, there was another reason I completely understood. Bill spoke out for them.

"Do you have fire in your realm, James?" he asked.

"We do," I replied.

I told them of the game Alana had taught me where players could create, by imagination, images of animals in the flames. The others playing would have to guess what the animal was. They had no idea we were able to mind block or in fact read each other's minds, which created another stir. Bill took my drift.

"That's the point, James. Since ancient times on Earth, people have socially sat around fires, stared into the flames for inspiration and have talked between themselves. They have told stories, shared problems and news and created friendships. A fire is not only for warmth, it creates community where people can come together and help each other. Yes, of course we want to avoid this damned cold, but in allowing a little comfort, much, much more could be achieved," explained Bill.

I linked to Thomas, who confirmed there were no fires because of the comfort element. I then heard Arthur say to Thomas: 'Oh no, here we go. You see the problem with these Harpies is they need to transform everything. And I know you can hear me, James'. I smiled into his mind and winked.

I placed a large circular firebase at the centre of the clearing between the huts where we were standing. It threw light and warmth in every direction, as it crackled and glowed brightly with flames rising to tease the night air. The expressions of delight coming from people were instantaneous, their smiles touching my heart and those of Thomas and Arthur.

All of the group moved forward simultaneously to sit around its perimeter. A few people attempted to take burning sticks back to their dwellings but on reaching a few paces from the fire, the flames extinguished themselves. They returned, complaining bitterly. Bill calmed them and brought the reality to what was happening.

"Folks. This is a gift in the moment. Even James does not have the power to change something as fundamental as allowing us to live with fire. Let's just enjoy and talk, as we are both enlightened by its glow and the glimmers of hope James brings to us."

There were noises of acknowledgement and agreement from our gathering and the thought entered my head that Bill was not far away from leaving this realm. My next thought was; his success would be a loss to others.

I wondered whether if given the choice, he would undertake front line work back in this realm until he next revolved, not as a guide, as this would require lifetimes of awareness, but as a mentor. It struck me, just how archaic the control systems were in these realms and the lack of awareness or interest in the quality and effectiveness of support for people residing in them.

"Can you make any chickens then?" a young girl called Britney chirped in. She was a young teenager, with dark hair and thickly set. She had preyed on old people in many successful street robberies before being killed by the wing mirror of a van, whilst running away from one.

"Do you know what a phoenix is?" I asked.

"Dumblefart, or was it Dumblefort? You know, the old wizard off Harry Potter, he had one."

"That's the one." I created its shape, allowing it to fly around in a circle just above the flames, before letting it rise into evaporation.

"Are you a wizard?" she asked.

"No. I have lived now for nearly five hundred years and after my first lifetime have returned to be born on Earth again for a further eight times. As you develop, it seems you can do more things," I replied.

This brought us back to the subject of fresh starts and the questions came thick and fast about, why, when and what did you go back for and did you get a choice to be part of a rich or kind family.

Having described the basic process, I told them that a point came when you had developed enough in terms of knowing yourself, where there was little point in going back to Earth. You could then remain in Realm Four and work like we were doing, most as guides or catchers. If you chose to develop further, you could move to the next realm up.

The overwhelming sense was, there were many things, they had not been made aware of which they could look forward to, when they had freed themselves. One of the strongest views on what stopped them leaving was it was hard to forgive, when you could not forget. Although the current quality and depth of support seemed to be focussed on reflection, without a compassionate and knowing mirror to gaze into and be guided by, nor a clear picture of what you might aim for, their progress was slow.

"After what you have just said about the chance to go back to Earth, wiped clean of your past memories, I will aim for that. I will make sure I get it right next time," said Marjorie.

"But you will not be conscious of getting it wrong in your last life time?" I replied.

"I think I will just know, not to get it wrong," she replied.

"You need not think to know. To think is to reason and to feel is to gauge. Knowing is instinctively accepting the truth before taking any action which may bring consequences for you or others," I said with knowing.

"Like allowing you mean?" said Bill.

"Yes, allowing. But not allowing that part of you that is the foundation upon which we build structures of denial, protection and avoidance, to prevent us from realising and accepting that for which we are responsible," I confirmed.

The point had arrived when we needed to be moving on and leaving this part of Realm Three's residents. Perhaps not in peace, but with a sense of being listened to and for what I intended, some rays of hope. It was obvious in my mind that things could change for the benefit of the whole system, if these people were a representative sample of the entire 'three' population.

"I am not a wizard as I have said, nor am I a high planer. I cannot create these things you would like just like that, without talking first with those who will have the attitude of: 'you don't fix, what's not broke'. However, I do have a voice in my realm and I will champion your cause because I think, sorry Marjorie, know, a few changes are needed. I am not choosing sides in this, but I can see by common sense that your future wellbeing has a far better chance of materialising faster for you, if things were evolved. So I will do my best," I said.

"No one has talked to us in the way you have. I for one, believe you can," responded Bill.

"Shit or bust then, Bill?" I winked at him.

"For shit or bust. If I had a glass of bloody flower juice, I would toast you. Thanks for coming, James."

"We have got to go now folks, look after yourselves and each other. I hope we will see you again soon, in our realm. I have some bad news though, I have to take the fire with me, sorry, even I am not sure of the consequences of leaving it."

There were a few grumbles and moans, but most understood why.

"However, there is a small pale of butter in that box next to the nearest dwelling," I said.

I watched the confused faces in the circle for a moment and told them they would understand shortly.

We said our goodbyes and disappeared. As the fire reduced itself and the embers crumbled and extinguished, fifty baking hot potatoes emerged from the ashes.

During the conversations, I had linked to Arthur and Thomas and so as we left the hamlet, we relocated to another area on the coast, so that we could talk. I lit another fire and we sat around it enjoying the flames.

"I know this has nothing to do with you, Thomas, but this situation is ridiculous. We are not helping these people; we are just letting them struggle along themselves." My delivery was frustration laden.

"I know, James. Using and, rather than but, this is the way it has always been," he replied.

In my view, the Dark Realms were prisons. There was even less rehabilitation and restorative intervention than provided in prisons on Earth. I was trying to work out if the powers controlling these realms from Realms Five and Six were just apathetic because of it being always like this, or there was an actual agenda to slow progress.

"I work with the dark dwellers because I agree with you something isn't right. But I work within the guide rules and at the same time, try and help them as much as possible. Whether it is because of who you are, I don't know, but you just do what you think is right without seeming to be concerned about the consequences?" said Thomas.

I explained to Thomas, not showing respect for an ethos or system was different from not showing respect for the orchestrators or those who manage it. It seemed, even over here in the after world, there still remained a risk of people taking things personally even amongst high planers. This was evident from Thaddeus's threat. I was not being arrogant, but when I say I know what is right and my actions follow accordingly; I don't think I know something is right, I know it is. And so did Thomas.

I was formulating a change plan and I needed to pilot small instances of change to gauge the effects, like rocks, fire and a small dog. If I didn't, I would not have evidence to back up my plan. The fact that what I did, would have been observed and there would be consequences, was a consequence of those who were in power, not wanting to change, or satisfying a need to remain in control.

Thomas's view was I had not sought permission, so I reminded him we were dealing with orchestrators who had been managing these systems, in my opinion, poorly for hundreds of years. These systems in no doubt, had been devised and created by the Collective itself, who seemingly ordaining high planers to manage them without consequence to date. Their view was probably one where in the absence of retribution or guidance from the Collective, they were allowing themselves to think they were doing it well.

My concern was millions of Earth dwellers were facing mortality due to global damage and we desperately needed to come up with alternative after world energy sources to slow it down. If there were high planers who chose to avoid change by adopting a reactionary stance, they must then take the responsibility for Earth bound genocide. In my view, they had probably contributed to causing it.

"I am poking them, Thomas, that's all I am doing. I know they are going to respond; I have already felt the displeasure from one of them. I need to see their true colours, not seek their permission. I am not concerned for myself, being extinct helps me overcome this, but if I smell injustice or prejudice based on any premise, I will go for the source. We can dance around permission and residual egos during the negotiations afterwards. The prize of patience is patience, as you know Thomas, but not in this situation."

"Nicely conversed, gentlemen. However, I feel the need for a lighthouse. Do you fancy a glass of tune juice whilst we watch the ocean?" enquired Arthur.

"I don't mind if I do, thank you," Thomas responded.

"Not for me on this occasion, gents, I am off. Thank you so much, Thomas, for guiding us in the dark, I have learned a lot and a lot has been revealed. See you later, Arthur, cheers," I said.

"You are welcome, James. I know you are right, so good luck. I shall look forward to the calm after the storm and what is washed up after the waves have subsided," said Thomas.

I smiled at him, locked onto Alana's vibration and disappeared.

Commanding Respect

As Scout, Greg and Simon returned to the ranch from Boreray Island, Simon reflected on the experience of stepping back into heaven.

I took a moment to appreciate how lucky we were to be able to transport across vast distances and through dimensions with such ease and speed. Sarah was down by the river talking with the horses. The two mares were nodding in agreement to whatever she was saying, one stamping its hoof occasionally, in an attempt to interrupt the other who was dominating the conversation. Behind them, the river lazily made its way across the land, slowed by the tranquillity of its surroundings. It willingly played host to the hundreds of insects, rising and falling, as they danced above its surface.

The contrast between Realm Four and Between Worlds continued to strike me every time I returned. Over here, you no longer had the sense of looking into the world, separated from it, you were once again part of a world. It was like being alive on Earth, except the levels of abundant beauty and serenity were further reaching and complete. I walked over to join her whilst the others stood chatting.

"Went well then, Simon darling?" Sarah asked.

"Yes, like clockwork."

"How did Greg get on?" she enquired.

"He's good. We have learned much from him already. It is a real advantage to have someone with you who thinks strategically and just 'does'. I know we have a fire power advantage over the Leaves, but I feel much safer having him with us," I said.

"That's good. He is a dark horse but his heart is true."

"I agree."

Scout had been earwigging on our conversation and I could tell there was an air of excitement with his sense. Prior to us re-joining them, he had already ascertained from Greg, that he had never transformed into an equid before and was posing the question of whether he would like some instruction on how to achieve it. Following their link, where Scout had furnished him with the skeletal and musculature connectivity and stance, Greg engaged his transitional will.

The result was spectacular. Standing in front of Scout was a black coated Arabian of about fifteen hands. With a refined wedge-shaped head, small muzzle and large eyes. He was a good-looking horse. His broad forehead sported a white diamond mark, the only white hair on his lean and muscular body. The high tail carriage portrayed his alert and high-spirited persona, masking his overall calm nature.

Arabians were bred to be warhorses, which fitted appropriately with his history. The shiny black coat and lean lines causing a stir amongst the mares in the herd, many jostling for a better view.

"I don't remember you ever transforming to a horse, Simon?" said Sarah, her interest heightened being a natural horsewoman.

"No, never done it. I'd probably be a donkey," I replied.

"Never. You are more of a Suffolk Punch or a Shire. Powerfully steady."

Both Scout and Greg were still facing each other, whilst Greg bounced up and down on his four quarters.

"How do I look?" he asked.

"Superb, my friend," replied Scout.

Greg settled, stretched his neck and squinted his eyes at Scout, letting out an enormous fart. Scout laughed in appreciation.

"I say, there is something very rewarding in horse farting," said Greg.

"Big cheeks, much echo. Wanna race?"

"Show me how," replied Greg.

The two of them shot off at speed, followed by three mares. As they raced off into the distance, I linked into Tarquin, who knew I was about to call.

"I added an extra passenger to that last island shipment," I said.

"I know you did and I understand your decision. I will give him a couple of days to really get a feel for what it is like being trapped there, then we must release him back to Lambeth."

"Can we hang fire until we have captured the Commander and his lieutenants from Tower Hamlets-Hackney. I would like him to see them arrive, so he can take back the news."

"Yes, I agree," confirmed Tarquin.

"How is it going anyway?" I asked.

"Alana and James have been irking a couple of high planers, one of them from six. Their expeditions have exposed some very questionable practices in the Dark Realms and revealed a hidden Harpy Whale line. A line which appears to have been manipulated to ascertain information the Sixer can control," said Tarquin.

"Can't say I am surprised, you are talking about James and Alana. I am aware of the whales as Sarah had linked into Alana and I am disturbed by what has been going on. It's amazing isn't it, we all thought this was heaven," I said.

"It still is, Simon, but my concern is there are those of us in Realm Five, who are supposed to know, who don't know the full picture. We have some interesting times ahead of us. Good luck, back in London, be on your guard though."

"I will be. Touch base soon." I broke the link and downloaded the conversation to Sarah.

The residual thought from both Sarah and I was, who exactly was in control of the system? If practices like this could go on seemingly undetected or overlooked, what had happened to the ethos of the freedom to personally develop. And in the case of the Dark Realms, for people to be supported to move on from them, rather than just treading water in what appeared to be just holding realms.

In addition, from our experiences in Between Worlds, it was obviously created, but without laws, perhaps because it was not envisioned as somewhere which might grow out of control?

"If we listen to ourselves though, darling, I hear us speak of control and controlling, instead of allowing, which is fundamental to the Collective," said Sarah.

"If the Collective had a house which had caught fire, it would control the fire to reduce the damage it might do," I said.

"Would it though. Or would it adapt to the changes the fire created, allowing another course of events to ensue? Think of plants whose seeds germinate only because of fire," she proposed.

"Or it's got to a point where it needs our help to control the fires?" I said.

One thing was certain; we were facing uncertainty. By this time, Scout and Greg had returned and were trotting across the open ground towards the house.

"So are you a skilful will horse or a strong will horse, Greg?" asked Sarah.

"Definitely skilful. I have made up my mind already. I am going to be a horse in my next life."

"How many have you had anyway?" I asked.

"I have had twelve lifetimes and the reason for that is, as a soldier, your lifetimes tend to end prematurely."

"Right then people, the East End awaits us. Can you locate our next Commander please, Greg?" I said.

"Will do. Is there a horse word for 'yes' Scout? I guess 'no' is Neighhh?" asked Greg.

Scout blew air through his lips in a short burst, letting them vibrate.

"That's yes. Am I bothered, on the other hand or hoof, is more to do with the other end," said Scout.

"You are such a horse Scout," said Sarah.

"I am a horse," he replied.

I caught Greg's eye, he nodded, transformed and engaged the task at hand. Moments later, he revealed the Commander of the combined borough was in an empty warehouse in Spitalfields. His name was Trevor Green, a white east end born and bred Londoner, with a long list of crimes against others including firearms, organised prostitution, rape and extortion.

"I thought we were going for the Newham Commander first. Why the plan change?" I asked.

"We are. There must be some sort of meeting taking place because the vibration of the Newham Commander, Janice Dawson, is coming from the same location," Greg informed us.

Splitting to review their position revealed a dimly lit, dilapidated large building with roof lights missing allowing the rain to wash in and the local pigeon population to come and go as they pleased. The far end of the building was shrouded in darkness with sixty metres spanning between end walls. The group were standing watching a desperately young heroin addict lying on an old and stained mattress cluck his way into his next existence, having overdosed on his last fix. They were betting on the seconds he had left, some goading his immanent transition.

"Bastards," said Simon. No catcher would dare enter to guide him.

Trevor was with three lieutenants displaying similar woeful credits in their histories and two other Leaves, one of them a woman. Janice held a history of two murders with a bladed weapon, drug import and human trafficking. Her three lieutenants were two women and one man. It seemed that all four were killed at the same time when a rival gang gunned them down in a private nightclub in Canning Town.

"We will have to transport in at close range and take them out swiftly. There are ten of them in total, so I am hoping this should be straight forward as it was in Lambeth. We will do as we did last time, capture them and take them this time to Whitechapel Station," I detailed.

"Commanders first again. I will take Janice and her three, if you Simon can take out Trevor and the two lieutenants closest to him at the same time. You Scout can go for the remaining three. Everyone ready? Let's go," instructed Greg.

I was about to take my second shot, having grounded Trevor, when a hail of light fire slammed into the rear of my shield from the other end of the warehouse. Greg instinctively hit the floor, rolled and elevated his line of fire from the ground completing his task. As for Scout and myself, being less well trained, we span to look at what was firing at us and in this error opened the opportunity for the remainder of our original targets to open fire.

Although we were shielded, the impact of multiple headshots hitting my shield at full force was disorientating and I was starting to become dazed. Scout stood there in full square stance, shots bouncing off him as he maintained his rapid fire into the shadows at the back of the warehouse.

Using this as a distraction, Greg shot at the remaining members of the Commander groups and caged them to halt their fire. As he joined us, I heard his mind link into Scout, who walked forward with his blue and white auric field building in intensity. As he transformed into his Pegasus, the warehouse was suddenly blasted by intense white light, illuminating and temporarily blinding the group of fifteen Leaves using the darkness as cover at the other end. By the time I had taken down four of them, Scout and Greg had disabled the remaining eleven.

"Wooohoo!" shouted Scout.

"You can't beat a good fire fight. Nice and spicy, well done chaps. Let's cage them," said Greg.

"That was bloody scary for a while. I have never taken that much fire before and it was starting to drain me," I admitted.

"Horse energy, channel strong will into your shield. I was showing Greg this earlier when we were horse playing," said Scout.

Suddenly, the silence and gloom of the warehouse was shattered as light bolts slammed into us from different locations around the internal structure. Greg had counted a further twenty Leaves in our close vicinity and was picking them off surgically.

"Strong will, Simon, use my horse link!" shouted Scout.

It was like having my head inside of a bell as someone else was ringing it. I engaged the link and the vibration and noise reduced significantly.

"I can't hold the cages, return fire and take this level of light blast," I said.

"Nor can we," confirmed Scout.

"Transport out on my signal," I ordered.

"No, wait. He who dares wins. Come close, we will set a dome shield over us and chill for a while," said Greg.

"I thought your motto was death or glory?" asked Scout.

"No, that's the Lancers!" replied Greg.

"Ah, that's why it is familiar," he replied.

Once inside the dome, we all assumed raptor form and perched quietly as the combined firepower of forty-five Leaves ricocheted off the surface.

"Any daring suggestions, Greg? Perhaps pop out one of those mines that knocks everyone over?" enquired Scout.

"That is what I had in mind, but most are guarded now so it will have less of an effect," he confirmed.

"No. I have an idea which will really shit these Leaves up and leave a lasting impression," I said.

"Bring in the cavalry in full battledress?" asked Scout excitedly.

"Exactly."

"Woohoo, this should be fun," exclaimed Scout.

Scout linked into Greg, demonstrating in his mind how to transform to a Harpy warrior in battledress. Greg's response was amazement and anticipated mastery.

An order was given from the Commanders to seize fire and having formed a ring of Leaves around the dome, Trevor and Janice approached us.

"Are you little birdies coming out to play?" said Janice sarcastically.

"Call yourself eagles, you are nothing but chickens." Trevor proceeded to strut around flapping his elbows to his sides, amusing the entire Leaf company.

"If Audaz was here, Trevor what have a mouthful of feathers by now," said Scout.

"We are telling you, not warning you. What you are doing is going to stop. You Commanders and your Lieutenants are going to come with us. No choice," I demanded.

"We are going nowhere. We have even sent invites across London so others can witness your demise and watch you run away empty handed," Trevor arrogantly informed us.

"Bonus," said Greg.

I linked into Sarah, gave her the building layout, the Leaf numbers and key members, and a view of what I was seeing.

"We need some backup, darling, and there is a particular dress code for right of admittance," I said.

"Gotcha. We will be with you less than shortly," responded Sarah.

Trevor had verbally wondered into a monologue of his hatred for self-righteous people and as he cursed and attempted to belittle us, I watched the hardly noticeable light disturbances as the 'split' windows appeared in various locations in the warehouse.

Seconds later, five huge Harpies materialised opening fire and throwing hypnic topplers to disorientate their targets. At that exact moment, Greg, Scout and I also transformed to battledress, opening rapid fire at the Commanders, flooring them. Sarah came to my side and we assumed back-to-back positions, as had James and Alana, Audaz and who I realised, must be Conchita, rotating slowly to cover all angles of fire.

The sound of head shots was deafening, the light from weapons discharged, illuminating the internal space like a strobe. Scout materialised and dematerialised in different positions, caging the fallen and connecting their holding lines to different members of our group. Greg who had obviously found the battledress a little cumbersome, had changed back to human form and was running, rolling and firing at Leaves to lessen their impact on the others.

With the majority of the Leaves having shielded themselves, we were gaining ground slowly. Then the guest Commanders, from three other boroughs arrived with their legions and tipped the scales in their favour. All of us were taking heavy fire and although we were standing our ground, the situation was becoming futile.

Being linked in to everyone in the group, I posed the retreat and regroup question, then heard an order being given to Greg from a voice I knew well:

"Transform to battledress now. Do not disobey my order!"

Greg immediately transformed as an intense white light shone suspended towards the roof apex of the warehouse. It pulsed slowly and drew everybody's attention as light fire subsided. The explosion of light was immediate and deafening, ripping through the Leaves, rendering them unconscious and inert. The blast from a Realm Five Harpy was capable of cutting through any light shield a Leaf could raise.

"Work quickly. You have less than five minutes before they come around. Sorry about the order, Greg, but you could not have withstood the blast undressed. I'm Nevaeh, nice to meet you."

"Me too. At your service, ma'am," he replied in awe.

"Thanks, Nevaeh, it was getting a bit intense," I said gratefully.

"You are welcome, Uncle Simon. Now let's get these Leaves swept up."

The other meets and greets were postponed until we had finished our task. Lower rank Leaves were separated from the five Commanders and a total of seventeen lieutenants. The guest Commanders had come in from Camden, Croydon and Haringey and had all brought witnesses with them. With all Leaves caged, I addressed the gathering.

"You will never see these people again, so say your goodbyes now. If anyone is thinking they may take over where they are leaving off, think again, because you will be next. You can tell Dexter, the Commander in Westminster, that we will be back for him," I said.

I then caught site of Nesta, who with a catcher was attending to the young man, who was thinking he had tripped into some nightmare world and was trusting neither of them. We exchanged smiles and a thumbs up.

It had been arranged that James, Greg and I would transport the captives to the island and we would all meet up in Capri with everyone else, afterwards. We all disappeared, releasing the remaining Leaves and the three of us transported our cargo.

We arrived at the island still in battle dress, landing and uncaging the group we had brought. All immediately attempted to transport out, but failed. In the distance were a group of other residents who vanished and reappeared at our location.

"There is nothing here!" complained Kingsley.

"What did you expect, a bag of weed and a minibar? Wake up. There is only one way out of here. You have a choice. Talk to the guides," I pointed out to him.

"Bumbaclaat!" Kingsley turned and walked away with his group.

"Clive!" I called out to a young man who was following Kingsley.

I told him he could go back to Lambeth if he wanted, as he did not deserve to be here with the others. He drew out his decision, sheepishly avoiding the damning glare from Kingsley. Letting James jumble any island co-ordinates he had in his mind, I opened a channel to Lambeth and told him to think of where he wanted to go.

Before he left, I instructed him not to tell others about the island, knowing the knowledge of its existence would be all over London by tomorrow and half way across the country by the end of the week. With him gone, we headed for Capri.

Sanction to Proceed

As Simon, Greg and I arrived back in Capri, the others were in full-animated flow describing their personal experiences of the warehouse battle.

"Welcome aboard, Greg, are you happy to join us?" I asked.

"Absolutely. Beats guiding, that's for sure. You have been a soldier, haven't you James?" Greg asked.

"I worked in intelligence during the Second World War," I replied.

"Good to meet you. I am glad we have some common history."

"So Simon. While I have been mooching around in the dark, you have been having loads of fun!" I said.

"I did feel you would be a tad envious, as we have had some real battles. I tell you what though, James, it is out of control in Between Worlds and we have only just scratched the surface in London. There are places all over the Earth which will be as badly affected," said Simon.

"Are there enough Harpies, that's what I am wondering, because we can't sort it out on our own?" I asked.

"I don't know, there are many still hidden. Apart from you, who takes every opportunity for a raptor reveal? I heard you even exposed yourself to Adolf Hitler."

"Yeah well. Harpy and proud I say. As for Adolf, I wanted to leave my stamp on him."

"I thought it was Arthur who did that?"

"Ummm, yes. I felt for Arthur that day."

We joined the rest of our group. As usual, it was Audaz who had had the most challenging of Leaves to overcome and it had been his skill and intuition that had vastly contributed to our success.

"I see that two years in the after world has not changed you, my dove," said Conchita, confirming our impressions that Audaz could embellish even the most insignificant of stories into an epic.

"How would you know; you were fighting with your back to mine. I would prefer also, if you did not call me 'my dove' in front of my friends. It is almost as bad as being called a chicken. I am neither, I am a—"

"Yeah, we all know, you are a Harpy Eagle," everyone joined in with the response.

"I was going to say: a lot bigger and much more handsome," replied Audaz.

We all laughed and Conchita introduced herself to Simon, Greg and I. Also a rainforest Harpy eagle like Audaz, their plumage was identical having dark grey feathers, a white underside and a black neckerchief. Again with a fan of grey feathers crowning their heads, there was only one difference, she was a lot larger than he was. It appeared that Conchita had also been shot by farmers, although these were clearing ground for palm oil plantations. Unlike Audaz' shooting, she had been killed outright.

"Did you go through an awakening?" asked Alana.

"I recognised him as soon as I saw him. I mean, who would not recognise such a 'handsome' bird," she said this with a wink which Audaz missed, as he raised his beak slightly and tilted his head to the side in self-appreciation.

"After that, it was pretty rapid and I knew exactly how I fitted in, hence the reason I was able to change to full battledress so soon after arriving here," she said.

"How many lifetimes?" asked Sarah.

"We have both had fifteen in total, so I think we have done what we need to. It is always a few more revolutions for us than you, as our lifespan is normally about thirty years. I feel ready now to work from the realms and from what Audaz has told me there is much to do," she replied.

We sat out on the veranda drinking in the views and the sunshine and relaxed. Audaz had taken Greg, Scout and Conchita for a flight across the water and to explore the islands Alana and I had created. His request was slightly veiled, as he was interested to see Greg's skill in the air. Conchita on the other hand, had never seen a Haast eagle and had persuaded Scout to fly with them.

Because we were all linked in our minds, everyone was up to speed on what each of us had encountered during our expeditions. However, it was not long before Simon, Sarah, Alana and I were speculating on the concerning practices and situations emerging. Part way through our discussion, Tarquin and Nevaeh arrived.

"Greetings all. That was slightly intense, wasn't it? Just a little more organised than we thought perhaps," said Tarquin.

"They have been left for too long without some kind of order being put in place in my view," added Simon.

"Speaks the man with the experience."

According to Tarquin, that was just it, there was no order. The ancient stories said that Between Worlds was created as a contemplation buffer on Earth to provide a choice for those few, who chose to take more time to think about moving forward to the after world. For thousands of years, Earth dwellers appeared to accept their responsibilities during contemplation, then crossed to whatever fate awaited them.

It had been during the last couple of hundred years' numbers had grown significantly and over the last century, they had escalated. The numbers were still increasing dramatically especially in the Western world as religions declined and values had become more self-centred.

Although exact numbers were not available, guide estimates were in the region of six and a half million Leaves in the UK and in excess of thirty million in the USA. We already knew the guesstimate for the Earth in total was about six hundred and fifty million Leaves. The plan to dramatically reduce Leaf activity in London had worked and guides had reported many boroughs being quieter than usual.

Evidently, there had been seventy-five defectors from the tube station incident in Lambeth with a steady trickle of Leaves approaching guides for transit in the other boroughs Simon's team had visited.

"It is not going to stay quiet indefinitely though and this kind of activity is happening all over the world. We cannot cover everywhere," said Simon.

"We know that. One of the ideas Nevaeh had, was to put out a Harpy call. No one knows just how many there are of you who are currently in the realms at present because you have all remained so hidden. I understand that Greg has even been able to alter his vibration to remain even more secret," said Tarquin.

"I estimate using ancient knowledge and speculation based on Harpies born since extinction, numbers are a little over four hundred thousand. Over sixty percent of those are currently on Earth, some are resting and others like you, are now working from the realms. I think those who are realm-based total about one hundred and fifty thousand. Therefore, with a coordinated approach, a considerable number of Commander-type Leaves could be removed if a combined Harpy offensive was instigated," detailed Nevaeh.

"Assuming you could rally such a force to remove darker Leaves, where will they be removed to and what about holding them. Boreray Island isn't big enough?" I asked.

"We have been looking at the larger picture which includes dealing with an Earth catastrophe," said Tarquin.

Nevaeh and Tarquin had been in dialogue with Realm Sixers. Alana's investigations on the Mariana Trench raised concerns for long-term holding solution of revolved spirit people post a climate change catastrophe. There was need for an alternative holding area or sort of realm to take the pressure off the after-world systems should significant numbers die on Earth. It would also have to be somewhere they could not revolve from.

"Are you suggesting we use Between Worlds as a temporary realm? So those poor people going into it, get the crappy end of the stick. It's hardly heaven, is it? And for how long, hundreds of years, more?" injected Alana.

"The problem is and as we have discussed, if a catastrophe at worst halves the Earth population, if the majority come to Realm Four, they will want to revolve within a short space of time as usual. This will not be possible because birth rates on Earth will not recover to enable them to, for a long time into the future," confirmed Tarquin.

"Come on, Mum, what were you like when you hit the point when you needed to revolve again," said Nevaeh.

"Grumpy, irritable, frustrated and itching to get back," said Alana.

"Times that by three billion," summed Nevaeh. Alana saw her point.

"What is your plan for Between Worlds?" I asked.

Tarquin briefed us that he, Nevaeh and a number of other Realm Fivers had proposed splitting Between Worlds into a dual realm. This involved creating a dark realm within Between Worlds to separate dwellers of the main lighter realm from those who, if they had gone through the current self-judgement system, would have gone into Realm One or Two.

Because Between Worlds had been set up originally as a contemplation zone, it meant that people going into Between Worlds could avoid judging themselves until they chose to go over to the after world with a catcher. This was causing the problem.

The implication of this dual-realm model meant in order to separate the darker candidates, pre-self-judgement had to be facilitated by someone or someones who could ascertain the likely outcome of a judgement taking place, as per the current system, between that person and the Collective. For a more developed spirit, the history and current mind set of an individual could be easily revealed, hence Simon being allowed to make decisions on Commanders and Lieutenants.

For segregation to be achieved successfully in the absence of an automatic judgement system, this meant that guides and catchers would have to be present at the death of individuals without fail and be responsible for the judgement made before individuals were able to orientate themselves to passing from Earth to Between Worlds.

Training would have to take place, not only to ensure correct judgement happened based on thresholds, but also to facilitate the relocation of a darker individual into the darker realm. It had been proposed this Dark Realm be based on the same model as Realm Three.

"Where would this Dark Realm be situated?" asked Sarah.

"Within the same location as Between Worlds but in another dimension. It would be the same as realm separations in the after world," replied Nevaeh.

"Big question. What about all of the darker individuals currently residing in Between Worlds, what will happen to them?" Simon asked.

Tarquin paused in an attempt to add reality to the necessary action. If these darker spirits were alive on Earth, they would have been sought by Earthbound police and processed by judicial systems which would separate and incarcerate them. If they had gone through the after-world judgement system and deemed themselves to be Dark Realm candidates in that moment of truth, they would be segregated to those realms automatically. They were in Between Worlds because of the absence of judgement. Therefore, the darker ones would have to be located, judged and segregated into the Between Worlds darker realm.

"A mass hunt you mean?" said Alana.

"Let us be under no illusions or delusions. I know the term 'hunted' echoes with deep foreboding amongst the Harpies but your extinction was not justified. What's more we are not exterminating them. At the same time, we are creating an environment in the lighter realm in Between Worlds for spirits in contemplation to live more peacefully and without threat. Concurrently, we eliminate the threat and interference to the current Earthbound," clarified Tarquin.

"In essence, you are preparing the Between Worlds lighter realm for a massive influx of spirit from Earth, when the climate change catastrophe takes place. It could become an alternative to that influx ending up in Realm Four, where they would want to revolve," I said.

"A way of keeping the grumpy and frustrated would-be revolvers out of heaven?" added Alana.

Tarquin suggested that was not the main aim. It was about providing a type of heaven on Earth where dwellers would have access to a virtual world facility like in Realm Four to imagine and build homes and create their own pockets of heaven to live in if they chose. They would not be restricted in travel throughout Earth and would remain undetectable to Earth dwellers, as Between Worlds occupants currently were.

The idea was that in still being connected to Earth and being able to experience it, albeit from another dimension, dreams could be realised, relationships could develop amongst occupants and communities could thrive. Due to its location on Earth, there would be less of an anxiety in needing to revolve and more of an acceptance, that this was actually heaven.

Guides would still visit the lighter realm post influx but the work would be more about guidance at that level and living in that realm. Guide identities would be such that they would be seen as higher realm spirit people from a realm which may be accessed should dwellers progress in Self-development to a point where the system allowed them to move on.

"The system meaning who exactly? It would not be the Collective would it, so you would have to have another within-system judging facility," said Sarah.

"That would have to be for those in Realm Six or Seven to decide. It is about maintaining balance and metering the flow of spirits revolving in the face of an adversity we cannot predict," said Nevaeh.

"And once those progressed spirits had reached Realm Four, they would learn that Between Worlds isn't actually the heaven they thought it was," I said.

"They would experience Realm Four as another heaven, but within the after world, with the opportunity to revolve back to Earth. Guides would also visit the darker realm to help people to Self-develop. The reward for those there would be to join the main lighter realm. Any dark dwellers who wanted to face their responsibilities and go to the actual Dark Realms in the after world, would be allowed to do so," said Tarquin.

I aired my concern about another situation which would occur if this plan was achieved and the Earth catastrophe took place. This was, post catastrophe, all of those who had been killed, as well as existing Between Worlds residents, would continue to witness further destruction and suffering taking place on Earth, as the Earth readjusted to new climate conditions.

"It will be like witnessing hell on Earth, not being able to help them," I said.

There was a momentary silence amongst us. Tarquin responded meaningfully and purposefully.

"Yes, this is a difficult one and we have had Realm Seven input on this dilemma. They are of the view that where suffering is caused, denial of responsibility does not foster change or growth. We are the Collective. All of us, on Earth, in Between Worlds and in the after world have a joint responsibility to maintain balance in all worlds to ensure our survival. Those casualties entering Between Worlds will face the consequences of all of their races on Earth failing to take collective responsibility for climate change. They are unmoving in this and I agree with them."

"We are all going to suffer with them anyway," said Alana in acceptance. "But what about the animals and other life forms?"

"They will have safe passage into Realm Four. We will need to restructure and expand habitats and look at ways to manage their instinctive revolution urges," replied Nevaeh.

"Can I have that job?" asked Alana.

"This catastrophe hasn't happened yet. Come on, we need to refocus on our current plans if we are going to slow this damage or stop it. Can I take you back to those proposed plans?" asked Tarquin.

Everyone was getting caught in the finer detail and the issues which would arise. Tarquin's response was that higher planers were not trying to organise a work based social. They were attempting to restructure Between Worlds and modify the flow of spirit from it and into Realm Four, to facilitate revolution back to Earth in a fair and transparent way.

Both Nevaeh and he were aware there was much fine detail to be worked out, for example, where do people go when they graduate from Realm Three or might those in Realm Four be allowed to relocate to Between Worlds? Conceptually, however, the consensus was building in the proposed idea's favour.

"Coming back to the Harpy call, it is a call to arms. With all due respect, the guides do not have the abilities to be able to exclude the darkest and most dangerous of Leaves. All here are aware of the ferocity of firefights involving Commanders and even though we have more effective weaponry and armour, these adversaries had proved to be well-defended and organised. To put it simply, we will need a global task force who are instinctually predisposed to hunt and work covertly if necessary," Tarquin said, lowered his brow in respect.

Nevaeh reconfirmed there were about one hundred and fifty thousand Harpies currently hidden in Realm Four, disguised in raptor, horse and human Harpy lines. It may be that some would not want to be involved. However, like Greg's admission, with an ancient history of being hunted and always having to hide, to achieve the opposite, may provide an opportunity to lift that sense, from one of oppression to one with a higher realm sanction.

"I am not being disrespectful, Nevaeh, but you sound like a recruitment officer trying to rally troops. 'Join the Harpy army, travel the Earth and shoot humans'. I think there are Harpies out there like us and they will rise to the challenge of doing their part for the whole of the after world," said Simon, sensing a little manipulation in her words.

"I know there will be those who will want to do their part, but we should not underestimate the latent disquiet coming from perhaps an unconscious part of us. We may not seek retribution or revenge, but there is an undercurrent beneath the surface, which questions the motivation for our extinction. I know what Greg said about his reflection in Realm Three for motives to join the SAS and Scout's comment about legitimate hunting. The ember glows in us still and clearing the darker Leaves from Between Worlds may just offer some reprieve to Harpies," Nevaeh responded.

"What do you think, Tarquin?" I asked.

"I trust in what Nevaeh is saying. We are not trying to manipulate anybody, other than the dangerous Leaves. We need a job to be done and the Harpies are the only ones who can make it happen. That's the reality," responded Tarquin.

I asked Tarquin about timings and how soon they expected a sanction from higher up. He divulged it had already been agreed and sanctioned at Realm Seven level that Between Worlds should be divided into light and dark realms because of the threats and activities currently apparent in its lawless state.

The construction of the new architecture was achievable on a majority vote which had already been taken. Acting as a majority, Realm Seven spirits could access energy from the Collective system to orchestrate the reconstruction. It was not something the Collective had to create itself. This was happening now and would be complete within a day.

The current system of catching Earth dwellers as they died and taking them over to the after world via their own judgement would continue to operate. The encouragement of existing Leaves wishing to pass over would also continue up until a point where global threat was considered immanent.

When this happened, all passings to the after world would cease until the extent of the impact on Earth populations could be assessed. There would be no changes to the light realm within Between Worlds, such as the integration of a virtual world facility, until that same point was reached.

Pre Earth catastrophe and once full separation and segregation of Leaves had been achieved, the plan was to initiate the active encouragement of Leaves to pass over to Realm Four for the purposes of additional energy transfer. It would be at this point and with the supervision of guides, that our religious colleagues, Matteo, Haadee, David, Aarna and others would become involved. They would be invited to organise their followers to help to enlighten Leaves from the light Between Worlds realm, to the security and benefits of passing over to Realm Four.

There would be no free movement of light realm dwellers into the dark realm and as with the current Realm Three criteria, minors warranting realm one or two judgement would go into the Between Worlds Dark Realm, but with additional guide support. With actions already in process, it meant there was clearance to proceed with segregation very shortly, however the Harpy call had to go out, meetings had been arranged and training must take place.

"You two have got your work cut out for you, especially you Nevaeh trying to mobilise thousands of Harpies," said Alana.

"Thankfully, I am not the only Harpy in Realm Five. There are quite a few actually. You will also be pleased to know there is a Harpy presence in both Realms Six and Seven as well. We have a far-reaching voice," said Nevaeh.

"That is good to hear as our recent adventures have revealed some interesting characters who could do with a refresher course in allowing, empathy and compassion," said Alana with guarded criticism.

"When will we get to meet Robyn, your mate? I assume she is from Realm Five too?" added Alana.

"I will arrange something with her. She is busy with the animal zones at present. Actually, she would be the person to talk to about that job you were interested in. But I hope you will not need to take it on," replied Nevaeh.

The four flyers had returned, one by one gracefully landing on the veranda and transforming as necessary. They momentarily paused to connect to the conversations which had been going on, before meeting and greeting Tarquin and Nevaeh.

The rumblings that had gone on at Realm Five level once the news of current questionable Dark Realm operations and the indiscretion from Thaddeus had broken, had caused some unsettlement. A realisation, even at that level, that assumptions had somehow replaced the need for involvement even through interest, had created a wakeup call.

Controlling the Dark Realms had always been seen as an onerous and depressing task, therefore once the role had been delegated, the spirit in charge was left to get on with it whilst reporting into their immediate line supervisor. Gerry had undertaken the role because, it had been delegated to him by a Realm Sixer, who was keen to offload the job and Gerry was keen to have that Realm Six profile of responsibility. As Tarquin said, there were no prizes for guessing who that Sixer was. Members of Realm Seven had been involved in preliminary discussion with both of them, but no action had been taken as yet.

"What would action look like?" I asked.

"Side tracking, meaning less involvement in systems management and at worst, a realm demotion. You have to realise, in the higher realms, ways have been more reactionary, as there are individuals wanting to maintain the purity and originality of the Collective's ethos," confirmed Tarquin.

"But the Collective's ethos is to evolve and change, is it not?" I said.

"There has been no need to evolve and change the system for thousands of years and as I heard recently, 'you don't fix, what's not broke'. We just need an audit and an upgrade where the powers that be, accept we need to evolve quickly and in line with Earth. Thankfully, we are making headway. But the priority is to action the changes Between Worlds and because you all have been involved in the pilot action, I need your help to make it happen," said Tarquin.

"As a matter of interest, could the likes of Thaddeus or Gerry choose to reside in Between Worlds?" I asked.

"And why would they choose to do that when they could stay in the afterworld realms?" asked Tarquin tracing my thoughts.

"Feeling ostracised and disgraced may cause the extreme. They would have more power in a newly under developed realm so close to Earth, as that also, goes through its own new beginnings," I posed.

"Fallen angel syndrome you mean? Let's hope not, at least for the time being," he replied pensively.

Nevaeh, party to our conversation, diverted my attention, which I chose to flow with.

"You created quite a stir in the Dark Realms, with your approach to people and understanding of their predicament. Those you saw in Realm Three want you back, with the fire and tune juice this time. We will be lobbying for changes supporting personal development within these realms and will sort out the Harpy Whale situation. But as Tarquin said, we have a priority," reconfirmed Nevaeh.

We all knew what each other felt and there was a unanimous response to take action. Nevaeh would put out the Harpy call to arms following the meeting. Tarquin requested that Simon, Greg and I be tasked with identifying those Harpies coming forward, who had combat experience. It was a good job we were able to mind link and assess on masse, otherwise we could be interviewing for years.

Once this was achieved, we would be able to assess any leadership shortfalls and embark on identifying individuals for leadership training. With Audaz and Scout as part of our core team, they would act as the main points of contact and reference for raptor and horse lines during this task. It was likely their lines would respond better to like kind initially and during the delegation process.

Alana, Sarah and Conchita would play integral roles with the rest of us in training. When it came to the sorties themselves, they would have a choice. Because of what Sarah had said previously about being in combat, an option was offered where they could work with guides and catchers on site to help lighter Leaves come over to Realm Four. I already knew which option Alana would choose without hesitation. As for Conchita, she made it clear she was in it for the hunt.

"Nevaeh, about that weapon you used at the warehouse, which was capable of blasting through shields. Can you show me how?" asked Greg.

Nevaeh smiled. "It's a little above your vibration level, sorry Greg. However, I know you have provided some effective modifications to light weaponry, so you may find others who have developed their own armouries," she replied.

"We must get on. Thank you for the efforts and achievements so far. I for one am looking forward to embracing these changes and continuing to work with a team I hold much love and respect for. Good luck. Nevaeh will be in touch shortly," said Tarquin.

They both disappeared.

"Tune juice anyone. I think we deserve it?" asked Alana.

"Make mine a bucket," replied Scout.

Harpy Call

Contacting thousands of individuals simultaneously was thankfully a straightforward task within the realms. Whether they chose to respond or not was a different matter. When in existence on Earth, Harpies chose to lead lives away from human influence. As birdmen and women, they became objects of fear and superstition, but were also envied by men for their ability to fly. Religion, not able to categorise them as angels, deemed them to be creatures who must serve the devil.

When conflict occurred, their aim was to scare humans away. However, their innate transformational powers enabling them to assume a battledress appearance, confirmed the church's suspicions that they were in fact devil creatures which must be exterminated. A covert edict was initiated whereby Harpy tribes were systematically hunted by zealots empowered by the will of God to purify Earth, ensuring that only those of his image remained. Although purging them of their sins through death, much torture and suffering came with it.

Scattering across the Earth, many escaped persecution from this source for generations. However, indigenous cultures were also afraid of their sudden presence and their persecution continued. They had been wiped out three hundred years before religion finally hit the shores of the Americas.

Nevaeh's point to Simon was the Harpy race all carried the historical memory of persecution by humans. Whilst ignorance could be forgiven and the existence of the after world confirmed to them that not all humans were evil, beauty and powers beyond human capability were a source of envy and difficulty. Although they could not revolve as their race back on Earth due to extinction, they still chose to remain hidden during rest times in the after world because the echo of fear and non-acceptance still remained.

The task, if they chose to become part of it, would necessitate exposure, but with the acceptance that only their race could meet this task. To ignore the underlying historical resentment towards humans would be foolish because in a group context, it would emerge. If the opportunity to relieve and repair some of this sense through conflict with humans Between Worlds, who chose to remain malicious and to achieve a better way of living for the majority, the task would become a double-edged sword.

The call could only be initiated by Nevaeh with the assistance of a Realm Sixer who could channel the energy needed to make the broadcast. Ethan was an Alaskan Bald Eagle Harpy of immense presence and knowing. Having lived on Earth when Harpies were alive as a species, he was able to recount stories about tribal life and struggles towards their final demise.

Realm Six residents were of less form and more light, although the choice remained to maintain form. When addressed, facial features and body shape outline came into focus, then diffused again to a shimmering light body presence. At times, it was possible to see the light connections flowing to and from them connecting to other beings or systems.

Although Nevaeh still described them as a person in terms of presence, they were much more connected to the system. She was aware that as a spirit progressed through the realms, identity and individuality became less important. Those surpassing Realm Seven, were absorbed into the Collective, becoming part of the knowing and consciousness which orchestrated stability across all realms and Earth.

Like those of Realm Five, sixers just knew, however, were more aligned to realm diagnostics and changes within them. This made dialogue unnecessary, as they were able to think into and sense any information or feeling another spirit may have in their long and short-term memories as well as know where a line of thought was going to take them. Conversation still took place as part of the etiquette of social exchange, plus fives and sixers had an internal switch which could momentarily suspend the immanent knowledge of what dialogue would be spoken next.

"Now, I want you to speak clearly and concisely into the microphone, breathe easily and let the following word flow from the previous. And remember the line, 'if necessary, we will fight them on the beaches'. You will be fine," said Ethan, keeping a straight face.

"Memories are funny things, aren't they? But to all who heard that message when it was delivered, they could only imagine what they were about to face.

Although this isn't a war, I hope our race realises, they are really needed in coming forward."

"Think of it as uniting the tribes in the face of adversity. Their role is importantly integral in moving the whole plan forward," advised Ethan. "Ready?"

Ethan energised, allowing connections of energy to join with him from the immediate surroundings. Concentric rings of white light energy rose from his feet and on reaching his heart chakra, he blended his own powerful Harpy essence with it making the signature of the transmission readable only by Harpies. As they ascended past his throat chakra, the light changed to a sky-blue colour before raising upwards to form a vortex. The highest rings pulsed outwards in all directions as they reached the top level. Ethan looked at Nevaeh and took her words.

"My name is Nevaeh, a Realm Five Harpy and direct descendent of the Radak tribe. This message can only be heard by those of Harpy descent. The realms and the Collective needs our race's help. For most amongst us, we have remained hidden within the realms and on revolving back to Earth have been forced to use the vehicles of human, raptor and horse lines to complete our development towards knowing.

"Today, I am speaking to members of our race from all lines. Although it was the humans who decided our fate a thousand years ago, consciousness and understanding has evolved amongst humans in the higher realms and we are accepted as an equal life force as part of creation and evolution. Acceptance in Realm Four has not developed for different reasons.

"This may be due to us choosing to remain hidden amongst the humans; because your Harpy heritage remains hidden from you and because we have not been encouraged to reveal our true identity to protect their insecurity. This is something that requires righting," Nevaeh continued.

"Most will know, on Earth, in their ignorance and greed, humans have damaged the Earth to a point where a catastrophe will take place and millions will lose their Earth lives.

"Some may say, yet again, it is the humans behaving in their own interests without concerning themselves with the consequences of their actions. Therefore, this issue may be considered as their problem. However, this Earth issue affects humans, Harpies and all Earthbound life and threatens the entire existence of the after-world realms.

"Preparations are under way to modify Between Worlds, converting it to a world of both a light and dark realm. The light realm will temporarily accommodate the influx of people and any Harpies coming from Earth as a result of the catastrophe. Realm Four for reasons which will become clear, cannot take in these numbers.

"At present and for thousands of years, Between Worlds has remained a lawless state of pre-judgement where dark and light souls, the Leaves, have resided together. Dark souls have become organised to manipulate, abuse and control vulnerable others for their own gain and have found ways to negatively affect the Earth dwellers.

"A small Harpy warrior force has been instrumental in segregating some of these darker elements in London, England and they have been judged and will now be transferred to the dark realm in Between Worlds. It was these Harpies who initiated this course of action, supported by me and others in the higher realms. Their success is based on attributes and skills such as instinct, transformation and animal species communication which are not available to humans. These have enabled them to capture some of the heinous Leaf leaders involved in this abuse of innocents.

"I am asking for your help, to join others like these warriors and fight to clear Between Worlds to make it a safe place to live. A gathering to discuss plans and raise questions will take place at this time in two days and the meeting coordinates will be sent at the end of this message. I understand that not all will wish to fight, however, of those who choose not to, we can still use your support to help vulnerable Leaves to pass through to our world.

"This is not a duty. This is a choice to help shape our future and that of all life. And a choice to enable our visibility and acceptance within the realms. Another of our race, wishes to add his message. Thank you for listening I truly hope you will come."

"My name is Ethan. I am a Realm Six Harpy and the coordinator of this task. The time has come to awaken to your role in safeguarding this after world. We all search for meaning as part of our development, however meaning will evade us without the true embrace of our identity, an identity we keep hidden and some deny. Come to, come back to awareness, Harpies of all lines, our future is in doubt without you. We are needed to help preserve Earth and we need to forge that pathway towards our acceptance together, in order to stand in our true light, purpose, meaning and value. Hear our call and come to meet with us," Ethan delivered his message weaving an ancient Harpy distress vibration into the last pulse.

"I think there was more of a choice in my request," said Nevaeh, concerned she had not emphasised the absolute importance of the call.

"There was still choice in my message, but left for the individual to decide based on the power of a greater need to respond. We have no choice; we need their help. Our future is less certain without them," confirmed Ethan.

The message would have been heard by all Harpies whether awakened or not. For those not yet awoken like Scout was when James first met him, there would be immediate confusion, however, the power of instinct was always greater than intrigue and it was hoped they would respond.

Training would have to happen in smaller groups; however, the initial meeting would be arranged with all attending. Considering that football stadiums on Earth could seat in excess of ninety thousand people, constructing a stone amphitheatre with the same or a larger capacity for all Harpy lines, was easily achievable for either a Realm Five or Six dweller.

Nevaeh and Ethan jointly created the structure at their location within virtual world, in the design of traditional concentric platforms, the lowermost at ground level to accommodate horses. In the middle of the theatre, a large stone dias was positioned to enable speakers to project by voice to the outer gallery. Once erected Nevaeh made it permanent within Realm Four itself.

As she and Ethan sat on the uppermost rim, a considerable number of materialisations and dematerialisations took place as beings visited the location as if to check it out.

"We appear to have some interest!" stated Ethan.

"Look up there," Nevaeh directed Ethan's attention to six raptors circling the amphitheatre at about three hundred metres. "I'm going up to get a feel for their interest."

Nevaeh transformed to her sea eagle and flew upwards to meet them. Rather than disappearing, they held their presence. Interestingly they were all of one species, the Steppe Eagle and Nevaeh could detect they were all linked in to each other.

"I take it you are here to get an idea of where the meeting will take place?" asked Nevaeh.

"We take it, you are Nevaeh and that is Ethan below us?" said one of the birds.

"That's correct. I also detect that you have all known each other through many lifetimes and your awareness is great."

"We are of the Atassu tribe with our homeland in Kazakhstan. You are right about the lifetimes and about identity in your message. We have completed our revolutions and find ourselves in a place where we cannot progress further whilst maintaining our secret that we are in fact Harpies. Without acceptance from the humans or having more developed Harpy mentors, we are stuck in limbo."

"I hear non-trust," said Nevaeh.

"We are not like them. Humans find it difficult to accept other races actually existed on Earth. They have conveniently placed them into myths and legends, as a way perhaps of trying to cover their guilt. Maybe, in Realm Five, there are humans who have the ability to understand the language blend of instinct and dialogue, but not in Realm Four. My name is Erasyl; it is good to meet with you."

"I think you will have found a way forward, if you come to this meeting to understand what we are proposing. I think this is what we all need. My sense is you are from the raptor line? Do you transform to human form?" asked Nevaeh.

"We are raptors. We do not live in the animal realm because of our mental abilities and there is a limit to how much contact you can take from purely instinctive animal spirit. We live amongst ourselves and will periodically mingle with humans in their form. But we are always looking in from the outside," said Erasyl.

"How many of you are there?"

"Twenty-eight. We have created our own area to live. And yes, we are a warrior tribe."

Nevaeh smiled and experienced the feeling of emotion building around her heart. It was a feeling of having found a pocket of spirit from her own kind, who needed help and mentoring and who needed to belong.

Erasyl explained that they did not seek vengeance. They were warriors because that was the message which came down the generations, to fight to maintain their existence. Even when this cause was lost to extinction, the traditions held strong to remain in a place to defend. They had always been a peace-loving tribe but had low tolerance and no respect for others who preyed on the vulnerable and less able.

"Will you bring your tribe to the meeting?" asked Nevaeh.

"We will be here," replied Erasyl, who then disappeared with the rest of his group.

Nevaeh transported back to Ethan's side.

"So proud and yet at the same time lost, aren't they?" said Ethan.

"Yes," said Nevaeh.

"Let's change this, Nevaeh."

"Yes. Let's change it," she replied.

The Gathering

The morning of the gathering was bright and sunny, with a cooling breeze blowing in from the south. Rolling grasslands punctuated with poplar trees, undulated in all directions from the site of the amphitheatre situated on higher ground. From the time of early dawn, the location had been a hive of activity with frequent visitations from the various lines of Harpies, perhaps confirming the location and to serve their curiosity.

Nevaeh had met previously with us all at Sarah's ranch to discuss how she saw the meeting progressing and the importance of recruiting as many Harpies as possible. The task of separating the dark Leaves from the light across the expanse of Between Worlds which circumnavigated the entire Earth, was mammoth in its conception. It was hoped that teams of Harpies would operate in the countries and continents of their origin, thus providing familiarity with and knowledge of locations, towns and cities.

The plan was each team would be accompanied by a guide and catcher to facilitate cross overs to the after world by those Leaves wishing to and being encouraged to pass. Although this could be to any realm from one to four, it was of paramount importance to harvest accrued energy from the Leaves to counteract overpopulation on Earth.

Judgement of dark Leaves would be facilitated by trained Harpies from each team, giving them the authority to transport dark Leaves into the dark realm. A Realm Fiver would scan all transfers to ensure correct judgement had taken place.

Before and during the mission, Simon, Alana and I, were to act as the key reference point for human form Harpies. Audaz and Conchita would be the raptor link and Scout, backed up by Sarah because of her wide horse-based knowledge, would provide key contact for horses. Greg was assigned as head of combat training. All would be located upon the central dias during the meeting, alongside Nevaeh, Tarquin and Ethan.

In consultations held by Tarquin, the ethos behind the plan of action and the re-modelling of systems control to manage the impending impacts on Earth, had been received with concern by Matteo and Haadee. They were to be representatives of the largest religious followings on Earth and in the after world.

However, the majority of those in Realms Five, Six and Seven, had decided, choice was the integral factor within the concept of evolution at all levels. The assumption that the Collective would ordain non-action based on a fatalistic premise, was too risky. Not to take action, negated the entire ideal of existence, to strive to achieve more developed levels of consciousness and knowing. It was the collective knowing of the majority of higher planers which drove the changes. In the main, other members of the religious consultation group had accepted the high plane guidance.

The amphitheatre was starting to fill up as the time for the meeting approached. Thousands of Harpies from all three lines populated the stone terraces and patiently awaited the arrival of others and those orchestrating the gathering. Tarquin joined me just outside the perimeter.

"Quite a day for your race, my friend?" stated Tarquin.

"A revelation would be one way of describing it. My heart grows in realising my place amongst my kin and to connect with the potential we hold as a whole," I replied.

"A potential you rightly deserve to at last engage the kinetic will of Harpies as a whole, to change that which must be changed for the future of all," said Tarquin.

"It is nice to be needed in purpose. There is something else which we need to talk about."

"Yes, I know. Once the training and the Between Worlds task is underway, I need you, Alana and Sarah to work with me in sorting out the Dark Realms in the after world."

It appeared that there had been some embarrassing and difficult meetings which had taken place involving Gerry and Thaddeus, following an investigation by Realm Seven spirit beings into Dark Realm operations and systems management.

Assumptions and the archaic way of managing where 'everything appears fine' had drawn attention to the fact that equal opportunities were not being observed and upheld in all parts of the after-world system. Tarquin had been asked to step in as a caretaker to oversee the Dark Realms until a long-term overseer could be found. He would report into Ethan in Realm Six.

"Are you all right meeting this request? I am aware it is not an enviable job," I asked.

"I see it as an opportunity to put things right. I would like you to work with Arthur as part of a team, to investigate, then suggest what changes could be made within the Dark Realms. In particular, the system of moving people forwards and the way we will manage the kick back, if any, from those who currently reside in Realm Four. The kick back, meaning those who may find the notion of 'not on my doorstep' difficult to swallow," stated Tarquin.

"As I said, nice to be needed. I am sure Sarah and particularly Alana would wish to be involved. I will talk to Alana and Arthur, will you speak with Sarah and Simon?" I asked.

"Yes, I agree, it is an important job and I need Simon to focus and head up the Between Worlds operation. Anyway, we have a meeting to attend."

"Harpy Whales?"

"Nevaeh will keep an eye on them in the short term. They need to stay where they are at the moment because they fulfil a key role. She will then hand over to a Realm Six spirit called Hils or Hillary, as she knows the oceans. Come on, let's go," added Tarquin.

With fifteen minutes to go, the amphitheatre was almost at full capacity; however, Harpies continued to arrive targeting spaces amongst the audience. Ethan linked a message to all present and requested they all sit tight as he created an additional stone level at the top of the structure to enable guests to spread and enjoy more comfort and space.

As he walked to the centre of the stone dias, he was followed by Tarquin and Nevaeh. Simon led the second group including Alana, Sarah, Audaz, Conchita, Scout and myself to join the high planers, standing in a semi-circle behind them. Ethan opened the proceedings.

"I am Ethan. Harpies! You are welcome."

The cheer which rang out was deafening. Raised wings and arms waving and manes shaking, acknowledging their energy and will to be seen and be amongst their own kind. Materialising in the sky directly above, an aurora shimmered and glowed, coloured with green, blue, indigo and violet light, responded to the vibrancy of the crowd. Nevaeh stepped forward to speak.

"And I am Nevaeh. Your presence here today has already created an important point in the history of our race. If you take a moment to gaze upon the faces of those around you and greet them, you will be doing so in the majority of cases, for the first time. We have hidden ourselves for long enough and perhaps this is so, not only because of the messages of protection passed down from our tribal elders, but because our identity and purpose has evaded us. We now have an opportunity to stand in our true light and embrace that purpose."

A further cheer sounded loudly, before Nevaeh continued.

"We are needed, for it is only the skills and capabilities of Harpies who can forge a pathway forwards for those who orchestrate in the after world to follow and construct a safe haven for those in need."

Changing her tone, she confirmed there was shadow in our history with humans; however, a thousand years in hiding had also taught us compassion and acceptance. These enabled us to accept that individuals from any race or creed, could develop consciousness and knowing based on the quality of the mirrors gazed into.

Self-development was accrued by individual realisation and we had a choice to show empathy and respect for those who were not blessed by the instinctual insight we possessed. If we did not, we would lose an opportunity to act as mirrors for them and accept the value of the mirrors they reflected back upon us.

"We ask you to fight in this ordeal with a common aim, to help the Collective restore balance on Earth and for the security of all life in all realms. We fight as Harpies because although we have chosen to live and let live peacefully in our history, we have always remained ready to fight and that is who we are," asserted Nevaeh.

The realisation and acceptance of identity echoed wildly around the amphitheatre and regulated into a purposeful common chant of Harpy, Harpy, Harpy! Tinges of red joined the colours in the aurora, coursing through the other colours in rhythmic spikes indicating the vitality behind channelled passion and the defence of Self. Ethan raised his hand in order to speak and in a short moment, all was quiet.

"The Collective in creating Between Worlds, intended its purpose as a space to provide newly passed spirit from Earth who were uncertain, time to contemplate their decision to proceed to the after world. For thousands of years, the time in contemplation was mostly short-lived and numbers remained small."

This Ethan said was in part because belief was confirmed by the existence of a life after death on Earth. But it was also combined with an inherent trust in those visiting from the after worlds and the strength of personal moral responsibility. This triggered an innate truth supporting their decision to pass.

With the process of self-judgement happening at the point of transition into the after world and the absence of any type of judicial system, Between Worlds had become a haven for those wishing to pursue their own desire for power. By avoiding personal responsibility and the after world Dark Realms by not passing, an opportunity presented itself for individuals to dominate and manipulate other more peaceful and vulnerable Leaves.

Most importantly, this darker element had become successful in affecting Earth dwellers, whose sensitivity and vulnerability opened their minds to negative suggestion. Those Leaves in positions of power were motivated by control and to perpetuate suffering. They had become organised in threatening and recruiting others to achieve their aims.

"These activities must be stopped and those individuals provided with a choice. The choice to transition to the after world to face their own judgement, or be transferred to an alternative realm within Between Worlds, in a dimension away from the Earth," Ethan concluded.

Nevaeh took up the mantle and explained the alternative realm had already been created by spirit from Realms Six and Seven and that it was based on the model of the Realm Three after world Dark Realm. Its first occupants were those commanders captured by the Harpy team operating in London.

Describing the system of judgement and transfer to this darker realm, she outlined the global objective to purge the negative influences and relocate them. Lastly, she detailed how catchers would now be responsible for allocating the appropriate destination for newly passed Earth dwellers wishing to remain in Between Worlds. These combined actions would create a safer realm for others to live in.

"I am Tarquin, of Realm Five. Yes, I am human, but in my defence, I have secretly always wanted to be a Harpy."

This raised a rolling laugh from the audience. Tarquin introduced the reason for taking this decision to create a safer realm, was also to plan for the future. The consensus of belief in the higher realms was that the Collective was over populating the Earth in an attempt to maximise enough energy return, should a global catastrophe take place. Rather than if, it was more likely to be when.

High planers were in agreement, a sizable influx of Earth dweller casualties would cause havoc for the revolving process. This was due to the reduced numbers of new born humans available to revolve back into, caused by the Earth catastrophe culling their numbers. Therefore, it had been decided, in such an event, casualties would be accommodated in Between Worlds where facilities, making it more 'heaven like' would be introduced. Ethan continued after Tarquin.

"We know as high planers, we are taking the destiny of all of us into our own hands. However, it is felt that the Collective is giving us a choice to do so. The Collective is an ancient identity derived from all of our consciousness and knowing, but we understand that part of it, is a system."

Due to its own laws of revolved spirit on Earth not knowing of their part in the whole structure of the realms and especially over the last near two hundred years, Earth dwellers in their ignorance, had caused the Earth itself, major damage.

High planers believed the Collective did not anticipate this level of damage occurring. After all, it had no control over the presence and use of natural resources on a planet which has been created by the solar system forming itself.

"By making these changes to Between Worlds, we are freeing a contingency energy and accommodation resource. I say energy resource, because each Leaf transitioning to Realm Four, brings with them higher levels of energy the Collective can use as an alternative to overpopulating. We are instigating radical changes and the Collective is not stopping us from doing so," said Ethan.

Ethan's last words sent ripples through the audience. However, the voices were not raised in objection. The murmurs were based on the instinctual realisation of the need for change. At that moment, Ethan and Nevaeh knew they were dealing with an instinctual collective consciousness and the smiles spread across the faces of all on the dias as their thoughts dissipated. Nevaeh held up her hand to still the audience.

"If we capture this moment, we realise who we are. Never in my history have I had the opportunity to feel what it is like to be separate and yet so connected to so many of my own kind at the same time. Together we are more than just who we are, together, we know our own strength and accept the instinctive truth that will drive us to right the balance of compassion and justice," Nevaeh continued.

"The task, should you choose to join with us, is challenging and as I have said, global in its magnitude. Before you choose, I want you to know exactly what to expect. With the help of Ethan, I will transmit the episode of one of our missions in the East End of London where a number of Leaf Commanders were captured. Have no illusions, we fight hard for what we know is right. At its conclusion, we accept there will be those who choose not to join with us and no judgement will come to bare upon their decision. Ethan, if you will?" said Nevaeh.

The entire scene and course of events in the Spitalfields warehouse was transmitted to every Harpy present including Nevaeh's appearance and the transport of the five commanders and seventeen lieutenants to Boreray Island. Everyone on the dias, with the exception of the three high planers waited anxiously for the response.

There was much shock and surprise coming from the audience in particular, the horses. The overwhelming feeling was the surprise that many Harpies had no idea of the ability to transform to battledress or into Pegasus form. Nevaeh waited a while during which conversation reverberated around the amphitheatre. As the noise subsided, she spoke again.

"That is the most intense it has been. If anyone of the team had been captured, we would have got them out. As you can see, the teams have Realm Five firepower and support behind them and in less than two days, seven Commanders had been captured. The resultant effect in the London boroughs, has been massively reduced Leaf activity and the breakdown of organised control. On the back of this, many disillusioned Leaves have taken the decision to pass over to their rightful place in Realm Four, surrendering the valuable energy they have accrued through this acceptance," Ethan stepped forward.

"Harpies, hear our call. Will you fight with us?"

The resultant cheer was momentous in its spontaneous delivery. The Harpy chant expressed the majority feeling and commitment. On scanning the gathering, Ethan detected of the near one hundred and twenty thousand present, less than eight thousand either had decided not to be involved or doubted their ability to be of effective use in the call to arms.

He spoke in example to Nevaeh saying of the thirty-six thousand cities and towns in the United States, if Harpy numbers were divided into teams of three, optimistically, the States could be cleared of significant Commander Type Leaves in a few days, at most a week. Ethan again raised his hand, this time to quell the euphoria to enable Nevaeh to speak.

"We take it, that's a yes then!"

The laughing and cheers reverberated around the stone structure followed instantaneously with an influx of green light into the aurora in an expression of unconditional love through cohesiveness. This time, Nevaeh raised her hand.

"We need to assess your skills for combat readiness and train you if it is necessary, to provide you with arms enabling your effectiveness at task. My friend and colleague here, Greg, will be ultimately responsible for bringing you to that point. He needs to know which of you have combat experience in your Earthly incarnations, as once briefed, you will be involved in the training of others who have not. For your information, Greg revolved as part of the human line, however, he is a Black Eagle."

A cheer rang out from the southeast section of the amphitheatre as Greg stepped forward and waved his presence into the crowd before speaking.

"We thought it best to appoint representatives from the teams involved in the London and other covert missions to act as focal points of contact for each of our lines. Scout and Sarah here, will represent the horse line, Audaz and Conchita our raptor line and James, Alana and Simon the human form line. Simon is a Between Worlds veteran. He spent four hundred years in Between Worlds as a gatekeeper. He will be responsible for mission operations. What he does not know about Leaves is not worth knowing," added Greg.

Each of the team stepped forward in turn to show their identity.

"Some of you may not be aware as yet of our capabilities. When I speak of lines, there are in fact no lines, there are only Harpies. However, each of us has a raptor, horse and human form as part of who we are," said Nevaeh.

Nevaeh, signalled to the group on the dias, who transformed simultaneously into each form to demonstrate. Sarah's intuition had been correct as Simon transformed into a Suffolk Punch. She gave him a horsey grin and whinnied in appreciation. Simon snarted for effect, much to Scout's amusement.

"Finally, a fart buddy! I knew you had it in you."

"Had," responded Simon, smiling at Scout.

The group then transformed into human and finally raptor form.

"There are some skills which are unique to the lines and you will discover these as part of your progress. In particular, it seems that some of us have mythological roots," added Nevaeh.

Scout turned and trotted to the back of the dias before galloping at full speed towards the front edge and transforming to his Haast eagle. He took off beating his wings hard to rise in parallel with the top of the amphitheatre before exploding like a phosphorescent firework into his brilliant white Pegasus form. His two friends from Sarah's ranch also transformed to join him. Surprisingly, seven further Pegasus horses took off from the base tier to join the three in the air above.

There were expressions of awe as those present were amazed at what befell their eyes. Point made, all those airborne returned to their places. Nevaeh pointed out it appeared we had some among us, who had been extra vigilant in hiding their identities. An identity available to all those of the horse line. However, she warned them to let their new image, should they choose to embrace it, remain amongst us, as other dwellers in Realm Four tend to struggle with mythological beings. She continued.

"As I have said, we need to train and at the end of this meeting we will inform you of the next meeting. In order to reduce the training time however, you will have access to the skills we have been using in our battles to date. Some of you will know of these already and I ask for your patience. At the end of the meeting, I also need those with combat experience to make themselves known to our team here with me, so please remain in your places. With Ethan's help, I will mind link now," said Nevaeh.

The link engaged and all of the team's expertise was relayed to each and every Harpy. Sarah stepped forward and addressed the meeting. She commenced by saying it was recognised, not all would wish to fight.

"I will fight when I need to, but my nature chooses to listen and support. In our time in London, I witnessed the power and cruelty bestowed over and against vulnerable Leaves. Leaves who are frightened, manipulated and abused by both male and female Commanders and their followers. Many of these victims are children. I have been able to free some of them which for me, has made my presence in the team invaluable, because these spirits pass with the energy our Collective needs. Most importantly for me, I have helped them to trust. No team will be complete without a member who is attuned and focussed on helping the casualties of these dark pursuits. This role will be responsible for liaising with guides and catchers to help considerable numbers pass to our realm once the Commander operations have been arrested. This is good and valuable work. I say let the warriors be warriors and they let us do what we do best, heal."

Cheers rang out from individuals in all quarters in the amphitheatre, cheers filled with compassion, love and knowing, their owners identifying the other key quality of what it is to be a Harpy. Sarah continued.

"We need those who support and I will be responsible for coordinating this part of the operation. Warriors will respect you if you need to remove yourself from the conflict to do your work, but your team's welfare and support is your main priority."

This time, the audience responded with applause, stomping and high-pitched calls of respect. Sarah caught Tarquin's eye, as she turned and sent him the message that she needed to do this, rather than work in the dark. He acknowledged and respected her choice. 'You are who you are Sarah and I would not have it any other way'. 'Thank you, Tarquin'.

Ethan then closed the gathering.

"I have had the privilege today to enter the minds of each and every one of you. At essence, we are strongly cohesive. We instinctively act as one in our separateness and in case you have not noticed, we are far from extinct. Our task ahead is an arduous one, obviously one without the risk of death, but one which requires our unique abilities to trail blaze a route through to our after world's security. I am humbled to know the resilience of our true essence has not been lost through the ages and I am proud to be known as a Harpy. I send you the information concerning our next meeting. My belief is to see you all shortly. Thank you."

Nothing could be heard for the next three minutes as all present confirmed their respect and commitment. As the cheers reduced, individuals transported out to leave those with combat experience remaining.

The Warrior Tale

As others disappeared, Ethan confirmed those now remaining, numbered an astonishing seventy-five thousand.

"I think one to one interviews are going to be out of the question," stated Greg.

As a group, we all stepped forward, raising our arms with an open palm. "Warriors!" we all shouted in unison.

There was a rapturous response as seventy-five thousand voices returned their shout and salute, the horses drumming their hooves. Greg assumed pole position.

"It appears although our purpose has remained hidden for all of our lifetimes, we seem to have unconsciously been aware of our need to remain prepared. I assume that those of you as horses have ridden into battle and as raptors, you have fought adversaries as part of your status in the natural Earth world. I take it, those amongst you in human form will have had incarnations involving conflict. All of you are honoured for your knowledge and skills and all of you are needed."

Simon and I addressed the audience and through Ethan, transmitted all of the conflicts the Between Worlds team had been involved in. We included planning, reconnaissance, action and Leaf response. The action plan was for those with combat experience to lead teams of three warriors, a Harpy Leaf support officer, a guide and a catcher. The latter two would be familiar with the locations and Leaf Commander operations and would be substituted as teams progressed geographically. The leader of the team would be ultimately responsible for the decision to transfer Leaves to the darker realm.

"I am being informed by Ethan that as a whole, you represent all continents on Earth. We welcome your suggestion as to how we approach the fight. Whether you operate in your homelands individually as teams or clear continents one at a time as a total force," asked Simon.

The consensus of opinion was to clear continents between compass points. The rational was by acting on mass in one continent at a time, they would be able to clear wide geographic areas quickly and the flow of information alerting their actions would be slowed to other landmasses because of the oceans between continents.

"Specifically, your targets are those Leaves who would be candidates for either Realm One or Two if they chose to pass through the judgement process. A conscious information source has been generated for you to refer into, to check this status. You are at liberty to access the guide and catcher network to seek the support of those who are familiar with your target locations. Some degree of flexibility may be required as they will need to delegate their normal duties to meet with your requests," I instructed. Greg followed it.

"Teams. Having three highly experienced Harpy warriors working together may improve your odds of success, however, it will potentially reduce those odds for less experienced teams. You will have your personal agendas, whether they be tribal or friendship based. However, we are intuitively one race with the consciousness to know others and we are asking for your cooperation in forming effectively operational teams throughout the entire force. Can you put together your teams in the days after this meeting? If resolution is needed, come to us openly and we will resolve your issues," said Greg.

"Weapons," said Scout. "Our newest team member, Greg, when he arrived, was packing weapons we had not come across before. These were extremely effective in our sorties. Leaves are basically armed and do not command the variety we have in our arsenal. Ethan is now transmitting a data bank reference point to you, which when accessed contains weapon type, use of and contexts most effectively used in. My request is you access this bank and upload the same type of information on weaponry you are aware of, which are not included on our list. This will then be made accessible to all."

"Transformation," introduced Audaz. "Earlier it was made clear for those who did not know, we could transform into each of the different Harpy line forms. There will be times when you will need to present yourselves in the different forms, whether that be in Pegasus form for our horses or human form when we are covertly mingling amongst Leaves. Our signature form is raptor, not only because this is part of our heritage, but as well-known by our raptor line, flight and height provides massive advantage in combat. We would ask you to practice transforming and becoming familiar with your other line identities.

Unfortunately, for those in human and raptor form, you cannot achieve Pegasus status. This is something only our horses can achieve. So, be nice to your horse colleagues, as riding a Pegasus is an experience you definitely want to have."

There was a loud response of neighs and whinnies from the horses present. Audaz looked at Ethan who confirmed 'very few were aware of our battledress' back into his mind.

"I have something more to add. I refer you back to the episode you watched in the warehouse. Harpies are the subject of myth and legend for another reason. When we were being hunted on Earth, it was the females of our race who attempted to scare the humans away, so we might live in peace. As you may know, they were considerably larger and more powerful than us males. Conchita, Alana and Sarah here will demonstrate the formation of the ace up our sleeve."

The three females transformed to a level of full exposure with skin splitting, wings unfolding and faces contorting. At full height, they towered above the males in the group and screeched a menacing banshee call into the amphitheatre. There was silence for a moment among them, then six individuals followed suit. Ethan connected to all of the warriors keying in the transformational process and in a short period of time seventy-five thousand screeching Harpies in full battledress filled the theatre.

"Would you be afraid?" Audaz assertively challenged his audience.

"They will be," was the resounding response.

Alana, still in battledress raised her arm.

"We as the females of our race are more powerful than our males. That is the evolutionary product of our roles. Remember girls, the temptation to assert control through genetic power is strong, however, we must be fair and allow our males to equally assert theirs."

A cheer was raised from almost half of the audience, followed by a humorous response triggered from the acceptance of ancient social undercurrents within the race. Alana continued.

"Be mindful. Our society is based on a higher order of learned equality, however, in conflict it has been our female's instinctive role to protect. In battle, I experienced my nature to take control and eliminate threat and was able to overcome this urge by accepting the value of all who were in my team. Passion raised through instinct is powerful. Power can be harnessed by the team, but be aware that unbridled power can also undermine it. Fight together with one instinctual mind and with one aim. Just because we are bigger than them, ladies, doesn't make us better."

The murmurs of acceptance of Alana's words of wisdom reverberated amongst the crowd with many glances of acknowledgement shared between the sexes. Ethan raised his hand once more for Simon.

"I am glad I am on your side, Harpies. We have work to do. I look forward to meeting you back here in four days, at the same time. Bring together your teams and find your Leaf support officers. We will see you all then."

All on the dias saluted our respect and the huge gathering commenced its departure, to the sound of 'Harpy, Harpy, Harpy!'

After the last of them had left, Nevaeh created a cushioned seating circle for all the group to sit and voice their views. There was quiet and reflection for a few moments as everyone contemplated over the justification and concerns for what had just emerged for them. Ethan named the overriding notion in everyone's thoughts. It was followed by the thoughts of each member.

"We have just created an army. Probably the first of its kind in the entire history of the after world," said Ethan.

"This is true," said Nevaeh.

"But we attack to defend," said Tarquin.

"We attack to free others from oppression," said Sarah.

"We attack to restore order," said Simon.

"We attack those who are less defended and less powerful than us," added Scout.

"We attack to preserve balance," said Conchita and Audaz simultaneously.

"We attack, to eradicate what stands in our way," I added.

"And we attack in the doubt that whilst attempting to restore the order of systems that we believe to be right and true, we do so without the Collective directly initiating its impetus," summed up Alana.

"I think that sums it up. Cohesion fosters growth and we see and learn with new eyes. There were well over a hundred thousand Harpies here today who agree with our need and will follow our cause, because they believe what we do is right," said Ethan.

"How do you know? There are probably a hundred thousand plus Harpies out there, itching for a scrap. Because, they need to alleviate nearly a thousand years of self-oppression and denial of their true identities," I said in quick response, regretting the burst as soon as I had said it.

Ethan looked at me and smiled. I looked into my own palm as it met my face. "Because you are from Realm Six?" I added.

"I did not get to where I am today young James by not knowing," he replied.

Ethan delivered this in a West Yorkshire accent, weaved with humour. I laughed, as did the others. The journey towards knowing for all Realm Four residents was one racked with the instinct to be impulsive with etheric and disjointed reasoning. I put it down to seeking to be heard when struggling with the truth of justification, in order to alleviate the state of becoming overwhelmed by responsibility. Ethan caught my thought.

"I know you connect to what I have just allowed you to see about those in Realm Four struggling to know."

He then addressed us all by saying justification in taking any action against others was not always true. Justification conjoined with belief, was pivotal between doubt and faith. Both were brought by all of us in the reasons justifying our attack upon these darker Leaves. Matteo and Haadee had also expressed their views of believing the Collective operated by ultimate divine design and order. We always had the choice to do nothing, then sit in denial with the guilt of inaction when increasing difficulties revealed themselves and threatened us. Or we could act.

The only way to manage our own sense of being overwhelmed by responsibility was to consciously move to a place of faith, for within faith, lies trust. Faith was not a 'poof moment' where every doubt was magically dissolved. Faith was a state of being which provided clarity and the stability needed to trust our actions and achieve our aims more responsibly. By doubting least our own abilities within our move towards accepting faith, we would succeed in changing systems which pretty much every high planer, knew, needed to change.

"Let us bestow that faith upon our army and trust they will succeed," concluded Ethan.

Every member of the group including Nevaeh and Tarquin voiced their acceptance of Ethan's words. Ethan reminded us that he was not in need of our humility and that he was the same as us, just knew a bit more.

He also knew that he was responsible for recruiting, requesting and motivating our involvement in a monumental action, which would purport all worlds into a new way of order. In support, he covertly transmitted portions of divine will from his own personal reserves to each of us, which would act as a personal faith fertiliser.

"I must raise a concern," said Sarah. "It's about helping those Leaves who realise their true path means passing to the after world. I can foresee the leaf support officers, getting side tracked and bogged down by the potential numbers wishing to pass."

"We are aware of that," replied Tarquin. "Nevaeh and I are endeavouring to gain the support of the religious groups. Rather than waiting to engage their groups after we have segregated the darker Leaves, we think they should join us on the ground as the clearing is taking place."

They both envisaged the support officers referring Leaves into the religious teams, or delegating support actions to them. They could then arrange block transitions with catchers, thus relieving the pressures on the combat teams to maintain their momentum. Their other role would be to encourage other Leaves who were unsure, to make that transition. They had enough numbers to effectively maintain a constant flow.

There was an uneasiness amongst us concerning the religious groups, put in place by their struggle with us as shown at the initial meetings with them present. Ethan picked it up.

"I wish to quell your angst. During the gathering, Nevaeh identified the shadow that was cast upon us in our history by humans. That shadow of difference was driven by religion. It is a fact and we must accept that every group strives to maintain their difference in the light of what they believe to be true. Much as we do. At core, all religions hold the same essence."

"Each religion wants everyone to follow their religion," interrupted Simon. Tarquin answered him.

"They believe peace is achieved through unity and it is. But it is unity with the acceptance and compassion of difference, which is essential for growth. Their agendas are based on the paradigm inherent in all sentient beings: how do I keep myself safe, in order to live peacefully. We need to help them accept the bigger picture of how we keep our entire existence safe and in balance. My belief is they will be motivated to help others. Their challenge will be to do so impartially as ambassadors and representatives of the after world, not as recruiters into doctrine."

"In my experience, many Leaves have turned away from religions and they are cautious of guides and catchers. If they are unable to achieve the challenge you identify, many Leaves will not trust them enough to transition," said Simon.

"Have faith in Tarquin and Nevaeh, as I have faith in those religious groups, they seek cooperation from and watch this space," concluded Ethan.

Everyone was clear on what needed to be done and it was agreed we would meet back at the amphitheatre an hour before the start of the next meeting.

"A big thank you to all here who are making this happen. I could not do this without you," expressed Ethan.

Saying their goodbyes for now, the three high planers dematerialised.

"Are the rest of you coming back to the ranch?" asked Sarah.

Audaz and Conchita said they were in need of some forest, so would catch them later. Alana and I had a date in Capri and Scout and Greg had decided to visit Scout's sanctuary which I had created for him, what seemed like a lifetime ago.

"I want to show Greg what it is like to be a Pegasus, albeit in virtual world. We will join you later," said Scout.

"Before we all leave, was your partner here today, Greg?" asked Alana.

"She was, but she knew I was tied by all of this, so didn't approach."

"You must introduce her to us."

"Warrior or healer?" asked Sarah.

"Definitely warrior. She is, how can I say, very unique. He will show her true self when amongst friends though," Greg replied with a smile.

Each of the group experienced a double take on Greg's words, but did not pursue the subject further. Alana entered his mind at the same time linking to me.

"Please, both of you come to dinner tomorrow night in Capri?"

"We will be there. Thank you," he replied back through the mind link.

Hugs and kisses exchanged, all of the group transported out.

Normalising

On our arrival back in Capri, we relaxed on the veranda. With Alana sitting into me and my arm folding around her, we both stared blankly out to sea. Straying from my mindless absorption, I slipped into household routines from distant memories. Alana, reading my mind, went with my flow.

"Shall we see what's on TV or just read for a while?"

"No, I fancy doing some gardening. But we could go out for a walk if you like," Alana responded.

"Ohh… Just remembered. We better collect Tiggles from the cattery," I said.

"It's okay; they said they will drop her off later."

"Why did you call her Tiggles anyway?" I asked.

"Because she likes it."

"And I suppose she told you, did she?"

"No, you numpty. She likes Tiggles."

"Whatever. Any chores to do?"

"No, I did all of them yesterday."

"Oh, thank you, you are a star. I do my fair share though, don't I?"

"Yeah, most of the time, even though I might have to ask you more than once."

"That makes me feel just, a little less guilty."

Alana sat up and met my eyes. The words 'bloody hell' were spoken in unity.

"We are a part of this," exclaimed Alana.

"I know. Just to think, I was a fifteen-year-old schoolboy on earth, less than a year ago and you were waiting for me to come back. Now we are involved in restructuring the after world."

"Odd how we just chose to fantasise about the mundane, when the practice is normally done to engage in what is far removed from it?" replied Alana.

"Ummm. I think it is just a polar response to normalise the fact that our realities are the subjects of fantasy and the responsibilities of the mundane, are a contrast to momentarily avoid the massive responsibilities we are now facing."

"Can I get you a drink?" asked Alana.

"Yes please. Got any lager? If not Lennon flower, will do nicely," I said, linking to a nostalgic memory.

We both laughed with and at each other in trying to observe yet another normality which on Earth, may hold the promise of the ability to avoid that which was pressingly important. Instead of alcohol numbing the senses, John always enabled an absorption into his emotional genius, lifting the mind to an alternative.

My thoughts strayed to the Dark Realms and I could feel Alana enter my mind.

"I am up for it you know," she said.

"I know you are and of all the people in the universe, you would always be my choice to accompany me back into them."

"Sweetie!"

"I know we are who we are and have chosen each other by design, yet we are a perfect match. It's funny when you fall in love, you somehow feel you know the other, or all is suspended leaving only a clear view of your total need for them. Yet when you gain knowing, all of the things which would distract or divert from that clarity, do not and the view remains clear whatever."

"Put simply, you mean you really love me, don't you?"

"Yes, of course I do," I said smiling at her.

"Why is it, James, you spend time becoming involved in the intricacies of understanding processes which need nothing more than your thought free acceptance of them? I tell you what, I like to visit your mind but I am thankful I can return to mine. I'd go nuts if I had to stay in there for too long."

"Oh, thanks. It hasn't made me nuts though?" Responding with the slightest of an imagined wound incurred.

"We have only a few hours before our guests arrive, let us not enter that arena of debate," Alana raised her eyebrows knowingly.

"Bastard," I said.

"Complex git," she replied.

I took her in my arms and squeezed her affectionately.

"I wouldn't ever, ever, ever be without you." I smiled into her eyes.

"I wouldn't ever, ever, ever be without you either."

Her returned smile and look confirmed her eagerness for intimacy. She led me to our domed sanctuary and we kissed searchingly as if trying to find a miniscule thread of doubt which if detected, we would both lovingly hold safely for one other. No such doubts were existent between Alana and me, because we had a gift beyond doubt.

We held, loved and experienced each other within an imaginary window of time pressing, not allowing the time to make any difference.

Harpy pairings were somehow, divinely arranged when we were jointly created. It was true on Earth, many humans believed in the relational concept of the 'one', therefore this arrangement might even exist for them also. However, it was rarely found, perhaps because they lacked the level of instinctual knowing we evolved to possess.

If the ideal of the one was abandoned by them in pursuit of security, they learned to compromise and with it, developed that hunger to know or deny the truth. This, I speculated, was a hunger baited by the Collective, an influence inherent in all, to foster change and accrue energy for the ongoing maintenance of the whole system.

I was so glad I was Harpy. Lives hold many doubts and in truth, so have mine and Alana's. Yet even when we had to separate, having only met for a short time during Earth revolutions, we parted always knowing we would come back together.

I decided, of all the doubt life entailed, not having doubt in relationship, was the ultimate state to achieve. I did not know why humans were not like us in evolutionary abilities, but I did feel sorry for them for not having the instinctual trust we had and the capacity to read and accept truthfully.

"Realm Four, calling James."

"I am here. I am just thinking."

Although being Harpy at core, we still lived in the belief we were human whilst on Earth. With it, we were party to the need to assume roles and deliver psychosocial and cultural expectations. These like the words of our parents, follow us into the future, some remaining more dormant than others as we carry them through our progressive lifetimes.

I could sense Alana's delight wrapped in the risk of choosing her next line, however, she concealed it from me. Whatever it would be, I knew it was loaded to exert pressure upon me to respond to her need for security. A security engineered from these social expectations that were now purely delivered out of nostalgia rather than actual need. It was a bit of a game really and at the same time, reminded us of the vulnerabilities we had experienced. The choice was whether to play or not.

"Why don't you cuddle me longer after we have made love?" she asked.

"Dunno really, got things to do, my car needs washing and the match is on later."

"Is your car and the match more important than my feelings then. Sounds like they are?"

"No darling, course not. You know I love you and when we are apart, I think of you loads, honest."

"I love you too, but actions are more powerful than thoughts, are they not?"

"Ah, I get it. I am thinking you are looking for a bit more action?"

"No. Go and wash your car, James!"

The realisation for both of us was, we were doing it again. We were polarising away from the massive responsibilities we were taking on.

"I trust the high planers, James, and I have faith that we are acting in the best interests of the Collective."

"I think we are experiencing that faith, doubt and responsibility dilemma, Ethan spoke to us about. I also think that having revealed it to us, we have a clearer view that what we are doing is right," I replied.

"I agree. We will be fine. Have faith. Mine is growing stronger as we speak," reassured Alana.

"Yes, mine too. What are we having for dinner tonight, darling?" I asked.

"Oh my God, it had totally slipped my mind. What's the time? What about a take away?"

"Perfect. Greek all right?"

"Lovely."

"I will give them a call. Let's hope they deliver."

We smiled widely at each other and laughed.

"If you can't beat them, join them I say," said Alana knowingly.

"Thank you. A generous concession to accepting I am perfectly sane!"

"Enough! We have about twenty minutes before Greg and…umm, arrive. Do you know her name?"

"No idea. That's odd, Greg chose not to reveal it. I don't know what kind of raptor she is either, possibly a Black Eagle?" I asked.

"No idea either?"

The evening light glowed with blushes of pinks and soft reds as the sun made its decent towards the horizon. Above the rosy border, the sky darkened to deep blues and then blackness with stars making their presence known, as shards of light splintered from their source in a helical display.

Alana had created a welcoming atmosphere with the position of small soft candles set next to potted plants and shrubs. I had strung fairy lights in our lemon tree, accentuating the hanging fruit and set a fire pit ablaze to take the edge off the cooling night air and to also act as a beacon for our guests. Our favoured fragrance of jasmine hung in the air, provided by the huge plant which had grown and spread across the doorway to our villa from the veranda.

As we sat on the stone balustrade blending with all which was around us, a feeling of peace met with our awareness. Yet, an element of intrigue befell us both in the wait for their imminent arrival.

Two black silhouettes came into view above the island opposite, then dived steeply for the water. Flying centimetres above the surface, they were only just visible as they made their way across the inlet before disappearing beneath us and rising to the veranda edge. We both stepped back giving them landing space. The two birds alighted in synchrony with Alana and I presenting ourselves in our raptor form out of respect for our own race. She was a Black Eagle like Greg.

"Alana, James, this is Ichtaca my mate," introduced Greg.

"Hello, good to meet you at last. I was starting to think Greg was hiding you away from us. Ichtaca? Isn't that an ancient Aztec name, meaning secret? I thought your tribe was based in Ethiopia? How did you get that name?" asked Alana, who was searching like mad, trying to find a way through Ichtaca's mind defences.

"My human shoe size is seven, if that is important as well," she replied with a gesture designed to repel and blunt the intrusiveness.

Greg and I caught each other's eyes, him responding with a slight raise of his brow. He said nothing and continued to watch and listen. Alana transformed to human form, as did I, followed by Greg and Ichtaca.

"Pleased to meet you, Ichtaca. Come let's sit. Can I get you both a drink? Elderflower and Jasmine, suit you?" I said, them both accepting my offer.

I could tell Alana was a little perturbed, as she was only trying to make conversation and had not meant to offend. I linked secretly to her to sooth her angst.

"I am picking up shy and a little introverted. That's all darling, there are no worries here."

To look at, Ichtaca was slightly darker skinned than Greg, tall and with fine, yet strong features. Her hair was jet black and shoulder length and her eyes dark brown. With broad shoulders and long limbs, she was narrow at the waist, lithe and held the look of a warrior. She was both beautiful and handsome at the same time.

"My shoe size is six," said Alana with a smile. "Please forgive me, I did not mean my opening words to be like an interrogation. If I proceed gently in trying to get to know you, would you be more at ease? For I sense you have had to remain hidden and defended at another level, alongside that of our race having to?"

"And I sense the meaning of serenity emerge through your name Alana. You are correct in your deduction. My lifetimes have not been easy and I have learned to use judgement in reverse on those who judge and when they have not stopped, I have hidden myself away. I can be a bit defensive when I meet new people, as to truly know another, one has to present oneself as you truly are. I am not ashamed of who I am, but if I show myself, there are always questions and uncertainty and in some, fear and aberration. Even now, I can pick up your intrigue and detect your thoughts and feelings oscillating in possible enquiry," replied Ichtaca.

I chose to sooth. "Let me use the words you have heard thousands of times, however, base them on your knowledge of the actions we take in service to the after world. You will be aware from Greg what we do. I open my mind, feelings and knowing to you, as I know Alana will also do. The word is trust. But also know that if your experiences are different to those we have or know, we would choose to be able to share them with you. Not only to satisfy our curiosity as that is how we learn, but to understand and be able to empathise with your feelings and lives' journeys," I requested.

Ichtaca looked at both Alana and I and then at Greg. He smiled at her and in it reminded her of his total acceptance for who she was. Ichtaca transformed into her true eagle. She had brilliant white feathers, pink ceres, feet and talons and bright blue eyes. She shook her feathers readying herself for inspection.

"So you are a white version of a Black Eagle. That is very rare. I can see how you would stand out and be noticeable amongst your tribe," I said.

"That is just stage one," said Ichtaca and transformed back to human form.

Instead of our impressions taken in when we first met her, her dark colouration had been replaced by a pale white skin, white hair and the same-coloured eyes as her eagle. If she had kept her wings in a scale befitting her current form, she would have looked in image like an archetypal angel.

"Been there, done that. Let me tell you, it doesn't go down too well." She read my thoughts.

"You are albino, aren't you?" said Alana. "I can understand that you would be highly visible to others around you and the subject of wonder."

"Much more than wonder, Alana. I have been called many things which express others non-acceptance of who I am."

Having refreshed the drinks, we retired to the cushioned stone semi-circle which part surrounded the fire pit. We had all decided we were not hungry, although I promised to rustle up some pudding later, if anyone was feeling peckish or hungry. All of us lost ourselves in the flames as we reflected on the difficulty of difference. In that moment, I was reminded of Bill in Realm Three.

"Are you all right, Greg? You seem a little quiet," asked Alana.

"Yes, I am fine. I have spent the day trying to fill it with mundane things in light of what we are about to embark upon."

"We have done exactly the same and had some really random conversations involving gardening and washing cars," I said.

"Yep, I've been cutting lawns and picking black berries in the hedgerows. All memories of course. Although I could have gone into virtual world and scythed a meadow or two," he replied.

As we sat watching the flames flicker and caste shades of light and shadow upon our faces, I noticed Alana taking occasional glances at Ichtaca.

"Are you watching me, Alana?" she asked.

"Yes, I am. You have an amazing face. As the light from the flames brightens and subdues, your face seems to change. It is almost like you shift between being beautiful and handsome. Please do not misinterpret me, they are of equal attractiveness and honestly, I find you mesmerising, like your face is telling me stories. I find your face attractive," declared Alana.

"Are you attracted to me?" she asked in response.

Alana linked to me. I knew exactly what she was talking about.

"I am, but I don't understand how I am."

I looked at Greg. My need to also be open with Ichtaca was sent to his mind and he responded with a smile and a nod.

"I also feel this attraction and like Alana, do not understand how I am either," I said.

Ichtaca took a deep breath and declared her stage two was her shift from her eagle to her albino human form. However, her stage three of disclosure was she was both albino, male and female.

"I am different from humans because I am Harpy, different because my look is extreme and different because I am of both sexes. My last difference has been a curse," she divulged.

Sadly, both males and females from Harpy and human races saw something in her which when they are not aware, propelled them to seek relationship or a sexual encounter with her. It seemed she did not have the same value and respect of those who are single sexed in comparison. It was as though she was fair game, something pursuable without her need to provide consent being important to them.

There had been many cruel acts played against her and this had been the same in each of her lifetimes. She had even lived one lifetime in prostitution believing her purpose was to be a whore, but it did not serve her truth, so in others she remained a secret.

"I am glad you have told us, and I am glad you chose for us to experience the hypnosis of your appeal. Both James and I are aware beings, yet we were drawn to your enigmatic vibration. You are truly beautiful and unique, and yet have such a heavy responsibility as well as having to deal with the painful consequences of just being you," said Alana.

Alana rose from her seat and faced Ichtaca with open arms. She assumed nothing and was prepared should she choose to defend. Ichtaca smiled at Alana and met her embrace, a blue collar of light appearing level with their throats.

"As you have said Greg, you have a very unique partner and I now understand your words before we left the meeting, which made Alana and I double take," I said.

"It's a real pain in the arse though," he replied.

Both Alana and I were a little taken back by his unsupportive response, yet Ichtaca did not respond at all. I looked at Greg with a tone of slight disapproval, and aimed a message of 'be a little more supportive, it must be very hard for her'.

"It wasn't aimed at her. She is more courageous than me," said Greg.

Greg transformed into a white eagle.

"Now I have loads of questions," stated Alana.

"Thought you might," said Ichtaca, smiling at Greg who had transformed to his albino human form. She continued:

"Having been embraced in a collar of blue light with you and experienced who you both are; we will always be straight with you. Just know us through our disguises and let us decide on the trust of others along the way. By the way, Greg calls me Taca. You may too, if you wish."

"That makes sense. Kabalarian origin, isn't it?" asked Alana.

"It is," confirmed Greg.

"Let us tell you," said Taca.

The foremost thought in Alana's mind concerned children. They had had two together in all of their lifetimes and it was possible for them both to carry a child in human form. Even on Earth as humans, if either of them became pregnant, others just saw what was obvious to them.

They were created from the same Harpy source, however, genetically they both carried anomalous genes which appeared in human and raptor form. Other than themselves, they were not aware of others like them and it was not until their third lifetime did they realise what they thought of as a curse, held a further gift within it. This was the gift of being able to present to others in the guise of the opposite sex, as well as being able to change appearance on Earth to obscure their albino condition.

These gifts had been used in their frequent military vocations in either covert ground-based operations as teams or on their own. Being natural shape-shifters provided effective disguises. Although they were different personalities, their instinctual awareness was the same and there were no misunderstandings between them, which might have been created by gender difference. It was obvious both Greg and Taca were perfectly matched, a match made in heaven as one might say. But one which came at great cost, however, with the potential of great knowing.

"Would you two be happy to work together with us as part of our team?" I asked. Alana acknowledged and supported my question.

"We would. Since Ethan transmitted battledress ability at the meeting, I have been imagining the dark Leaves faces when one of us in albino form materialised in front of them. Thank you for accepting us as who we are," said Taca.

"Thanks for coming. We will introduce you to the team. I think you will find, as you have experienced, Greg, but not yet revealed, you can be yourself among them. Anyone fancy some pudding yet?" I invited.

"Yes, we can do pudding. We will trust the surprise and your judgement we will like it," replied Taca.

Four steaming bowls of strawberry jam roly-poly and custard appeared before us. We all tucked in and having cleaned our bowls, shared our stories late into the night.

Preparations

The day after dinner with Greg and Taca, we all met up at Sarah and Simon's ranch. When Greg introduced Taca to everyone, the welcome she received convinced her she was among true friends who would hold her concerns in their hearts. Within the space of an hour, both she and Greg had revealed their secret and shared their vulnerabilities and worries behind their choice to remain hidden. With time allowing, Taca was able to get to know us more. In particular, she was drawn to Scout.

"Greg has spoken a lot about you, Scout. It seems you and he have become good friends," said Taca.

"I trust him completely. He has taught me a lot in combat and he has an ability to know my horse sense at a level beyond others. I like him and I am glad he is part of our team."

"I hear you took him to your sanctuary in virtual world to go Pegasus flying?"

"Yes. We had great fun. It makes sense now, why he chose to imagine himself as a white horse. Funny, I thought then he looked virtually real. You know us don't you, like he does, I mean us, as in horses," said Scout.

"We have the same instinctual ability, that's true. During lifetimes on Earth, animals were mostly my friends, however, I was able to understand horses the most and they accepted me unconditionally. Greg was the same. I think it's because Greg and I possess a finely honed awareness of transitional will, as do horses."

"I am still perfecting the transformation to other lines. I have been a horse all of my lifetimes and James only woke me earlier this year. I know the sense you mean though," he replied.

Taca transformed into her horse. Scout, not even the slightest bit shocked, stood his ground admiring her form. She snarted loudly.

"Excuse me," she said.

"No need to snart around me, or excuse yourself, you just blast away. I am picking up two breeds. Lipizzaner and something else?"

"Yes. I am mixture of both Marwari and Lipizzaner and an albino version of course."

"You are beautiful in our form. Greg is a lucky Harpy. You must know, I say this in light of what you said before about others being attracted to you. What stirs in me is something which is a little different. It makes me want to protect you," he said.

"I know. In my lifetimes of feeling unsafe, it has been horses who have transferred this sense to enable me to feel stronger. They have always been my closest. Speaking of closest, where is your partner, Scout?" asked Taca.

"Still on Earth, although she is an old mare now. I visit her occasionally and as you would know, she knows I am there. I do not wish for her to come here sooner, she will come in her own time and I will be here to meet her."

"What is her name?"

"Suleta."

"That's North American Indian, isn't it? As in to fly, to fly around?"

"Well, Scout had his eagle, didn't he?"

Taca changed back to her human form smiling her response to his comment.

"Do you think they will let me work with you as part of the Harpy Horses, I would like that. Greg has a lot to do in his role and I want to fit in somewhere?"

"I happen to know; Sarah really wants to be more involved with those who will help Leaves come over. She may be happy to relinquish her contact point role for the horses for you to take on. Come on, let's go back and talk to everyone about it," said Scout, optimistic of the idea.

Their discussions revealed Sarah's concern for not having enough time to supervise and help Leaf Support Officers and she gladly received Taca's considered request. With a job role confirmed, Taca became one of our team.

The day of the meeting came and as a full team, we arrived at the amphitheatre an hour before the start as arranged. Tarquin received Taca warmly and the proposal for her role. It appeared that Ethan had speculated upon her emergence and knowing both her and Greg's histories, had briefed Tarquin and Nevaeh previously on their true status and abilities. Tarquin gave Nevaeh's apologies, as she was elsewhere on important business with the religious group leaders.

"Were you able to gain any support from the religious groups to help our teams?" asked Sarah.

"Yes. Ideally, they see this as their contribution to the campaign and will be on call to Leaf Support Officers when conflicts take place. However, dialogue is necessary in order to balance representation and decide who will head up their support force. Therefore, a little more time is needed to secure the macro, whilst others have been sorting out micro details," responded Tarquin.

Their resources ran into the millions and an interreligious dialogue council had been set up to ascertain the best course of action. Having been made aware of many Leaves not trusting religions, it was suggested multi faith teams were created so that each belief, where possible, was represented in one action. In the face of interreligious rivalry, this also encouraged transparency to the methods of enlightening prospective transitionary Leaves.

There was active discouragement in Leaves being told, part of the Earth was about to destruct and they would be better off in heaven than staying Between Worlds. It was agreed the choice to come over must be based on personal will and not on some fear placed to evoke a result and a proviso that a religion be adopted to facilitate salvation.

Ethan arrived and with him was Hillary, his Realm Six colleague, the high planer now holding responsibility for the Harpy Whales.

"Morning, everyone, this is Hills. We thought it better if she was the communicator for the support element of the teams, whilst I focus on the warrior's meeting. The plan is we separate them, hence the addition of a smaller amphitheatre for their use. We have also added to the main one in anticipation of more attending."

Hills, a golden eagle Harpy, with a history in the human line, introduced herself to everyone and in particular Sarah. She made Sarah aware that she knew of her wanting to focus on the support group. The two of them had a short conversation in preparation for the meeting.

"How is Theseus?" asked Alana.

"A little on the jealous side. He would have loved to have been involved in the forthcoming events, now that you have shown him how to cross to Between Worlds and transform to his raptor. He has made a few trips since you met him, as has his partner," replied Hills.

"We didn't mean to cause a problem," I added.

"You didn't, James. He knows his work is important to us and his trips are not detracting from it. I am happy he can experience another degree of freedom in addition to the oceans. I am also happy others in the tribe will become aware of their ability to transform. All of his tribe are aware of Thaddeus's departure from his responsibility and my new role," reassured Hills.

"Tarquin, has there been any progress on planning for catchers to intercept dark individuals coming from the Earth plane into Between Worlds as soon as they pass?" asked Simon.

"That is the great bit of our news. Although it has been less than four days, we have communicated with and instructed the entire guide and catcher network. The new system of 'on death' judgement, has already been instated and is operational across two thirds of the Earth. We expect global coverage within the day," confirmed Tarquin.

"Any issues?" asked Simon.

"Yeah, a few and those few have been given the opportunity to go to the after world or have been returned to the lighter part of Between Worlds. We expect issues, but where errors are made, those returning, do so with the knowledge of a not so nice place to live. I am sure they will be telling others about it," said Tarquin.

"Design errors, or errors by design?" I questioned.

Tarquin responded in a way which understood my point, but maintained the credibility of catcher's instruction. Changing the subject, I confirmed Alana's agreement to come into the Dark Realms. Tarquin had already happened to bump into Arthur at a guide and catcher meeting and broached the subject with him. He was happy to come with us, although said he would be careful where he trod this time.

"Thomas, your Dark Realms guide is also up for working with you again. He speaks highly of you and enjoyed your ethos and methods, although at the time was worried about the backlash from Gerry. He sends his regards. Why does he call you bird boy?" asked Tarquin.

I laughed and told him that whilst we were sparring, we had reduced our dialogue to name-calling and I had nick named him mop head in retaliation.

"What has happened to Gerry and Thaddeus?" I asked.

"I can't really say, James. I haven't seen Gerry since the meetings he had with the higher planers. It has been a Realm Seven issue," replied Tarquin.

As the time to start approached, each level of the theatre was filled to capacity. Word of a quest to unite and emerge had enticed many more to join those from the previous gathering. Ethan and Hills counted one hundred and forty-two thousand in total, not far off the total population of Harpies currently present in Realm Four. As last time, our group walked onto the dias to the sound of cheers, whinnies, shrill cries and applause. Simon and Sarah walked to the front edge and silence befell the arena.

"Decided to come back then?" shouted Simon in a broad Yorkshire accent.

Laughter filled the entire amphitheatre, followed by cheers after which Simon continued.

"Welcome, Harpies. I salute you. Your presence warms my heart and strengthens my courage. This new feeling of suddenly not being as alone as I thought, empowers me to face this task with added purpose. A purpose not just to free Between Worlds from oppression and tyranny, but a purpose to unite our tribes and race to take our rightful place in heaven's society, as who we are. Many more of you have come today and we are over joyed for your company as well as the Harpy skills you bring."

Introducing Hills, Simon explained that she and Sarah would coordinate and brief all those wishing to support the combat teams and help Leaves pass over. A separate meeting had been arranged to facilitate this. He then introduced Taca, who would take Sarah's place as the horse focal point with Scout. She transformed to her horse form and to introduce familiarity, farted loudly, much to the delight and vocal appreciation of the equine warriors and Scout. Simon raised his arm to speak.

"Thanks for that, Taca, and just to say, Greg will be discussing weapons shortly. I must point out, however, we will be following the protocols of the Earth-bound Chemical Weapons Convention. Therefore, the use of chemical weapons is not permitted during this campaign."

Laughter again filled the amphitheatre.

"Non-toxic varieties, however, may be used at the discretion and free-will of the instigator, as I understand from my friend Scout, it is an integral part of Harpy horse communication," said Simon.

Following the humour break, Simon detailed that Leaf support officers would have a direct link with the followers of the religious groups, who would back up the teams enabling other Leaves to pass. This would allow Leaf Support Officers to move on to the next conflict area with their team.

It was made clear that other than guides and catchers, only the combat team leaders held the power to judge Leaf candidates to go into the new Between Worlds dark realm. Others including the support officers and religious group members would not have this responsibility. They would have access to the likely realm destination database for potentially passing Leaves and were there to guide, inspire and enable choice.

Sarah stepped up and made them all aware of the other meeting venue, giving the coordinates of the smaller amphitheatre.

"LSOs, we have some important information of our own to cover. Let's all relocate now."

Ethan calculated the total number of warriors remaining at one hundred and five thousand and Hills, the support officers at thirty-seven thousand. This meant there would be thirty-five thousand teams with an excess of two thousand support officers who would be allocated amongst them. Ethan spoke to the warrior crowd.

"With the numbers present today, we will have about thirty-five thousand teams to do this job. It may seem a formidable task when you consider the Leaf population stands at six hundred and fifty million and our targets, we estimate to be in the region of fifty million individuals. Simon and Greg will take you through the maths shortly and explain what we are up against. Simon has chosen the UK as an example as this is where his battles have taken place." He handed over to Simon.

"There are forty-nine thousand cities, villages and hamlets in the UK with less urban concentrations in Eire. So, you could say with our number of teams, we could clear the UK and Eire in twenty-four hours, as not every populated area will have dark Leaves." He handed over to Greg.

"It is possible yes, but you have to consider the size of the cities and the concentration of targets. We hit only five main areas in London and captured a total of thirty-one targets within thirty-six hours. We got lucky on the final sortie because one Commander had guests. Realistically, we were capturing about four or five targets per mission," explained Greg. Simon continued.

"On a global scale, with the number of teams achieving three strikes in twenty-four hours, capturing and then redeploying targets to the dark realm, we reckon we can clear the planet in three and a half months. It is more likely to be four because the religious teams will want Sundays off and we need them to follow up our trail blaze," proposed Simon.

A single cry went up from the audience. "Is that all. I want at least a six-month contract!"

A bolt of laughter echoed around the amphitheatre and Ethan confirmed to the team that the consensus of opinion was four months was acceptable. One of the benefits of being able to instantaneously transport home during rest periods.

"You, my friend, can stay on for twelve as a mark of my respect for your commitment," said Simon.

"Seriously, there will be work afterwards for those who wish to remain involved. One thing that will slow you up is Leaf Commanders and seniors running and hiding," said Greg, Simon expanded.

"We relied on our own team members, like Greg to track unique vibrations when we were in London, to locate displaced Commanders. Ideally as teams, you will need some reference point to connect into, like the realm destination facility to check the dark status of Leaves," said Simon looking at Tarquin. Tarquin stepped up.

"We have achieved this. All of the guides around the world know or know of the Leaf targets we are seeking. They have uploaded every vibration into the same database. If one of the team's targets runs and a guide or assigned reconnaissance team member is not available, every combat team member can access this directly. A link system providing known associates is automatically triggered when a particular vibration is accessed and identified," explained Tarquin.

"Taking out the Commanders is the main priority. We must maintain momentum when driving through continents, therefore if team leaders consider time is more important than capturing a missing accomplice, leave them. We will know which have been missed and teams can choose to redeploy once the main campaign for a particular continent is completed. So, for the hungry Harpy wanting overtime, there's your answer!" said Simon.

There was a cheer of enthusiasm, before Greg spoke again.

"Weapons! A big thank you for all of your weapon uploads. There seems to be a lot of consistency with what we are already aware of and have used in the past. I do have a particular favourite though and we now regret making this exercise anonymous. Who, if you would like to declare yourself, uses a pink powder-puff grenade?"

There was silence before a young man stood up and raised his hand. "Me!"

"Are you up for telling us how it works? There is no pressure."

"No pressure hey, having just got me to stand up?" he replied.

"Well, would you like to demonstrate it?" asked Greg.

The young man disappeared in an instant. Reappearing beneath the dias, he threw the grenade and vanished, returning back to his seat. No one with the exception of Ethan, who had moved out of the blast range, was expecting him to take such an action. Everyone hit the deck with no time to transport out.

The grenade exploded in mid-air above our group, covering everyone with a fine pink dust. The effect was immediate with group members laughing then starting to hug each other. There was absolute uproar as everyone joined in, laughing at the humorous scene confronting them. In just less than three minutes, the effects wore off to silence on the dias as our team members composed themselves. Then all of us burst out laughing and applauded.

"Young man, your new code name is Powder Puff. That was brilliant. How does it work?" asked Greg.

"It's a chakra happ-e-hour cocktail, designed to divert the victim's attention. The pink light dust causes the victim to feel overwhelmed with happy emotions and makes them want to hug people. Should cheer the miserable bastards up a bit before things get dark for them," he replied.

The place roared to his suggestion.

"Thank you, young sir, perfect. With all your permissions, Ethan will now link in and update you with the content of the arsenal and the contexts of their use," said Greg. Simon continued.

"Teams. Ethan informs me you have mostly formed your teams. With the majority present from the human line, it will not be possible for each Harpy line to have a presence in each team. For those who yet need to find members and wish some help to do so, Ethan has created a database site which he is now transmitting the link for. Don't ask me how he does it but when you upload your vibration and the numbers you require, you will find compatible team member vibrations. His knowing is based on friendships, personalities, expertise, experience, decision-making abilities and of course, personal knowing. He informs me his equations encompass everyone. We will have a thirty-minute break now to enable you to locate your comrades," instructed Simon.

"Ethan, when you say the teams are mostly formed. Does that include the support officers?" asked Simon.

"Yes, it does. Hills has just briefed the support group on the same link. They are also having a break to enable support officers to locate warriors and vice versa," he replied.

The amphitheatre was active with individuals transporting to various locations for a meet and greet with new members. Powder puff reappeared, but this time on the dias.

"Excuse me; it seems that I am in a team with you, Taca and Scout. There must be some mistake. You are, you know, the leader Harpies and I am a foot soldier."

"No mistake. Do you think we were going to sit around whilst you lot had all the fun? We are going out there with you," replied Taca.

"Who is our leader?" asked Powder Puff.

"She is," answered Scout, motioning towards Taca.

"Whilst code names are all good and fun, what is your name?" asked Taca.

"I am Roman."

"Well, pleased to meet you, Roman. What training have you had?" asked Scout.

"I was in the army serving meals in the officer's mess. I did some boot polishing, ironing and some light dusting too, but I really wanted to get out there with the other boys and fight," he said.

He was met with silence and open mouths.

"If you could see your faces," he said smiling. "Not really, I was in the Russian infantry, specialising in mortar fire and hand to hand combat. I can also put a grenade in a bucket from fifty metres."

"Hence the accuracy of your powder puff pitch earlier. What's your raptor, Roman?" asked Taca.

"White tailed eagle and my horse is a unicorn."

"A unicorn! Never. Unicorns are mythical creatures," said Scout.

"Says the Pegasus himself! You are right, joking aside, I am a Prezewalski wild horse. We are pretty hardy," he replied.

"Sounds good. Last interview question, can you fart?" said Scout.

"Remember what I said earlier?" said Simon who was ear wigging.

"Take no notice of him, his horse is a Suffolk Punch. Large backside, incredible reverberation," said Scout, smiling at Simon.

"Yeah, I've been known to blow a tune or two through it," Roman answered.

"Excellent, you've got the job, welcome on board. We are about to start again so we will see you later," said Scout.

"Simon? Conchita and I do not seem to have a team?" said Audaz.

"You haven't. I need you in a more important role."

Audaz raised his head feathers in recognition of his status as he elbowed Conchita. Their first mission was to accompany the teams through South America, as this was difficult territory to navigate and Simon needed their expertise in advising on jungle and rainforest habitats. They also had vast knowledge of Spanish traditions and customs.

After that, he wanted them to act as field generals, which would entail them supporting and motivating the teams in the fields and personally updating them on the progress of others.

"I am happy for you to lend a hand in the fight, as and when necessary, but do so at the command of the leaders," added Simon.

"Generals Audaz and Conchita, reporting for duty. Thank you, sir."

Simon readdressed the gathering.

"Can I have your attention? It appears we have acquired all of our teams. Thank you."

Simon broached next, the subject of training. Ethan downloaded the procedure necessary for the team leaders to transport dark Leaves to the darker realm. Then sent out reminders to enable access to database information on Leaf vibrations and likely realm destination. In addition, guide and catcher network access and weapons arsenal, was also reconfirmed. He linked to Hills to provide the same information to the support group who then returned to the main amphitheatre.

"Welcome back, support officers. I understand Sarah has told you of her need to be involved in some of the conflict when we were in London. She had no choice when having to disarm captors or when caught in a firefight. For those reasons, support officers need to know how to defend and attack tactically. If you thought you would disappear when the shooting started, this is not a mission for you," said Simon.

"Everyone is aware of their responsibilities and what others expect of them," responded Sarah addressing the audience.

"Small point for everyone then. Am I correct in assuming you can all fight?" asked Simon.

Every one of them laughed and cheered their acknowledgement and Ethan and Hills confirmed it. It was decided combat training would use necessary mission time and would only prove what was already apparent. After all, Simon's team had not trained when they commenced their sorties into London.

The mission was planned to start in South America moving northwards. Next would be Africa, Asia and China, then Europe moving east across Russia and into the far east. The force would then come south finally into Australia and New Zealand. As not all teams would be needed in the final territories, they would pick up other land masses and islands.

"It is now Tuesday and the mission will commence next Monday. In the meantime, we practice. One country I did not mention was the UK. That is because we will use this and Eire as a trial run," said Simon.

The task, as a complete force was to clear it of Dark Leaves, moving south to north, within a thirty-six-hour window, commencing 05.00 hours this Thursday morning. Unlike other countries, Leaves were aware of our past operations and would be on guard. Guides and catchers had already been briefed and each would link to the teams. The religious group attendance had yet to be confirmed, but should they be absent for this mission, the UK was a small enough landmass for them to come in after the event.

"Targets," said Simon. "Realm Six, under the direction of Ethan and Hills, have organised team targets with associated vibrations via the database. Known locations will also be given at the same time. This is to increase our effectiveness and stop more than one team targeting the same Leaves. The same back up will be available for the mission proper. Once you have dealt with your target, access the data for the next and move on. Any questions?" instructed Simon.

Ethan picked up that as populations became sparser the further north, not all teams would be needed.

"Ethan heard your main question and if your targets are completed, access the database for those missed and retarget. Support Officers can return to their battle points and help the Leaves which the religious groups would have picked up if they had been in situ. Regardless, I do not want anyone still on the ground after thirty-six hours. Clear?" instructed Simon again.

"Clear," a unanimous shout from the crowd.

"We meet back here on Thursday at 04.30 and again on Saturday at eleven for a debrief. See you all then," said Simon.

Rapturous cheers, squawks and whinnies filled the arena, as they all started to transport out.

More Winds of Change

During the time before the UK mission, the atmosphere amongst the team was confident and motivated. Simon, Greg and Sarah, prepared their interaction plans in the field to support teams moving through the UK during their battles. Audaz and Conchita planned their field visits, routes and progress update formats.

Scout, Taca and Roman had met up with their support officer Victoria, a human line Harpy concealing an Australian wedge-tailed eagle raptor persona. Although she presented a strong challenge in battle to any adversary, her heart sat with helping those who were vulnerable and easily manipulated.

She and Roman naturally synchronised with Scout and Taca with a knowing, in a way in which to an outsider, would have marked and shown them as part of a well-seasoned and experienced team. They used time to re-run the London sorties and discuss planning and action from initial targeting to the delivery of dark Leaves. Being part of the force did not detract from Scout or Taca's responsibility as horse liaison officers, being at hand for communications or concerns from the horses, although they were sparse.

Alana and I twiddled our thumbs a bit. We were both restless and keen to get on with our missions back into the dark. As planned with Tarquin, we would not start these until the main advance into Between Worlds was underway. From this point, Alana and I would relinquish our responsibility of Harpy human contact, deferring it to Greg, Sarah and Simon.

We met with Arthur and Thomas at Arthur's lighthouse for a glass of tune juice and a preliminary discussion. We talked about identifying those in the Dark Realms who were ready to move to the next level up, including those in Realm Three, ready to move to Four.

Under the previous control systems administered by Thaddeus and Gerry, there were many who had been purposefully overlooked. Although you could argue what we were doing in Between Worlds was similar, in so much as we were introducing our own judgement process, our motives were sound and sanctioned. Thaddeus and Gerry had interfered in a process which the Collective should have had full control over, automatically enabling the transfer of Dark Realm inhabitants when they were ready.

It had been revealed, their motive was to keep Realm Four, as an archetypal 'heaven' allowing only selective ex-offenders to transition through to the higher realm. This meant those in Realms One and Two could move forwards as per the Collective's design, however, a barrier had been put in place preventing the movement from Realm Three to Four. To achieve this would necessitate great power and knowing, plus an ability to interface with the Collective's fundamental control systems. It was still unclear how they had done this.

I had learned from Ethan, via Tarquin, that it would be very unlikely for a Realm Sixer like Thaddeus to be able to achieve this with his own level of development, suggesting someone or others higher up were involved. Whether it had been done by a Realm Seven spirit or had involved the Collective itself, had not been determined, as Thaddeus refused to divulge the source of his abilities.

Ethan had decided with consultation, to maintain the barrier between three and four until it could be determined how many would be likely to transition and the impact on Realm Four be assessed.

Other factors we considered with Thomas and Arthur about Dark Realm systems were to review facilities accessible to inhabitants; improved developmental support work to help people gain personal reflection skills and greater transparency of move on destinations. We included in our discussions a new idea of probation, if this was possible.

If it was, whilst on probation, people who were close to move on could spend trial periods of time in the next realm up, which may act as a motivator to develop and provide insight by hearsay to others not yet ready to transfer. The other big consideration was the rehabilitation of those moving to Realm Four and dealing with the potential of them not being welcome. Both Arthur and Thomas were also raring to get started and these six days were dragging.

Alana and I decided we would visit my grandfather Tom and Hazel his mother, who were currently living in Realm Four and who had met me when I had first passed over from Earth. This was one Earth year ago and I had stayed with them for a while before Alana found and awakened me. We thought we also might take a trip back to Earth to Denby Dale to visit my grandma and mum, whom I had not visited for over eight months.

I supposed for most, keeping in regular contact with family and friends back on Earth was a high priority; however, I seemed to have packed my time with discovery and new encounters which had diverted my attention away from them. There was a sense of guilt, but since passing as a fifteen-year-old, I had been awakened to my older self and with that was able to access nine previous lifetimes, opening memories of many parents and families through the centuries.

Being my last Earth-bound family, did however strengthen these particular bonds, more so because they were alive on Earth and continuing to suffer with my loss. I could hear them call from time to time in their grief and I would send back healing thoughts filled with hope and future reconnection.

Our plans to visit family were another attempt by Alana and me to normalise our lives prior to our next mission. There is nothing like family to put things in perspective and reintroduce a sense of mortality within our immortality. For Alana, although she still had two daughters on Earth, all other relatives had passed. She had brought them up with her knowledge or belief of the after world and perhaps this had closed their minds to its possibility, or they decided not to pursue her eccentric personal fantasies. She decided she would not visit them on this occasion.

Although I had kept in touch with my grandfather, Tom and Hazel periodically, we had also not visited them for nearly four months. Following our mission to rescue Tom and free Simon from Denby Dale, he had become more acceptant of my abilities and knowing. I was aware he missed the young John he knew. This was the name I held on Earth prior to my awakening but the adoption of my name James, was the one I had held for centuries.

Tom was a loving, traditional and proud Yorkshireman, remaining focussed on protecting and maintaining the loving bonds of familial relationship, with less interest in the larger picture of after world events. Life to him was about keeping things simple and straightforward, doing your time and enjoying your experiences. I respected his choices and also knew they were determined by the experience and knowing he had achieved from just his one lifetime on Earth.

"Grandfather, it's me James, can we come and visit?"

"Hi, John, we haven't seen you for a while, do you need to borrow some money or something?" Tom replied.

"No, not money, but if I can borrow your lawnmower, that would be handy."

"All right, than'os, I will put a drop of fuel in her and she'll be ready to go. When are you coming?"

It was easy to look between the lines of wit and detect his disappointment based on my neglect. It was just his way of saying 'yes, it would be great to see you' whilst letting me know how he really felt at the same time. Funny or was it sad, why people need to veil an intended wound, so you can choose to wound them back, confirming to them, they are not worth visiting anyway or you are just visiting out of duty? 'Only joking', as always the saviour of such transgressions.

"We'll be with you in ten minutes, if that's okay."

"Splendid. I will put the kettle on and let Hazel know. Bye for now."

"He still calls me John you know, Alana."

"Your folks on Earth are not the only ones who are grieving, James. He has lost someone too, his little mate and he is unsure of how to receive you."

"I know it will take time. I am just not used to his non-acceptance, when that is all I received from him whilst growing up. At least Hazel is more in tune and talking of her, are you picking up an immanent revolution?"

"Yes. Not the best time to be reborn back on Earth, is it? If I could choose my location, I am not sure where would be the safest, with a better chance of survival."

"Higher ground, a temperate climate and away from volcanoes?" I proposed.

"Yes, but the last time we spoke to her, she was thinking coastal, north of Japan. That is if she can choose, which I believe is a Collective decision, not up to her," said Alana.

Once she had revolved back to Earth, we would not know who she was or where she was. This was a Collective design based on providing the person revolving with anonymity to live a lifetime as determined by what potential experiences were required to further their personal development. Whilst the potential experience opportunities may present themselves, it was always a matter of choice as to whether to engage with them.

The other reason for anonymity was to cut all ties with previous loved ones in spirit to halt visitations. This was two-fold in reason. One was the returning spirit's loved ones remaining in the after world would experience a loss, almost similar to a death on the Earth plain and therefore would go through a further essential grieving process as spirit. The difference this time was the assured knowledge that life continues.

This was the Collective's way of reinforcing loss, an emotional package, all beings feared as part of relationship. It sat in the unconscious and was there to drive us to maintain relational bonds. Unfortunately, it worked both ways, as if loss was experienced on Earth, it deterred some from re-engaging in relations for the fear of losing someone else again. The challenge of overcoming this fear was also something the Collective wanted us to achieve. If we did, we achieved both knowing and accrued energy.

It was still a death of a kind to those left in the after world, as reconciliation was not possible until both were able to access previous lifetimes and locate vibrations. Many lifetimes and many families would have been experienced by this point and those journeyed with, would have lesser emotional significance.

The second reason was for the returning spirit to feel the necessity of being alone. This, of course would be dependent on the attachment style or lack of, of their Earth-bound parents or care givers. This would also determine the way they related to others around them and hence, opportunities presented to them in the future. The Collective's aim for the individual was, in their sense of aloneness and separation, they would generate knowing and energy by pursuing right relation, symbiotically satisfying their own and other's needs positively.

The lifeline was ever present though, as the spirit element, the soul, woven into the Earth body retained a sense of still being connected to the Collective, the choice to feel and strengthen this, determined by belief. I remembered my last Earth lifetime, where although I had family and some friends, I craved like kind, felt separate from the world around me and harboured a hidden and elusive sense of purpose. Then I got run over by a truck and a short while afterwards, it all made sense!

"You didn't choose to get run over by a truck, James. And I cannot say I was pleased you did, because I would have waited for you anyway. But maybe the Collective needed you back over here to meet the purpose thing you were trying to work out?" stated Alana.

"If I hadn't died, I would have carried on living my life, searching for my meaning. The Collective obviously needed me to die at that time and I have re-found my like kind in you and our friends and am now involved in a hell of a purpose. I had done my time and I am happy I died."

"Splendid. Can we go and see the rellies now?" asked Alana.

I tuned into Grandfather's vibration and linking into Alana, we transported to the garden of Mill Cottage, my great grandma's house. They were both sitting on the patio enjoying a cup of tea in the sunshine.

"All right, than'os, how's yah bum for spots?" opened grandfather.

"James, Alana, how lovely to see you again. How are you both? There's tea in the pot," added Hazel.

We walked over to greet them and shared hugs and kisses before joining them sitting down at the table.

"We are both fine and happy, thank you. Busy and involved in lots of stuff to do with this climate change situation on Earth," I replied.

"Yes, difficult time for the Earth folks. So much ambiguity and worry about what might happen," said Hazel.

"And both James and I are aware you could go back at any time?" added Alana.

"Yes, but life is what it is. I cannot deny the feeling building inside of me. I don't feel complete, if that's the right term of phrase. I need to learn more about myself and Earth's 'harder knocks' are the only ones which really ground the experiences and knowing as you learn along the way," she replied.

"We just want you to be safe and live a fulfilling life this revolution and we will miss you very much," said Alana.

"It is sad this has to be an ending. Once I am there, I will be none the wiser anyway, but you two, Tom and my friends will just know I have gone back, with no more knowledge and a slim chance we might meet again. It may be hundreds of years before I will know enough to remember all my lives and whom I have journeyed with. Tell me, are family of previous lifetimes important to you two?" asked Hazel.

"Not really, other than Simon, Sarah and Nevaeh, but they all re-emerged serendipitously and have been integral in us getting involved in the work we are now doing. Apart from them, all others have faded. The strongest bond remains with your last family on Earth and those who have come here from it," I said.

"Seems a bit harsh to me," said Tom. "I died on Earth and remember the folks back home and they remember me. When Hazel returns, I will remember her, knowing I have been wiped from her accessible memories, so she cannot remember me even when she next comes back here."

"If you think about it though, Tom, many on Earth, with the loss of a loved one to death, hope the person will rest in peace and look down on their family occasionally. They don't really know what happens to them and future generations only have a vague knowledge, if any, of ancestors," said Alana.

"That being said, Alana, there is a lot of talk here about many of the Earth born trying to trace their ancestors through their DNA. I wonder whether it is revolved spirit, having gone back, unconsciously trying to find another way of tracing the loved ones they lost here?" said Tom.

"I can't see the point though because the body containing the DNA is just a vehicle. It is the spirit, us, who revolve into random family trees as selected by the Collective. I think the Earth born are searching for meaning and identity, but instead of belief in what the future may hold, they are using science and fact to look into the past. Which is in the opposite direction of where they will end up," I said.

"Barking up the wrong family tree you mean," said Tom.

I laughed. "Exactly!"

"Well, at least we know Hazel will continue to exist and hope her future journey will be absent of suffering and be a beneficial one. As you said, Hazel, it is a sad time and yet we see birth as a happy occasion and rebirth as another opportunity to choose wisely," said Alana.

"Talking of choices, I don't think anyone is listening to me about my choice of Earth destination," said Hazel.

"Thing is Hazel, you are never going to know and neither are we. You just have to trust, you end up where you need to be and whom you need to be with. I do believe the Collective orchestrates that from the beginning of a new revolve, then leaves it up to you to choose how to deal with the consequences as more choices become available to you," I said.

"I am afraid it is beyond me to understand why things are the way they are. I believe there is a greater plan and I accept the Collective must have a purpose and a reason for doing things the way they are done. I shall miss you though, Mum," added Tom.

"I don't think you will be alone for long though, Tom," she replied.

Both Alana and I looked at Hazel and Tom, knowing immediately Hazel was thinking of my grandma Audrey back on Earth. Last year, her stomach issues, which she had ignored for some time, had flared up and again she had done nothing about it. I knew about this from grandfather previously and had accepted his comment about her being as tough as old boots.

Like him, she was a World War Two child and had learned to put up and shut up. In her world, doctors were busy with other people and you didn't trouble them unless absolutely necessary. Even when necessary entailed a degree of suffering which could be coped with.

She had finally submitted and been given a diagnosis for primary stomach cancer, with no further secondary issues as yet identified. The prognosis lay in her hands as she had not decided what to do as yet, meaning, seek treatment or let it run its course.

"Mum doesn't know, does she?" I said.

"No. You know what grandma's like and with you dying last year, she did not want to add to your mum's suffering or worries," replied Tom.

"Seems like she is choosing to let it run," I said.

"I can't choose for her and when I visit her, she tells me she misses me a lot and she's tired. She knows I am here waiting. She also knows you and Alana are over here and alive and well. She does not think or believe you are, she knows. That makes a big difference when deciding what she might do next," said Tom.

"She is seventy-six now, isn't she?" I asked.

"Yes. Same age as me."

Perspective always played a massive part in after world discussions about the death of Earth folks. Our experiences confirmed the sadness remained with those left on Earth. There was no such thing as a timely death. It did not matter when a person died, young or old, only to those left behind. With no knowledge of our world, only a hope remained. Choosing to extend an Earth life was part of the journey. Choosing not to and facing the consequences, was also part of the same journey. It came down to choice.

"We are going back to Denby Dale after we leave here. The plan was to pop in on grandma and visit mum too," I said.

"You can't persuade her either way, John," said Tom.

"I know. I just want to gain a feel for where she is. Whichever she decides, she is going to end up over here anyway. Mum is surely going to miss her and I think she has a right to know, but mum is not sensitive enough to hear me," I said.

My grandma was an amateur channeller who had become more successful at linking as she had become older. She had been aware of Tom visiting her since he had passed over and Alana and I were able to communicate with her through pictures and energy transmission. Mum was more sceptical, although had accepted small pieces of evidence from us via grandma.

We spent the next hour, catching up on news and developments and shared what information we were able to without divulging the plans for Between Worlds and the Dark Realms.

We could tell that Hazel was restless and looking forward to re-joining the Earthlings to continue her journey. As with birth on Earth, an exact time was never given, but you knew you had about twenty-four hours when you started to experience distortions in your vision. These were like circular or wheel like movements in the light. When the time came, the circle would spin slowly and open to reveal an entrance to a tunnel, similar to the one entered when leaving the Earth world to come here.

At the end of that tunnel, your arrival coincided with the exact moment of conception and your new life on Earth began.

"Let us know when you are getting close, won't you, Hazel? We want to see you before you go," said Alana.

"I will," confirmed Hazel.

"I think there will be quite a few present to see you off from what I have heard, so we will have to get plenty of tea and cake organised for the baby shower afterwards," said Tom.

"Another 'rite of passage' among the many," I confirmed.

"Indeed. That's life," replied Tom.

"We must be off now. I want to catch grandma before Earth dark. It's good to see you both in good spirits, especially with the immanent change. We will be seeing you both soon anyway I think," I said.

"As important as that is, don't stay away too long between visits John. I miss you. I also happen to love you very much and like to hear of both of your adventures," said grandfather with a slight difficulty in expressing his emotion.

"We won't. I love you too and there is nothing stopping you from having your own adventures," I said.

"I'm too old for all that."

"And there speaks a man who at seventy-six, is a sixth of my own and Alana's age. Too old, on yer bike!" I replied with eyebrows raised.

"Point taken graciously, it's all still a bit strange for me."

We hugged our goodbyes and left them to the rest of their afternoon. Setting a course for my grandmas, we transported to the back lawn of her house and looked in through the kitchen window.

Never Alone

Grandma was sitting at the kitchen table with her head down, concentrating intently on a crossword puzzle. As we sat opposite to her, I could see how she had aged. Darkened rings sat beneath her eyes and her skin, having lost some of its lustre, was starting to tighten across her features where she had lost weight. I watched the goose bumps rise on her forearms and looking up, she sniffed the air, squinting in our direction.

"I know you are not Tom and I sense you are nice, give me a clue?" she said.

I was sad she did not detect it was us but our absence of visits had not enabled her familiarity with our vibration. To add to her surprise, I chose not to use my riding bike symbol by which I knew she would identify me.

Scanning her cryptic crossword clues, I ironically found the perfect one. I sent her the symbol for two down, two arrows facing downwards and added a picture of a Yorkshire dale. Two down quoted 'Small man with staff would afford carriage', 6'4".

"A crossword clue. Very original. I have scanned that already and told myself I would come back to it." She went to task verbally exploring her thoughts.

"Umm. Rich man with servants buying a carriage, but not very tall. Dwarf, little man? A picture of a dale or a moor too."

"Is she any good at these, otherwise we might be here for hours?" asked Alana.

"She is. She'll get there," I replied.

"Carriage. Not wheels, carry, to carry. Afford to carry. A ford, like a car. A big car, so the man looks little, umm?"

"Dum-de-dum dum... What's for tea, James?"

"Prize of patience, Alana."

"Another ford, I know, like a stream and would, as in sounds like, meaning wood. Wooden staff or trees, or it could be both."

"I'm off for a short tour of Scotland."

"Alana!"

"I know the answer and the, dale clue," she announced.

Her eyes welled up and she smiled widely in our direction.

"Little John and Alan-a-dale. Where have you been? I have missed you. I thought you had forgotten about me."

"Impressive!" said Alana.

"Runs in the family, darling," I replied.

We both touched her hands and transferred strong pulses of loving energy into her. She shivered and held her hands to her cheeks. Getting up from her chair, she walked around to our side and opened her arms to us. Encircling her with our arms, we generated a warming bind, enabling her to feel loved, protected and eased from her suffering.

"I take it you know about me from Tom then?"

I sent a tick symbol inside a tear shape.

"It's not sad, John, I am old and tired. I have what I have. I don't know if I am supposed to have this cancer and die from it, or to suffer getting better. And at my age, is there a point in getting better?"

Small bird.

She knew this was our symbol for my mum, her name being Jenny.

"Wren. Jenny wren. She will be sad, but she will cope. She still grieves your departure, obviously, but she has become stronger. That time you visited and helped her see the truth about the lock of hair in her locket, which only she and you knew about, sparked her faith in you continuing to live. She misses you desperately, but she knows you are all right. As do I and I know Tom is with you too."

I sent her a picture of two open hands moving up and down.

"Balance?"

A traditional picture of a weight moving upwards, I sent to clarify.

"Weight up? Weighing up you mean?"

Tick.

"Yes. I might be all right with the treatment, but I don't really want to be ill and become dependent on your mum. I may not be ill. I don't know. If it works and I go into remission, how long will it be before I die of something else. I am going to die anyway," she responded.

It was really difficult to transmit images for etheric concepts like hope and trust which I wanted to say. Alana squeezed my hand and reminded me this choice was in her hands and I could not provide weight to either side of the decision.

"I do know; it's been three years since your grandad went over and I miss him. We had and I suppose have been together since we were teenagers, but I really want to see him again, cuddle him and share what life brings wherever we end up. I know I said on one occasion you visited, I didn't relish the idea of living with his mum, Hazel, but I am sure I could get used to it. We could spend lots of time on our own, couldn't we?"

Alana looked at me and said, 'good luck trying to explain this one'. I sent grandma a picture of a nut, I had used as a symbol for Hazel previously, followed by a gravestone and finally a baby.

"Hazel, death, baby? I've no idea what you mean?"

I followed it with a picture of the Earth and a metronome in movement.

"Time running out for the Earth?"

I sent tides moving in and out.

"Back and forth, back and forth? You mean she is coming back to Earth, what, she is going to visit me too?"

Alana laughed.

"Well, I am glad you find it funny, Alana. I'd like to see you try and work it out, if you were me."

Alana and I looked at each other, with the same question in our minds.

"Don't worry, Audrey, I am constantly deciphering what James is thinking," said Alana.

Audrey looked down at the table, placing a waggling finger in her right ear.

"Something has changed. Say what you just did again, about deciphering, James."

We proceeded to look at each other in total surprise.

"We haven't somehow brought her into Between Worlds, have we?" I said.

"Brought me where? Slow down, I can just about work out what you are saying. I think I can hear you speaking. Retune or something, I want to hear what you are both saying."

I mind-linked to Alana, enquiring about the sudden clairaudient shift and whether her absolute belief, coupled with a closer distance towards death, may be opening an audible channel for her.

"Shocked you into silence? I have been hearing more from Tom ever so recently, just occasional words."

We placed our hands on Audrey's and both generated waves of blue light moving from our throat chakras, through our arms and directing it upwards, rotated the light as a ring around her head. Alana signalled a synchronised pulse of energy from both of us, magnifying the intensity of the blue halo. We watched her blink her eyes whilst raising her brows, as if trying to work something out.

"Is that better?" I asked. Her expression was charged.

"Yes, I think I can hear you, but not voices. It's like voices in my head, rather than hearing someone actually speak to me. If you see what I mean? It's hard to work out whether it is you who are actually speaking to me or I am imagining it?"

"You have got £27.32 in your 'change for everything piggy pot' on the dresser grandma. Do you want to check?" I said to build her confidence.

She left the table, returning with the pot and emptied it out to count it. The exact figure was £27.33.

"I have an extra penny, you miscounted," she declared with playful sarcasm.

"No, because you need to spend one soon," I replied.

"I do need the loo actually," she paused and asked, "do you know everything?"

"No, not everything, but I do know you can hear us now," I replied.

Audrey beamed widely, with tears in her eyes and clapped her hands together.

"I feel I have really got you back now, John. And Alana, it is lovely to meet more of you. I am so excited."

"Don't get too excited, Audrey. Not before you have dealt with the matter at hand," said Alana.

"Oh, yes. Don't go away, will you?" she said.

Grandma excused herself and I looked at Alana, who felt the sudden onset was nothing to do with approaching death. It was more likely to do with her belief shifting to undoubtable fact, combined with her natural sensitivity. I wondered whether contemplating an acceptance of an ending given her nature and her knowledge of us, had provided a handle by which to open the door, slightly more through to our world. Alana agreed. Grandma returned to the table refreshed and sat down.

"What were you trying to say about Hazel, just before?" she asked.

"I was trying to say she is about to reincarnate or revolve back to Earth. That is something we do after we have been in the after world for a while," I said.

"So she won't be there when I get there you mean?"

She tutted at herself and apologised for her tone, explaining she did not dislike Hazel. When she and Tom had started courting seriously, Hazel had given her the impression she wasn't good enough for her Tom and it had caused her some resentment. Grandma suddenly went quiet.

"When will your grandad be coming back?"

"No one knows when they will come back. Both James, I mean John and I have done our revolutions, so we will not come back to live here again," said Alana.

"Why do you call John, James?" she asked.

"That has been my name through the centuries and one Alana has always called me by," I replied.

"How long have you two been together?" Audrey asked.

"Nearly five hundred years. But we haven't been with each other all of that time, we have had to live our own lives on Earth for some of it. We have always found each other again though," said Alana.

"Five hundred years! We have no idea here, do we? So Tom could return at any time. I need to get over as quickly as I can, so we can spend lots more time with each other before either of us returns," she responded, her mind seeming to indicate a mission.

"Quickly?" I asked with some concern.

"As quickly as however long it takes for me to die. I am not having the treatment. Life is too short to carry on living and I have too much to live for after I am dead."

She paused to rephrase her last words.

"What I mean is, too much to live for on your side. I need to be with Tom for as long as possible, before I lose him again."

"Are you sure, Audrey?" asked Alana.

"As sure as knowing I am sitting here talking to you," she said with determination.

"You need to tell mum then. Telling her before your departure becomes immanent, will help her start to grieve before you go. It's a kinder way," I said.

"Never been one for fuss, me," she replied whilst avoiding where she imagined my eyes to be.

"Let her give. Supporting and fussing over you will be the last gift she can give you and your last gift to her," I advised gently.

"You've gotten very wise since you have been over there, John."

"Five hundred years is a long time to develop wisdom grandma, if you choose to. When will you tell her?"

"She's coming around after work to drop off some groceries. Will you both stay while she is here? I could do with your support. I don't think she is going to take it too well."

I knew from the time on the wall clock, mum would have left work and probably be at the supermarket. She worked for Kirklees Council in Huddersfield, which was a thirty-minute drive away and I planned to accompany her on her way back in the car. Alana acknowledged my thoughts and elected to stay with Audrey. I told grandma who was pleased, intending to ask Alana lots of questions in my absence. I transported out and followed mum's vibration.

When I arrived, mum was pushing the trolley towards the back of her car. Memory served me to open the boot and help her off load her shopping, but my status resigned me to watch and accept. Sitting in the front passenger seat, I watched her get into the driver's side, exhale deeply and begin to chat to herself.

"Another day, another; why do they say dollar? We should have an English expression, something like: another palaver, another pound. Wasted me, I should be working in advertising," she said.

I tuned into her mind and listened to her internal dialogue. I could tell she was in a marginally light mood. Her reconfiguration of the saying did make me laugh though, which resulted surprisingly in her pausing, turning in my direction and shivering. She shrugged her shoulders and thinking of me, wondered if I had to do boring things like go food shopping.

"No, I always have everything I need, or can think of," I replied.

There was no response other than a momentary tidal return of sadness. She allowed it to wash over her and accepted her reality, as she ordered her planned activities for her evening at home.

I had lost many family members and loved ones during my nine lifetimes and during a lifetime of loss, it was time passing which dulled the sharp edges and immediacy of the emotional distress. I have found the internal occupation becomes one where you wrestle between the absence of that person's love and your guilt and regrets, which handicap your own need to enable you to love yourself again. You never forget people and that is the saving grace in remembering their will to bolster yours to carry on with your own life. Of course, sadly, some don't, but mum was a fighter and I also felt she would fight to keep her mum with her too.

She started the car and the CD loaded into her deck, restarted. Mum was a mid-seventies child and her needle had stuck on the tracks of the late eighties and early nineties. We had enjoyed lots of music together and her choices had widened but she remained faithful to her core. Serendipity works in timely ways and we were part way through 'Back to Life' by Soul II Soul, as we headed out towards Wakefield Road.

Mum cheerfully sang along with the lyrics and the next one by Marvin, which was a little early for her, so I reckoned she must have made her own compilation. Next, she belted out 'Like a Prayer' with Madonna and I enjoyed the links she created with her own memories, as she relived her emotions and experiences from the past.

Interestingly, they resonated with a current point of joy, but one wrapped in hesitation and doubt, albeit with a hint of hope. I left her side and transported to the source of this hesitant joy out of intrigue, returning a few minutes later before the next track had ended. Sensing her feelings in the silence of the engine running, her mind was trying to link to something elusive about loss.

She ejected the disc, viewed the oncoming traffic, then leant across me retrieving another disk from the glove compartment. It was marked 'Whitney Mix' and I knew she needed to balance the partial elation evoked from the previous tracks. Selecting track five, we waited for the unmistakable spiritually channelled clarity of Whitney's emotional resonance.

The first two lines of the Greatest Love of All slid between both mine and mum's emotional memory folds and teased the lumps in both of our throats to submit to our tears. Her thoughts confirmed that I was the future which had been taken from her, however, with her belief strengthening, she was slowly starting to find the courage to love herself once more, as Whitney inspired.

When we as spirit visit loved ones, the greatest joy is to feel you have made a connection and I wondered if she had picked up on my 'wrestle thought'. Unlike people like grandma, most Earth bound have lost the ability to listen to the sound of silence and trust to accept the thoughts and quiet voices without dismissing them.

The track complete, mum selected seven. I did not know this one, but felt an emotion coming from her which might be described as her opening her arms to receive what might be given. The track was a duo with Mariah Carey called

'When you Believe'. I listened to the lyrics with her and felt her wrestle with the gravity of her own pain of loss, as it fought to disable the will to lift her to her own personal miracle.

"Fill your heart with love, Mum. There is no fear if you do, just miracles waiting to be believed."

She placed her hand upon her locket from outside her blouse, the one containing a lock of my hair. The tears started running down her cheeks. I could sense she was at a point of adjustment and wondered which track she may choose next. Whether sad to depress her mood further, or something to elate her, to maintain her flight. Although we had about five minutes before we would be in Denby Dale, she checked the surrounding traffic and once again leaned over me to retrieve another CD.

The case had 'Mishmosh & Randoms' written on the front. Track eight was Good Life by Inner city, obviously something that had slipped in from 2006. Her mood was coming up and Mum bounced slightly in her seat, as she sang along. It was the nodding dog head movements which were the best. I could feel her heart lift and the grief take its reprieve. As we pulled up the drive, I transported back to the kitchen and sat next to Alana.

"She is about to arrive," I said.

"Good trip, John, how is her mood?" asked Grandma.

"It's not bad; we listened to Whitney together on the way back. She is struggling but she is taking some positive steps forward," I replied.

The front door opened, as mum let herself in and called out to announce her arrival to grandma.

"In the kitchen, Jenny," she responded.

"Let me see how she is, before I let her know you are here," said Grandma.

We agreed. Mum came in and put the groceries away as grandma enquired about her day and how she was feeling.

"Yes, I am okay. Had an interesting trip back from the shop. I am not sure how it is supposed to feel, but it felt like John was with me and it was nice to have him around. Probably just my imagination," she replied.

"Well, he is your greatest love of all. Next to me and dad of course," said Grandma.

Mum turned and scrutinising her face, confirming she was listening to Whitney on the way back. She continued to study her, as I fed grandma information.

"Well, miracles can happen, if you believe in them. I think you have to believe in yourself first and not let the fear overtake you," Grandma proposed.

"Okay, mystic Meg, you have either become an overnight Whitney expert or your powers of clairvoyance are getting stronger?" Mum replied.

"Just wishing for a good life, or what's left of it. Who was the group who sang that, Outer Town, wasn't it?"

"Inner City. You know he was with me, don't you? Is he still here and is dad or Alana with him?" Mum spoke quietly and determinedly.

"He says you ought to keep your CDs in your door pockets and not stretch over to the glove compartment whilst you are driving. Oh, and get a nodding dog to dance along with. He's with Alana," translated Grandma with a big smile on her face.

Although mum's eyes welled up, she kept her composure and waved a randomly directed greeting to us both.

"Hi John, hello Alana. Mum hasn't spoken of you being here for a while, are you all right?"

"Relieved and happy you are getting stronger and starting to love yourself again, little steps at a time. They are fine. Alana has been telling me they are involved in trying to help Earth with the global warming problem. This is why they haven't been back to see us recently."

I could tell from mum's thoughts, she was wrestling with the doubt and acceptance of what she was hearing, still trying to balance her reality with that of grandmas. Many had become conditioned to uphold their sense of Earth's reality, which now dominated over the innate sense of instinctual belief relied on by our ancient forbearers. Unquestionably, doubt is essential to our survival, however it is a difficult sense to be burdened with in its pervasiveness.

"You must be reading and translating their pictures really well mum. You have given me some very accurate information?" Mum asked.

"No Jenny, something has changed. I can hear what they are saying to me in my head now. It's very clear. It's the same as having a conversation and it helps if I believe what I am hearing. John has grown up now. Alana has been telling me they both look about twenty-six and Tom has turned back his clock and looks thirty-five. It's so different over there and yet similar to here. It seems they have a good life."

Mum looked across to where she thought I might be sitting. "Do you know why you had to die, John?"

"He says you are never sure why, but he thinks it was just his time. He saw the spirit person at Ashe Cottages on his way home that day, the one who met him after he had just been killed. So, those in heaven must have known he was going to die before he did. This suggests a God plan. He and Alana have discussed it and they are both involved in important work at the moment. They think God needed him back. They confirm, God or the Collective as they call it, is connected to everyone on Earth and over there."

"It is almost as though death is just a change, a different direction and yet it is so hard for us who are left behind. Why don't they just tell everyone on Earth about it and make it reality?" asked mum.

"Alana says it is the Collective's law that the Earthbound are not definitively informed of what happens," said Grandma.

"They are telling us!" Mum pointed out energetically.

"John says there are many who claim to know the truth, but the majority do not believe. Of those who do, some follow the religions, yet there is much doubt. He says, can you imagine having a conversation with Mr Foster, your manager at work, telling him you were speaking with your dead son yesterday and heaven does exist?" said Grandma.

"How does he know about Mr Foster?" Mum's reply, a blend of suspicion and surprise.

"John says he was crossing your mind quite often whilst you were listening to your eighties music and he says you might choose to blow upon that ember."

"John, can read my mind?" asked Mum.

"When he feels it is proper to do so."

"This is a different world. This is…" Mum placed her head in her hands.

"John says, unbelievable? Are you all right, lovey?" asked Grandma.

"You are amazing, Mum. What would I ever do without you?" she said.

The silence in the room suddenly became deafening, as grandma had turned quiet and looked down. She offered mum a cup of tea which she accepted. As she was brewing, mum asked where we lived and grandma translated our favourite house was a cliff top villa in a place like Capri. This sparked many questions. After answering them, Grandma sat down again with the tea.

"Just before, you asked what you would do without me. One reason John and Alana are here, other than to see us, is… I have hard news which affects us all."

"I knew something was wrong, I am not blind, Mum, I just wish you would share your troubles to take the guessing out of it. It's not cancer, is it?" she asked taking Grandma's hand, her bottom lip dropping and tears filling her eyes.

"It is, but I don't want to suffer, Jenny, or be a burden. But I might just need you to hold my hand and let me hold yours while I go through this."

"You know I will, if you let me."

Grandma smiled into her eyes and squeezed her hand.

"Perfect, grandma," I whispered.

"Where's the primary and have they identified any secondary as yet and what about treatment?" Mum asked.

"I have to confess now, even to John and Alana," said grandma in acceptance of her situation.

Our attention was heighted, as I had not explored grandma's mind around the cancer.

"Stomach is the primary and they think they have also found it in one of my adrenal glands. They have told me they have not decided what course of treatment is best yet."

I put a call into grandad and told him he should join us, uploading the information on the cancer declaration to him. He was standing behind grandma with his hands on her shoulders in less than two seconds.

"Hello, darling, come to join the party? Dad's here, Jenny," she declared, patting her left shoulder with her right hand.

"Hi, Dad. I think you can see; we have standing room only," Mum replied, smiling out of imagined acceptance.

"She told me nothing about the adrenal stuff John, it's worse than I thought," declared grandad.

"That depends darling on your interpretation of worse. Not for you and me it isn't. It will be harder for Jenny though."

"Bloody hell, you can hear me!" he said, totally surprised.

"No swearing in front of the children please! Yes, I can. John and Alana have clarified it for me. Okay let's get down to business. Heaven family, you can do what you do; I am getting the gin out."

Grandma retrieved the gin from the kitchen cupboard and the tonic from the fridge. Mum sliced the lemon. I produced a bottle of soulful tune juice and three glasses. I wasn't sure if I could do this in Between Worlds, yet fortune enabled.

Grandma asked if we had something to share a toast with, to which I acknowledged.

"There are never endings, only new beginnings along the way. Cheers!" proposed grandma.

We all replied cheers other than mum, who managed only to raise her glass. She reminded everyone that cheers were not coming her way, that although she was here, she could not hear the conversations and it would remain as if she was alone with grandma.

"I am lucky to be able to hear and sorry you cannot and are just left to try and believe. As you have come to understand today, there is much evidence to confirm those you love are around you. All we ask is you continue to believe and believe mostly in yourself," said grandma.

Both Alana and I knew that most adrenal cancer diagnoses were not picked up until advanced tumour stage and cancerous cells would be pumping themselves around the lymphatic system affecting other parts of her body. Treatment was possible but the uphill was steep. Grandad picked up on my thoughts.

"What do you want to do, darling?" asked grandad. Grandma told mum his question.

"I know in myself that this has got hold of me. I am uncomfortable and I can't sleep at times, but I can bear it at present. I know this may sound defeatist Jenny, but I want to go. I do not want to go through all the treatments and tests to possibly get to the stage where I am in remission, then fear it could come back at any time. It may sound selfish to you, but I want to be with my Tom. We all know John died, but he hasn't really and neither shall I. I will only be one-step away. I will just miss you and continue to do so, as do the others here," said Grandma.

Mum allowed the tears to flow, wiping her cheeks and nose on a tissue before responding.

"I know I don't have a choice in this, like with John's death. And I am weighing up the value of withdrawing from you to try and satisfy the wound I am feeling, verses helping and supporting you towards your ending. But I know it is now about making the quality of our lives memorable for me before the inevitable. It is your journey, mum. I will be here with you until your new beginning."

"I can see where you get your words from James," said Alana.

"Probably from me too," said Grandad.

"True. I have been fluent in 'West Yorkshire mill-hand' from an early age," I said smiling at him.

Kneeling down beside mum, I placed my arms around her and created two lilac light vortices, drawing energy from the Collective ether. One I placed above my head and the other above hers. Slowly enlarging them, I brought them downwards, linking them together, until they encompassed us both, then I flooded them with divine will energy. Alana and grandad added to the energy, drawing it up from the Earth to overlap the vortex at her heart level. Working together, we sent pulse after pulse into the vortex from our own reserves.

"Can you hear us now? You are not alone," we all spoke at the same time.

Mum stood up with an expression like she had just emerged from freezing water. She shook the shiver away from her and rubbed her tingling hands together. Grandma looked at her with a surprised smile.

"Not alone, are you, Jenny?"

"I think I heard them. The feeling was beautiful; they told me I was not alone." Mum burst into tears.

"Thank you, I do believe you are all here. Just help me with mum and be with us at the time she leaves me to be with you."

"They all say they will, Jenny," said grandma.

"I miss you, John and Dad, and love you both very much. Alana, thank you for looking after John. I will look forward to meeting my daughter in law, when my time comes," said Mum.

"We need to go, grandma." I nodded to grandad; we were off.

Although we could have spent more time, I felt unsettled about what I had experienced today, things I hadn't yet shared with Alana. Grandma stood up and I hugged her closely. I whispered, 'take your time and let it happen, no willing'. As Alana hugged her, I cuddled mum and told her I loved her, then warmed the seed to blow on the ember. I had taken a few minutes to visit Mr Foster on our journey home with mum to check out his intensions. He was true, kind natured and he liked and admired her. Alana kissed Mum's cheek and saying our goodbyes and good luck to grandma, Alana and I vanished.

Believe It, It Is Happening

"I am wondering what was so unsettling that we needed to leave when we did? I understand about the sadness your mum will have to face, but your thoughts seem to be drifting between reality, belief and the unknown," said Alana.

I had transported Alana and me to Windwillow Cross on the outskirts of Denby Dale. We sat on the bench in the cold November air, staring down Unwind Hill, the gateway to my new beginning when I left Earth a year ago. We were faced by the bleakness of our surroundings as winter strengthened its hold, deepening the slumber of the trees and hedgerows, as they turned inward.

"They are drifting. I really felt Mum's struggle with belief today. I am sitting with the imbalance between us knowing the truth and them wrestling to believe through the uncertainty of life after death. But not just that."

I had experienced things today which made me think it was the same for this global warming issue on Earth. Even though there was greater evidence of that unknown approaching, there seemed to be an issue with people on Earth believing it. In our world, we were driving our actions because we knew what was happening. In comparison, there was progress on Earth to contribute to slowing climate change, but it was not happening fast enough, nor with an intensity or global commitment.

Up until recently, the after world had been run by the Collective and nothing had changed until we realised we needed to change it in line with what was happening on Earth. On Earth, things were constantly changing and now when they needed to change behaviour rapidly, they were slow or hesitant to counteract the dilemma.

We needed the majority on Earth, to change attitudes and mind sets to make a difference towards changing this dilemma. Not just leaving it to governments to propose and instigate change. This issue would affect everyone on Earth. It was a certainty, not unlike death or taxes.

When chatting with Ethan at the gathering, he had told me eighty-five percent of the adult population in the UK were concerned by global warming. And I bet many worldwide, felt the same. This concern needed to be transformed into a change in behaviour.

"I am wondering, within the Collective's law governing the disclosure of the after world to the Earthbound, whether there is a way to transform the awareness of this issue. Transform it into a belief that disaster will happen and then into action, to slow it down or reverse it," I proposed to Alana.

"You don't have the power to do that, James. This law is fundamental to maintaining the basic laws of the existence of spirit and spirit in matter or people on Earth," said Alana.

I looked around at the cold, bleak countryside.

"What if it was always like this here, this wintery state, never changing, nothing growing. Or global warming affected the seasonal tilt of the polar axis. Where a permanent shift resulted in Denby Dale being thrown into darkness for three months during the winter, like North Norway? Like the Earth people, we don't know the extent of the outcomes either," I said.

As we watched the glow of orange sodium street lamps mark the location of Huddersfield in the distance, I told Alana about my journey home with mum. I had watched the traffic commuting from work to home, travelling in opposite directions and how most were single commuters. Lights burned everywhere, along the streets, in shops and businesses and in people's homes. A billboard advertising a faraway holiday destination, encouraged commuters to imagine they could be flying to somewhere else, rather than sitting in traffic queues.

Prior to travelling back, I had seen Mum load her shopping into the boot of her car. I could not help notice the amount of red meat, dairy and palm oil products she had bought for her and grandma as part of their next week's meals. Also, when I had left mum to check out Mr Foster, I had found him in a burger restaurant. It was packed full of diners, many queuing, whilst more were serviced as they drove through on their way home.

"Are you linking the farting cow problem with your mother, where methane is thirty times more potent as a global warming gas compared to carbon dioxide?"

"Yes, that and the high carbon footprint of animal feed production and the amount of energy used unnecessarily, which I saw today. Mum is just a typical example of current inaction. She is my closest relative on Earth and I know she is aware of the issue and yet it is almost as though she feels her contribution to warming is unimportant. Or is not believing it is," I confirmed.

"What do you want? A global warming warning on each cattle based and palm oil product? Like: 'This product was sourced from an animal which produced one hundred and fifty kilos of methane before it was slaughtered for your enjoyment. Weight for weight, your quarter pounder represents 48.7 grams of methane, or the equivalent of 1.46 kilos of carbon dioxide, now floating in the atmosphere, warming your climate. Please note: Flatulence may occur as a result of your purchase. The manufacturer cannot be held responsible for you carelessly contributing further to any climate catastrophe both locally or globally. Have a nice day', sort of thing."

I thought this was a great idea. There were other warnings on dangerous products, for example tobacco. Some governments were brutal in forcing manufacturers to place pictures of dissected tar filled lungs, impotent couples and even dead people on cigarette and tobacco packaging. Why, because it costs health services millions to deal with the consequences of their consumption.

With warming, however, the consequences would be much greater, costing not just billions in currency, but billions in lives also. Currently, there was a lack of action to change everyone's small contribution accelerating the arrival at a devastating result. The responsibility seemed to be currently denied by, 'my contribution won't make any difference'. It was time to wake up.

"Even with the informative packaging, why do you think people continue to smoke when faced by such horrors backed up by the research?" asked Alana.

"I think they are aware of the damage it causes, but they do not believe the bad outcome like cancer, will happen to them, or hope it won't. There is a significant shift or event which moves people from a stage of awareness to belief. It is a personally empowered will and it has the power to effect a change in behaviour," I said with commitment.

"Is it direct personal experience?" asked Alana.

"Smokers can over time, develop their own health issues. They know it is the tobacco damaging their health and yet they deny the symptoms will continue to get worse over time and end in premature suffering. That's direct experience, not affecting behaviour, so it can't be totally due to direct experience," I countered.

"Yes, but there is an extenuating factor. They are addicted to needing to consume nicotine. That's what strengthens the consumption behaviour."

"That's my point. What extenuating factor is stopping the majority from changing their red meat, dairy or palm oil consumption? If it continues, it is going to contribute to the cause of a global catastrophe on the very planet they are relying on for their survival? People on Earth consume and they individually underestimate the power behind it," I said.

"Your point is valid, but what about those smokers when faced with a choice to carry on smoking, take up vaping or even quit, still continue to use tobacco because that's their personal choice," said Alana.

"But their personal choice and addiction is contributing to their continued behaviour and that behaviour, unless they are smoking over somebody else, is only affecting them. If smoking tobacco was not addictive, I think many more would give up, knowing the risks."

What I was trying to get to was I wanted to know what it would take to change people's behaviour on a massive scale when the risk of continued consumption of those types of foodstuffs and fossil fuels would end up in disaster?

"If we used, say, the consumption of red meat as a gauge of one thing within population's power to reduce, which directly affected greenhouse gas emissions, it would demonstrate an awareness in action," I said.

"Why aren't you more interested in the reduction of fossil fuel consumption? They are much more significant to increasing global warming," asked Alana.

I said I was, but people relied increasingly on governments, industry and technology to drive changes in energy production sources and develop innovations like electric cars. With this, people had become reliant on consuming energy to drive equipment which provided convenience for them.

The convenience freed them to maximise their leisure and pleasure time. Realistically and in the case of personal transport, faced with a choice to go electric, it came down to affordability and reliability supported by an extensive recharging infrastructure, verses maintaining the use of fuels which progress towards climate catastrophe.

"But realistically, James, even if people switched to electric vehicles, the majority of the electricity generated for their use would still come from fossil fuel generators," said Alana.

"Yes, but EVs can travel up to three times further than fossil fuel vehicles for the same cost of fuel and they do not emit carbon dioxide or pollutants into the air. Therefore, it is a way of slowing down greenhouse gas production and generating the time needed to develop and increase non-carbon emitting energy sources."

Populations needed to recognise, out of all the resources available to them, time was the one which was going to run out first.

"But, again realistically, average and below average income consumers and families cannot afford to change their vehicles," added Alana.

"I know, not without help."

In addition, watching the traffic when I was travelling with mum, I felt people were not going to change their commuting behaviour, which is their largest fuel consumption element. Car sharing and public transport eroded people's flexibility and independence. Nor were people going to stop flying for business, the largest profit sectors for airlines, or taking foreign holidays by air. Not when foreign holidays provided opportunities to experience more of the world's pleasures. These kinds of reduction compromises would regrettably happen later rather than sooner, unless something drastically changed.

"I think as the concern intensifies, the degree people hoping that everything will be all right, will also increase. Therefore, my feeling is, at present, people believe they are limited in their perceived power to change these things and become active in doing so," I said.

"So, if they drastically changed their beef, dairy and palm oil consumption and evidence backed up the reasons for it, it would demonstrate an increasing dynamic voice of global warming concern. Like an indicator of action, you mean?" said Alana.

"I think so, because it is under their direct control. And I think this kind of collective consumer voice would instil confidence in them to pressure governments to act in other areas. Such as, nationalised electric vehicle production at low margin, supported with other financial incentives. This would massively speed up the withdrawal of fossil fuel engines from the roads."

"That's going to cheese off the competition and where is this government going to make them and by who?"

"There will always be more well-off individuals who want a more luxurious model and suppliers could continue to produce these. If you remember during WWII, the western governments commandeered and standardised production to efficiently produce tanks, planes and munitions in a very fast response time to the threat. Their united front and drive maintained this for five years. Is there a difference? Are we not at war?" I asked.

"And for the petrol heads refusing to vape, if you get my link?"

"Increase the tax on domestic fuel purchases and stagger a withdrawal from the launch of the Gec-ko."

"Gecko?"

"Government Electric Car Knock Out, where the fossils get knocked out."

"Designed the TV advertising as well, James? I can see the plan and it has your idealistic finger prints all over it and I know why you are wanting this but this will be a next step."

"We need to take steps quickly. They could do it. In 1937 in Germany, they produced the Volkswagen, standardising car production. It became the people's car," I said.

"Yeah, and we all know whose idea that was!" replied Alana.

"Yes, all right, he may be an evil stain, but it was a good idea. Just because the originator is an abomination, should not stop people from adopting the concept. Different nations could produce different styles of basic vehicle, so long as they were internationally compatible, so as to maintain choice," I said.

"You are right. But before you can get people to buy into this kind of idea, you need to get them to activate their choice to make a difference at a smaller level. How are you going to get people to start with beef reduction and what about the beef farmers and the effects on dairy industry?"

"Industries will be faced with a need to adapt to a change. As with every war, there are the few who are sacrificed for the need of the many. Everyone fighting this war, which needs to be everyone, will all need to adapt," I said.

"Adaptation is an action. Why not get the government to ban red meat or beef to start with? If you think about it, they are very quick to ban chemicals, pharmaceuticals or products which cause health and safety risks and the products you are suggesting, present a risk. That part of the problem is then solved," said Alana.

"Yes, and who likes being told what to do. This has to be a collective people's choice. The power to change things only accumulates the momentum to further change things, when it is based on personal choice and volition. It becomes a personal commitment to the greater good when the choice is affected by a belief. A belief that others are needed to accept the same belief collectively, in order to change the outcome of the threat," I said.

"Then you would have to believe there is a threat. By looking at the symptoms, the damage currently happening in the world perhaps?" said Alana.

"World populations live with the symptoms every day, they are not important enough, obviously. And in the words of Theseus, our whale friend, the ones who do care are not strong enough to convince the ones who don't, or are apathetic, to start to care seriously."

"We need a big event then, maybe something that shocks?" suggested Alana.

"Think about Grandma Audrey and her link strengthening, so she could understand us better."

"That's not going to happen. As I said, you are undermining a fundamental law and you cannot possibly conceive the consequences and effect over time. Revealing our world might incur more devastating consequences to the Collective's energy needs than global warming as we know," reconfirmed Alana.

"Not to the level grandma is able. I am thinking about the increase in the strength of the existing connection between the Collective and everyone on Earth. Like a fibre optic broadband upgrade. I just want to rebalance scepticism and apathy against a propensity to believe, by allowing them to feel a little more connected to everyone else. There would then be a greater chance of people acting together."

"Ummm. That's interesting and it may be possible I have to admit, but I am sure the level is set to some ancient formula and cast in stone. Tell me more because, if you were to propose a change, you would need a strong argument," requested Alana, formulating the arguments in her own mind.

"We have to consider the need and nature of the Collective's connection and how it will have been impacted upon by social and societal changes happening over the last few generations."

We knew that in the human condition, unlike Harpies who were naturally evolved to balance instinct and consciousness, humans were not. They, in their development still struggled with fear based survival instincts and the need to procreate. The resultant feelings created an anxiety based existence which faced into the risk of the unknown and the eventuality of death or the commencement on a pathway towards it. That was because they thought they were mortal. A growing feeling of 'you only get one life, make the most of it', had caused distractions away from holding a belief in an existence after death. Perhaps in part due to the monopoly of those vehicles, the religions, maintaining the same stories to support their beliefs which had remained unchanged for thousands of years.

Now in developed global societies, evidence and fact were becoming of greater importance and the religions had been unable to provide rational evidence of immortality. Consuming and experiences were now the vehicle for providing the solution to an unfulfilling life, the bucket list replacing belief. That was not to say religions were not growing, they still were. But not in those societies which dominated global power, led consumerism and innovation and were the main contributors to global warming emissions.

As self-centredness increased, it also affected the way we related to others. This sense of anxiety and mortality had been orchestrated by the Collective and supported by the strength of connection between the spirit element in Earth dwellers and itself. This Earth-Collective connection also served in part to help manage instinct in a young, Earth bound and developing race. Humans could feel the dichotomy of being separated and alone verses something built-in, allowing them to feel connected to others or something unknown. This uncertainty drove the need for relationship, which is what the Collective wanted, perhaps based on its own instinctual needs, or losses.

In relationships, a belief is fostered that by not being alone, your experiential horizons widen, which further builds the desire to be connected to others. Without relationship, the feeling of disconnection to the 'other' increases and with confidence lessened, can cause you to feel more isolated and misunderstood. At that point, there is a question mark around how significant and valuable you might feel. Without feeling significant, you are less likely to believe you can make a difference.

"But you and I both know, the number of single adults is increasing in the western world and although marriages are on the decline, the largest percentage of people are in a relationship."

"Not like ours!" I said.

"We are different and you know that."

"I mean right relationship. Knowing, communicating and responding supportively to each other's needs, fears and desires. Many people can be in relationship yet feel alone, isolated or even controlled and undermined. If they suffer, they can insulate themselves, feeling insignificant and devoid of making a difference."

"I think I can see your point. I see that most people who feel like that, whether single or in relationship will move to self-protect and sooth. Many will hide and lose their sense of being able to make any difference, even if it is for themselves.

The fastest growing family group is the cohabitees. Playing devil's advocate, it makes me wonder how many of those relationships are convenient, or even co-dependent?" asked Alana.

"Also, in western societies, there is a growing acceptance of single people. They do not need to be in relationship in a traditional sense. They may seek social contact, but there does not have to be any commitment or compromise. This social change is supportive of both sexes and it drives independence. Independence is single mindedness, where with support you can disconnect and become strong in your own agenda needs and less concerned about what others or the majority feels," I added.

"So what you are saying is, the nature of relationships has changed. Particularly in the last hundred and twenty years, as has the coherence with belief and the level of distraction from consumerism. But the frequency of the Collective's link has remained the same for however long."

"Yes. I think we need to boost the signal not change the frequency. The Earthbound are increasingly bombarded by multi stimuli which are distracting. Successful advertising, for example is about airtime, interest and repetition. Add to the stimuli, the growing fear of not being independent and in control and the underlying connection to the Collective becomes increasingly lost in the overall distraction," I said.

"In addition, I suppose there is the growing feeling that in independence you build self-reliability and arguably, it is less painful to criticise yourself for your imperfections, than take the punishment from others," said Alana.

"Especially in a world where people are increasingly and publicly bombarded with the non-acceptance of imperfections and the fear of failure to achieve unrealistic standards. Self-criticism causes you to withdraw more and believe less in yourself or cushion yourself from the views of others, good or bad," I said.

"Playing devil's advocate again, do you think there is a coercive Collective impetus to educate people into the mentality of 'every man, woman and child, for themselves, because come disaster, it will be like that? After all, the Collective will need survivors," added Alana.

"I don't know. Safety in numbers also wins that argument. Whatever it is, it's about getting through to people. I think they've just stopped believing in whatever they think they are supposed to believe in and are now afraid of the thought, that it is going to take everyone getting together to sort this mess out.

That is a daunting prospect, when many believe it should be the government's responsibility to do that," I ventured.

"There are a few small hurdles to overcome in all of this. Like how much energy it would take to boost the signal; whether it would be a permanent or a temporary adjustment and whether the Collective was agreeable to taking such action to alter a course which may be part of its plan," Alana pointed out.

I felt it did not have to be permanent, but continue for enough time to instigate radical change to alleviate the threat. Ethan and Hills may have a better idea of the implications and feasibility. There was no doubt if the campaign was successful Between Worlds, there would be a massive energy influx which may power the idea.

"I think it is worth an attempt to invigorate the link?" I said.

"We both do. Let's go through Tarquin and Nevaeh," confirmed Alana.

"Hi, Tarquin, Nevaeh. We have a few hours before the UK Between Worlds trial starts. Can James and I come and see you to bounce an idea around?" asked Alana.

"What? To talk about upsetting and undermining the Collective's spiritual power network it has in place with the Earthbound?" questioned Tarquin, knowing exactly the purpose of our request.

"That's the one," I said.

"Yes, of course. See you shortly."

The Magnanimous Seven

We knew from the connection with Tarquin, he was not only with Nevaeh, but also with Ethan and Hills. Following the vibration, we transported into a Thai coastal like landscape created somewhere in the Fourth Realm. The four of them were sitting on an ornate wooden jetty protruding from a stilted residence, supported just above the crystal-clear blue sea. In the backdrop, the dense rainforest had proceeded down the hillside to meet the water and teemed with wildlife of all kinds of species.

"Hello, everyone, thanks for seeing us. Nice spot, but I thought you had your own realms to play in?" I asked, smiling widely.

"The wildlife in Realm Four is a bit more prolific than in our realms. Call it mixing business with pleasure," replied Tarquin.

"Greetings, James, Alana, nice to see you as always," said Ethan, accompanied by a smile and a nod from Hills. Nevaeh rose from her seat and hugged us both warmly.

Tarquin took up the conversation.

"The question of whether the Earth dwellers should be made aware of our domains has been debated ever since the existence of consciousness. Changing it would be a constitutional breach of what is seen as the fundamental foundation of the whole Collective system."

"But consciousness has evolved and knowing expanded since that time. Am I correct in thinking the connection between the Collective and beings on Earth has not altered since it was first initiated?" I asked.

"We understand the level of connection was set to enable free will and doubt to manifest. At the same time, imagination, the bridge between the known and the unknown, was enabled to allow the personal evolution of the imagined, into the believed. With a leap of faith, this manifests into conviction," Hills detailed.

"We take it, that is a no then?" suggested Alana.

"It is a no, Alana," added Nevaeh.

I responded to Hills saying I thought there was an issue in the chain she had just described. The one involving free will, imagination, belief, faith and finally conviction, the certainty to behave in a certain way with justification. It was to do with the security of informed choice and the development of consciousness now fuelled by multi sourced information, evidence and fact.

Earth dwellers, in my view, were naturally insecure. I believed having been made so by the Collective as a condition requiring a choice needed to elevate themselves beyond that insecurity. The choice being bound by moral codes inter twined within the same connection with the Collective.

"Yes, I can agree with that," she replied, so I continued.

"Earth dwellers still achieve their convictions; however, the growing consciousness increasingly follows a sequence of free will, imagination, seek fact or evidence and information reliability, then conviction. The security required to believe or have faith, unless it is in an information source, has reduced significantly, because these concepts are etheric rather than evidence-based actualities. Look at religions and how the followers in the more technologically advanced countries have fallen," I said.

"I think that is a reliable theory, please carry on," said Hills.

I used a business analogy, explaining we used to have the monopoly on the belief market before information and communication became apparent and widespread. We had lost market share because our product had not evolved at the same pace as the competition. That was not surprising because in their world our competition's product was a reality.

Knowing in part, came from information, so we could argue they are following the evolutionary path the Collective desired. But at the cost of belief and faith? Two essential ingredients needed for personal development and right relations with others. These were also needed to achieve greater knowing, enabling access to spiritually guided intuition derived from the Collective.

In my view, people on Earth were withdrawing from this source and were losing faith in the term 'safety in numbers'. The result was, they did not believe enough people cared or have the conviction to make changes with a combined voice, choosing not to involve themselves.

"They are losing their belief in their own abilities and their sense of being significant. You might ask, is the Collective deserting them, because it knows of something, they are about to find out?" I said.

Alana mind linked on our deepest channel to evade detection. "Let me," she said.

"That's it, isn't it? It is deserting them, much as it is letting us change and take control as we are doing in Between Worlds and the Dark Realms. It probably thinks it is all going to crash and burn anyway, so could blame the ones who took over towards the end and tried to fix it, when they did not truly know what they were doing. There is no point, is there? We are fighting a losing battle," said Alana, her words tinged with apathy.

Tarquin and Nevaeh replied in unison that there was a point and for her not to lose faith.

"I don't think I am the one to be concerned about here," said Alana, continuing by saying the Earth folks were not getting the point.

In her view, they were losing their abilities to see the value of faith and were afraid of something which was stopping them from taking personal responsibility as part of a whole. They had become dependent on information and were frightened to make decisions wrongly for fear of the judgement of others, who judge to cover up their own inadequacies.

Alana voiced that Earth had become a planet of beings who were afraid to get it wrong, who won't risk being exposed and criticised. Many also believed their voice was insignificant on its own. This was because they were too frightened by rejection or the fear of being ostracised by others, for taking action based on a belief not supported by categorical fact.

"Inert, you mean?" said Ethan, having kept quiet for the discussion so far.

Alana looked at me and I took back the lead.

I acknowledged Ethan, agreeing with his description of inert. Alana and my own view was that this condition was linked to the rapid change in information technology and within it, the speed of communication. We felt the Earth dwellers, from an individual level to those in national and international control, were at a loss as to how to manage the way forward to counteracting the global warming threat. There were obvious radical solutions which would slow it down dramatically, but it would come with implications including the cost of adversity, sacrifice and international destabilisation.

Information technology had enabled world powers to assimilate consequences based on predictive scenarios of change. Economic and political effects could be forecast by varying the continued use of resources which increased global warming. The result meant that hard evidence was available to enter into global debate, where if drastic change was made, drastic economic consequences and shifts in power and security would result.

Inertia was the result of trying to find a way through the complexity of competition, to reach cooperation on a global level to halt the very pursuits causing a threat to everyone on Earth. Although the evidence of global damage was in plain sight, information technology could not predict the scale of disaster or the time scales associated with it. This inability to predict had created a false sense of security, which delayed the level of action required to counteract the building evidence.

At an individual level, in their perceived powerlessness, people were left to deny their world was going to change drastically, with their fate and that of their loved ones, being too frightening for them to conceive. The speed of information change and social pressure to adopt evidence-based information had for many, collapsed the Collective faith link. The adopted position for the individual now, was to have faith everything would be all right, based on information fed to them. I added and summed up our view.

"As we know, personal responsibility doesn't work like that. Because the Collective requires them to choose to take right action, but they do not know what right action to take. That is because nobody is telling them, or the voice providing the message is no longer clear or loud enough amongst the distractions of life. I do not think the Collective foresaw this coming. As the Collective is in fact, the collective conscious of both after world and Earth world beings, I am suggesting part of the Collective's consciousness has become inert as a result. Hence lower order overpopulation systems kicking in," I said.

The entire scape surrounding the jetty was suddenly flooded with phosphorescent white and violet light. Even Ethan and Hills shielded their eyes to the undetected arrival of a Realm Seven spirit. The two colours oscillated within a column like structure, losing their intensity to become a glowing being, unmistakeably powerful. It spoke slowly and deliberately.

"Representatives from Realms four, five and six in one meeting place! Your command of the immanent Harpy invasion of Between Worlds, not the topic of debate? Instead, I hear you question the divine authority and prowess of the Collective's design. Next topic, a coup d'état perhaps?"

I could tell that no one in our group was capable of reading this being as he maintained an impenetrable guard and therefore we were at a loss to truly decipher his intensions. The expressions on their faces, including Ethan and

Hills, were nothing short of shock. I knew I had to trust what was in my heart because I knew this being would be able to clearly see our intentions.

"I fail to see how this is any of your business," I said calmly.

I kept my face straight and my mind as guarded as possible within my Realm Four capability. A painful silence ensued with further expressions of shock from my colleagues, except this time in my direction. Then the being burst out laughing. Not a chuckle but a 'heart of your bottom' laugh which continued until every member on the deck had joined in.

The being transformed from its glow and into an ancient and majestic Harpy. He was tall, erect and handsome; his raptor like facial features sharpened his image. His torso and arms were human in form with huge dark brown wings draping down his feathered back, overlapping his tail feathers. From the legs down, he was avian. His legs reversing out backwards at the knee joints and feet replaced with powerful talons. He tilted his head and studied me intently. I held my hand out to greet him.

"I am James. I am very pleased you got my joke, I got yours."

"I know exactly who you are and that was, funny. I haven't laughed like that in a long time, so thank you and pleased to meet you. My name is Torfaen."

"Likewise. You are my first seven."

Ethan and Hills had met with Torfaen on numerous occasions previously, as he was their mentor, but had not been able to see him through his guise. He introduced himself to Tarquin and Nevaeh and finally Alana.

"Torfaen is a Welsh name, isn't it?" asked Alana.

"It is. It means breaker of rocks," he replied.

Alana smiled at him as he winked at her. She subdued the intrigue and delight, but shared the relevance with me. I could tell Torfaen was a golden eagle like Hills and I, his tribe flying the South Wales mountains and valleys when eagles still populated the area, probably eons ago.

"I am aware of the discussion you have been having. I am also aware of what you and Alana have debated prior to arriving here," said Torfaen.

"Can we turn up the volume?" asked Alana.

"Can the Earth stop mining, drilling for and consuming fossil fuels? There is much to consider, Alana," he replied.

"We thought there would be, but is it worth consideration?" I asked him.

"James, you have said that there are consequences to information technology and that is to do with those consequences of change being easier to identify and then assimilate into potential vulnerabilities as well as beneficial outcomes. You know here in the after world we are not limited by information technology. But we are still faced with managing the implications of change. Changing the connective link would have far-reaching consequences. Would we all not agree?" asked Torfaen. Tarquin responded first.

"I see the connection between the Collective and the Earthbound as a blended set of frequencies designed to stimulate responses. Some are default such as procreation of the species which connect directly with instinctual behaviours. Others are higher order, such as the desire and need for relationship, again based on fundamental needs to survive, like attachment. The highest order is in the area of belief and faith in the more than, the more than being a presence or power which is beyond comprehension yet influences life paths and one could argue, fate. The link provides a feeling that someone has your back when you are solely responsible. The mechanism is complex and connections innumerable," proposed Tarquin. Hills continued.

"Yes but, within that highest order, the stimuli can be misinterpreted. You may believe you will be repeatedly forgiven for your sins if you ask for forgiveness and direction. Also, that life paths are at the will of God, so discounting responsibility. They may consider they are acting in God's name or nature, choosing not to learn along the way, believing they will be saved regardless. The connection therefore allows free will but strives to foster balance overall," added Hills. Ethan continued.

"Belief and faith are like power. They are neither positive nor negative, inert unless choice activates them. They are a catalyst for something else in the process for taking action, acceptance. This may be of something factual or etheric. Maybe the Collective did anticipate the implications of information technology in its entirety. It may have anticipated a move away from belief into evidence-based decision-making. It has upheld the law of the free will to choose and it may have understood humans needed this chance to experience it. Therefore, the intricacies of involvement are unfathomable," injected Ethan.

Whilst I loved and respected high planers, they had a tendency to explore the menucha of meaning more than Alana accused me of doing. I checked my patience chip and although we still had time before the Harpy send off, in my view, we needed to move this along.

"We accept there is a global warming issue on Earth. We didn't arrive at that acceptance through a source of facts we can share with the Earth bound. We are aware because we have a greater ability to know. We cannot share this knowing with Earth dwellers either, because it is based on our acceptance of belief and the Collective forbids it. The problem is, given the urgency of this matter, the Earth bound at their level of development, cannot access knowing through current levels of belief," I said and Alana followed.

"You are all aware of mine and James' conversation before we came here."

She identified the Earthbound could not predict the scale or type of damage the Earth would respond with in reaction to their neglect. There was a fear of global political backlash which was preventing governments from instigating action. The reason for this being that effective action would result in the destabilisation of their own or other country's economies, creating conflict and potentially, global war. The problem was this precarious status quo limited the progress to reduce the threat.

"James and I are saying that the evidence on Earth to support a disaster is etheric. They will not gain the evidence via facts because the facts only support possible outcomes. We need to escalate those possibilities to the level of likely and then to probable. A probable status can still remain inert and that is why we need to increase the sense of personal responsibility towards others at the same time. That is not just accepting the concept, but believing that personal involvement will make a difference," said Alana. I continued.

"We are proposing that elements of the Collective-human connection be amplified," I said.

We were unable to know to what extent, as our knowing did not stretch that far. However, we saw that altering it would increase positive attachment to the Collective and to other fellow beings as a result. This would increase security and a sense of safety in numbers.

However, the intension was not to allow people to feel secure enough not to act, by believing God or a higher power would save them. The basis of the connection change would be to create a sense of increased spiritual cohesiveness between people. This may increase a resurrection in the strength of belief in religions, which was not a negative side effect. But the other intension was to help people to realise their own significance and in joining with others in the same behaviour, it would be a demonstration of that.

"It is not about getting people to take up arms against governments, it is about demonstrating a cohesive energy which can be harnessed to change something. This results from people starting to believe they can. Choice and free will must remain the constants. Currently, people will not act cohesively because the global warming crisis is shrouded in too many possibilities. Outcomes are uncertain and likelihoods and concrete probabilities etheric. There is a lot of information about the causes and they can see the effects and symptoms of damage, but they cannot see a way forward on their own. We have the power to make a difference. By doing this, we are helping them to help themselves," I proposed.

Torfaen stroked his beak with his fingers. I could tell he was thinking, not only of the global consequences of such an action, but also, if he chose to support the idea, whether he could gain enough support to effect it.

"If it happened, we could not evoke a reaction on a shock level. I am also seeing it would be temporary until we saw the effects of changes on Earth." Torfaen blew out air in an expression of the difficulty to balance the proposal.

"What level of behaviour change resulting from a change in the connection, are you looking for?" he asked.

"We are looking for indicators of involvement through consumerism, because they all consume. My idea is to use red meat and palm oil consumption as an indicator of personal commitment, making a difference on a collective scale. As simple as if you eat beef, cows will continue to add greenhouse gases to the climate. Once people see that their personal actions can change contributing factors, I believe there will be a greater impetus and a united volition to change other contributing negative influences. I realise it is unlikely the Collective will send subliminal messages through the link to focus action; however, there is concern and awareness building already on Earth, which would be amplified by their presence. I think, once people see they can make powerful changes, this will strengthen their resolve to making further ones with a greater acceptance of the costs and consequences," I said.

"These are uncertain times. Not only for Earth folk, but us also. We have and are about to make further changes. Like you and Alana have said about Earth outcomes being etheric, we also face unforeseen outcomes. I know from all here, you are in favour of trying this, although there are some reservations around side effects," said Torfaen.

"Are there others who break rocks in your realm?" asked Alana.

"We will need to consider the proposal and gauge the after-world support for it. If we reach agreement, others and I from my realm will then need to blend and create ourselves into a key in order to access the consciousness of the divine ether. This ether, being the glue which adheres to all and knows of all. I will be in touch, I wish you well for Between Worlds and your investigations in the dark. Not my business…" Torfaen disappeared with a laugh accompanying him.

"Ladies and gents, that was good work. Thank you, James and Alana. We have no time to spare and have a pressing engagement, let's go," said Ethan.

Alana and I let the others disappear, then hugged each other, smiles beaming.

"Fingers crossed we have said enough," said Alana.

"I hope so, darling. You know, the Collective is the master of subliminal messages. It wouldn't harm to add one or two maybe?" I thought.

"Let's see what comes. Can't believe you said that to him!" she replied.

Let's Go

Alana and I transported in to find the rest of our group already present.

"Nice holiday, you two?" asked Simon.

"You know, family and friends," I replied.

I opened a link in for Simon to review the very recent meeting we had had with Torfaen and the others and invited other members of our group to see what we had been trying to achieve.

"Going up in the after world, brother. Conversations with Seveners. Good on you and Alana for having the balls to take the chance. Let's hope it pays off," he replied.

"So Realm Seven Harpies present in our ancient guise. Amazing, but I suppose they have nothing to hide from," said Audaz.

It was just after 04.00 and the amphitheatre was full. Hills confirmed all were present from the last meeting. Conversations and greetings reverberated around the circular structure as they waited patiently to commence some seemingly routine event.

"What is the overlying feeling, Hills?" asked Alana.

"Poise. Followed by focus and intent to complete. They want to beat the thirty-six-hour deadline, mop up thoroughly and return valiant and victorious," she described.

"On point then," Alana added.

Ethan, Hills, Tarquin and Nevaeh called our group closer to update us on the accompaniment of the religious groups into the UK and global missions.

"They have got through their discussions and are ready to support us," said Ethan.

"Who is leading the movement?" asked Simon.

"No one on their own. They have had to settle on a committee. Representatives from each religion will be part of a panel which will handle any issues arising," added Nevaeh.

"Haven't they got someone in Realm Five or Six who could head up their involvement, like you are doing for us?" asked Scout.

"There are no religions past the level of Realm Four Scout. Knowing replaces any need to follow them," said Tarquin.

"So why are they all still believing in and following their religions?" he said.

"It's called free will. We all believe what we wish to, until such time when a belief no longer serves a new reality we find ourselves growing into," said Ethan.

"How many will accompany the force into the UK?" asked Simon.

"Three hundred and fifty thousand. Ten per team. They have nearly a million in reserve for this mission should the numbers not be great enough to keep up with the combat teams. They have an additional two million available for the global mission," said Nevaeh.

"Those are incredible numbers. Have they been briefed on what we are doing and the dos and don'ts of supporting the vulnerable Leaves?" I asked.

"Tarquin and I have been meeting with them. They know exactly what is expected of them. They did want more power like the ability to judge and send Leaves to the darker realm, however, have accepted their role will be invaluable in increasing energy flow as Leaves come over to Realm Four," added Nevaeh.

"I am sorry. I struggle with religion, having sat in Between Worlds for all that time feeling shameful, guilty and afraid because of religious doctrine. Each to their own, but I hope we don't get situations where transfers are conditional and reality is manipulated. Any energy accrued from their transfer will be lost if Leaves choose to go back," said Simon. Ethan then sought to broaden his view.

"This, as far as I know, is the first army which has been raised from the after world. This is not a holy war and they know that. This is a combined force whose job is to clear dark Leaves and facilitate an energy surge into the Collective. Much as you are the most vocally suspicious of the religions amongst us, there will be the more zealous individuals amongst them, who are there to further their cause. I should also imagine, within our Harpy force, there are individuals who will be competitive and I expect this to be the same of the religious groups. Dark Leaves caught verses Leaf souls saved. Better you save your energy for coordinating Simon, the UK is a trial run by your design, so let's see what happens," said Ethan.

"Okay, thank you and point taken. Let's do this," replied Simon.

Our group made their entrance onto the dias to a rapturous response. Simon held up his hand in salute until all voices were silenced.

"Can someone remind me, what are we here for?" Simon asked the audience in his sarcastically playful tone I had seen him use on other occasions. It always delighted the audience and after they had quietened down, he spoke again.

"Oh yes, autumn has come, my friends. A time to sweep up the Leaves who are rotten and polluting so as to allow others to grow safely and in peace. I ask you to meet your task with compassion. The adversaries you seek have become whom they are through the wounds inflicted by others when they were unable to defend themselves. Rather than seeking to heal, they have chosen to perpetuate their suffering through the suffering and control of others more vulnerable. We seek them for this choice. Our weapons are effective, but they can cause suffering. Minimise this suffering by showing compassion and deal with these Leaves efficiently and quickly." Sarah followed his opening address.

"Support Officers; the religious groups have delivered," said Sarah.

She detailed they would be supporting teams during this trial and the global mission. Ten would be assigned for officers to refer into, with more in reserve. Hills transmitted the reference point entry to the database through which each officer and team member could access the vibrations and identities of their support team. The religious support teams would also have the facility to access combat team information. Additional reserves could be accessed via the same portal.

"Their objective is to support, advise and encourage and are aware they must work effectively and keep up with the geographical progress of the teams they are assigned to. These teams have the same start coordinates as you do and will meet you there, then follow," informed Sarah, who then handed over to Greg.

"When James, Alana, Scout and Audaz were in Denby Dale dealing with a problem Leaf, they discovered a caging system used by the Leaves to hold people. You are well aware of this and it will be one of your most frequently used pieces of equipment. My point is, as you proceed, it is possible you will come across other methods or weapons we are not aware of. You must upload these into the weapons interface on the database as soon as possible, so others will know of their operation and presence. I will send out alerts via Ethan and Hills to advise you. I will also be in the field, keeping an eye on how you are getting on, as will Audaz and Conchita. I wish you good luck," said Greg.

Simon stepped forward again.

"Harpies, we do this together because we are the best at what we do. Good hunting, see you Saturday. Let's go."

There was an instantaneous departure as thousands of Harpies including, Audaz, Conchita, Taca and Scout, who left with them. I listened to the sudden silence and compared it to the conflict that was now underway on the British mainland.

Ethan had created a visual display and accessible portal to monitor the geographical progress and dark Leaves exiled to the Between World's dark realm. It also tracked the number of other Leaves deciding to transfer to the after world. As teams drove northward, after a while, it became obvious the religious groups were lagging behind. This was probably because supportive encouragement was taking more time to effect transfers.

Sarah took the initiative and liaised directly with the interfaith committee to coordinate additional support needed by the combat teams. Their response was rapid with additional reserves being deployed immediately on her command. She then facilitated direct communication via Hills to inform the relevant Support Officers of their increased resource.

"It must be amazing to be able to communicate so specifically and instantly, over a broad field of recipients. We could not do this without the abilities you and Ethan command. It would be an uncoordinated bun fight," said Sarah.

"You do what you can, like I see you and your friends do every day. Whilst I find James a little beyond his station at times, I watched him earlier challenge a Realm Sevener, because he and Alana believed in what they felt was needed to happen. All of you have tremendous courage and skills and we could not achieve this without you either," confirmed Hills.

Sarah smiled and thanked her.

"I am so pleased we from different realms can work together. I thought wrongly in the past, that you were all a little unreachable," said Sarah.

"We are here because there is a need. The after world has just bumbled along in the past, as we have tended to our business. These latest events necessitate our presence and we are demonstrating our commitment to act, as you are," replied Hills.

The results were accumulating quickly as the combined forces tracked, dispatched and encouraged in their task. With time flying, the offence was two hours in. We could see from the geography that the teams had slowed up around London with the increased concentration of targets. Greg checked in with Taca.

"How's it going, Snowflake?" he asked, using one of his pet name for her brightness. She replied with one of his.

"All right, Firefly, couldn't have wished for a better team. Your buddy says hi. He misses your creative acrobatics during the shootouts. We came up through Brighton and are slowing down because the targets are becoming more intensive. There are a lot of teams operating in London."

"Where are you now? By looks of things, you are in Westminster," asked Greg.

I noticed Simon turn to listen.

"We are on the top of this cylindrical tower on Churchill Gardens Road adjacent to Johnson's Place. Our target is in a vacant building a short distance away. He is some guy called Dexter. Scout knows who he is, he overlords the Westminster borough."

"Did Scout somehow elect to get that target?" Greg asked. Simon was now connected to the conversation.

"He says he might have had something to do with it. Unfinished business he says."

"Taca, it's Simon. Are you linked in Scout?"

"Yes, I am," Scout replied.

"You two, you Roman and Victoria, be very careful of this Leaf. Westminster is a prime crime borough in London and Dexter will use everything he can to defend his patch. He is connected and it is likely will know there is a force on its way who will target him and his closest."

This Leaf, a well-presented white Englishman, was a little more sophisticated and intelligent than the other London Commanders we had captured. His delusions of grandeur were fuelled by his belief he was on God's mission to organise crime, thus controlling the chaos which would otherwise happen without him. Being clever and manipulative, he had killed under the radar when alive on Earth and was never caught for the seven murders of those who he believed threatened his mission. It was very likely he would be vigilant and well defended.

"Should we be scared now?" asked Taca.

"No. Just hyper aware and prepared for heavy firepower," replied Simon.

I could read from Greg he was uncertain as to whether to join them for this sortie. So, I assured him I would handle any issues until his return.

"I am coming to join you, Snowy, if that's all right with you and the others," said Greg.

"Honestly, we will be fine. We have already done a recon and there are about twelve of them in this social centre," said Taca.

"All right, keep on your toes," Greg replied.

I linked with Alana to place her on alert to the possibility we may be needed in this fight. Simon's description concerned me and I was thinking of scenarios of how I would defend myself if I were Dexter.

The minutes passed and we waited. We knew they would be in the thick of it and concentrating all of their focus on their adversaries. I put a link into Scout, just a welfare echo check, nothing which would distract him if he was in the midst of conflict. It bounced back.

"Greg, I can't get through to Scout, check Taca," I said.

He achieved the same result. Both of us looked at Simon.

"I am linking into the guide and catcher now. Sharna, Pierre, have you got sight of the team?" said Simon.

Pierre responded negatively. They had watched them dematerialise and then had relocated to hide in view and in earshot of the building. They had heard a number of shots and then nothing.

"We were presuming it had been an easy hit and everything was under control. We were just waiting for their call," reported Sharna.

Greg, Alana and I instantaneously split, projecting our consciousness into the space the team had materialised into. Rather than twelve, there were over fifty hostile Leaves who must have transported in on a signal when the team arrived.

According to Greg, there were familiar faces present who he had spotted in Southwark and Lambeth and then his last sortie into Tower Hamlets, where Camden Leaves had been present as guests. It appeared, Dexter had taken advantage of the other Commander's absence and been recruiting aggressively.

Our team were caged, held sitting on the ground, sixteen power lines transversing their prison to the Leaves engaged to hold them. Dexter was gloating at the success of his masterful plan and the predictability of the team's approach. He had ordered roof top vigilance and the team had been under surveillance since their arrival.

Anticipating their move, he had created a light cage encompassing virtually the entire room. Our team had no idea they were about to transport themselves into a trap. Unaware of the scale of our National operation, he chastised them for their weakness and futile attempt to capture him, the only ordained Commander in the land, who answered only to God.

"It seems like God's having a laugh, Dexter, because we are acting on its command also and we cannot both be right," said Taca.

"God is not an it, he is a he and he has placed his faith in me to order the Leaves under my control, structuring our existence here, providing purpose and meaning," replied Dexter.

As we half listened to the conversation, we scanned the environment and assessed the Leaves present. When we freed Simon in Denby Dale last year, he was also held by a light cage and as it was then, the Leaves powering this one, did not have the power to achieve this and shield at the same time. The difference was, only four held Simon and he was just able to communicate out of it. With sixteen, all communication was blocked other than verbally to those closest to it.

"And such high order purpose and meaning you dictate, Dexter. You create misery and suffering in those around you and who are under your influence. You do not serve God's interest; you serve your own. You may inflate your intelligence and spirituality all you like. You will always be a scumbag, who hasn't quite worked it out," Taca, purposely chipped away at his ego.

Dexter raised his hand and a volley of headshots slammed into the sides of the cage. The team maintained their guards, unflinching to the barrage.

"Are you going to hold us forever, Dexter?" asked Taca.

"Indefinitely was more my thinking. I have enough resource under my command to do so if I wish. I would torture and kill you all if I could but God seems to have taken those pleasures away from me. I will just wear your shields down gradually until you are able to feel the misery of our weapons wounding you into hopelessness and despair."

"I am pretty used to misery and despair. All of my lifetimes have been filled with them, they have been very hard," replied Taca, who was now subtly changing her approach.

"Lifetimes? You blaspheme. There is only one lifetime. My predicament and that of others around me is a lifetime extension. In my case, because I have not completed God's task. When I do, he will welcome me warmly into heaven."

"As I said, Dexter, you are one who hasn't quite worked it out. This is a shame because you appear to be a powerful and influential man. Tall, handsome and focussed, a natural born leader others want to follow. Actually, a man who interests me on lots of levels."

We watched Roman and Victoria turn to scrutinise Taca as she conducted her interaction with Dexter. Being linked to Greg, I could feel him smiling, as he watched his partner seduce her captor with words and feelings in order to enter his mind and explore his desires. As she had been speaking with him, she had slowly and subtly altered her features, form and tone into a projection which stirred him.

"Please let me out, Dexter, I am seeing now that it is you who is the more powerful in this fight. I will follow you and help you achieve your desires. With my knowledge, we can do it together. If you search your heart, you will see?" Taca wooed his ego softly.

It was obvious Taca had made her connection as Dexter stood more erect and puffed out his chest.

"Get ready to release the cage. I want the others still held but her to be freed," ordered Dexter.

Taca mind linked with the others to be ready to instigate a full frontal attack as soon as the cage was dropped.

"Thank you. God has chosen well to place his faith in you. I will never be a regret to you," Taca said.

"Dexter sir, it's...not the same woman," said one of his lieutenants nervously.

"Of course it is. I see what I see," he replied.

He looked around at the faces of his own men and women present, who were shaking their heads. The same lieutenant raised his hand ordering the others to open fire. He shouted at them to obey when they hesitated. The noise and distraction disempowered Taca who was unable to maintain the hypnotic mind link on Dexter.

"Seize fire!" ordered Dexter, his mind clearing, though his sight still saw the object of his desire.

"Witchcraft! However, I could still use someone like you, although I could never trust you. You would always be caged. Maybe you could be trusted over time," he said, still partly caught by Taca's hypnosis.

Greg linked to Alana and I and we pulled back out of the split. We were joined by Simon for an update.

"She normally wins them over, but there were a lot of them, weren't there?" said Greg.

"They are stuck. Shall we order another team in there or are you going to handle this yourselves?" asked Simon.

"No. I will sort it out; I have an idea. Can you split again to monitor and come in on my signal? We will need help to cage and sort these Leaves," Greg asked Alana and I.

"Who dares, hey?" added Alana. "See you back in there."

Alana and I split immediately and in time to see Greg materialise inside the cage. We had no way of linking to him as he had just cut himself off from us. We could not understand how he had made such a stupid mistake. Alana wondered whether he had followed Taca's vibration specifically in haste, not thinking about the cage.

Fifty Leaves including the Commander opened fire as he arrived, uncertain of his abilities. Greg crouched down on the floor with his hands over his ears in submission. He mind-linked to Taca and Scout. After the fire had stopped, he got up and stood facing Dexter.

"That was bad luck. If I had known there was a cage, I would have avoided it and then you would all have been sorry," said Greg.

Dexter looked at him confused by what had just happened and decided he must be an idiot.

"Well, it is nice to see that even the dim-witted make it into heaven!" scoffed Dexter.

"I was lucky, there were no exams or anything to get in, I just arrived there. Funny really," replied Greg.

Dexter burst out laughing followed by the other Leaves present. As they amused themselves, he linked to all four members of the team, requesting Victoria and Roman listen while he spoke to Taca and Scout.

"We are getting out of here, enough time lost. Tristar Scout, it will flatten everything, guards, shields and all. I have James and Alana on standby to help us clear up," said Greg.

"It doesn't exist; it is a myth," Scout replied.

"No Scout, it isn't," confirmed Taca.

"It is impossible; we would need three Harpy horses," said Scout.

"We have three, Scout," said Greg.

Scout looked from Taca's face to Greg's as they smiled at him. His eyes welled up as he told them fondly, they would never cease to amaze him.

"I am inputting the tristar download, Scout, we need to set a formation and get Victoria and Roman inside our triangle. We will transform to horses first, get in position and then follow my cue," instructed Greg.

The Leaves had finished laughing at Greg when Dexter focussed his attention on him once again.

"What do you do in heaven, idiot?" asked Dexter.

"Well, it's a bit embarrassing. It may sound strange to you, but I am a horse really, not enough humans would volunteer to come and get you. We can talk in heaven, but we don't much. I don't know, just graze and walk around. We are not too bright really. We thought it would look odd if we did not come as humans to try and catch you. I can show you if you like," said Greg.

"Do what you like, you are not getting out of there," said Dexter.

Greg transformed to his black horse and told Dexter that two others in the group were also horses and would it be all right if they transformed, as being in a human shape was a bit uncomfortable.

"Please yourselves," was his reply.

Taca and Scout transformed to their horses, Scout neighing and farting loudly as a distraction. The room erupted as Greg and Taca followed suit.

"Formation!" instructed Greg. Roman and Vitoria moved into the centre of the triangle the other's hindquarters made, as they faced outwards in different directions.

"Tristar!"

What Alana and I witnessed from our split position was nothing short of incredible. All three horses raised on their back legs and transformed to Pegasus's, wings elevated and facing forwards, meeting at the tips. White light started to swirl around them rapidly increasing in velocity as it shot upwards into a vortex, crested and plummeted to the ground forcing its way outward as a powerful wave in every direction. Everything in its path was knocked flat, lying motionless on the floor. Alana and I transported in and gave them a round of applause. All three transformed back to horse form.

"Masters! That was brilliant, never experienced anything like it," I said.

"We had a good teacher. He was very wise and never disclosed our ability to transform to our Pegasus. He is the only other we know. You met him earlier, although he was a Sixer when he came across us," said Taca.

"Torfaen you mean?" asked Alana in surprise. Taca nodded.

"Thanks, buddy, I had no idea that was possible and I could do something like that," said Scout.

Scout dropped his chin and placed his forehead on Greg's, so their faces and muzzles were aligned. He blew up Greg's nose, to which Greg reciprocated in close friendship and respect.

"Are you and Taca going to confess that you are Harpy horses really?" asked Scout.

"We're not, Scout, we are just, I don't know, something weird," said Greg.

"Excuse me, guys. How long before these Leaves wake up?" asked Roman.

"They will be out for a while, but let's get them bagged and tagged. Roman, can you and James get all the non-dark realm candidates together. Of them, Alana, can you identify potential realm three Leaves with Victoria, we need to keep them all caged until after the support arrives. Greg and I will sort out the dark and get them transferred. I am not going to wait till they wake up, they can wake up in the dark," said Taca.

Greg and Taca's job done, Victoria contacted Sharna and Pierre to attend and be ready for the big wake up. She also requested support from her religious colleagues who had now been affectionately nick named the God Squad. Taca, Roman and Scout located and then departed to their next target in Essex. Greg, Alana and I transported back to Simon with whom we shared our experiences after Greg had uploaded the cage trap scenario Dexter had used, to the database.

"Will you upload Tristar?" I asked.

"No. The teaching and practice takes much time and commitment. Plus, there are not enough horses to go around," replied Greg.

"I am amazed, Greg, by you and Taca, amazed," I told him with total respect. He smiled and winked in reply.

The mission we had just been involved in had resulted in the capture of one commander, 11 lieutenants and eighteen other dark realm candidates. Of the Leaves left, twelve had decided to defect to the after world.

Mopping Up

Alana and I spectated, watching Simon and Sarah coordinate the task force with Greg's input. He dipped in and out of Between Worlds to check on progress or respond to teams who were slowed down and needed direct support.

Taca and Scout had been fighting their way through Newcastle Upon Tyne at the fourteen-hour check-in, with other teams heading up the west coast. That was three hours ago. They were now wading through rural Northumberland picking up sporadic targets on their way to Edinburgh.

Ireland had been cleared, although there was intensive fighting in Belfast and Dublin. The heaviest resistance had been met in Glasgow and Paisley in Scotland. Here teams grouped together to improve their odds, with Audaz and Conchita flying in to bolster confidence and get involved themselves.

The wake left by the teams was far reaching. Half of the God Squad reserves had been deployed, with reports coming back that support in many cases had been turned into time consuming counselling sessions. Sarah had had strong words with their committee, to be met with, 'We are doing God's work'. Her reply was that we were all doing God's work and they just needed to pull their finger out and get moving with the teams.

She spoke with Nevaeh to arrange a debrief meeting as in her view, they were more likely to encourage defectors soon after a conflict had happened and word was hot off the press. Nevaeh agreed to arrange this. The main problem was the coordination of God Squad teams. Like the committee, they were not led, so no one was ultimately responsible for driving ground squads forward.

"James speaks dog really well. Perhaps he can recruit a couple of thousand Collies to help move them along next time," said Sarah.

"Aunt Sarah, that is just a bit harsh. You have been spending too much time with Uncle Simon," replied Nevaeh.

As we approached the twenty-first-hour time marker, the dark leaf capture figures were slowing down on Ethan's scoreboard. The defector totals, however, were still growing healthily. Teams were now involved in the mop up operation and were retargeting individuals whom they missed or had escaped them on the way north. Simon kept tracks on the locations teams redeployed to in search of targets, via team leaders accessing the database. Ethan kept him abreast of the general movements.

"No offence, Ethan, but I could do with a couple of assistants for the global mission."

"Me too, Simon. This is quite a challenge," responded Ethan.

"Us too," said Sarah and Hills. "It's intense fun though."

"Liberating is my chosen description," said Nevaeh. "However, frustrating at times."

The number of targets totalled three hundred and forty-seven thousand dark realm candidates and at the twenty-five-hour time elapsed marker, there were two hundred left to capture. Most of the combat teams were now working alongside their support officers and the God squad to encourage other Leaves to pass over. The remainders had transported back to Realm Four, some to the amphitheatre to touch base and share their experiences with their comrades.

With Tarquin now being responsible for the Dark Realms in the after world, he had taken responsibility for the dark realm within Between Worlds. His role was to ensure no dark Leaves had been transported into it, whose historical and current actions did not justify seclusion.

He and Ethan had decided, of those wrongly transported, they should be given time to get a feel for the environment, spending time there before Tarquin transported them back to the Between Worlds light realm. They wanted a message taken back to those Leaves who were of Realm Three potential status, that a reward existed for them, should they negatively persist in affecting others.

At twenty-six hours, all targets had been successfully transferred and those in error returned. With the warrior's and support officer's tasks complete, they shipped back to Four. The God squad continued to help Leaves come to Realm Four or to Realm Three should they wish to face their responsibility. The incentive being they could restart their journey towards being reborn back to Earth in the future.

Within four hours, willing Leaf potentials had dwindled and the squad also returned. Ethan had previously messaged the guide and catcher network to be alert to stragglers wishing to transfer once the squad had departed. He then called a meeting to congratulate us all on our roles and a brilliant job well done.

Other than the targets, a little over one million Leaves had decided to defect; however, he anticipated ten percent of these would drift back. Half of the influx of new Realm Four dwellers were met by family and friends. For those whose close ones had revolved leaving them without a connection in Four, realm guides were on hand to help them acclimatise to their new home.

It would be some time before the additional energy influx would make a difference to population growth on Earth, the main effects anticipated once the global mission was under way.

"If I could tire, I would be tired now. What an experience, even for Hills and myself. Although I know, if I didn't, Leaves left in the lighter realm are going to find themselves living in a more peaceful environment. As for the Earth bound, I wonder what their sense is now to have negative influences suddenly taken away? Let's hope the crime rates reflect, the change," said Ethan.

"What about the Limpet Leaves?" asked Sarah. "Many are not even of Realm Three status and although, overall Between Worlds will be more peaceful, they will continue to affect people."

"We know some will be freed from Commander influence but without help and support they are likely to persist in their attachment. Tarquin discussed this at the guide and catcher meeting and now the darker Leaves have been separated, guides will focus more effort on supporting the Limpets. This will also take place globally. Perhaps you might choose to have input into this task once the global clearing has been achieved?" replied Hills.

"Yes. I would like to contribute to increasing their wellbeing, they have had a rough ride," responded Sarah.

"Speaking of resource, although this mission worked well, it has shown me we need additional help to coordinate our side of it when the global mission starts," said Ethan.

"Simon? Conchita and I will help you and Sarah when the global mission starts, if you wish? We found we were interrupting the teams more than supporting them in our role. Although the combat opportunities were good fun, we feel our service would be better used in the command centre."

"That is fine, Audaz, offer accepted, thank you. Thanks, Conchita. Come Monday though, you still need to advise teams travelling through South America as we discussed before," said Simon.

"We will and will transport in if needed," confirmed Audaz.

"Ethan and I feel we need two more Sixers for the global mission who can work with us and we will arrange that by Monday," said Hills.

"Hills and I must go. We will see you back here tomorrow at 11.00 for the debrief." They both disappeared.

"Us too," said Tarquin. "James, Alana, I will be in touch. We need to talk through the after world Dark Realm visit. I am not available on Sunday, so it will be before our meeting tomorrow."

"Right you are. We will wait for your call," I said, pleased we could finally get moving.

As our team came together, the focus was on Greg, Taca and Scout. Watching Greg in action with Dexter was like poetry in motion. He played a game with him, projecting his mocked idiocy, refrained from using monologues or threats, engineered his strategy and when the moment came, without drama, just executed his plan. He was a true professional and highly trained. As for his and Taca's ability to achieve Pegasus, their skills and abilities were far reaching into incredible.

"I have to say you two, you are spectacular in battle. How come you can achieve your Pegasus?" I asked. "You are both human line Harpies."

"We don't know," replied Greg, Scout giving his view.

"They are like horses. They understand me and know how I think and feel. They also know at a horse instinct level. It is really useful when you are in the thick of it. What's more, Tristar is an ancient legend where three horses joined together to create a huge tidal wave which washed an enemy away. Virtually, every horse is aware of that legend. To be part of something I thought of as just a myth was mind blowing," said Scout.

"Taca and I have thought a lot about our situation over the centuries. Pegasus originates from Greece and we wonder whether centaurs actually existed and somewhere along the way there was a highbred whose light energy was mixed with Pegasus and which was somehow introduced into the Harpy raptor line," said Greg.

"There are a lot of ifs, maybes and a possible in that," said Simon.

"Well, that's our theory anyway. It is a bit more romantic than accepting you are an abnormality," added Taca.

"What does Torfaen know about it?" asked Alana.

"He is in our line; we are descendants connected to him. Our guess is he knows, but he has not divulged anything to us other than he says its occurrence is something to do with awakening to a need to remain previously hidden. Think what you like of that, we have tossed that one around ever since he said it to us," explained Greg.

"Do you have regular contact with him?" asked Alana.

"No. We have seen him three times in all of our lifetimes," said Taca.

"As for uploading Tristar as an available weapon, I think it would cause more problems at this stage with having to reorganise the teams to put horses together. We have it as a backup if needed," said Simon.

We all agreed. With less than twenty-four hours until the debrief, we said our goodbyes and arranged to meet up just before the next meeting started.

As Alana and I were shortly to commence our mission and could be occupied with our investigations, I thought I would gain an update on Grandma Audrey. Linking into Grandfather, he had been to see her a number of times, she describing her sense of being as 'soldiering on'. She had already visited the doctors to explain her decision not to go ahead with treatment and had investigated what kind of support she and Mum could expect as the time for her to come over approached.

"She has always been organised, John. It will probably be planned out until the last minute," he informed me.

"Grandad, Alana and I could be away for a little while. We have a mission and you may not be able to reach us. Can you keep us updated on Hazel, regardless please?"

"Will do. Anywhere sunny?"

"I can't really say, shouldn't think so. We will keep in touch as and when."

"All right, John, keep safe and see you soon. Lots of love."

"Love you too, Grandad, and love to Grandma and Hazel."

Debrief

By 11.00, the debrief meeting was underway, the atmosphere lively and electric. As many stories were shared amongst the warriors and support officers, a green and yellow aurora capped the amphitheatre in response to their mood. Morale was definitely high, as was that of the committee of the religious group who were also present. At her own debrief meeting, Nevaeh's faith in their intensions had been restored, as rather than a recruitment drive, the God Squad had upheld their part of the mission to facilitate passing based on after world reality. This was confirmed by the number of Leaves drifting back to Between Worlds, which had been lower than expected, at only a four percent. Simon spoke into the assembly.

"I think you misheard me. I said thirty-six hours, not twenty-six."

There was a rapturous response as the whole amphitheatre erupted in laughter and cheering. As it settled, Simon spoke again.

"Harpies. You have earned your place in history. Valiance, comradery and compassion. Qualities of the finest of warriors with no exceptions. For I know that those among you who chose the role to support, earned respect and admiration for your bravery and commitment," said Simon.

Sarah raised her hand in salute to the support and an agreement of recognition echoed around the circle as Ethan took the stand.

"Our race, once lost and scattered comes back together. I am of the same spirit and my spirit calls to you in admiration for what you have just achieved. We now move as one to the next phase of our mission, however, we now move with experience and friendship which will help us to remain victorious in our task. Three or four months is a long time to maintain your efforts to achieve victory. I wonder what you might need to maintain your focus and morale?" asked Ethan.

A single voice shouted out:

"Chocolate bars, fresh socks and some of those rude postcards you get at the seaside."

There was a burst of laughter from the crowd.

"I know who that is," said Scout.

"Me too," said Taca.

"Powderpuff, check the pocket of your coat," said Ethan.

"Thank you, sir!" he replied and Simon retook his place at the front of the dias.

"What Ethan means is what further support do you need and what would you change to make operations more efficient?" said Simon.

A ten-minute consultation took place before the thoughts combined and acquiesced for Ethan to gather and pass on to Simon. It appeared, weaponry and information accessibility were on point. Some of the Harpies originating from other places on Earth struggled with cultural information. Although language did not present a barrier, there was a request for a portal to provide downloads on the country's societal culture, taboos and consciousness.

Nationalistic mentality and emotional differences were apparent between the five countries making up the UK and Eire and within them, regional variations were obvious. The request was based on having a greater insight into behaviour and cohesive norms between Leaf adversaries. With one hundred and ninety-five countries in the world and multiples of regions and sub cultures, the Harpy force needed to be better informed. This importance was agreed and Ethan immediately connected to five other Realm Sixers, who helped him update the database with all information necessary. Ethan then made this available to all Harpies and the religious support groups.

The other and main concern was the religious groups themselves. The consensus was they did a great job. However, when additional volunteers had been deployed, the combat teams and support officers were struggling to know whom and how many were following their team. With no one ultimately responsible for coordinating each group, contact points were confused and valuable time was lost accessing the database and then contacting multiple people.

"They are requesting the God Squad introduces a chain of command in the field. Having one point of contact who can make decisions to redeploy their team members and bring in reserves, will obviously make operations more efficient and effective," said Ethan, linking to all on the dias.

Nevaeh linked to the religious committee to inform them of the feedback. After some deliberation, Matteo confirmed that this was possible; however, they would require Hills's assistance with communication in order to make it happen. Hills acknowledged this.

"If we upload this information on the database also, all of the religious followers and Harpy teams would be able to access it," Hills confirmed to Matteo.

Simon readdressed the gathering and confirmed their requests would be actioned. Ethan transmitted the access codes to enable download of this information. Simon then advised the religious group team leader information would be available before the mission start.

"We have made changes as well. Audaz and Conchita who were in the field will work in operations with Sarah and I. They will still be on hand to help out with information or knowledge as you are ploughing through South America. Ethan and Hills have recruited two additional Sixers, Tabatha or Tab for short and Xian."

The two new Sixers materialised on the dias waving and then spoke into the crowd to register their voices.

"They will work in relay with Ethan and Hills, as other duties continue to command their attention," said Simon.

"So do you want to know how you did?" Simon asked the audience.

His question was met with a resounding 'Yes'.

All three hundred and forty-seven thousand dark realm targets had been exiled. Between the support officers, the religious groups and a large number of warriors who were mopping up, just over a million Leaves had trusted them enough to make that leap into Realm Four. Energy wise, Leaves carried five times as much energy over when they chose to defect.

"If you consider, just under fifty-eight million people pass over from Earth every year as a matter of course, with two or three units. In comparison, your efforts have made a massive difference to our support of the Collective. Imagine what the next mission will bring. As for those left in Between Worlds, thanks to you, their lives will be much more peaceful. We salute you, as we do the religious groups. Together, we are a force to be reckoned with."

The entire amphitheatre erupted with cheers, stomps and shrieks. Simon linked into Matteo and his colleagues and having personally thanked them, requested they pass on his salute and appreciation to their ranks. When quietness returned, Simon gave a short message.

"Are you ready for Monday?"

A synchronised 'Yes' resounded.

"Remember to take time out during this campaign and combine your teams to effect this if necessary, because three and a half months will be a slog. I will see you at 05.00 on Monday. We will check in, count down and sweep the planet. Cool your jets till then."

Everyone on the dias saluted and waved watching the mass exodus.

A Step Towards the Dark

Alana and I transported back to our Capri home from the command centre and spent the next few hours floating on the breeze at high altitude, enjoying the sun on our backs. It all seemed to be about waiting at the moment. My mother's words, 'the prize of patience' drifted through my mind as they did often. As we perched on an island hilltop across the strait from our villa, the call came in from Tarquin.

"I am at Arthur's with him and Thomas. Can you join us or shall we come to you?"

"We will be with you in a tick," I replied, Alana and I dematerialising and appearing on the top deck of Arthur's home.

"Good to see you again, Thomas, Arthur. I bet you have been busy in the last day, Arthur?" said Alana.

"Nonstop, Alana. The presence of the combat teams and the religious support made a real difference to a lot of Leaves opinions of us in the after world. Many believed we were trying to help them in their world by taking away the negative influencers. But more than that, I felt they were more trusting of our message that it was safe for them to come over and their lives would be more fulfilled," replied Arthur.

"It was an extremely successful trial run. Everybody carried out their roles brilliantly. Now, let's get Dark," said Tarquin, focussing our attention into the seriousness of our next task.

He had discovered since taking the responsibility for Dark Realms, the system for move-on had been disabled between the borders spanning one, two, three and four, not just between three and four as originally thought. There was still no indication of the source of the power which had enabled Thaddeus to erect these, but they could be deactivated.

The Collective's Self-perpetuating system where individuals developed their sense of Self-awareness, forgiveness and responsibility and automatically moved on to the next realm up was still in place; however, people were currently blocked from crossing the boundaries.

Operating without blocks, individuals would be given a sense that movement was immanent, then find themselves in the next realm, providing they chose to go. There had been no transitions from Realms One or Two in the past one hundred and fifty-seven years.

Over the same time span, people moving from Realm Three into four had been selected. The automatic system when operating freely, enabled the orchestrator time to forge connections between the graduate and any loved ones in four or in their absence, alert guides to meet and rehabilitate them.

"Why don't you just remove the blocks and let them flow naturally?" asked Arthur.

"There would be a mass transition. I am not yet aware of the actual movement numbers. The movement from Realm Three into Four, could be in the millions. Maybe as high as the numbers defecting out of Between Worlds from the entire planet," replied Tarquin.

"It is not as though they could not be accommodated though, is it?" said Alana.

Accommodation was not the issue. Guides were the issue. Over the next three to four months, many guides would be tied up supporting the combat teams placing abnormal pressure on others to achieve their day-to-day roles.

If we were to break the dam, tens of millions of people would flow into Realm Four from Three. It was unlikely the majority would have family or friends still living in Four to settle them in because of the time elapsed since the selection practice started. This job would fall on the guides and there were not enough of them to meet the task.

"But surely with the Dark Leaves exiled to the Between Worlds dark realm, that will free up time and numbers to meet this task?" asked Thomas.

"We cannot abandon those Dark Leaves. They must and will continue to be visited and supported by guides," replied Tarquin.

"Are you suggesting we delay the Dark Realms rebalance until after the Between Worlds global mission?" I asked.

"That is one option," Tarquin replied.

"Are there any others?" asked Arthur.

"We could encourage them to move to the Between Worlds lighter realm. It is placed on Earth; they can enjoy all of Earth's beauties again, albeit from a nonphysical perspective and still have the choice to transition to four when they chose to. With the Dark Leaves removed, it will be nicer place to live," Tarquin proposed.

"It's hardly heaven though and if it was me, I would choose to go to four as soon as I could. That is unless you are thinking you will upgrade the facilities like virtual world integration, as we are planning to do when there is a massive influx of Earth bound?" I responded.

"No. Upgrades will happen as and when that situation arises," said Tarquin.

"I think you are just moving the problem sideways. Those in three know the next move is the heaven move if they work hard. Take that away and you will demotivate them and that is at the very least. If it was me who was affected in that way, I would revolt," I said.

"Ultimately, James, we do not need to take action if they do," said Tarquin.

I mind blocked and linked into Alana. That was the first time I had heard Tarquin respond to me where the pressure of his new responsibilities had interrupted his line of empathy and compassion. Metaphorically, I sheathed my broadsword and sighed.

"There may be another way we can deal with this without a delay. The four of us touched on this idea when we met recently. It does, however, contravene what Gerry and Thaddeus were trying to preserve, meaning the archetypal heaven experience. However, the truth is we need that energy as soon as possible and this may work," I said.

The idea was based on the fact nearly fifty-eight million people die on Earth each year and on average stay about ten years before revolving. Other than those who get diverted to Between Worlds and the Dark Realms, there are about half a billion residents in Realm Four at any one time, waiting to revolve. Rather than resting in peace during that period, I wondered how many would volunteer to help rehabilitate ex-offenders into the realm.

Once the basics were explained with the dos and don'ts, those transitioning could be left to live their spirit lives. Because the guides would be temporarily deployed aiding combat teams and rehabilitating Leaves in four, perhaps others from the general population would be prepared to meet this task. There may even be numbers from the religious groups who could do this until they were needed Between Worlds.

"We could stagger or meter the flow from Realm Three during those three months, then free the system to operate, as it was designed by the Collective," I suggested.

"It could work. I know you are aware of the 'not on my doorstep' principle, but if Realm Four residents could be persuaded that their help and flexibility is also required at this difficult time, it may be possible," said Tarquin, Alana now adding her point.

"That change in acceptance is the crucial factor. Putting that aside, if you think about it, we may stay for a maximum of three days in rest homes to acclimatise when we first come over from Earth. In this situation, it isn't all new for those in Realm Three, they know they are in the after world. Therefore, they would only need to know the basics when they arrive in four, which would take a day at most, with some sign posting afterwards. If we could recruit one percent of Realm Four residents and they helped two days a week, one on one, we could rehabilitate ten million people a week. This could be many more if more than one at a time was achieved," suggested Alana.

"As I say, I am not aware of specific numbers yet, but if we could achieve what you are suggesting during those three or four months, theoretically, we could transition a hundred and fifty million. That would be way in excess of our needs. My guesstimate is there are a little over a hundred million in Realm Three in total, with over half of them developed enough to move on. Okay, that sounds like a plan. I will discuss it with Ethan and he can bounce it off the Sixers and Seveners," said Tarquin.

Next, we discussed what our objectives were as of Monday next week. During the first half of Monday, we would show the three realms to Alana, so she could gain an idea of the terrains and people living in them. After, that we would go back into each realm and start to gather information on potential improvements. As a group, we could find out what additional issues had arisen due to the backlog created by the blocks.

If the proposed plan went ahead and the backlog from Realm Three was cleared, all the blocks between Dark Realms could be removed. There were a few concerns with Realms One and Two as with blocks down, individuals would transition of their own accord. However, with the length of time the twos had been kept in the dark, those ready to transition to three would be facing quite an adjustment. We would need the help of Ethan to identify those individuals whose shift could be pre-empted by the Dark Realm guides to ease them in.

The work in Realm Three would be more involved. With almost half of them transitioning, the social infrastructure would be drastically altered. To be faced with half of your friends disappearing, rumours would be rife as to why the sudden change. We needed to think around how this could be managed and the level of information provided. We did not want people to think they had just disappeared mysteriously or rumours circulate they had been taken and held captive elsewhere.

We also needed to decide whether to expose the fact the system had been corrupted. The repercussions of which may incite anger and frustration in those who may have been released into Realm Four many years ago. Those who remained may also feel the injustice, wondering whether a corrupt system was still operational now. The major factor would be how we built a level of trust back into, the non-trusting Dark Realms.

As Tarquin had said, in basic terms we need not take any action and leave them in the dark about everything. After all, they were in the dark by their own choosing. I understood what Tarquin was saying between the lines, however, the rest of us and him in truth also, purposefully upheld the rights of the Dark Realm inhabitants.

The Collective had managed the system for thousands of years based on the principles of the opportunity for choice and Self-development. These were maintained even in the Dark Realms and we had to decide how well they were informed to facilitate their faith being restored in them once again.

Informing all of the Dark Realm inhabitants was obviously something we could not do without mass consciousness communication, facilitated by someone from Realm Six or some form of update via the guides. Tarquin would consult with Ethan as to the best way to do this.

When Alana and I met with Arthur and Thomas previously, we had talked about improvements across the Dark Realms. These included updating the Dark Realm systems, reviewing facilities accessible to inhabitants; improved developmental support work; greater transparency of move on destinations and the new concept of probation.

After orientating Alana, we intended to gather information in the different realms to broaden our knowledge of what people's views were of what they may change to help them develop. The current system was simple and one size had fit all for thousands of years. What was lacking was a person-centred approach, where people had the opportunity to input into their own development, encouraging their support of others at the same time. We knew we would be powerless to facilitate everyone's desires and wishes and that was not the point.

The point was to kick-start the system by introducing transparent and achievable outcomes which may just motivate people to move forward positively.

After Tarquin had discussed with Ethan the support of Realm Three graduates by Realm Four residents and if it was agreed, we would likely become involved in building the consciousness of their acceptance of them. Once momentum had been achieved from people moving through and forward into Realm Four, a steady flow of more valuable energy would become available for the Collective's use.

With the initial plans set, we arranged to meet Arthur and Thomas at the amphitheatre at 04.00 Monday morning, before Tarquin closed the meeting.

"I will be in touch again to update you on facilities which will be of use to you on your mission, such as ways to identify those ready for move on. We will use the database system we have used for Between Worlds. See you all on Monday."

Alana and I shipped back to Capri.

Not of Earth

Later on Saturday, Tarquin had been back in touch to update us on resources we could tap into to gain information on Dark Realm inhabitants. The main bonus was an agreement with Ethan that we were enabled to identify, via vibration, which of all three realm's populations had qualified to make a transition to the next realm up. This fact would remain unknown to the qualifying candidates, but we were aware that many individuals would be feeling this pre-movement sensation, however, would be unsure what it meant.

Although this move would not happen until the blocks had been removed by the Seventh Realm, we were at liberty to tell individuals of their current status. The first of the blocks to be removed would be between Realms One and Two and would affect twenty-three thousand dwellers. As the influx would be small, transition would take place without guide intervention. This would happen the day following our arrival.

We were planning to spend seven consecutive days in the dark gathering information. Tarquin required us back after this to start to make plans for the integration of those from Realm Three, into Four. Ethan had agreed our idea to recruit Realm Four residents to act as temporary guides, therefore we were needed to instigate the recruitment drive and work with those full time guides available, to standardise the approach and content of each induction.

I was really pleased there was not going to be a delay. It was great to see the attitude of higher planers, was to move things forward on all fronts as soon as possible. However, it also indicated just how serious the need to move quickly was. Whilst in Four, we were also to report on any 'not on my doorstep' feedback. Not so action could be taken against perpetrators, more so to understand the concerns and prepare to alleviate them. Ethan was more in favour of exposing the wrongdoing of those in previous power to the Realm Four residents, explaining why blocks were put in place.

Although they could now expect a massive influx, without the blocks, people would have previously transitioned naturally to assume their rightful place. The backlog would be described as a result of overzealous control and this now needed to be rectified and rights of Dark Realm spirits as ordained by the Collective, restored.

Once we had recruited, we then had to formulate a system to connect candidates with temporary guides to ensure the inductions took place. I could foresee another database system being designed, in order to inform both parties of whom they should expect.

We could feel Tarquin's rising but controlled frustration, as transition times and numbers were based on the Collective's automatic system and he would need the cooperation of Ethan or someone from Realm Seven, to meter the flow by lifting then reinstating the blocks. The problem was there was no way of controlling how many transitioned at one time and that would affect those meeting them.

An information source was contrived to monitor the real time number of those transitioning, so the cork could be put back in the bottle to stop the flow. His admission that Nevaeh would need to take more of his responsibilities to monitor the Between Worlds dark realm during the global Between Worlds campaign, was a reflection of the daunting task now facing him.

Finally, the border between Realms Two and Three would be opened after six weeks. Tarquin had already contacted the Dark Realm guide network and granted them access to a portal providing each of them with vibrations of those ready to transition. Their task was to meet with each of these and brief them on the forthcoming change. The guides were free to explain the move and what those transitioning could expect in Realm Three. This task would stretch the guides considerably during that time, as candidates numbered five million individuals.

The official guide network in total was immense. It consisted of individuals who had achieved their revolutions to Earth and back and who now resided in Realm Four. Although there was a choice not to work, the vast majority used their time to increase their knowing by helping others.

Guides were divided amongst three areas of responsibility; working in the Dark Realms, working with Realm Four residents and working on Earth with people as they went about their everyday lives. Although direct Earth dweller contact was forbidden, unless there was absolutely no risk, Earth dwellers would be supported, seeded and echoed in their thoughts.

As an immanent Earth dweller's death approached, guides would also work with the catchers to aid a smooth transition to the after world or Between Worlds if so chosen. Earth guides took responsibility of their Earth charges when they chose to go to Between Worlds to maintain continuity. The difference was in the Between Worlds context, residents and guides could now see and communicate with each other, if the Earth dweller chose to.

With the invention of the Between Worlds dark realm, Tarquin had not made it clear as yet that Dark Realm guides would also oversee this realm, or if Earth guides would continue to support them. Being involved at this kind of level of change, made Alana and I so much more aware of the intricacies and scale of responsibility the high planers now had to manage.

For thousands of years, the system had been run on auto by the Collective and high planers made sure systems ticked along without real responsibility. Vigilance was even greater now, as it was apparent that the system could be manipulated and personalities existed who would pervert the natural course of events, believing they were acting on the idealised faith.

This was something which resonated inside of my head often. It was the question of whether we were acting from the same premise by changing systems as we saw fit, when the Collective might be running with a natural course of events in its own plan for us. In essence, we were protecting ourselves from what the Collective may know to be an evolutionary necessity in the overall plan. It made me wonder often about whether the Collective was being managed itself in its direction and behaviour by an even more powerful source.

As we ran into Sunday, Alana and I spent much time thinking and talking about what we were collectively doing to correct issues like global warming, the Between World issue and re-booting the Dark Realms. I could remember times in our ignorance when living on Earth, we would consider the enormity of the universe, what kept it in balance, the question of life after death and the purpose of existing.

Our conclusion was, although we were who we were and we lived in the after world, there were uncertainties as to what it was all for. The Collective's plan was unclear. Sure, it let us take control of our own destiny, we were part of that, as were the Earth bound, but consciousness does not always lead to the wellbeing of the majority, it can lead to disaster.

Yet it would seem the Collective was there to allow and accept the consequences of our actions as part of our evolution and perhaps of its own. We were more aware in the after world, but there was still evidence of shadows. It made me wonder, why part of the system was held out of our view.

"The much higher planers must know the answers, so what is the danger in letting us know. It cannot be arrogance of status?" I asked Alana.

"Maybe we are just a collection of beings who consciously evolve to different levels. We form a collective and that is the purpose," replied Alana.

"You mean we exist for the sake of it?" I said.

"Yes, basically." We sat silent for a moment wondering.

"This sounds odd but I remember back on Earth, the amount of airtime extra-terrestrials used to get in the media and how some thought there was a cover up about their existence," I said.

"Yes, I remember. The conspiracies suggesting governments held the proof, but refused to release it for fear that they would lose control should the masses realise there were significantly greater intelligences whom were more obviously in control. Why do you remember, anyway?" asked Alana.

"How come we don't hear of any in our realms? We don't see ships or beings, do we?"

"Would you know? There might be beings which live amongst us, who are from outside our system. If we were to walk around in our ancient form, half raptor, half human, people would probably think we were aliens," said Alana.

"True."

"What about if early cultures thought we were aliens because we were birdlike and could fly. Think about it. How many cultures around the world carved images of us into their temple stonework or painted us on the walls, Horus for example? What if, however, they were symbolic descriptions, rather than literal, meaning because ancient images had wings or bird features, they represented beings originating from the sky?" suggested Alana.

"We didn't have space ships, so it could have been literal, but even today, people all over the Earth world report flying ships. There must be something in it."

"You know what, James? Remember we had that normalising day when we first got involved with all of these changes and we talked about mad things like washing the car and watching the television?"

"Yes, I do?" I replied.

"We are about to go into the dark and here we are talking about the unknown and the uncertain. Perhaps we are doing it again. The dark can make you feel insignificant and powerless and without light, lost and alone."

"You are probably right, darling."

"I usually am, but I don't mind waiting for you to catch up."

We were silent again for a while, staring out to the horizon from the veranda. I could see something twinkling in the far-off distance.

"You know I was talking about spaceships?"

"Yes?"

"Look at that."

Currently set on the horizon was a bright white and blue pulsating light, getting larger in a short space of time and coming towards us. Even from our vantage point on the terrace of our Capri home, where we had relocated to, neither of us could gain any sense of it.

"I am staying put, it's not as though it can vaporise us if it is a hostile alien ship," I said bravely.

Coming in over the island adjacent to us, the sphere descended to our eye level and started to compress from the top and bottom poles to form a disc shape. The blue light now circumnavigated its outer edge. We could tell it was not solid in structure but of solid appearance.

"It's a bloody spaceship, Alana. How weird is that."

"I am not sure. This is, weird," was her response.

Suddenly, the disk split, creating a slit like aperture on its front elevation from pole to pole and a creature of brilliantly coloured lights emerged and moved towards us. At five metres in height by a metre wide, it moved closer revealing a cylindrical structure. Within it, a multi-coloured helix, not unlike a DNA strand, rotated slowly. The strand alternated with rainbow like colours as they ascended inside.

We could not detect anything from this being, other than its brilliance. Then, two beams of white light shot forward and intercepted our forms. We were powerless to transport away from its grasp.

"It's scanning us, but I can't detect anything hostile in the scan."

"Me neither, James."

"Weird thought. The internal structure is like DNA. Maybe it is communicating in a way we would recognise the symbol. Showing us it is like us, it is friendly," I proposed.

Its voice boomed out towards us, words cutting through mine, as I finished my sentence.

"You are not alone. You are never alone."

The ship disappeared and the cylinder of light transformed into Torfaen. He walked across the air path between us and stepped onto the terrace. Our faces had provided him with exactly the prize he was searching for.

"Did you like that?" he asked light heartedly.

Neither of us could find words to respond to our experience, nor the imaginary links to what we thought, might just be a UFO. Alana's voice emerged following a significant pause with her mouth still agape and her mind scrabbling for an opener.

"Are you an extra-terrestrial?"

"I am a being and I do not reside on Earth. So I must be, mustn't I? And I guess, well know, so are you two, like every other being in the after world."

"But you, yourself, are you really from another galaxy?" she asked.

"What? You mean because of the space ship thing? No, I was listening to the conversation, you were having, I thought I would become part of your possibilities. I am from our after world, however, the people on Earth might think I am from elsewhere," he replied smiling and raising his eyebrows.

I suddenly had this wild thought and Torfaen smiled at me. I could hear Alana's mind rapidly trying to work out from his smile whether he was joking or not.

"It's no joke; I do it every now and again. It is a Sevener privilege. I fly the ancient Earth grid lines. They are a Collective network, not unlike an irrigation system which blanket the Earth with the energy emitted from them. The energy is most intense on or above those lines and when I fly across or along them, my level of energy synchronises with the line energy enabling me to materialise."

"I do not fly to show myself to masses of people, just random ones. That is apart from when I am flying high up in the atmosphere sampling and am available for viewing by many more if they choose to look. I use the shape of the ship you have just seen. It is a classic and I make it visible, when I choose to. I also do it because Earth is such a beautiful planet and I like to continue to explore," said Torfaen.

"Do you ever appear as yourself?" I asked.

"No. Although historically, other Sevener Harpies have."

"So all the UFO sightings are Seveners out on a jolly?" asked Alana.

"I would say, quite a few."

"And the others? You are suggesting there is something else?" I asked.

"Well, it makes sense, as we cannot be the only colony in the universe, can we. Let's say, there has never been intentional harm done or threat made."

"But why fly around in a spaceship with the intention of being seen, if only by a few?" I asked.

He explained they were not trying to create evidence, much as they upheld the law of not letting the Earth know definitively of our after world. He used my grandma and our communication with her as an example of one person, who has no credibility to change a world's view. The individuals who saw his ship were similar. Appearing was an opportunity for them and others to believe in a phenomenon that suggested Earth people are not alone. Our whole system was based on belief, believing in ourselves and our connection to something greater, the Collective.

Belief was the same vehicle and process whether it was purporting that person to accept the existence of God, the after world or aliens from outer space, or facilitating it based on truth. It was a small logical step, in the advent of further information, that those believing in alien existence would accept aliens were really us, who do not visit the Earth as often as we did do thousands of years ago.

"Hence the paintings and carvings?" I asked.

"Yes, and the fact that Harpies were alive on Earth for thousands of years and would have been seen by humans," he replied.

"So why do you fly around in a space ship?" asked Alana feeling like some of his answer was missing.

"To reinforce belief in something that cannot be proved as yet. To allow people to feel they are possibly not alone. To maintain that invisible, intangible sense that everyone on Earth, in this case, is connected to the more than, which instils a sense of believability. That leads me onto why I have come here to see you two," said Torfaen.

"Why didn't you just link in and tell us you were on your way to talk about our idea?" asked Alana.

"Books tend to sell because of the story, Alana," Torfaen replied.

"Did you break rocks?" she asked.

"I did, we did. Interesting times. It was the business analogy which caught their attentions, much respect to you two. I would promote you if we were working for me in my business. But you are not, so you will have to settle for an imaginary £15 million bonus and the possibility of a flight in my space ship one day."

"I can't wait to be a Sevener. Sounds fun," I said.

"When will the signal change?" asked Alana.

"We hope, very soon."

Torfaen explained the complexity of the process of Collective contact. Whilst the majority had to agree on the purpose for contact, the combined knowing of sixteen Realm Seveners was required to open a portal to the Collective itself.

With their combined consciousness, they made the request and they received only a feeling of serenity if the request had been accepted for consideration. They had never been ignored in any of their proposals made and a response had rarely exceeded three days. The request had been made two days ago.

The implications of such a move, were far reaching as they were asking for a fundamental shift in the attachment. The last thing they wanted to unbalance, was the sense of personal responsibility, where the Earthbound would feel their actions to rectify climate change and factors attributing to its escalation, were out of their hands. Increasing the strength would increase a sense of security, however, the consensus agreed a feeling of believing they would be saved, needed to be avoided.

The overarching aim was to increase the feeling of being connected to others and personal volition to achieve collectively through individual action. However, it was necessary to maintain each individual's sense of feeling alone in the world at the same time. Torfaen's group had to leave the change in elements to the Collective. They merely requested it increase the presence of its own nature, of all as one in the Earth bound for a set time period to enable disaster to be avoided. Upon request, the feeling received was serene with an underlying element of respect.

"We took this to be a positive initial response," said Torfaen.

"How is the energy transmitted?" I asked.

"We don't know. However, we know there are three vehicles; direct, via others and through the lines."

"So we may just see an increase in Seven ships materialising?" I asked.

"Maybe?" Torfaen replied.

"How will you know when or if your request has been agreed and when a change will occur?" asked Alana.

"We just know and with that message, it will tell us when. We asked for immediate change," replied Torfaen.

"Something that baffles me is, if you and your colleagues are Seveners and highly integrated with knowing and the Collective, why didn't you know of the idea to increase the strength of the attachment to build belief?" I said.

"We all knew of the idea, but being who we are, we are detached to a degree from the detailed reality of Earth social consciousness. We see the macro picture and are aware of historical change, but information technology has evolved really quickly. It is not until spirit like you and your friends, who are operating on Earth and have recent experience of it, who voice that knowledge and back it up with evidence, does it become focal to our knowing. You have to remember that the after world has been an automated system up until these recent changes and realm roles have been clearly defined. You have actively developed links with higher planers, like Tarquin, Nevaeh, Ethan and Hills and you have chosen a route to manage upwards."

"And is that acceptable?" I asked.

"Allowing and guidance are fundamental to the success of any structure seeking the aim to build consciousness and knowing. Since these changes, it will now become necessary to change the way we manage the after world. Who knows, perhaps this is part of our evolution where we become more independent of the Collective, like a child on Earth does from its parent as it grows. A time may come when the Collective may no longer feel it is depended upon and return to its own source, leaving us to manage, having done its job."

"Is this an idea, Torfaen?" asked Alana.

"You mean; do I know it will?"

"Yes."

"That answer lies beyond Realm Seven. To know it, you would have to become part of the Collective itself," he replied.

"And when you do and it returns to the source, you will go with it then," I said.

"I think it is the same model replicating itself. You revolve back to Earth a number of times to develop knowing. You then choose to develop greater knowing if you progress through the realms. The Collective is increasing its knowing of our races, as they evolve in the context of Earth and in time, will absorb us from Realm Seven into itself when we reach our 'known' saturation point. When it is satisfied, we can manage alone as a system, it may just return to its source with all of its accumulated knowing and be absorbed into that to enable its source to evolve. If I go with it, it matters not to me. However, cells divide and perhaps it splits or replicates itself. It may leave part of the knowing accumulated to become an offspring which remains and continues its purpose as a descendent of itself. If I am part of this, I will not have left."

"Why don't we know these things?" I asked.

"The other fundamental element of the whole system is trust. Without trust, there is no belief and without belief, there is no trust. That is why changing the degree of attachment to the Collective is so sensitive. We must maintain that crucial balance of believing in yourself, but not trusting all will be well without taking responsibility for yourself and others. Change is a challenge, without it, we do not reach out and come to know who we truly are," he replied.

"A bit like shining a torch into a shadow or dark place to understand what it may reveal," said Alana.

"I am obviously well aware of the four of you going into the dark. I can also read you have allowed your minds to resurrect that inherent fear of the unknown within it. My advice is to maintain that level of vigilance and allow it not to become overwhelming. There are things in the Dark Realms, especially One, we do not fully understand. These are ancient practices which thrive in shadows. You will need to determine which can be trusted and to what degrees, but beware of Greeks bearing gifts, as it is possible to become lost in the dark."

"Lost?" I asked.

"Thomas will tell you of stories where guides have gone missing, sometimes for weeks. When eventually found, they are dulled in brightness, drained of energy and amnesic of their experience."

"I have seen this, it happened to Arthur," I said.

"No. Not Stains. This is something more powerful."

"Great. Nothing like a bit of danger," I said facetiously.

"I am sure between you all, you will be watching each other's backs, but I am giving you a gift to take with you. You can transform in the Dark Realms, but your status does not allow flight. I am now transmitting that ability for you to be able to do so. Don't be surprised to receive a few strange looks of wonder."

"A bit like flying spaceships on Earth then?" added Alana.

"Exactly. Good luck, be aware," said Torfaen, who then dematerialised.

"I am sure we will be all right," said Alana.

I reassured her we were travelling with an experienced guide and between the four of us, we could look after each other. It was strange though to be placing yourself at risk, a phenomenon alien to our realm and more associated with Earth. At least we could fly away if it got too scary.

D-Day

When we arrived to meet Arthur and Thomas at the amphitheatre, our team were already set up and awaiting the full arrival of the global combat teams. We checked in with Tarquin and acknowledged our readiness to depart as the teams departed themselves. He was aware of our meeting with Torfaen and the issue raised and he reassured us he would be keeping his eye on our progress. There were many embraces between our team members in mutual love and support of our own immanent adventures about to commence. We promised to check in with the others in seven days' time, although it was made clear, current tasks aside, to shout if we needed assistance.

The God squad had met the request and appointed their own team leaders in the groups backing up the combat teams. All relevant vibration and identification references had been uploaded for access and their teams were poised to arrive on location when the combat teams landed. They had learned from their experiences in the UK to remain out of sight until the combat teams had acquired their targets and would then be called in by the support officers when assistance was needed.

With a full assembly, as promised, Simon kept his address short and to the point.

"Have you all checked in?"

A resounding 'Yes'.

"Are you all ready to change the course of history?"

Another resounding 'Yes'.

"Good luck, go and get them!" Simon saluted them all.

Within three seconds, the entire gathering of Harpies had vanished and all eyes switched to the score board. Within fifteen minutes, it was starting to register their progress. This was our cue to depart.

Thomas having already set a location in Realm One, linked into each of us to follow. I had enabled Alana to access my experiences from my last trip, providing her with a description of what it was like in each of the realms, so she knew what to expect on arrival. I felt her shiver as soon as we entered the domain.

Arriving on a ridge just beneath a steep mountaintop called Le Griffe, we could just make out the horizon in the dim light. Although there were plateaus and saddles providing some flat ground, the entire terrain was mountainous, steep elevations of black rock rising from cavernous ravines and chasms. There was a drizzle hanging in the cold air which on fabric would have soaked and chilled the wearer to the bone in no time.

"Cheery place, isn't it?" said Arthur, breaking the dowdy spell we were succumbing to.

"How about thirty-minute breaks back to your lighthouse Arthur, say, every couple of hours?" said Alana.

"You feel how it draws upon you, don't you? This is the story of this place. Pretty much everything in it wants to draw what you have from you, having been depleted of its own energy by others around. Because we are light beings, we become the lure or the bait."

"You don't get squid down here, do you?" asked Alana in jest, suddenly reminded of her dark ocean adventures.

"No," replied Thomas, reading her mind's untimely distraction. "In all seriousness, can I suggest you respond to my instruction to reduce your radiance when I tell you to. I am very used to noticing the signs of immanent multiple interest and approach. We have three dwellers watching us at present who have moved closer to us four times since we have arrived."

"I didn't see them or any movement," I said.

"Too busy getting sucked into the surroundings. You need to keep a focus on your will to keep your head above this blackness. Drowning in the darkness is a common occurrence for trainee guides," added Thomas.

"Where are they, Thomas? They do not seem to have a vibration which is easily detectable," asked Alana.

Dark realm dwellers vibrations were much lower in frequency than our own light form and it was necessary to recalibrate to detect the dull ebb they emitted.

"Lights out now!" ordered Thomas.

We moved quickly into a tight group, as Thomas threw a shield dome over us to evade the attack. Just as it activated, three black smoke like forms slammed into its outer boundary before they slumped to the floor. They squirmed into their separateness and hung, suspended without solid form, sensing what our presence consisted of. The one on the left opened a surprising dialogue in a very cultured accent.

"I say that was bloody miserable. All I wanted was a friendly chinwag, you know, see where you come from and all that. I don't know who these two are, never seen them before in my entire life and frankly, I wish they would bugger off!"

The form's consistency changed as a red glow started to swirl inside it. Thomas mind linked to us to watch what he was about to do. The other two forms retreated a matter of feet away, but not far enough to evade two vapour like tentacles which extended from the being and enveloped them in what looked like black and red smoke. It tightened its grip and small pulses of energy were transferred from them, along its extended arms and into the form's structure. The two others screamed and desperately fought to escape from its hold.

"At my leisure, gentlemen. Alas, such meagre pickings, now, as I say, bugger off and don't try to muscle in on my prey, sorry, friends again."

He released the other two who slowly retreated, perhaps because their residual energy reserves allowed nothing hastier. As he was seeing them off, Arthur profiled our visitor. He was a sixteenth century landed English gentleman. However, far from gentle to the fifteen young women whom he had whipped and then strangled. His intelligence had served him well, as their bodies had never been found. It was his mother who had helped him develop his behaviour, by beating him naked in front of the female servants of their home.

As he materialised to his human form, his dashing good looks and obvious charm were evident and had more than likely made it easier for him to manipulate his victims. There were no elements of remorse or empathy present within him.

"Hugh. Pleased to meet you all. Never been one for surnames. Always preferred a little anonymity, being well off and all that."

"Do you think he's a Greek, James?" Alana asked me in a whisper, which he heard.

"No. British thoroughbred, well English. Who are all of you then?"

His social charm smoothing over the fact that he had labelled us as his prey a few minutes earlier. We introduced ourselves and explained we were in the Dark Realms to find out what would help people to move forward into lighter realms.

"What would you like to improve your life here?" Alana asked.

"Well, I think I am in the wrong place anyway, I should be in a much nicer place. But, err, I suppose I miss killing things really. You know hunting and trapping, then looking into the face of your prey as it realises it is not going to escape with its life. You know, sport."

"You mean the look those fifteen young women gave you, as they were pleading with you to let them go back to their loved ones." Alana's tone was cutting and spiked with malice.

Thomas reenergised the dome as Hugh started to power up for a shot.

"Come out here and say that Missy. And magic up a mirror to watch your own face, as I take your last breath," Hugh spat back.

"I am already dead, knob head. You are a sad man, Hugh, and I feel you are a long way off finding yourself. I am afraid we cannot recommend your suggestion, but are willing to try and get you more help," said Alana.

"Listen, bitch, I am not insane, you know. I know what I did, but I just don't give a damn."

With that response, he evaporated back to his smoke form and quickly moved away.

"Knob head? Interesting description Alana," said Thomas.

"I know, sorry Thomas, but fifteen young women? You have a hard job; you must be very patient."

"Progress is slow, but every spirit is worth the patience," he replied.

"Thanks for being so vigilant. They came in at speed, didn't they?" said Alana.

"Yes. Don't be fooled. They may come over with low brightness, but they find the energy when they need to." Arthur and I also thanked him.

"Good start, lady and gents, now let us descend."

"Do you want a piggy back, Arthur, to avoid treading in anything?" I teased, and Thomas smiled at my quote.

"I have learned my lesson, James, thank you."

Thankfully, we were in a different location to where we were before so may avoid a repeat meeting. I did wonder if whether our runic conversation and Arthur's transmission had made any difference. Alana was quick to remind me of my tendency to explore the extremes of delusions of grandeur, however fleetingly.

As we appeared in the depths, I was instantly reminded of my first experience in the dark, although this time, I had Alana's hand to hold. The darkness crowded in from every direction, again limiting our visual perception to a few metres. She tightened her grip as her anticipation levels heightened in parallel with an age-old fear of the unknown which lurks in blackness.

"Why don't you set the dome?" asked Alana.

"It's all right. There is nothing in the immediate vicinity. However, the level of your voice has just diverted some attention towards us," Thomas replied.

Thomas intentionally lit an arc of ground in front of us to reveal two Stains shuffling and sliding across the rocks to where we were standing.

"Why the light? You are going to draw their attention more. And wouldn't the dome be a good move now?" Alana questioned Thomas again.

"No need, but you 'need' to meet this spirit and his friend. They are…unusual, if not rare," replied Thomas.

As the two stains reached within three metres of our position, they both transformed to human appearance.

"Good morning, Max, Ted. How are you both?" asked Thomas.

"Faring well, my friend, although it is always this time of year that the darkness seems to encroach a little more. But my hull and within it, my heart, remains secure," Max returned the greeting.

Alana and I quickly scanned both of them, our suspicions raised to the potential of their vibrations. Both were Realm Three if not Four candidates. We both mind linked, sharing the same notion of 'what the hell are they doing here'. As we introduced ourselves, Thomas transmitted their identities and history. It appeared that Max was a WW1 U-boat commander, responsible for sinking many tons of shipping and with it, the lives who were aboard them. Ted, was an American B17 bombardier and responsible for releasing thousands of tons of bombs onto German cities during WW2.

"You must have been asked this question a number of times. You were acting under orders and yet when you judged yourselves, you chose to come to the worst place possible, why?" I asked.

Both Ted and Max turned to face each other and raised their eyebrows, as they looked down.

"I can speak for Max as well in this. During war and in the intensity of battle, how would you say, indiscretions happen. An indiscretion in that context, describes an act under your control where you may have selected a target and obliterated it, based on your own personal anger or loss. Many civilians died or lost their homes as a direct result of my decision. I know that Max succumbed to the same impetuous where he sank ships, perhaps, when he might have chosen to let them to sail on," answered Ted.

"We could have gone to a less harsh place, as was offered to us, but separately, we chose to come here, because we felt the magnitude of our actions deserved a befitting reward," added Max.

"Having met each other, what distinguishes us from others around is we accept our responsibility and we have grown to trust each other. I have been here seventy-five years and Max, a little less and we both hold this fantasy that things will get better for us. They haven't other than in what we make for ourselves," said Ted.

"What do you do here?" asked Alana.

"Apart from run and hide and make like a dull-looking stain, you mean?" replied Ted.

"Yes," Alana smiled at him.

"We find others who have started to glow a little and we try to build trust to support them. It's a one in a thousand task. This is an 'every man and woman for themselves' sort of place. People are very isolated here because they are too afraid not to isolate themselves," said Max.

"So in effect, you are doing guide work?" said Arthur.

"Well, we have to, because this lot are rubbish," said Ted, laughing and pointing at Thomas. "That's not fair really, Thomas is all right, although nothing seems to change much."

"What if I said there has been an indiscretion which has directly affected you two and others here," I said.

"Meaning?" questioned Max.

I explained the embargo which had been put in place by Thaddeus, although could not provide them with a detailed reason behind it. As both of them had been here a shorter time than it being operational, they would not be aware of the way and how the system moved them forward automatically, which I explained.

"You two will have a choice to move forward, if not to the second but one Realm along, but quite possibly into Realm Four where we come from. I say possibly because you Max are holding onto something you have not reached far enough into yet," I announced.

"That would be Persia. My biggest regret. You English have an expression about a wolf in sheep's clothing or Greeks bearing gifts?" said Max.

"That's true," replied Alana.

"I chose to attack without warning, sensing the wolf, but I really wish I had not rushed the shot and torpedoed her from the other side, so more could have escaped," said Max remorsefully.

"Talking of which, when will we escape?" asked Ted.

"Within eight weeks. But expect some movement after a day or two, when you will relocate to the next realm up, if you choose," I said.

"We want to come back though. After a bit of a break, of course, to carry on working with those trapped in the depths. I feel I owe it to them," said Max.

"As Dark Realm guides?" asked Arthur.

"If that is what you call them. Thomas here could do with more support and to be honest, he doesn't know the half of what goes on here," replied Max.

"If you make it as far as Three or Four and I put my neck on the block and say I will make this happen, would you be prepared to train guides and go back in on missions?" I asked.

"Most definitely," was his reply.

"You have a deal, Max, choosing forgiveness is your route forward," I said.

Alana was in my mind as I said this and combined the green light energy emitted from my heart chakra with her own to wrap around Max's chest and head. We watched as his smile grew to a grin, before he thanked us.

"We have one more question for you," said Arthur. "What would you change or make available here which would help those living here?"

Max looked at me and asked me to confirm a feeling he had that I had been a spy at some time in the past. I told him I had and gave him the context.

"Then you will know the meaning of a safe house. I do not know if this is possible, but if there were places where people who are growing, could congregate together, with access denied to the wolves, we could support and teach in greater safety. People would thrive more amongst like kind. I am not saying exclude the others, but you could base entry on the same principle as movement to the next realm level; a readiness to accept," proposed Max.

"Or even create a realm within a realm, like Realm 1A," I suggested.

"Forgive my partner, Max. He is always the one to come out with the grand idea," said Alana.

"There is nothing wrong with grand ideas, Alana. Other than the disappointment of the originator, when it becomes actualised into a lesser vision than originally conceived," said Max.

"Story of my life. Thank you, Max," I said in agreement.

"We will let you good people get on with your visit. Thank you for talking with us and speaking for both Ted and I, we hope to meet you again. Good bye."

Both of them waved and dematerialised back to smoke, moving quickly out of sight.

"Wow, Thomas. One word, amazing," I said.

"I thought you would be. I have wished on many occasions to be able to work more closely with them, but it has not been allowed," he replied.

"That is another suggestion we put to Tarquin on our return," I said.

"Look up there. Somebody else is using chakra light," said Alana, pointing to a green glow located a short distance away and half way up a steep, nearly vertical cliff face.

"No. There are no more guides operating in this area. I don't know what it is," said Thomas.

"Well, let's go and find out. It looks pretty sheer, but it is hard to see. Alana and I will fly up there and have a look for a safe place for you to transport to," I suggested.

We transformed to our raptors, to be reminded by Thomas, we would most likely draw attention, as there were no birds or animals in this realm. We took off and flew through the darkness towards the source. As we approached, we could see there was a shelf like pathway that led up to an elliptical cave entrance from which the glow originated.

Outside of the rocky aperture and spewing down the rock face beneath, was a black smoke-like substance, similar to the disguise the spirits used in this realm. It pulsated occasionally, as if trying to free itself from the rock.

"This is strange James. If those are dark spirits, maybe something is trapped inside, which has become developed enough to repel these unwelcome visitors, but cannot escape."

"Maybe, I don't know. I'll tell the others," I replied.

I mind linked to Thomas and Arthur and let them see what we were watching. Thomas had no idea what it could be, having not come across anything like it before. He did agree that whatever was making the glow, had developed in some way to be able to emit light as light emission was usually a sign of awareness and will operating. They transported up to us and onto the pathway as we changed back to human form.

"These are spirit dwellers, lots of them. Except they are really low in energy. It's almost as though they do not contain enough to move away. I don't like this. This is something we need to avoid," said Thomas.

"Come on, Thomas. You have already introduced us to two remarkable dwellers who are very different from others. This cave could be a refuge to one just like Max or Ted. Perhaps someone, who is hiding and trying desperately to protect themselves from these others who are trying to attack them," I said.

"It may be a young woman, vulnerable and alone, who does not know who to turn to or cannot get out to seek any kind of help," added Alana.

"Alana, it does not matter if it's male or female. Dwellers are here for good reason. We should be extremely cautious. I can feel the vibration of whatever it is and it's different from what I usually pick up down here," said Thomas.

"Max! The two birds!" shouted Ted.

"They must be something to do with Thomas and his friends. It looks like Thomas and Arthur have joined them. We need to warn them," replied Max.

"We are not going to be able to make it up there in time, but we must try. Come on!" said Ted.

We approached the entrance to the cave very slowly, having agreed to transport out quickly if need be. I was reassured by the colour of the glow, which was the colour of the heart chakra we had projected before. I was also optimistic we could help another who had been trapped by the embargo and denied its rightful realm location. Alana shouted a hello into the entrance, with no response.

I split and projected my consciousness inside the cave. As it arrived, I was sure I had caught sight of a movement, yet all was now still. The cave, consisting of the same wet, hard black rock, was of a shallow dome shape with a flat central area, surrounded by jagged tooth shaped rocks. At its midpoint stood a naturally formed stone font, from which the now eerie green light emanated. I returned to show the others what I had seen.

"It's empty, no one is in there," I reported.

"Don't be so sure, James," warned Thomas.

Moving along inside, the passageway doglegged to the left, obscuring the interior. There was a noticeable rise in temperature, increasing as we progressed and a vague hint of oranges and mustiness in the air. Alana was gripping my hand tightly, as we turned the corner with Thomas and Arthur directly behind us. Unlike before, a young girl was now sitting at the font, her head resting on her forearms which draped over the rim. She was weeping softly.

"It's a child!" Alana shouted, and ran forward, dragging me with her.

"Alana! There are no children in Realm One. Transport out; go to the lighthouse!" Thomas shouted back at her.

Stopped, dead in our tracks and unable to move, we were all caged by some sort of energy I had no understanding of. The girl looked up and scooped the green phosphorescent liquid from the font, pouring it onto the floor. We watched as it slithered towards the entrance and sealed us inside. Her words in a whisper which echoed around the chamber, were designed to chill and instil fear.

"At last, a feast befitting my own majesty."

Ingram Content Group UK Ltd.
Milton Keynes UK
UKHW020613070423
419773UK00007B/631